MOORLAND BLUE

MOORLAND BLUE

CHARLIE GIBB

The Book Guild Ltd

First published in Great Britain in 2019 by
The Book Guild Ltd
9 Priory Business Park
Wistow Road, Kibworth
Leicestershire, LE8 0RX
Freephone: 0800 999 2982
www.bookguild.co.uk
Email: info@bookguild.co.uk
Twitter: @bookguild

Typeset in Adobe Garamond Pro

Printed and bound in the UK by TJ International, Padstow, Cornwall

ISBN 978 1912575 855

British Library Cataloguing in Publication Data.
A catalogue record for this book is available from the British Library.

I dedicate this book to my ever-loving wife for if it was not for her endless patience and fortitude, this novel would not have been possible.

1

"What do you mean he's not there? I told him 11am sharp... OK, well phone Danny; see if he can get over... Well I don't bloody know, you'll just have to manage by yourself... No, I can't, I have to be at Whitechapel by 12... Mark? Mark? Oh, please yourself."

"Trouble at mill?"

"Oh Solley, I didn't see you there. What can I do you for?"

Solley sat provocatively on the edge of Paul's desk and started to finger his Tower of London paperweight. "You know what you can do for me lover boy."

Paul had always found kind of hard to accept a gay Jew. Sure, they must exist but Solley was the only one he actually knew of – and he knew a lot of Jews, the property market was more than well represented by them in this part of London.

"I'm very flattered but my bread's not buttered that side."

"How do you know until you have tried? One night with me and you'll be a new man."

"One night with you and I will be a new man, Kim would cut my balls off! Now do you want something or have you just come round here to piss me off and drink my coffee?"

"Well now that you mention it, there is something..."

Solley did not look at him, but eased off the desk, made his way over to the sun-bleached sofa that sat pride of place in front of the large plate-glass window, and flopped into its dusty embrace.

Paul could see tiny particles filling the air. "I don't know why I bother," he sighed.

"Sorry?"

"Twice a week I pay her to come in here and clean this shithole."

"Not with you."

Paul then realised that, with his back to the light, he was totally unaware of the fine cloud of detritus surrounding him. "Never mind," he said, "so what is it?"

Solley leaned forward and placed his bone china mug onto the coffee table. "I have a business proposition for you."

"I told your old man twice, Corn Lane's not for sale, how many more times?"

"This has nothing to do with Corn Lane. I have chanced across a property that's just crying out to be converted into flats."

Paul eased back into his chair, a look of suspicion etched across his face. "Hold on a minute, am I reading you right?" he said. "You want to go into partnership with me?"

"Kind of."

"I thought the Solomons had a *Family Only* policy when it came to business."

"Times change," he replied, looking a little uncomfortable.

"Not that bloody much they don't!"

"Ok, so this is a little different from our usual projects."

"Look, if your old man's not interested, then neither am I."

"Well at least you could hear me out; you might change your mind."

Paul looked at his watch. "Ok, but be quick, I have to be over at Whitechapel by 12."

Solley wasted no time, "It's an old nursing home, six acres of grounds. We could easily convert it into eight 4-bedroomed, six 3-bedroomed and nine 2-bedroomed luxury apartments."

Paul had to admit this did sound promising. "Ok, it almost sounds too good to be true. But why come to me?"

2

"Well a project of this nature, as you know, requires quite a lot of funding."

"There's something not quite kosher about this is there?"

"No, it's legit, honestly."

"Ha, honestly," retorted Paul. "So why is your old man not interested, or Michael for that matter?"

"Oh, it's nothing really…"

"Nothing?"

"They think it's too far."

"Too far?" he queried. "So where exactly is this place?"

"Up North."

"Whereabouts up North – Luton?"

"No, Yorkshire."

"Where?" exclaimed Paul, not quite sure if he was hearing right.

"You make it sound as though it is on the other side of the world," said Solley, now perched back on the edge of the desk.

"It might as bloody well be. And there's another thing you forgot too."

"Oh, and what's that?"

"The language barrier."

"What language barrier?"

"I was up there with Kim a couple of years ago, on one of her church things – likes to wander around them, cathedrals, that sort of thing. We went into this pub – couldn't understand a bloody word they were saying."

Solley ignored this churlish excuse, "You're just parochial," he said.

"Me, parochial?" he answered. "What about you? You all live within a mile of the first house your family moved into when they came here from Hungary and that was over 200 bloody years ago."

"There's something I haven't told you."

"Oh and what's that then?" asked Paul, a hint of misgiving in his voice. "You found a map with an X marking the spot where the buried treasure's hidden?"

"Not quite, but almost as good."

3

Solley looked about and leaned forward. "You know Marcus Goldman?"

"Yeah, of course I do, he's our local MP."

"He's also a sort of relative."

"Is there anyone round here you're not related to?"

"Look, I'll get to the point. This property was built in the late 1890s for chest problems, TB that sort of thing, so it's in quite a remote area, built away from pollution. That's why it's a giveaway at £500k."

"Oh, and that's supposed to make me change my mind is it?"

"No, but this will; the buried treasure – so to speak – comes in the form of HS2."

"Sorry?"

"The railway," he explained. "You know; the 200mph job that's got all those posh twats up in arms because it might come within a mile of their country piles."

"Yeah I know what it is," he replied impatiently, "but what does it have to do with this proposal?"

Once again Solley looked about him furtively and edged even closer.

"I'm not saying who but a little birdie has told me that the line is going to be extended to Leeds. It will come within a mile of the old Sanatorium."

All of a sudden Paul's scepticism started to evaporate in the light of this information. "How sure are you?"

"One hundred percent," he replied, springing back, a broad smile revealing several gold teeth

"One hundred percent?" he questioned, raising an eyebrow.

"One hundred percent."

"Ok, the initial investment of £500,000 purchase price. Is that fixed or is this place up for auction?"

"No, private sale; it went up for auction two years ago but got nowhere near the reserve of £550,000. It's owned by the Albright family."

4

"Albright? That rings a bell."

"Should do – Albrights biscuits and cakes? You must remember the double choc-chip cookies when we were kids?"

"God I would kill for a packet of those right now," he reminisced.

"They were bought out fifty years ago by one of these Swiss multinationals, but the old Lord Albright was a bit of a do-gooder in his time. He built homes for his workers and this hospital on the edge of their 15,000-acre shooting estate, specifically for the treatment of TB which was rife at the time. Mind you, it was not all purely altruistic. Keeping his workforce healthy was important at a time when labour was hard to find around there with so many people moving to London."

"Things don't change much do they," commented Paul, answering the phone. "Of course I'll be there... yes, at 12. Look Solley, all this sounds good but I must be on my way."

"Talk later?" he said, a pleading look on his face.

"Ok."

"Good, tonight at 7pm, The Pink Slippers."

"Ok 7pm it is, now piss off; you're making the place look untidy."

—◊◊◊—

"Liam, Liam!" called Paul. "Where the bloody hell is he?" he muttered. "Tells me to get over here for 12... Oh, there you are. I've been looking for you for the last twenty minutes. I busted my balls to get over here for 12 and I had to interrupt an important business meeting. So, what's the urgency?"

He followed Liam upstairs. This was one of his first properties purchased nearly thirty years ago; now he had twenty-seven in total. He watched as Liam removed a sheet of ply from where the old boiler once stood.

"Well, what?" he asked.

"Asbestos," he replied. "This whole partition and probably the ceiling; bomb damage."

"What?"

"Second World War bomb damage – quick, cheap repair."

"So what does it mean for me?"

"You'll have to get it removed by a specialist."

"How much is that going to cost?"

Liam picked up his tool bag. "No good asking me, Squire. But I can't do anything until it's sorted."

With that he stepped onto the small landing and disappeared down the narrow staircase leaving Paul staring at the hole in the wall that should have now housed the new boiler which, ironically, he was reluctant to install in the first place. It was Kim who was always onto him 'Do this, paint that.'

Not that he would have his tenants living in squalor or at any real risk, but then again, he had to turn a profit and of course if Ingram could afford a new Roller, then why shouldn't he? After all, business was not only just for the money, prestige was all part of it and he was not going to be shown up by that flash git.

Maybe Solley had something – branch out a bit. This game was changing fast in London and he did not want to get swallowed up.

2

"So this is how the other half live," said Ian as he sat down in Frank's office.

"You've been in here before, surely?"

"Not that I can remember – and I'm sure I would have done," he added, looking about.

"This Solley guy – I take it he's Jewish?" asked Frank.

"So what difference does that make?"

"I'm not over keen on them."

"Why, what harm have they ever done to you?"

"None that I can think of but they're really shrewd business people; I reckon you should look for someone else."

"I disagree, he seems to be just right. In quick, no nonsense, get the job done. After all, we don't want a repeat of last time. The quicker this is sorted the happier I'll be and, of course, the least questions asked the better."

"But there will still be the usual channels to go through."

"Look, all that will be taken care of, trust me," smiled Ian.

Frank Horton was not in the habit of trusting anyone, and especially not Ian Turnbull. But what choice did he have? He was up to his neck in it and he owed that psychopath Reggie Carlyle 12 big ones. Ian was right about one thing, the sooner this was dealt with, the better.

"So, Frank, you know what you have to do?" Ian continued.

"Yes."

"Look, I don't want anything to come back to me, understand?"

"If you don't trust me, why don't you…" Frank paused. "Of course not, I understand. What about my money?"

"You'll get that when you deliver. And another thing," he added as he got up to leave the office, "buy some paint and give this shithole a once over."

Frank eased back in his chair and waited for a few moments. He had already rehearsed what he was going to say at least a hundred times and picking up the phone, he took a deep breath before punching in the number.

"Philip Townsend speaking."

"Listen – don't speak," he said.

"Who is this?"

"I told you not to speak. A couple of years ago your wife was dragged from her car and assaulted by three men."

"Look, I don't know who…"

"Shut the fuck up and listen. I know all about what happened to her."

Philip's knees went weak and for a moment he even thought he might be sick.

"If you want to keep her identity a secret you must follow these instructions," continued Frank. "In the basement you'll find a filing cabinet, no. 1624. In there is a file that relates to the old mine workings on the Albright Estate, inside which are more recent documents in a pink folder. You are to take it and put it in the dumpster behind the kebab shop on the corner of Wellington Street, eight o'clock sharp tonight. Got that?"

"Yes, but I must have them back."

"You'll have them back in 48 hours. Don't try anything clever, I'll be watching you."

"That was delicious love."

"Ok?" questioned Kim, leaning back slightly.

"Ok what?"

"You only compliment me on my cooking when you're up to something."

"Me? I'm up to nothing."

"What date is it?"

"Err, June 9th?"

"And?"

"And?"

"Cast your mind back twenty years."

"Shit, I thought dinner was a bit over the top. Look I'll make it up to you this weekend. I'll book a table at Chino's."

"I don't want to go to bloody Chino's. I want an evening in with my husband."

"Ah, you see I told Solley that I would meet him tonight. Big business opportunity, too good to let slip."

"You promised me that you wouldn't go out tonight."

"Well, yeah, but in all fairness, I didn't know it was our wedding anniversary."

Kim got to her feet. "Didn't know? We have one every bloody year, on the 9th of bloody June! Oh, what's the point," she sighed. "You go and cuddle up to Solley."

"What's that supposed to mean?"

"Well it hasn't been all systems go in the bedroom recently has it?"

"That's a bit harsh."

"Oh, now don't get me wrong, if you're gay just tell me."

"I'm not bloody gay," he said, "just because I – well you know – can't at the moment."

"Look you go and do what you have to," said Kim, "I'll tidy this lot."

He put his arms around her waist. "I do love you, you know."

"You have a bloody funny way of showing it sometimes." She

kissed him on the forehead. "Go on, piss off, or your boyfriend will wonder what's happened to you."

"By the way," he said, half out the front door, "where are the kids?"

"Over at Julie's for the night."

Paul closed the door behind him feeling guilty. Not just for forgetting their wedding anniversary and all the trouble she had gone to getting rid of the kids for the night, but his inability to get aroused. Although Kim was in her mid-forties, she was still a stunner – good looks and a figure most women half her age would die for.

He would see Dr Green, get some pills. After all, there were plenty of blokes willing to see to Kim's needs if the desire took her. Not that he ever thought she would, but he felt it was a man's duty to keep his wife happy in every sense.

Not only that, he was missing out big-time himself. After all, it was nothing to be ashamed of; lots of men his age had difficulty in that department. It was time to put pride to one side.

—⚬—

Philip glanced nervously at the large clock above the door, its hands almost motionless. Never before had he known time to move so slowly. At last he removed the keys from his desk drawer and made his way out into the now deserted lobby and down to the basement. Once there he turned on the main switch and, shielding his eyes from the rows of bright fluorescent lights that flickered into life, moved tentatively between the serried ranks of filing cabinets to a section at the far end that was rarely, if ever, visited.

He placed both keys into the respective locks and pulled open a drawer revealing at least fifty files. Finally, after some searching, he found what he was looking for – the file relating to the ancient mine workings on the Albright Estate. Having removed the pink folder, he was tempted to see what it contained but then again, would it be best not to know? However, after some deliberation, curiosity got the better of him.

So, this is what they wanted, he thought.

No sooner had he started to read, then he froze as he heard footsteps coming towards him. He was not sure why he felt so uncomfortable – after all, he had every legitimate reason to be there – but he closed the filing cabinet and stuffed the folder up his jumper.

"Oh, it's you Mr Townsend," said Steve, the caretaker

"I wasn't expecting to see you down here this late in the day," he replied.

"Overtime Mr Townsend, apparently there's a …"

"Well Goodnight Steve," he interrupted scurrying past him heading for the lift, his right arm suspiciously held tight to his chest.

Philip felt a sense of relief as the metal door closed behind him. Why he felt the need to hide these files inside his jumper he couldn't say, but under the circumstances it just felt the right thing to do.

—◊—

The pub was packed for a Tuesday night. Despite its name, The Pink Slippers was not a gay pub – that honour belonged to The Elephant across the road. The Pink Slippers had got its name from the theatre that used to be next door, which had been knocked down in the mid-1970s to make way for shops and flats.

The only reason the pub survived was because the developers went under before they could start on phase two. Had it gone ahead, it would have resulted in the loss of many fine 19th Century buildings – unthinkable by today's standards. However, the mindset was very different back then. *More's the pity,* thought Paul. *Wind the clock back fifty years and I would be a billionaire by now.*

"You made it then," said Solley, glass in hand.

"Where the hell did you come from?"

"I was in the gents."

"Oh yeah?" he teased, nudging him in the ribs with his elbow.

"You can cut that out for a start, I'm not that type."

"No of course not," replied Paul, feeling a little ashamed.

"Come on," said Solley, "we're over here."

Paul grabbed him by the arm. "Wait a minute; I thought this was a private meeting."

"Oh there's plenty of time for that."

"Look, I want to talk to you privately for a minute. What about the gents?"

"I told you, I'm not that type."

"Very funny but I have just left Kim almost in tears."

"Why, what's up?"

"*You're* what's up!"

"Me, what have I done?" he replied indignantly.

"It's our wedding anniversary. Kim went to a lot of trouble to cook a nice dinner that I had to cut short to see you for this big deal of yours and now I find this."

"Why didn't you bring her with you?"

"Because, you prick, I thought it was supposed to be hush hush."

"I have to admit I'm somewhat surprised. You two always struck me as the type who confide in each other all the time."

"We do, well most of the time."

"Correct me if I'm wrong but I don't see you hiding something like this from her, do you?" he said, raising himself to his full height, looking down on Paul.

"For your information, I was not going to *hide it from her* as you put it. I just wanted to get a better idea of what's involved before I put it to her, that's all."

"Look Gary's on the wagon, do you want me to send him round

to fetch Kim? A bottle of bubbly and my extraordinary wonderful company might go some way to making amends."

Paul hesitated, not sure as to whether to accept this offer or even that Kim would accept.

"Come on, you know that little vixen's got the hots for me, all women do. Irony at its best – nothing like being a tease."

"Oh, fuck it, why not, she can only say no."

"Good man, about time you two let your hair down."

—ᴍ—

Councillor Roberts entered the all but empty chamber. "You still here Townsend?" he bellowed.

"Yes," replied Philip in a somewhat timid voice.

"What does that pretty wife of yours have to say about these late nights of yours?"

"She… she… doesn't mind," he stammered, his speech impediment always at its worst around Roberts.

"Well whatever it is you're up to, get off home."

"Yes C… C… C…"

"Oh just go!"

Townsend picked up his coat and briefcase and was just about to leave when the Councillor called out to him.

"Give Catherine my love… and if you don't, I will," he added, just loud enough for him to hear.

Philip stepped out onto the steps of the Town Hall to find that the light drizzle had now turned itself into an unseasonal monsoon. Pulling his collar up in an attempt to fend off the heavy rain, and with bag held over his head to provide some additional protection, he crossed the road, through the narrow alleyway that divided the parade of shops and out onto Wellington Street.

He made his way to the back of the kebab shop hoping there would be nobody there. Sure enough, as instructed, he found a large galvanised dumpster. He lifted the lid tentatively and dropped the pink folder inside before retracing his footsteps back to the bus stop to find a gang of surly youths sheltering from the unseasonal weather. *That's all I need,* he thought. If it wasn't for the rain he would have walked to the next stop. But then again, why should he?

Trying to avoid eye contact, he stared across the road, focusing his attention on the neon lights above the chip shop that flickered intermittently as water dripped onto the electrics from the building above. *I'll have a word with them tomorrow,* he thought, as in his mind it posed a possible fire risk.

"Oi, you!" called one of the gang.

He tried to pretend that this provocative outburst was meant for someone else other than him and focused even harder on the pale blue sign as it fused in and out of life, as if by doing so, he could somehow render himself invisible – something he had tried to be his entire adult existence.

Suddenly he bumped up against the cold steel pole, one of four that held the roof of the bus shelter in place and now knew that his attempt at invisibility had failed – as it always did.

"S… s… sorry," he said.

"Don't apologise to him," said one of the two girls, her hair short and her skirt even shorter. "What the fuck you looking at, you perve?" she added.

Philip lowered his eyes.

"Fancy her do you?" said the young man that had pushed him.

"Look, I don't want any trouble."

"Trouble, what makes you think we're trouble?"

"Oh no, I didn't mean…"

"Didn't mean what?" said the girl with the short skirt, her hand now in his coat pocket. "Got any ciggies?" she added. "No – don't tell me. You don't smoke, bad for your health. Or is it mummy doesn't want her little cherub smoking?"

He turned to leave but his exit was blocked by two other youths, these slightly older than the one who had just pushed him.

"Give me that," said one of them, pointing to his briefcase.

"I couldn't possibly do that, they're official papers."

"Oh, official papers?" mocked the other youth. "Give it here," he said, grabbing at the case.

But to his surprise, Philip's grip was extremely strong and the case remained firmly in his hand. This made the young man feel inadequate in front of his fellow peers and this loss of face – all be it minor – could not go unanswered.

Philip caught a glimpse of something flash past him. At first, he felt no pain but on removing his hand from his face, he discovered it was covered in blood.

The gang now dispersed and desperate for assistance, he ran over to the chip shop, only to have the proprietor scream at him, "Get the fuck out, what the hell do you think you are doing, spilling blood over my clean tiles?"

This potential refuge from the unpleasant events that had just befallen him now denied; he felt he had no choice but to return to the Town Hall and get David, the night guard, to summon assistance. However, halfway across the road, he remembered Roberts. The last thing he wanted was to be seen by him in this state, as sympathy for his plight would no doubt be in short measure.

He could see it now, 'What's the matter with you man? Have to stand up to these bastards. I bet you did nothing to protect yourself'.

He knew this ridicule would be too much for him, plus the bleeding seemed to have alleviated somewhat. He tried to remove the hanky he had clasped to his face in order to stem the flow of blood, but it seemed to have adhered itself to his cheek.

Better leave it, he thought, *or it might set it off again.*

It was then that the No. 37 came into view.

"You all right mate?" asked the bus driver as he stepped aboard, his deep West Indian accent feeling reassuring, as if there was someone who actually cared.

15

"Yes, I'm fine," he mumbled, not daring to look up as he handed over his money.

Philip sat just to the rear of the driver, this close proximity to someone who had shown concern to him, giving him a sense of security.

—⁓—

"So this is your all-important meeting?" said Kim as Paul turned to greet her.

"No, well, yes – you know what Solley's like?"

"I do unfortunately," she answered. "What a waste, and look what I have ended up with! You know, I reckon I could convert him," she added, looking across at Solley, his arm around an extremely good looking Armenian.

"Don't you start," said Paul.

"What do you mean by that?"

"Oh nothing – we'll give it ten minutes then we'll head off. Have some of that gateau you made."

"Bollocks," she replied. "I've only just got here and I intend to enjoy myself!"

—⁓—

Philip alighted from the bus, the driver's words ringing in his ears that he 'should get that looked at', and made his way up the tree-lined avenue. He now lived with his wife in the house he had inherited from his parents, buying out his sister's half. There was no way he could ever afford a property around here, especially a four-bedroomed one, that was for sure.

He pushed the garden gate open and made his way up the front path, the bright marigolds that lined it during the day reminding him of a runway at night. If Catherine had her way, there would be marigolds everywhere. She had always loved bright things – even the patterns on the curtains that she ordered for the kitchen mirrored their floral counterparts.

Catherine eased the sitting room curtain to one side. *Who would be calling at this time of night?* she thought. To her surprise it was Philip. But why hadn't he used his key? It then dawned on her that he had his bag in one hand and the other was holding what looked like a rag to his face. She put her knitting on the coffee table and ran to answer the door.

"What on earth has happened?"

"Oh it's nothing," he replied in a low voice, placing his case in the hallway next to the umbrella stand.

She took him by the hand and led him upstairs to the bathroom. "I'll have to soak it to get it off," she said, and using her thumb and forefinger she gently eased the blood-soaked hanky from his face, finally revealing the wound in all its gory detail.

"My God, what the hell happened? You will have to go to hospital for stitches."

Philip got up from the edge of the bath where he had been sitting, having finally summoned up the courage to see the wound for himself. The bathroom cabinet mirror confirmed his worst fears: there, some three inches long, was a deep gash. Catherine was right, it would need medical attention. He had hoped this would not have been the case as he would be asked how it happened and lying was never his strong suit.

"I'll get the car out," she said, leaving him sitting on the edge of the bath, hands between his knees.

There was no way he could tell her what had actually happened as she had always looked up to him. Was he really a coward? After all, had he tried to defend himself, things could have turned out a lot worse. Instead of a trip to A & E, Catherine could be on her way to… Philip put the thought out of his head; it was too terrible to contemplate. Not so much for his sake but for hers. As an only child of older parents, she had led a sheltered

17

life – how would she manage on her own? It was possible she could end up in the hands of someone like Roberts – literally.

—⁓—

Roberts answered his phone, "No I don't have them yet," he said, "this is not the place for that sort of thing; you never know who's about. I thought I would go over to his place – have a face to face, put the pressure on him there."

"Are you sure these documents actually exist and they're not a figment of your imagination?" said Reggie.

"Of course they exist; I wouldn't be going to all this trouble if they didn't."

Councillor Roberts put his phone back in his jacket. "Goodnight David," he said as he left the Town Hall and made his way to the waiting taxi.

"Evening Squire, where to?" said the driver.

"I want you to take me to Waverley Road, no. 64."

Roberts made himself comfortable on the back seat. He knew confronting Townsend in his own home was audacious to say the least, but if the shit hit the fan in any way, it could be helpful if it appeared that Townsend was implicated in some way.

"Wait here," he said to the taxi driver as they pulled up outside the house.

"Oh no you don't."

"Don't what?"

"You pay me first."

"I'm not going to do a runner, I'm a councillor."

"I don't care who you are mate," he replied, "you could be the bleeding Queen of Sheba for all I know. You just pay me first."

"Ok," said Roberts, "how much?"

The cabbie looked at his meter, "£14.75."

Roberts handed the driver £15. "Keep the change," he said sarcastically as he slammed the cab door and made his way up the path to Philip's house. "How the bloody hell can he afford this?" he said to himself. "Whatever he's up to, I want a slice."

He pressed the doorbell but there was no answer so tried several more times. *Where the hell could he be at this time of night? He's not the type to be down the pub, nor's that pretty little wife of his. I know where I would be…"* he thought.

He made his way back to the waiting taxi and took out his phone.

"Ah Townsend, it's Roberts here… What's that…? I can't hear you. You eating something?"

"No," said Philip, trying to ignore the pain. "I've had an accident."

"How serious?"

"Sorry? The line's not that good."

"How fucking serious?" repeated Roberts slowly.

"I am in A & E," he mumbled.

"I want you to come and see me first thing tomorrow morning."

"I'm sorry, I can't hear you. The signal's not good here."

"I don't care what the fuck is wrong with you, even if you're on death's fucking door, I want to see you tomorrow."

Philip hesitated for a second, he had always deplored swearing, especially from those who should know better, and looked up as a young male nurse approached him.

"Mr Townsend," he said. "Will you please come this way?"

"I have to get treatment now, I'll call you back later," he mumbled.

"Don't hang up on me. Townsend… Townsend? Bastard!" said Roberts, almost throwing his phone to the ground in frustration.

Philip watched as the nurse pulled on a pair of thin blue gloves.

"I'm just going to clean the area first." The nurse gently removed the gauze pad soaked in antiseptic to reveal the wound. "How did you come by this?" he asked, looking concerned.

Philip hesitated. "I fell over in the shed."

"Really?" said the nurse, cleaning the wound. "Right, I am just going to fetch a doctor."

"Why?"

"This is a serious wound you have. It may need more than just stitches; the last thing you want is infection."

Now left on his own, he was tempted to just get up and walk out but he knew that would be a foolish thing to do. He checked his phone; there was a missed call from Roberts.

Damn it, he thought, *he will just have to wait.* He looked up as the nurse returned with what he presumed was a doctor, although he only looked to be in his late teens. The young doctor introduced himself as Adam as he placed his forefinger gently under Philip's chin and lifted his head to one side.

"That is a very nasty cut you have there…" the doctor checked his notes… "Mr Townsend. The nurse tells me you fell over in your shed?"

"Yes, that's right. I caught a nail."

"That is most unfortunate. You have severed the muscles in your cheek to such an extent you will need surgery to affect a proper repair."

"Can't you just stitch it up?"

"I could," said the doctor. "But your face might well end up distorted and chewing could be problematical."

Philip thought hard. "I have a very important business meeting I can't miss," he said.

"I'm sure they would understand."

"If I don't make it, my company will go out of business and my employees will lose their jobs."

"This is not something that can be just patched."

Philip got to his feet. "Well in that case, I'll have to leave it then."

"Mr Townsend," said the doctor. "You must listen."

"No, you must listen. People are depending on me for their livelihoods," he replied, his lie sounding convincing.

"When is this meeting?"

"Tomorrow lunchtime."

"Ok, I will do what I can for now but you must return tomorrow."

"Of course, straight after my meeting."

Philip made his way out into the waiting room to find Catherine reading a magazine, her broad smile lifting his spirits.

"You all patched up?" she asked, looking at the large piece of wadding held in place by several strips of plaster.

He nodded.

"We'd better get you home, you must be tired."

"I am rather," he mumbled, looking at his watch.

"Still, not to worry," said Catherine, "you can have a nice lie-in tomorrow. And don't look at me in that fashion Philip Townsend! I won't take no for an answer."

Despite his reluctance to admit it, the recent events that had befallen him had left him in a state of shock. Maybe a day off wouldn't be such a bad idea after all. But what about Roberts? He sounded very upset – but then again, he would just have to wait.

This decision of Townsend to defy his superior was most unlike him but he was in too much pain to care.

3

"What time is it?" asked Kim, trying to lift her head.

"9.30," answered Paul.

"Oh shit, I was supposed to pick the kids up from Julie's at nine."

"Don't worry, they're downstairs. Here, drink this." He handed her a mug of hot tea.

She pursed her lips and sipped at the strong, sweet liquid. "God, that's good. What time did we get back?"

"Midnight."

"Well that's not too bad."

"No, I got back at midnight. You didn't come home until 5.30."

"5.30!" she exclaimed. "What the hell was I doing until 5.30?"

"The last I saw of you, you were doing a duet with that greasy boyfriend of Solley's."

"Duet?"

"Yeah, John set the stage up with his latest toy – a karaoke machine."

"Oh yeah, I think I remember now."

"Well that was enough for me but you insisted on staying on."

She lifted herself up onto one elbow. "I can't face the kids like this."

"It's ok, I told them you had one of your migraines."

"One of my migraines?" she repeated. "I don't get migraines."

"Well you do now," he said, removing the empty cup from her hands.

"Oh who the bloody hell's that?" she groaned as the phone rang.

Paul leaned across her and picked up the phone from the bedside.

"Get off."

"What?"

"Get off," she shouted as she threw the covers to one side and ran to the en-suite as he answered the phone.

"No you haven't interrupted anything," he said. "And by the way, what did you do to my wife last night?"

"Nothing," replied Solley. "She was just having a good time and it sounds like she's having one now."

"Hold on," said Paul as he made his way to the bathroom and closed the door to block out the sound of Kim throwing up. "Well she's paying for it now."

"What happened to you? One minute you were there, then you disappeared. I wanted to talk to you."

"I don't know about you Solley, but if I'm up for 500 big ones, I would rather discuss it in a more appropriate place. Like an office maybe?"

"Ok, keep your pants on. Guess you have pants on?" he added.

"What concern is that of yours?"

"Oh, nothing, just lying here with my cock in my hand thinking of you."

"You know what Solley? Sometimes you can be a right sick fuck."

"Me? No, not me, I'm a fairly regular guy compared to a lot of people. Anyway, I have booked a table at Gino's for lunch, my treat. It'll just be the four of us."

"And who exactly would that be?"

"You and I of course; Marcus and that beautiful wife of yours."

23

Paul turned to see Kim in knickers and bra staggering out of the bathroom, her make-up smeared across her face, giving her a clownish appearance, the ends of her long raven hair, wet and matted from washing the vomit from it.

"My beautiful wife as you put it is somewhat indisposed," he said as she flopped onto the bed with a groan.

—∿—

Paul placed the half empty bottle of Chianti onto the kitchen counter and made his way into the sitting room. "You feeling any better?" he asked.

Kim looked up, her eyes bloodshot. "What do you think?"

"I'll take that as a no then."

He crossed to the drinks cabinet. "Hair of the dog?"

"Piss off!"

"Please yourself," he replied, helping himself to a large whisky.

"So how did your little soiree at Gino's work out?"

"Not bad, the food was fantastic as usual and Gino gave us a bottle of very expensive wine on the house. There's half a bottle in the kitchen when you're feeling up to it."

"I should bloody well think so the amount of times you and Solley go there. Between the two of you, you've probably paid for his kids' uni fees."

"So what if we have? The food's the best for miles and his kids are good hard-working Italians – salt of the earth. Talking of kids, where are our two feckless layabouts?"

"Your children are back over at Julie's."

"They seem to spend more time there than they do here nowadays."

"Maybe," she said, getting up from the sofa, "they know where they're welcome."

"What's that supposed to mean?" he asked, following her into the kitchen.

"What do you think it's supposed to mean? You hardly make them feel welcome."

"That's not true."

"Not true?" she repeated raising her voice, only to clasp her head. "Now look what you've done."

"Well maybe I am a little off now and again but they're 18 and 20 years old. I had been working for five years at their age – full time."

"Things are different now."

"No they're not. They're just bloody bone idle."

"I can't believe you sometimes, talking about your kids like that."

"Ok, ok, I admit that was a little harsh, but they have opportunities that were never there for you and me and we have made something of ourselves. It just worries me that's all."

"I know, it worries me too sometimes but they're not Gino's kids, they're ours. They are what they are. Anyway," she continued, dropping two large tablets into a glass of water causing it to fizz and effervesce, sending a stream of white bubbly foam down one side, "how did the meeting with Solley and Marcus go?"

Paul was glad to get onto a subject that gave him a firmer footing. "Yorkshire," he announced with pride.

"Where?"

"Our next project – and it will be a big one – will be in Yorkshire."

"Are you winding me up? Because if you are, I can tell you I am not in the bloody mood."

"No, it's kosher. There's a large old Victorian hospital – they treated people for TB years back." He paused, "My dad died of TB, doesn't quite seem possible nowadays."

"No," responded Kim, knowing he had always been close to his father.

"Anyway, this find is a potential gold mine."

"Oh, and how exactly is that?"

"Inside information," he answered, tapping the side of his nose with his index finger.

"Ok, so where did this inside information come from exactly?" she asked, knowing full well it would have something to do with Marcus.

"Marcus, but you must keep this under your hat."

"Of course."

"This old Sanatorium is perfect for conversion to luxury apartments. The only downside is its location and that's where Marcus comes in."

"I thought he would," she said under her breath.

"Sorry?"

"Nothing, carry on."

"As I was saying, Marcus has information from a reliable source that the new northern section of the HS2 line will go within a mile of the old hospital. If we can get our hands on it, we'll make a killing."

"So how much is this going to set us back?"

"Well Solley reckons we could get it for as little as £500,000."

"And the refurbishing costs?"

"Well I haven't gone into any great detail, but from what Solley has told me he reckons around £1.2million, plus our initial purchase price. So, say around £1.7million with fees."

"And return?"

"Solley reckons – and I think he's about right – it should convert into 22 luxury apartments with a resale value from between £250,000 to £380,000. So that should give us a profit of around £4.8million or thereabouts."

"Mmm… This sounds all a bit too good to be true."

"Never look a gift horse in the mouth," said Paul. "Not only that, but you know how things are here. Every time a property comes up, it goes to some bloody foreigner at over the top prices."

"Yes, but that's a good thing. It increases the value of our portfolio."

"Yes, I know that but we provide a service to our local community."

Kim laughed. "You ought to listen to yourself sometimes Paul Goodman!"

"What's that supposed to mean?"

"Service to the community?" she repeated. "Sounds like you're running a charity."

"We do provide a service. Good homes for people to live in."

"Oh yeah, they're only as good as they are because I keep an eye on you."

"Well there you go then, what a great team we make."

She reached slowly across, picked her phone up from the coffee table and read the text.

"Who was that?" he asked, ripping the ring pull from a can of Best Bitter.

"Julie," said Kim.

"Well I can't drive and neither should you. If Julie or Derek can't bring them over, they'll just have to get the bus."

"They're not coming home," she answered, phone still in her hand.

"Oh, why not?"

"Derek's taken them to Margate for a few days."

"Margate, why?"

"We need to talk," she said, sitting opposite him.

Paul's stomach turned over. *I knew it,* he thought to himself, *she's found someone else and who could blame her. After all, I haven't been the most attentive husband and now this little problem – maybe she thinks I don't fancy her anymore and I'm just using my age as an excuse while fucking my way around London. Ok, there was that one time, but I was drunk and it meant nothing.*

He braced himself for what he thought was about to come.

"I saw the doctor a couple of weeks ago."

"You're not bloody pregnant again are you?" he blurted, immediately dismissing this statement considering the recent situation.

"No."

"Ok then, what is it?"

"There's no easy way to put this so I'll tell you straight. I have cancer."

Paul did not answer. For the first time in his fifty-two years, he was totally lost for words. It felt as if he had been hit by a train. He could literally feel the blood drain from his head as pins and needles fizzed through his fingers. He suddenly leapt to his feet.

"Where are you going?" asked Kim.

"I'm going to phone Craig."

"Why?"

"Get one of those Harley Street doctors he knows. I don't care what it fucking takes or costs, we'll beat this."

"Sit down," she said, raising her voice. "Please sit down."

Paul reluctantly did so.

"Look, I am perfectly happy with Dr Peters. And anyway, our private health care is as good as any."

"Ok, but it can't hurt to have a second opinion can it?"

"I have."

"When?"

"After getting the results from Dr Peters. I was in shock. Me of all people – I just couldn't believe it. I don't smoke, I keep fit, and I don't even drink that bloody much – not that you'd think that looking at me now."

"Who did you see?" he asked.

"I went as you suggested to Harley Street. Ruth's doctor."

"Solley's sister?"

"Yes."

"You told her before me?"

"Yes, what difference does it make? Anyway, I wanted to be one hundred percent sure before I said anything, plus I needed to hear it from someone else."

"And?"

"He told me the same as Dr Peters."

"And what exactly was that?"

"It's definitely cancer."

"Where is it?" asked Paul, lowering his eyes.

"No, it's not that type – it's melanoma."

"Skin cancer?" said Paul.

"Yes."

"But how? You're always so careful, every time you get near the sun I have to cover you in that bloody cream stuff until you look like a cross-channel swimmer."

"That's the thing."

"I don't understand."

"They reckon this melanoma could have been from exposure to too much sun maybe twenty years ago or even more. Back then, sun tan cream was just that – it was to help you get a sun tan. It did little if nothing to stop the UV."

"So where is it?" he asked gently.

Kim stood up, removed her top and turned around. Paul looked at her beautifully smooth skin, searching for some form of recognisable abnormality. It didn't seem possible that somewhere there was a life-threatening disease. He got up to take a closer look. "I can't see anything," he said.

She removed her bra to reveal a red, slightly inflamed area.

"Is that it?" he asked, trying to convince himself that this insignificant mark could possibly hold any threat to his wife.

When she did not answer he put his arms around her and kissed the nape of her neck gently. "We'll beat this," he whispered, feeling her body tremble.

"I'm so frightened," she sobbed.

It was this that really hit home. For all of the 22 years he had known Kim, she had never shown any sign of weakness. Even through childbirth, her first labour lasting twenty-seven hours, she saw it through with guts and determination. Refusing anything but gas and air, she was determined to see her first born enter this world.

"So how long have you known?" he asked as she put her top back on.

"I first heard from Dr Peters about two weeks ago."

"But why didn't you tell me?"

"I tried to block it out of my mind. I know it's stupid but I hoped it might just all go away."

"They say denial's very common. What about the kids, will we have to tell them? Unless of course you reckon we can keep it all secret. Yes, that's what we'll do; keep it secret until you're better. No need to upset them unnecessarily."

"They'll have to know, you can't keep radiotherapy secret," said Kim, picking the half-empty beer can off the coffee table. "You finished with this?"

"Err, yeah. So, when does your treatment start?" he asked as he followed her into the kitchen.

"Tomorrow."

"Ok, I'll phone Solley."

"Why?"

"To tell him this hair-brained scheme of his is a non-starter as far as I am concerned."

"No, don't do that."

"Why? From now on you're my only concern."

"I want you to go ahead with it."

"I don't understand," said Paul, feeling a little dejected.

"Look, this might sound a little strange – and believe me there's no-one I want by me at a time like this more than you – but I'm going to need some space, if you know what I mean."

The refusal of Paul's undivided attention by Kim left him feeling somewhat rejected. "I understand," he said quietly.

That night he lay there in the half light, his mind turning over at the news he had just received. He could not believe it was true. He looked at Kim, her chest rising and falling with each breath. How could this vivacious and beautiful woman have such a thing? He understood she wanted everything to be as normal as possible but how? Especially once the kids found out. He knew they would be devastated, and of course – the crucial question was when to tell them. He lifted the cover slightly and stared at Kim's back. If he could only suck it up inside him and take it for himself he would, without a second's hesitation.

4

"Where are you going?" asked Catherine.

"To work," mumbled Philip, slipping on his dressing gown and tucking his feet into his slippers.

"But surely you can take a day or two off. What did the doctor say?"

"It'll be fine," he answered, wiping a small speck of blood from the corner of his mouth with a tissue.

She slipped out from under the duvet. "I'll make some porridge."

You'll have to liquidize it, he thought as he made his way into the bathroom and picked up his toothbrush.

He squeezed the bottom of the tube, delivering a red and white slug to the surface of the nylon bristles then paused, the toothbrush hovering just inches from his mouth. He parted his lips just wide enough to place the brush inside and there it stayed for several seconds before he removed it. There was just no way he could possibly clean his teeth the pain was almost unbearable; it would have to be mouthwash.

—∞—

"Oh Solley, it's you," said Paul, answering the door.

"Of course it's me, Yorkshire, remember?"

32

"Oh, yeah of course, our trip up North to appraise this project of yours."

"*Ours*," he corrected. "Don't tell me you've forgotten already?"

"No, of course not, bit of a rough night last night, that's all. Come in, I'll get a few things together. Just the one night?" he added, making his way upstairs.

"Unless you fancy staying on a bit longer, experience the local delights?" he joked. "Oh, hello Kim."

"Morning Solley – and what delights might they be?" she added, holding up the coffee pot from where she stood in the kitchen doorway.

"Don't mind if I do," he replied, making his way into the kitchen. "To be honest, I think a night of drunken debauchery in that part of the world is probably out of the question." He turned to Kim. "Talking of debauchery, what did Paul have to say when you got home the other night?"

"Not much really."

"If that had been Marco, I would have gone through the roof."

"Ah yes, but Paul knew I had you to look after me!" she quipped.

"That's true," he said with a smug expression on his face as he took a gulp of coffee from his mug. "Mmm, not bad."

"Bleeding well should be! It's a Carmichael's import."

Solley placed his mug on the counter and moved a little closer to her. "Is there something wrong?"

"What makes you say that?" she said, her voice less than convincing.

"Oh nothing, just that Paul seemed a little vague that's all. Hope he's not getting cold feet."

"Don't you worry about him, he'll be fine."

"So, what do you think of the idea?"

"Well, I'll need more info of course, but on the surface it looks promising."

"I'm ready when you are," announced Paul. "Shove this in the car while I say goodbye to Kim."

"Err, yeah, sure," replied Solley, getting up from the chrome bar stool, taking the canvas holdall from him.

"I won't be a minute." He turned to Kim, "Are you sure you will be ok?"

"Look," she said, placing a hand on his shoulder. "Go to Yorkshire, do what you have to do. Staying here won't make any difference."

"What time's your appointment?" he asked, looking at his watch. "You sure you don't want me to come with you? I really don't like the idea of you going on your own and you might not be able to drive after treatment."

"That's all taken care of, Julie's going with me."

"Oh, well that's ok then."

"Now be off with you; that sounds like Solley losing his patience," she quipped, hearing the car horn blasting.

Paul kissed her hard on the lips. "See you tomorrow evening."

"That took you long enough," said Solley, starting the car.

Paul didn't answer and they drove in silence for a while before Solley spoke.

"I know what's up. It's Julie."

"Sorry?"

"Julie's taking Kim to the West End and I bet you were giving her a lecture on not spending too much. Well believe me, I have been there mate and it doesn't work, I can tell you that much. You should have seen what Marco came back with last week. I told him in no uncertain terms that most of it would have to go back."

"Yeah, that's right, she did say something about shopping with her sister."

"There you go, Solley knows you know," and with that, Paul was forced back into his seat as the powerful Mercedes accelerated from the slip road onto the M1.

"Did we have to come up here?" asked Frank as Ian drew up outside the old Sanatorium, its wide sweeping steps leading to two massive oak doors. "How the hell did they get anyone in here?"

"Round the back," answered Ian, undoing his seatbelt. "The front's just a façade to make it look like a grand country house. You have those documents I take it?"

"Yes, but first my money."

"Look, I told you, I'm in for a pay-off from these developers. As soon as I have that you'll have your money."

Fuck it! thought Frank, *I just knew this worm would try something like this.* He looked at Ian, "My money or you don't get the documents."

"Ok, six grand now and the rest at the end of the week. I'm not made of the stuff you know."

"Ok then," he replied, knowing full well he would have to make this compromise. He knew Carlyle would not be pleased with only half of what he owed but if he got it to him straightaway, he could perhaps fend him off for a bit longer.

Ian handed the money to Frank who reluctantly retrieved the documents from under his sweater and gave them to him. After all, what choice did he have? This was his only way out.

As Frank opened the door, the piercing wind whipped around his legs and up into the vehicle. Before Ian could close his own door, it had sent various papers swirling up in a vortex, some exiting the vehicle causing him to give chase, leaping and skipping through the coarse heather in a vain attempt to try and retrieve the wayward sheets of A4 paper.

It was almost as if the wind had them on a piece of string and every time he was within reach, it would lift them from his grasp. If one believed the elements had a will of their own, there would be little doubt that they were toying with him.

Finally, he gave up on the last sheet as it wafted high into the air like a wayward kite billowing higher on every gust.

"Fuck it," he said as he returned, out of breath, tossing the retrieved papers on the driver's seat and slamming the door. "Come on," he said turning to Frank, "Let's get this over with. What are you waiting for?"

"Two secs," he replied, mobile phone in hand. He texted two words, *It's off.*

"This place gives me the fucking creeps," he remarked as he joined Ian by the doors to the Sanatorium, his words carried away on the ever-present gale that seemed to frequent these high moors on a permanent basis.

"How important were they?" he asked, knowing full well that Turnbull wouldn't have gone to all this trouble for nothing.

"I won't know until I have read them properly. Anyway, that's none of your concern, ok?"

Frank reluctantly followed him to the rear of the building. From the lane below, the Sanatorium seemed quite diminutive set in the vast expanse of moorland, but up close one could appreciate the true magnificence of this Victorian tribute to public health.

Ian dug deep into the pocket of his wax jacket and retrieved a bunch of keys, one of which had red electrical tape wound round. It was this one he placed into the lock. It took some effort but finally the key started to turn, its metal teeth pressing against the levers that at first seemed unwilling to yield.

"Don't break on me you bastard," he muttered as he exerted more leverage.

Eventually the thin pieces of brass fell into place, drawing the bolt from its housing.

"That's got it!" he declared, the sense of relief palpable. "Frightened I might bust the lock like last time," he added, "that's why we came round the back."

The two men stepped into the gloom of this once busy Sanatorium, their footsteps echoing through the now empty corridors. Occasionally their footfalls would crush small pieces of glass that seemed to litter the once polished floors as they made their way into the bowels of this great edifice.

Once again, Ian fished into his jacket, this time producing a torch, its bright beam cutting deep into the heart of this imposing structure whose labyrinth of corridors led in all directions.

"I hope that torch doesn't go out," grumbled Frank, the hairs on the back of his neck at attention.

"You worry too much. This is it," he added, stopping next to one of the many identical doors that lined every passageway. "That's odd," he said as he tried the door. "It's locked."

"It can't be, who would have locked it?"

"No-one as far as I know, I'm the only one with the keys."

"Try it again," said Frank, impatient to do whatever it was Ian had in mind and get out.

"No, it won't budge."

"Here let me try." He clasped the handle and threw his substantial weight against the door as he turned the knob, only to be met with the kind of resistance that told him in no uncertain terms that their progress was without question impeded.

"Fuck it," he complained, holding his shoulder.

"You all right?"

"Yeah, fine, what do you think? Are you sure you have the right key?"

Ian didn't answer but held his hand up.

"What is it?" asked Frank in a low whisper.

"I thought I heard something."

"Look, you don't have to try and scare me, I'm shitting it already. I hate this fucking…"

"Quiet," hissed Ian. "Listen, it's coming from down there."

"Look, it'll be dark soon, let's leave it until tomorrow."

"What difference does it make?" said Ian, moving in the direction of the sound. "It's bloody pitch black in here anyway now it's boarded up, and the last thing I want is to come back here tomorrow and find somebody has ripped every last vestige of pipework out of the fucking place."

"Does it really matter?" replied Frank looking around.

"Of course it fucking matters, I have a reputation you know."

"Maybe we should call the police?"

No sooner had he said this than Ian stopped in his tracks, causing him to plough into his back.

"Have you lost your bloody mind? That's the last thing we want – that lot snooping about. Here, take this," he added, bending down and picking a lump of 4" x 2" and handing it to Frank.

"What the fuck am I supposed to do with this?"

"Cover my back, that's what," he said, arming himself with a length of old pipe. "It came from in here," he added, stopping outside one of the doors.

The two men listened intently, the oppressive silence almost overwhelming. Now deep in the bowels of this edifice, its thick walls insulating them from any outside sound, even the persistent howl of the seemingly ever-present wind now silenced.

"I can't hear anything," said Frank, hoping this statement would be enough to satisfy Ian's curiosity. "Come on, let's get out of here."

"What? You must have heard that!"

This time Frank could not deny the fact that there was indeed something, or someone, in the darkness.

"On the count of three," whispered Ian.

"Wait," said Frank. "On the count of three – then what?"

"We burst in."

"Supposing it's locked?"

"There's one way to find out. One, two, three…"

The door burst open and Ian immediately scanned the room with his torch.

"This place is massive," said Frank.

"It's the dining hall," replied Ian, making his way through the piles of rubbish that lay strewn over the parquet flooring. "Over here!" he shouted.

Frank left the sanctuary of the doorway and with his piece of timber at the ready, made his way to Ian. "What is it?" he said in a low voice.

"Look."

"What?"

"There."

"I can't see anything."

"Footprints in the dust."

"You sure they're not yours?" said Frank hopefully.

"Of course they're not mine you prick! They're fresh too."

"Ok, I think it's time we called a halt to this. That torch of yours is not going to last much longer and getting out of here without it is going to be almost fucking impossible. And if there is someone in here, one thing's for sure, they're up to no good and pipework or no pipework; I don't want to be in here with them."

"Yeah, maybe you're right," agreed Ian, examining the fading beam from his torch.

Relieved to be out of the old Sanatorium, Frank made his way to the waiting Range Rover but instead of Ian getting into the driver's seat as he had expected, he made his way to the rear of the vehicle, opened the tailgate and started to rummage around.

"What the hell you playing at, can't it wait until you get home?" he asked, impatient to get on his way.

"There it is," he replied, retrieving a large torch from the cavernous depths of the boot.

"What's that for?" said Frank, knowing full well.

"What do you think it is?" replied Ian, shining the powerful flashlight straight at him.

"Fuck off!" he exclaimed, shielding his eyes from the powerful beam.

"No-one's going to hide from this. Two million candle power," announced Ian proudly.

Once again Frank found himself unwillingly scouring the labyrinth of corridors. "Look, there's no-one here, it's empty."

"But those footprints in the dining hall came from someone," replied Ian dejectedly. He felt certain there was someone in there. "Look, how much of this place have we searched?"

"Feels like all of it," Frank replied, showing signs of disquiet.

"You know, I bet we have only searched a quarter of it."

"That might well be true but even that bloody searchlight of yours won't last for ever."

Ian knew he was right; he would have to accept defeat. Once again, Frank was glad to be out of that awful place.

"What is it?" he asked as Ian stood in the doorway.

"It's gone!"

"What's gone?" he replied, his mind still half on what might be lurking inside the old hospital.

"The fucking car – that's what!"

Frank paused in front of Ian and stared at where the Range Rover had once been.

You stupid bastard, he thought, *you were only supposed to take the documents!*

Ian pushed past and ran towards where his pride and joy had once stood; looking about him as though he might have inadvertently put it somewhere else. Frank joined him on the vast expanse of weed-strewn gravel that formed the driveway.

"But who?" he said. "There's nothing for fucking miles."

"I'll tell you who," replied Ian. "Whoever was in there," he added, pointing at the old Sanatorium. "That's fucking who."

"What?"

"The documents."

"What?"

"The bloody papers I was running my arse off to retrieve earlier. They were on my seat."

Frank knew they were important but was not fully aware of their true significance. Whatever they contained was obviously important enough to take Ian's mind off his very new and very expensive 4x4.

"What's in them?" he asked.

Ian did not reply but turned to him. "I want my money back."

"Fuck off," he replied, his tone defensive. "I earnt that money,

I did my bit. It's not my fault if you forgot to lock your bloody car, and I still want my other six grand."

Ian knew Frank was right, and if he wished to he could make things awkward for him, but he would do his best to get out of paying the other six grand.

"Give me your phone," he demanded.

"What for?"

"To call a fucking taxi, that's what for! Unless you fancy walking all the way back?"

—ɷ—

Maybe I should take up self-defence classes? Philip considered as he made his way up the steps of the Town Hall, but then again, would it only serve to encourage him to do something that wasn't in his nature? No, he had done the right thing, this was a one-off.

He remembered the dual between the youth and himself over his briefcase. *Maybe if my hand had been around that little runt's throat, the outcome would have been different,* he thought. This lack of total capitulation cheered him up to some degree.

—ɷ—

Solley flipped open the central console. "Fancy some music? They're all classics," he added. "Tell you what, here's a great one – *Hits of the 80s.* That's always good for a listen."

"I'd rather not, if it's all the same to you," replied Paul.

"Spit it out."

"Sorry?"

"Oh come on, there's something up. You're never this quiet so what is it?"

Paul knew he would have to give him something or he would never hear the last of it. "Oh, it's nothing really, the VAT man."

"Oh yeah, something I should know about?"

"No, just a misunderstanding, that's all."

"Well if there is a problem I want to know about it. I don't want to get into bed with you only to find you have the VAT equivalent of crabs!"

"Everything's kosher," said Paul. "It's all above board – you have my word."

—⚬⚬⚬—

"My goodness," exclaimed Mrs Grayson as she entered Philip's office. "What on earth's happened to you?"

"Oh, nothing really," he replied, "tripped in the shed. It was a nail."

Might as well stick to the original excuse, he thought, *after all, a little continuity couldn't do any harm.*

"So that's why you weren't here when I arrived. I said to Tracy – I said it's not like Mr Townsend not to be here before anyone else. But if there's anything I can do Philip…" Mrs Grayson rarely used Philip's Christian name but when she did it always made him feel a little self-conscious.

"I'll get you a cup of tea," she continued. "You can drink tea can you? Or would you like a can of fizzy drink from the machine? I think there's some straws somewhere left over from the adolescent *Get-to-know-your-Council* party. I said to Tracy, I said, what a complete waste of time…"

Philip raised his hand. "Tea please Mrs Grayson," he mumbled.

"Ok," she replied, and with that, scuttled off closing the office door with a little more force than would normally be required. This demonstration of disapproval at being dismissed in mid-sentence did not go un-noticed by Philip. He was fully aware of the vagaries that came with menopause.

His mother – a devoted wife for thirty years – turned on his father in a most unexpected manner, and this harsh treatment and short temper evaporated one day almost as suddenly as it had appeared. All thanks to HRT. However, even with the help of this wonder drug there were times when she had felt it difficult to control her emotions which would manifest itself in many forms, the most common being sudden bouts of tears, apparently for no reason.

He always felt that it was his father's devotion for his mother that saw him through this most awkward time. Hopefully he would be as gracious and understanding when his time came, although that was still many years away.

—⁓—

"Frank… Ian here. Can you spare a couple of hours this afternoon?"

"As long as it's not another trip over to that bloody hospital."

"No, there's something I think you should see."

"About 2pm ok?"

"That's fine."

—⁓—

"Mrs Goodman, the consultant will see you now."

Kim followed the short but extremely attractive young woman into the office, its large windows flooding the place with natural light. This room, like the rest of the building, was painted in soft pastel shades and dotted with evergreen palms although the colour combinations were not ones she would have approved of.

"Please Mrs Goodman, take a seat," said Mr Rathbone, waiting for Kim to be seated before returning to his chair. "I'll get straight to the point. We are going to attack this carcinoma with a course of radiotherapy once we have removed the melanoma itself today. I have read your notes from Dr Peters. Now if you would be kind enough to remove your top so I can have a look."

Kim did so, the young woman taking her blouse and bra and

Mr Rathbone examined her carefully, humming and ha-ing as he did so.

"Thank you, Mrs Goodman, you can get dressed now."

She redressed and sat back down to find him hastily making notes. He placed his pen on the table and looked up at her.

"It is advanced but not so much so that you should be concerned. We will have this cleared up in no time I am sure. We have a ninety percent recovery rate for this type of melanoma but as I said, it would have been nice to have caught it a little earlier. However, the odds are still very much in your favour. Anyway, as I say, the stage this melanoma is at will require a slightly more intensive programme of treatment. As a result, I am afraid there will be some side-effects."

"What side-effects?" she asked in a low voice.

"Well these are the most common – nausea, fatigue and unfortunately there will be some hair loss. Although you will be glad to know these symptoms are only temporary."

Hair loss – she knew that might happen. She had always been extremely proud of her hair but to hear this from the consultant brought home the severity of what she was to undergo and the realisation that this nightmare was for real.

"Mary will take you to the treatment suite. I will see you before you go tomorrow and if there is anything you wish to discuss – or just need someone to confide in – we have a person available 24/7."

"This Helpline – who will I be speaking to?" asked Kim.

"It will be one of our fully-trained nurses. Everything you tell them will be in complete confidence and of course, come straight back to me. I will be available during office hours."

5

Philip looked up – he knew that knock anywhere and sure enough, without waiting, the door burst open to reveal the not-so-diminutive Councillor Roberts, his massive bulk filling the doorway.

"Oh, so you finally decided to grace us with your presence then," blurted Roberts. "I called by the other night but you were out."

"Sorry?" mumbled Philip, having no idea what he was talking about.

"I called round, about 9.30ish."

"I w… w… was at the h… h… hospital."

"Yeah I know that," he replied impatiently. "So tell me, what's all this about?" he demanded, pointing at Philip's cheek.

I was attacked by an escaped tiger while saving a crippled orphan from a fate worse than death, by stabbing the out of control animal through the eye with my fountain pen, thought Philip before speaking to Roberts.

"You fell over in the shed? You ought to get yourself a bloody light man. Anyway, last night I was looking for some drawings."

"C… c… connected with what?" stammered Philip.

"They relate to some ancient mine workings on the Albright Estate."

Philip felt a sense of panic wash over him.

"Are you all right man?" asked Roberts.

"Yes, yes. These documents you want, I will have to get a request form from the Director of Information first."

"Can't you just go down there and get them for me, surely they're not classified?"

"I believe they are," he lied, "and even if they weren't you would still need permission to take them off the premises."

"Who said I wanted to take them off the premises?"

Philip felt his arse tighten, what the hell had made him say that?

Roberts moved a little closer. "Well as it so happens, I do need to take them home with me, just for a couple of days. Is there no way round this?"

"I'm afraid not," he replied, hoping this would be the end of the matter.

"You're up for promotion at the end of this month, isn't that so Townsend?"

"Y... y... yes."

"Well it would be a shame after all these years of hard work and loyal devotion if you were for some reason to be overlooked. See what I mean?" sneered Roberts, now so far across the desk; Philip thought he might fall into his lap.

"Err, o... o... ok, I'll see what I can do."

"I knew I could rely on you Townsend."

Roberts was just about to leave when he stopped. "Oh, by the way," he said in a low voice. "This is strictly between the two of us ok?"

"Of course C... C... Councillor Roberts.

—◊—

Frank opened the mail, a job Sharon – his girlfriend and part-time secretary – did until recently but since his divorce things had changed, Maureen had taken him for nearly everything and even now he found it hard to believe. Ok, so they had had their ups and downs, but then again what couple didn't? And it wasn't *that* bad compared to some. And that was another thing? What the hell did she see in that prick David? Ok, so he owned a car showroom and had a few quid.

He placed the paper knife onto his desk. *You know full well why your marriage broke up,* he thought to himself, *drink – not to mention the gambling.*

But he felt he had good reason, the death of his son at uni from meningitis had destroyed him. He tried to keep it together on the outside but that was only possible with the aid of alcohol. How Maureen had managed to cope had been a mystery to him. At first he had thought she was callous and even uncaring, but all she was doing was blocking it out of her mind as if it had never happened. This he realised when he came home early from work one day to find her washing their son's clothes.

His depression sank to new depths as he remembered the twelve grand he owed Reggie Carlyle. Still, if he could sort that out, stop the drink, get the business back on its feet then maybe he could win her back. After all that had happened he still loved her very much.

He lifted the receiver. "Frank Horton, private detective speaking... You want to meet at 1pm now... Hold on." He rustled some papers. "I guess I could reschedule some appointments... Very well, I'll see you at 1pm."

He could have met Ian any time that day but it didn't look good to be at his beck and call all the time. Anyway, this might be an opportunity to press him for the rest of that money; after all, he had got what he wanted on Philip Townsend.

For a while Frank thought he had finally found someone without a past and indeed he had. But that did not extend to that pretty wife of his. Who would have thought it of someone so prim and proper? He had done his bit and it was about time he got paid – papers or no papers.

—···—

Paul watched the traffic slip past them as Solley bullied his way down the overtaking lane. It had always puzzled him how someone that drove like his arse was on fire had never accumulated any points on his licence. He would not have believed it if it hadn't been for Solley's sister Ruth telling him she was as baffled as he was.

"Look before we meet this Ian Turnbull," said Solley, "you ought to know I had to slip him a few quid".

"Oh, and how much is a few quid?"

"Twenty big ones."

"That *is* a few quid!"

"But there's more once things are watertight."

"Go on," said Paul warily.

"Thirty."

Paul raised an eyebrow.

"But it will be worth every penny," added Solley in his defence.

"How come you didn't mention this before we got halfway up the bloody M1?"

"Dunno," he replied, shrugging his shoulders, both hands off the wheel, "just slipped my mind, that's all."

"£20k just slipped your mind?"

"You know me," he smiled.

"Oh I know you all right. I said to Kim there'll be an angle to this somewhere."

"Come on, you know as well as I do that sometimes you need to grease the wheels a little, so to speak."

"You can get a lot of grease for £20k."

"That may be so but we stand to make at least £2.4million each, probably more with the way the markets are going."

"Can this sweetener be traced back to you?" asked Paul.

"What do you take me for? I wasn't born yesterday, it's all cash."

"Well that's good. Can he be trusted? We don't want some minion have £20k crop up in his bank account out of nowhere, especially if it can be traced to us."

"Look, everything will be fine."

Paul had noticed Solley's stereotypical behaviour coming to the fore when money was being discussed – the tilted head, the hunched shoulders and the raised hands *'already'* – but other than that you would never know. His grandfather had been the last Orthodox in the family and passed away some five years ago. Over 200 years of living in Britain had reduced their religious zeal to nothing more than a custom, and if you wanted evidence of that then you just had to look in Solley's fridge.

He could still remember how as a kid, the first time he went to Solley's house for tea and they had bacon rolls and baked beans. He had just moved to the area and was getting a hard time from the local kids – although they had only moved a mile-and-a-half from their old house – but it was Solley who had taken him under his wing so to speak.

In spite of being the same age when they met – just eight years old – Solley always seemed much older and wiser back then, as opposed to the big kid he'd grown into. It was almost as if the older he got the more childish and irresponsible he became, and it was this tendency towards regressive behaviour that worried Paul. He had every faith in him as a businessman – and let's face it there was always risk in a project of this nature – but now Solley had given him the lowdown, might it be too risky? He would take it one step at a time.

—◊—

Once again, the heavy knock on Philip's office door pre-empted the arrival of Councillor Roberts.

"Find those files Townsend?"

"Err, n… n… no Councillor. I haven't had chance."

"Not had chance man, I don't buy that one. What's so bloody important? Ok, don't tell me, it's that roundabout at Waverley Cross. I noticed that bloody Clifton in and out of your office; thinks the whole bloody world revolves around his precious roundabout."

"Y… y… yes," he replied. This unusual tendency towards deception was getting easier with every lie. Even his demeanour felt more disposed to fabrication as there seemed to be a distinct advantage in doing so.

"Well I want you to look for them before you go tonight. I'll be here for the Extraordinary Meeting this evening. Meet me after 9pm."

With that, he left and slammed the door behind him.

Philip leant back in his chair, folding his hands behind his head. This relaxed posture, although unfamiliar to him, felt good. Deception – that was the key. But this flush of self-confidence evaporated when the thought of the blackmailer and what he had said about his wife, flooded back into his mind. Not only was he a liar and a coward, he was allowing himself to be blackmailed.

But then again, surely that was the point – one did not really have a choice when it came to blackmail. It was important he protect his wife at all costs, after all where would someone like him find someone like Catherine? At the age of 32 she was his first girlfriend and the thought of spending the rest of his life alone was unthinkable. But how did this person find out? Her name was never mentioned during the investigation, she was only known as Ms X.

Once again, his sanctum was invaded by Roberts. "When you see Clifton, tell him from me he can stuff his bloody roundabout!"

"S… s… s… sorry?"

"You heard."

Philip winced in anticipation of Robert's signature departure.

—⁂—

Ian looked at his watch. "Where the hell is he?"

It was then that Frank's car came round the corner and pulled into the layby.

"You're late," he said as Frank emerged from his vehicle.

"Well I'm here now."

"Come on, we'll take a walk."

The two men climbed over an old wooden stile half submerged in brambles. It was one of these tendrils with its accompanying hooked thorns that wound itself around Frank's leg just above his sock. "Fuck!" he shouted.

"What the hell is it?" asked Ian who had safely negotiated the overgrown obstacle.

"These bloody brambles, that's what. Look, I'm bleeding."

Ian took a casual glance at the wound. "You'll live."

Having disentangled himself from the shrub's deadly embrace, Frank joined Ian on the other side of the hedge. "What the bloody hell's all this about?" he demanded, his left trouser leg raised as he took proper stock of his injuries.

"I want to make sure no-one overhears us," replied Ian, looking furtive, although this was an expression he carried with him most of the time.

"Ok, I can understand that, but isn't this a bit over the top?"

"You can't be too careful with things like this," he said in a low voice.

"Well, what is it then?"

"Tomorrow I am going to meet Mr Solomon and his partner – a Mr Goodman – they're both coming up from London, 10.30am at the Sanatorium. I want you to bug the building."

"What? I can't bug that place, it's massive and even if I could, it would take days."

"No, not the whole bloody place, just the reception area, it's there I will get to the nitty gritty if you see what I mean."

"That's not a good idea."

"Why not? If I have them on tape discussing cash back-handers it will be hard for them to back out, and it will be a little bit of insurance for the future maybe."

"You mean blackmail?"

"Let's call it leverage shall we – blackmail's such a dirty word."

"If you want my help you have to give me the rest of what's owed to me."

Frank could see that this insistence of his did not go down well, but Ian knew he had to give him what he owed him at some point, and his help in this matter was essential.

"Ok," he said, "I'll give you your £6k tomorrow."

"Cash."

"Cash," replied Ian. "What's that?"

"It's one of those e-cigarettes."

"Here, have one of these," said Ian, sticking the open packet of cigarettes under Frankie's nose.

The sweet rich smell of the finest Virginia tobacco invaded his nostrils. "No thanks," he said, "I have been off them for six months now."

"Oh go on," he cajoled, "you know you want to. One can't do any harm and stop worrying, everything will be fine and if questions are asked – and they won't be – you know nothing, it's as simple as that. Townsend has no idea that it was you who got that information on his wife and I trust there's no paper trail?"

"No, of course not, what do you take me for?"

"Well then, I'd better get back, Frances will be wondering where the hell I am. I'm supposed to be taking her to the theatre."

"What you going to see?" asked Frank, a bit of a theatregoer himself in the days when he could afford it.

"Oh I don't know. Something to do with horses or some bloody thing."

Frank was not what you might call the nervous type but as he got older and his gambling addiction started to take a toll on his life, his self-confidence had taken a bit of a battering. Ok, so he'd had a few quid on the dogs now and again, why not, lots of people did. And that's all it had been for years, and then for some unknown reason it became twice a week and then every day.

When it came to gambling it was as if every day was the first, and what he hoped to win that day would wipe out everything that had gone before – until his finances had reached rock bottom. Fortunately, his wife had persuaded him to sign over his half of the house otherwise that would have gone too. But what difference did it make now that she was leaving him? So here he was – no home, no wife, no business, no money and twelve grand in debt to Carlyle.

"As I was saying, wiring that place – even part of it – is not practical. Plus, you might not be able to get them to commit to anything incriminating at that particular point. No, the best way is for you to wear a wire."

"You can do that?" asked Ian.

"Of course; I'll call round tomorrow about… You say your meeting's 10.30?"

"Yes."

"Ok, I'll be at your place at 9am. It will only take a few minutes to set up."

"No, not my place," said Ian. "Let's meet here at 9.30am."

"Ok," he agreed, heading back towards the layby.

"Wait, there's something else…" he called, his voice trailing off, end of sentence.

This, Frank did not like the sound of, and turned to face Ian, half obscured by the shade.

"Well?" he said.

"Those papers that went missing from my car the other day…"

"What of them?"

"They're still missing."

"And what about the car?"

"Oh, that was recovered last night."

"What was in these papers?"

"Well that's the thing, not much really," lied Turnbull, knowing full well their full potential significance and the pressure he could put on Councillor Roberts with them – the only downside being that it would involve that fucking psychopath of a brother-in-law of his.

"And that's what's worrying me," he continued, "these papers would mean nothing to a car thief, or anyone for that matter, unless…" Ian hesitated.

"Unless what?" asked Frank. "It sounds to me as though I'm being accused."

"What makes you think I'm accusing you of anything?"

"Oh come on – we both know those so-called unimportant papers must have some significance or you wouldn't have gone to all the trouble and expense to get hold of them."

"Look, I'm not accusing you of anything but you have to admit it does seem a little odd. Apart from me you're the only person who knew we would be there. And that's another thing. Whoever took the car – where the bloody hell did they come from, if not the Sanatorium? After all, it's important we trust each other."

"You're right about one thing; we do need to trust each other. So what exactly is in these documents?"

Ian took a deep breath and began to explain.

—m—

"This it?" queried Paul as they pulled into the empty car park.

"Yeah," Solley replied, leaning forward so as to get a better look through the windscreen. "Looked posh online."

"Posh? It's a bloody dump!"

"Never judge a book by its cover," he said, throwing his door open.

"But why this place?" Paul asked, closing his door as Solley opened the boot.

"It's close to the old hospital. We're really high up here," he continued, "Do you think it might snow?"

"Snow?" he exclaimed, "it's fucking June!"

Solley paused outside the entrance to the hotel, placed Paul's holdall on the ground and tossed him the keys. "Lock up old man, I'll check us in."

Paul closed the boot and driver's door. Pressing the small button on the key fob, the car dutifully locked itself, telling him it had done so with a beep and two flashes of its hazard lights.

He looked around him. Apart from the rundown inn there was nothing, literally nothing to be seen as far as the eye could see except empty moorland, mile after mile. He had often used the expression *middle of nowhere* but he had never expected to actually be there some day.

The piercing wind harried him all the way to the sanctuary of the hotel lobby where he found Solley at the desk chatting to a very attractive woman – mid-thirties he would say, with an air about her that suggested she was more than just an employee. He introduced himself.

"Good evening Mr Goodman, I'm Margaret," she replied. "Your room is ready."

This statement had an air of pride about it as though she had just accomplished something noteworthy. "So gentlemen, if you would please follow me."

Paul could not help but notice how well her tweed skirt fitted, her shapely legs and slim waist separated by the most exquisite arse, equal to that of Kim's, *and that was something!* he thought.

They reached the top of the broad staircase culminating in a wide landing, the walls festooned with black and white photos of local people mostly engaged in activities associated with the local estate and its 19th Century obsession with killing things.

He waited in anticipation of what his room would afford him though his hopes were not high, if what he had seen of this place so far was anything to go by.

Margaret placed a large iron key in the lock of his room. It required a defiant twist of the wrist to force the levers to submit which they did with a resounding *thunk* – a sound familiar to Paul from his childhood days. The house his parents rented in his early years must have been nearly as old as this place – although he hoped the hotel would at least have an inside toilet. An en-suite seemed too much to hope for.

She pushed the door open and stepped to one side allowing him to enter. What greeted him came as a complete surprise – the room was well appointed with the finest furnishings and tastefully decorated. Maybe Solley was right, you can't always judge a book by its cover.

Margaret moved to the room next door and with as much effort as before, opened the door to Solley's room. Once again it was a homage to good taste and fine quality.

"I'll have to get these locks changed," she said. "Some of our older clients find it quite difficult sometimes."

"Thought you might have done that when you refurbished the rooms," said Paul, standing in the doorway as Solley placed his bag on the bed.

"Oh I would have done," she answered, turning to face him. "Grade II listed you see."

Both he and Solley were familiar with the meaning of this and avoided any building that was in any way listed.

"It's taken over a year just to get the rooms sorted," she continued. "As for the rest of the place, well who knows?"

"I might be able to help you there."

"Oh, and how might that be?" she enquired.

"I have a friend – or should I say my wife has a friend – in English National Heritage. She's an interior decorator, might be able to give you a few tips, help make things move a bit quicker. Sometimes it's the little things that can hold everything up."

"Tell me about it!" she answered. "Take these locks for a start; they say they're intrinsic to the soul of the place. Anyway gentlemen, I have taken up enough of your valuable time. Dinner will be served from 7pm."

"Well I don't know if we'll be dining here," said Solley.

"No, that will be fine," added Paul.

Her departure was accompanied by the creaking of the old stairway.

"I thought we might drive into Leeds, it's only an hour or so."

"No, I've had enough of driving."

"Wait a minute, you fancy her don't you?"

"No," replied Paul, trying to sound convincing.

"You dog you!"

"I do not fancy her, although I have to admit she is extremely attractive."

"Get lost, she's bleeding gorgeous! Even I can see that and I'm as bent as a nine-bob note."

"Look, Kim's the only one for me."

"Oh yeah? That's not what I heard."

"Oh not you as fucking well, that was eleven bloody years ago. I was drunk and it only happened once. Kim means the world to me and if anything should happen to her, I don't know what I would do."

"What do you mean by that?" asked Solley.

"By what?"

"*If anything should happen to her?*" he repeated.

"Nothing, just a figure of speech, I'm going to unpack," he added, leaving Solley without an answer.

—✶—

"Well that's it in a nutshell," said Ian.

Frank felt numb. The consequences did not bear thinking about. What the fuck had he got himself into? Talk about a rock and a hard place.

"Cheer up, it's not that bad."

"Twenty years in the police, ten years as a private detective, and I always kept my nose clean."

"So? But you didn't hesitate when I asked you to get that info on Townsend."

"I am a private detective, that's what I do for a living," answered Frank.

"All that's as maybe but you're on the wrong side of the law now.

57

Remember it was you who blackmailed Townsend, not me. Look," he continued, "are you in or are you out?"

"Hold on," said Frank as he took his mobile from his pocket and read the text. It simply read *your wife.* Frank knew exactly what this brief message implied, who it was from and its consequences.

"Ok," he said, "you can count me in."

6

"Mrs Goodman, how are you feeling?" asked Dr Peters. "I am pleased to report that the operation was a success. I believe the follow-up treatment has been fully explained to you?"

"Yes," said Kim, her left shoulder raised off the bed by a large doughnut shaped piece of wadding.

"I hope that's not too uncomfortable," he continued, "but it is important to keep the wound clean and away from pressure – not always easy. Do you have any questions for me?"

She had many questions and no questions. Every thought was cancelled out by another and anyway, what was the point? She was totally in their hands.

"No," she replied.

"Well, if there's anything you wish to discuss, just tell the nurse and she will make a note of it. Mr Rathbone will see you tomorrow morning before you leave. Now try and get some rest," he added as he made his way to the door of her private room.

Once again, she was cocooned in silence, alone with her thoughts. Of course, there was the TV or radio, but watching or listening to other people going about their everyday lives seemingly without a care, made her feel even more isolated.

She felt like a shop mannequin, separated from the outside world by a thin sheet of glass, everyone totally oblivious of her plight. But then again, wallowing in self-pity would achieve nothing and after all, she was an achiever, she would beat this cruel disease. She knew a positive attitude was essential.

However, this moment of self-induced optimism evaporated as soon as she thought of the kids. Should she have told them? After all, it was naive to think that by getting her brother-in-law to spirit them away for a few days she could hide this from them.

She had always confronted things head-on but this was different, it was somehow silent and insidious, secretly eating away at her, almost cowardly. It felt as if it had a mind of its own, suddenly announcing its appearance from seemingly nowhere. What control did she have over it? After all, her body had allowed it to happen.

This sense of helplessness washed over her like a tidal wave of despair and big fat tears rolled down her cheeks. What she needed now more than anything was one of Paul's powerful hugs. She wanted him to squeeze every fucking ounce of this putrid disease out of her.

—⁓—

Townsend tidied his papers and looked at the clock above the door. Its wooden surround accompanied by Roman numerals spoke of a time that was more ordered he thought, as he watched the second hand emerge from behind the minute hand as it had done countless times before.

Contrary to his strict moral code he would leave early this afternoon, the first time in eighteen years of loyal service. It felt as though he was taking a plunge into the unknown. He knew everyone's eyes would be focused on him but why should he feel guilty? After all, he had been struck across the face with a knife leaving not only physical but emotional scars.

Another glance at the clock and this was it. Philip left his desk with haste, the key fumbling in the door as he locked it. The first to see this momentous event would be Mrs Grayson as he passed her desk; the next would be Amy and Rachel, then finally Nigel Hunter. Apart from Councillor Roberts, this was the person he hated most of all and he knew the feeling was mutual.

"Goodnight," he said to a stunned Mrs Grayson.

"Goodnight," she replied, taking a discreet glance at her wrist watch.

Fortunately, neither Amy nor Rachel were at their desks and Hunter's was empty too. Perhaps this early exit might not be as traumatic as he thought.

"Where the hell are you skiving off to?"

He turned to see Nigel emerge from under his desk, a box of paper clips in his hand. He had never considered himself to be a violent man, on the contrary, but if he had had a gun at this very moment in time, so help him, he would shoot the man down.

"It's my mouth," he mumbled.

Hunter moved closer. "How exactly did you get that?" he asked, pointing at Philip's face.

"I fell over in my shed."

"Bollocks, you never did that by falling over, I know that much. Someone cut you, didn't they? Was it that wife of yours? Got fed up with you shagging her brains out every night? Because if she was mine, I would."

Philip felt his blood start to boil and he shoved his face straight into Nigel's.

"You should see the other guy," he hissed, ripping the bandage from his face, revealing the massive open wound that lay beneath.

The sight of this traumatic injury and Philip's reckless indifference to it shocked Nigel.

"Ok, no need for that, just messing around. Can't you take a joke?"

For the first time since the attack, Philip's face did not feel as though it had been torn open with a red hot poker. Was there really another side to Philip Townsend? He was beginning to think there might be.

He burst out of the confines of his workplace and made for the bus stop with the air of a man on a mission.

—⚓—

"Why is Townsend's door locked?" said Councillor Roberts to Mrs Grayson, who now found herself in a dilemma – one she could not have foreseen. Should she tell the Councillor that he had left early, or make up an excuse? In the end it was neither.

"I'm not sure," she answered pathetically.

"Not sure?" he demanded, now leaning over her desk in a manner that could only be described as intimidating. "You must have some bloody idea; you are his secretary after all."

"As I said," her voice now several octaves higher, "I'm not sure where he is. He might be over at records."

"I know where he is," came a voice; it was Hunter.

"Oh, and where might that be?" said Roberts, his attention now fully focused on Nigel.

"He went home early."

"Oh did he, and why would that be I wonder?"

"Didn't say."

"Well perhaps Mrs Grayson can shed some light on Mr Townsend's early departure. After all, she seems to know everything else that goes on around here. Well Mrs Grayson?"

"I really don't know," she said, her head bowed.

Even Roberts knew he was close to overstepping the mark and the last thing he wanted was HR on his back, especially after that incident with Smithson last year.

"Not to worry Mrs Grayson," he said in a cheery tone. "After all, you're not his keeper. Dare say he had to get that cut on his face looked at and forgot to mention it to you."

"Yes, yes, that would be it. He did say something about…"

But before she could finish her sentence, he had turned his back on her and was heading for the stairs accompanied by Hunter. She watched the two men as they stopped at the top of the wide marble staircase designed by none other than Constantine Raboli, the famous 19th Century architect, its opulence and grandeur reminiscent of a bygone era, but its statement to supremacy still relevant to today.

"Fell over in his shed," said Roberts.

"That's what he told me," replied Hunter, looking a little furtive. "But have you seen it?"

"No."

"I have."

"Oh, he showed it to you?"

"In a manner of speaking," he replied. "It was all a bit strange really. I was having a bit of a joke with him – you know how much a stick in the mud he is – so I thought I would try and lighten things up a bit. Anyway, he shoves his face right up close to mine, I nearly lost my balance. He then ripped the bandage away to reveal this massive cut. It must be almost from his ear to his chin. I swear I could see some of his teeth through it."

"How strange," mused Roberts. "Doesn't sound a bit like the Townsend I know."

"And that's not the best of it" went on Hunter. "He then said *'you should have seen the other guy and that if I wasn't careful I would get the same'.*"

Roberts stepped back slightly. "We *are* talking about the same Townsend, aren't we?"

"Of course we are, it only happened ten minutes ago."

It took a few seconds for what Hunter had said to sink in. "You're a bright young man looking to go places I can tell," said Roberts. "You might be able to help me *and* yourself."

"You know me, always at your service."

—◊—

Paul knocked on the door.

"Come in, it's not locked."

He entered the room to find Solley, his back to him, stark naked. "How did you know it was me?" he asked, "and for goodness sake put some pants on."

Solley turned to face him, "No, I like the freedom."

"Well you might like the freedom but I don't want to look at your meat and two veg swinging about when I'm trying to talk to you. It's disturbing."

"It's magnificent, that's what it is," he replied, looking down admiringly at himself.

"Anyway, how did you know it was me?" Paul repeated.

"I didn't, I kind of hoped it might have been that gardener we saw when we arrived."

"And what makes you think he would come to your room, even if he were gay?"

"Magnetism old man – you either have it or you don't!"

And there was no denying it; Solley certainly did in every sense. "I know what your problem is," he continued, pulling up his underpants.

"Oh, and what might that be?" asked Paul, sitting on the edge of the bed.

"You were worried it might have been that filly downstairs. Once she had seen what was on offer here, you wouldn't stand a chance," he said, a big grin emerging on his face.

"How many bloody times must I tell you I am not interested?"

"Ok, ok, fair enough," he replied, sitting next to Paul and placing his arm around his shoulder. "Maybe you're finally seeing the light," he continued.

Paul stood up, shoving him back on the bed. "Don't you ever bloody give up?"

"Well one lives in hope," quipped Solley, now propped up on one elbow, but he could see his horseplay had not been taken lightly by Paul; he obviously had something serious on his mind.

"Hey you know I'm only joking, I would never try and… well, you know…"

Paul sat back on the edge of the bed. "I know," he said, his hand on Solley's knee. "You're the straightest bent guy I know."

"So what is it? You can tell Uncle Solley."

Paul placed his head into his hands and began to cry uncontrollably. Solley could not quite come to terms with what he was witnessing. "What the hell's wrong man?" he asked.

"It's Kim," sobbed Paul, "she has cancer."

Solley could feel his chest tighten, this unexpected and devastating news hitting him like a bolt from the blue.

"No fucking way!" he cried, leaping to his feet. "That's not possible. Not Kim?"

Paul removed his tear-streaked face from his hands. "She's in hospital right now."

"Well what the fuck are you doing here?"

"She wanted me to come. She said she wanted things to be as normal as possible."

"So what kind?" he asked gently.

"Sorry?"

"What kind of cancer is it?"

"Melanoma."

"Whereabouts?"

"On her shoulder."

"You know that kind of cancer's very common nowadays and most people make a full recovery. How long is she in hospital for?"

"24 hours," said Paul, wiping his face with the bed sheet.

"Well there you go. It can't be that bad if she's only in for 24 hours can it?"

"I suppose not," he answered, looking up at him.

"Look, we can go back right now if you want, or at any time, you just give the word."

"No, we'll stay and check this project out."

"Ok then," said Solley, reaching for his trousers, "in that case we'll hit the bar. They seem to have an excellent selection of Scotch I noticed."

Philip made his way up the garden path, this time oblivious to the floral display that Catherine had so painstakingly planted and nurtured to the point where it almost seemed artificial. He opened the front door, slamming it shut behind him and made his way down the hall into the kitchen.

"Darling what are you doing home so early?" asked Catherine, looking up from a colander of home-grown peas she was shelling.

He reached across the table and grabbed her wrist, pulling her from her chair.

"What are you doing?" she protested.

But he did not reply.

"What's got into you?" shouted Catherine as he lifted her onto the table.

He then ran his hands up her skirt and took hold of her tights and knickers, pulling them free.

"Stop it!" she cried as she tried to climb down, but he was too strong for her.

With one hand he undid his trousers while holding her with the other. He then pushed her back onto the table and drew her towards him, at the same time forcing her legs apart. Catherine reached out and grabbed the tall, pale green vase containing freshly cut flowers from the garden and brought it down on the back of Philip's head, this violent and unexpected show of resistance causing him to recoil.

—〜〜—

Roberts held the door to the Mason's Arms Public Bar open as Hunter entered the gloomy premises.

"What you having?" he asked, striding up to the bar to be greeted by a woman in her late fifties, her face thick with make-up almost to the point of making her look like some kind of overweight circus reject.

But the thing that had caught Nigel's eye was her dress. It could not have been cut any lower without her large and somewhat wrinkled breasts spilling out. The thought of these massive members dangling unbridled sent a shiver down his spine.

"Well, what you drinking?" repeated Roberts.

"Err, well, it better be Cola," answered Nigel, "I'm driving."

"Nonsense man, you can get a taxi."

"But I live over at Waverley Cross," he protested, "It would cost a fortune."

"That's no problem, haven't you heard of a thing called expenses," replied Roberts. "And by the way, I don't want to hear that word again tonight."

"Ok I'll have a vodka and lemonade then."

"A large gin and tonic and a large vodka and lemonade please Tina."

Tina, thought Nigel, *if anyone did not look like a Tina it had to be this woman.*

Roberts handed over a £20 note.

"That's ok," she said, "you can have this one on the house."

He led Hunter to a table in the corner away from the games machine.

"That was very generous of her," said Nigel as they sat down.

"Planning," replied Roberts.

"Sorry?"

"Planning – they want to extend the restaurant. No money in booze nowadays and as you know, I am Head of Planning," he said, taking a slug from his gin.

He placed his glass firmly down onto the table and looked Hunter directly in the eye. "I think you may be able to help me young man."

"If I can, Councillor."

"You see the reason I was so desperate to get hold of Townsend was because he promised me some files concerning the old Sanatorium out at Highgate."

"Yes, I know it. Doesn't it belong to the Albrights?"

"That's right," he said, finishing his gin. "These files, I believe, show the old mine workings in the area and if I am not mistaken they go under the hospital. Of course, you realise if they did it would mean that any development of the area would be out of the question."

"I guess so," replied Hunter, looking a little unsure.

"The problem is that these files are over 200 years old."

"Won't they be on CD now?"

"No, I checked, it seems not everything has been uploaded yet and I want to get my hands on these files before they are."

"Well Townsend is definitely your man."

"I know, but for some reason he's being very obtuse so I was thinking maybe you could get them for me?"

"That stuck-up old fart Townsend wouldn't let me anywhere near his precious documents."

"Surely he's not the only one with access?"

"Technically no, but you would have to go through the Director of Antiquities for something of this nature."

"Director of what?" he asked.

"Everything more than one hundred years old is automatically released. Well, almost everything," added Hunter, lowering his voice and looking a little furtive. "Some papers are still deemed to be too sensitive even after all that time."

"So basically, you're telling me we have no choice but to go through Townsend?"

"I guess so, unless you want it to be documented that you have requested these files."

Roberts leant forwards across the table. "Suppose Townsend was to – let's say – find another job."

Nigel laughed, "You would need a stick of dynamite to get him out of there!"

"Ok then, let's suppose for instance that he got the sack."

"I can't see that," said Hunter. "I couldn't imagine anyone more dedicated to his work than Townsend."

"Well you say that but he did leave early today."

"Yeah, well, it's hardly worthy of the sack."

"No, but add that to his behaviour – I mean he did threaten you, didn't he?"

There was an uneasy pause. "Err, I guess so."

"And from what you told me, he physically assaulted you."

"Well I wouldn't go that far."

"Did he or did he not touch you in an unfriendly manner?"

"I suppose you could say that."

Roberts sat back, a broad grin on his fat face. "Well then, and did anyone witness this?"

Hunter thought for a moment. "I guess Mrs Grayson would have seen what went on."

"Good, now let's just suppose he lost his job for improper conduct and violent behaviour. He would have to be replaced would he not?"

"Yes, yes of course."

"And by who better than you?" said Roberts as he got to his feet, raising his glass. "Another one?"

7

"Thought the place would be busier than this," observed Solley, making his way into the bar followed by Paul. Their only fellow guests seemed to be an elderly couple and four middle-aged women togged up for what looked like an attempt on the north face of the Eiger.

They made themselves comfortable at the bar and waited patiently for someone to materialise. Finally, his patience now exhausted, Solley leaned over in front of Paul, and brought the palm of his hand down on the brass bell that sat opposite four hand pumps, each with an ornate plaque proudly depicting their allegiance to the League for Real Ale.

Apart from drawing the attention of the elderly couple and the *Nanooks of the North* huddled around their table, it did little to summon the purveyor of the alcohol they so craved. Once again, he repeated the exercise much to the annoyance of the other guests who felt this show of unreserved attention-seeking not only rude but bad form.

"What does one have to do to get a drink round here?" he called, leaning over the bar.

"Sorry," came a voice from behind them.

They turned to see Margaret wiping her hands, her face flushed and her neat hair tousled.

"What can I get you gentlemen?" she asked, making her way behind the bar.

"Two large ones of your finest 12-year-old malt," replied Solley, loud enough for everyone to hear.

"You'll have to forgive me," she said, removing the stopper from a bottle of Skye Whisky. "We're a bit short-staffed at the moment. Actually, when I say short-staffed, I am the only staff."

"You mean you're running this place on your own?" enquired Paul.

"Crazy isn't it," she replied, placing their respective drinks on the bar. "The trouble is it's not easy getting staff out here. I can't pay much over the going rate and the time it takes people to get here, along with the cost of fuel – well you can see what I mean."

"Surely you have staff quarters?" asked Solley.

"Yes and no. The problem is when Mike and I took this place over we knew it needed quite a lot of work – actually to be honest it needed gutting and total refurbishment. Anyway, to cut a long story short, we spent the money on the guest rooms so as to generate some income and left the staff quarters until later. But…" Margaret's voice tailed off. "Oh, listen to me going on, that's the last thing you want to hear – my problems."

"No, we don't mind do we Solley?" said Paul.

"No, it's not as if we're going *anywhere else* is it?"

"Ignore him," said Paul, "he's only miffed because I didn't want to go into Leeds."

"Oh you should, there's a very vibrant gay scene there."

"Oh, Solley and I aren't – you know – a couple."

"Oh sorry, how presumptuous of me, I do apologise."

"No offence taken," replied Paul.

"No offence?" repeated Solley, "you'd be lucky to have someone like me!"

"Oh my goodness, is that the time?" said Margaret looking at the clock. "I must prepare the evening meal."

"No, have a drink first," offered Solley. "I'm sure we can wait a bit."

"I should really make a start."

"No, we insist," added Paul, "have a drink on us."

"What's that in the chiller?"

"This?" said Margaret, opening the chiller door. "It's a Meullier 2006, apparently a good year for Champagne."

"Ok then, let's have a bottle." He turned around and looked at those waiting for their dinner. "Better make it two," he added, "and when we have finished those, we'll have some more. And for goodness sake, let's get some music on."

"I'll give you a hand," said Paul, making his way round the bar.

"You can't do that," protested Margaret, "you're my guest."

"Nonsense," he replied, helping himself to some glasses. "It reminds me of old times. My uncle ran a pub in Southwark, London. I used to work behind the bar after school."

"School?"

"Things were different in those days," he explained. "So why no staff if you have the room? From my experience, people who do that kind of work aren't over-fussy – a lick of paint should do the trick."

"Quite simply things got a little difficult after Mike died."

"Mike would be your partner I take it?"

"He was my husband," replied Margaret. "It'll be a year tomorrow…" she cleared her throat, "… that he passed away. The thing is it's a little more complicated than just a lick of paint; we need to upgrade the fire escape for the staff quarters. At the moment it only serves the guest rooms and it has to be extended to the top floor. So until that's done, I can't get full-time staff as the Fire Service won't give us clearance."

"So how much are you looking for?" asked Paul, placing a cloth over one of the bottles and twisting the cork free.

"You know, I never thought of that," observed Margaret, changing the subject. "I have always been frightened of taking someone's eye out."

"Doesn't do to blind the punters," he laughed, pouring the contents into several glasses.

Solley got to his feet and tapped a glass with his pen.

"Ladies and Gentlemen, I have an announcement to make. On behalf of the management, there will be a slight delay with this evening's meal due to unforeseen circumstances, so if you would care to join us at the bar for Champagne in the meantime."

The second part of this statement from the tall man at the bar brought a positive response from the disappointed guests awaiting their dinner, and soon Solley was in full swing, topping up glasses and chatting up the ladies. All of the women thought he was wonderful.

"Is your friend always so generous?" asked one of the lady hikers to Paul.

"To a fault," he replied. "But don't think it's all generosity on his behalf, he gets a lot out of it too."

"Your partner – or should I say friend – seems irrepressible," commented Margaret.

"Oh he certainly is that. You would need a ton weight to keep him down and even then, I'm not sure that would be enough. Just be thankful you don't have a piano."

"We do as it happens; it's in the back storeroom, under cover. I just haven't had time to get it out."

"Do you play?"

"I try, Mike was the pianist."

"What's this I hear?" said Solley, sticking his head over her shoulder, bottle in one hand, glass in the other.

"Oh I was just saying to Mr Goodman…"

"Please – Paul."

"That there's a piano in the back room," she continued.

"Well what are we waiting for?" he said, turning to leave the bar.

"Please be careful, it's very heavy," she called, running after him.

—m—

"Excuse me," said Councillor Roberts as he took his phone from his jacket and left Nigel alone at the table.

"Oh, Reggie it's you… You sure? Ok I'll meet you in half an hour, the usual place."

The Councillor returned to find Nigel finishing his drink. "That's handy," he said. "I'm afraid I have to go." And without another word, he downed his drink in one and turned to leave.

"I thought we were going to share a taxi?" said Nigel.

"Keep your receipt," was the reply as Roberts made his way through the crowd, followed by a somewhat irate Nigel.

"I don't have an expenses account," he called.

The Councillor turned and made his way back to him. "Well if you play your cards right, you might have one sooner than you think."

And with that, he left.

—⁓—

Solley arranged his new-found companions round the upright, which took a little in the way of organisation due to the amount of Champagne everyone had consumed.

"Ok, on the count of three," he said.

They had gone little more than ten feet when the piano ground to a sudden halt, its brass castors biting deep into the plush carpet, causing it to ruck up enough to form an insurmountable obstacle.

"It's no use," said Margaret, fearing for her carpet. "It will have to wait until I can get some professional removal people," she added, hoping this might be the end of the matter.

"Nonsense," replied Solley, that irrepressible character they had spoken of earlier coming to the fore.

Cheered on by his half-cut supporters hell-bent on liberating this somewhat neglected musical instrument to its rightful place, Solley rallied his loyal troops for one more final effort.

"No, wait," shouted Paul, "you'll tear the carpet."

This statement of the bleeding obvious finally brought proceedings to a halt.

"Maybe you're right," admitted Solley. "It's a shame though, just a couple more yards and we would have been on the laminate – easy going from there."

"Wait a minute," said Paul, looking to the back of the room.

"What are you looking for?" asked Margaret.

"Something we were going to need anyway if you were ever going to get this to the bar without ripping up your carpet and parquet flooring."

"Thought as much," he said to himself, returning from the recesses of the storeroom brandishing two long lengths of plywood.

"It dawned on me that it must have found its way in here somehow without damaging the floor and that would have been achieved with these," he announced, laying the lengths of ply in front of the piano.

"There's one thing," said Solley, "why didn't you put it in the bar to start with?"

"That was Mike's idea. He felt it was best out of the way until we redecorated. I wasn't here at the time. Everything was shipped up while I was in Manchester as I still had three months to run on my contract."

"What line of business were you in?" asked Paul.

"Consultancy," replied Margaret.

"What sort?"

"Hydroponics."

"Sorry?"

"Basically, it's growing plants under glass with nutrient-rich water."

"Oh."

"Good," said Solley. "Now we have that cleared up, let's get this piano to where it belongs and then get these good people fed."

—⁊⁊—

"Ah Councillor Roberts, I have your table ready."

"Thank you, Mario."

"Are you dining alone or will Mrs Roberts be joining you?"

"Yes and no."

"Sorry?"

"Mrs Roberts will not be joining me but I am expecting someone."

"Very good Councillor, I will set another place."

Roberts followed the maître d' to the table and sat down in his usual spot. He liked this corner, it was slightly out of the way, affording a modicum of privacy but allowing him to see whoever might enter the restaurant.

"Your usual, Councillor?"

He looked up from the menu to see Mia standing there with a bottle of Chianti.

"That will do fine."

"Would you like me to pour?"

"No," he replied, adjusting his napkin. "I will wait for my guest."

"Very good," she said, placing the open bottle of red wine on the table.

Despite his vantage point, he was taken by surprise as Reggie Carlyle announced his presence.

"Did I catch you unawares Councillor?" he said, taking hold of the wine bottle and pouring a large glass as he made himself comfortable.

"No, I was just looking at tonight's specials." *It's no wonder they call you Creepy Carlyle* he thought.

"So, what have you dragged me out here for apart from dinner at your expense – or should I say the good people of our town's expense, who it must be said you care so much for and have given many years of selfless devotion?"

"Well I hope I can count you as one of those."

"Well that depends on what you have to say," said Reggie, placing his empty wine glass on the table and looking at Roberts to replenish it.

"Ok, I'll cut to the chase. You know the old hospital on the Albright Estate?"

"The nut house you mean?"

Roberts looked about him. "I think for all our sakes we should refrain from that kind of terminology," he said in a low voice.

"Ok, have it your way," replied Reggie, leaning back slightly in his chair.

"As I was saying, it appears they finally have a buyer for the place."

Immediately Roberts noticed a change in Carlyle's demeanour.

"Go on, I'm all ears."

"It appears that our mutual friend Ian Turnbull is leading negotiations for its purchase."

"Anyone we know?" asked Carlyle.

"No, this is a big outfit from London. They want to turn it into luxury apartments."

"Oh, and how does that concern us?"

"I have been doing a little digging around," he said, a slight smile on his large face as he thought of the possible mine workings that lay beneath the old hospital.

This facial expression did not go unnoticed by Carlyle. "Something amusing Councillor?" he asked.

"Oh no, nothing. Frank Horton."

"What of him?" said Reggie.

"He's in your debt."

"You know that."

"And you say he has paid you half of what he owes you?"

"You know that too."

"The thing is – where did he get the money?"

"That is not of my concern. I've no interest in where he gets it from, just as long as he pays me."

"Yeah, but think about it, he's broke, his wife took him for everything. Well everything that you haven't already got."

"It was his choice," said Reggie, looking at the menu. "I didn't force him to gamble."

"Of course not," replied Roberts, "no offence, the thing is I think I know where he got the money from."

"Oh yeah? Well seeing as you know, you might as well tell me."

"Ian Turnbull."

"Turnbull, why should Turnbull give Frankie six big ones?"

"Good question. Ah Mia," he said, as the young attractive woman stood pen in hand ready to take their order. "I'll have the Linguine and Wild Mushrooms."

Mia dutifully noted the order and then turned her attention to the Councillor's guest.

Carlyle looked up slowly from his menu, his eyes dark and cold. "What do you recommend?"

"What Mr Roberts is having is very nice," she said nervously.

"Don't like mushrooms."

"Very good. The deep-fried Calamari in Garlic Sauce is also very popular with many of our regulars."

"Don't like garlic."

She was starting to feel uncomfortable with this strange man, his eyes locked onto her in an unforgiving stare. It then occurred to her that the only starter that was garlic free would be the salad and if she was right, this man was a meat eater. She would have to think on her feet as she did not want to disappoint this character with his malevolent overtones. "We have a selection of the finest hams and fresh baked bread."

"Now that sounds more my style," said Reggie, "I'll have the ham sandwich."

Mia took their order and hurried away.

"I think you scared her," remarked Roberts in as joking a manner as he could manage.

"Me? Never, what would make you say such a thing?"

"Anyway," said Roberts, doing his best to change the subject, "as I was saying, Frankie doesn't have the means to pay that kind of money, let alone in cash."

"Where he gets it from would not normally concern me," said

Reggie, "but if it has come from Ian Turnbull, that does interest me, if you're thinking what I'm thinking?"

"And what might that be?" asked Roberts.

"You first."

"Ok, this is the way I see it. Turnbull's up to his usual tricks and this time Frankie is in on it somewhere and the money's for services rendered."

"And what kind of services would they be?"

"Well funny enough, the Albrights and Frankie have one thing in common – they're both skint, although for different reasons. The Albrights need to pay off death duties in order to keep the Manor House, it's been in their family for 330 years and you know what that lot are like when it comes to hanging on to the family pile? It's a matter of pride – they don't want to be the generation that loses it."

"Just get to the point," said Reggie impatiently.

The two men looked up as Mia placed their food in front of them.

"Can I get you gentlemen more wine?"

"No, later perhaps," said Carlyle curtly.

Mia wished them Bon Appetit and left them to their meal.

"So the connection is…?" asked Reggie.

"I reckon Turnbull has got Frankie to drag up something on the Albrights – and believe me, I bet there's plenty there. He's using this to blackmail them and the money he's giving you tomorrow is his payment."

"There's just one flaw in that scenario. If the Albrights are skint, where did they get the money from?"

"Well I think our friends from London will have something to do with that."

"Ok, so where do we fit into this?"

Roberts leaned forwards slightly. "I think I can get hold of some documents that could prove to be very lucrative."

"These documents you speak of, what's in them?" asked Reggie, finishing his wine.

"Well as I have said, the Albrights are desperate to get their hands on this money and they need it soon. The tax man won't wait for much longer and Ian's in it for something more than just doing their accounts."

"What the hell is in these documents?" he repeated, voice raised.

"It appears – if I'm not mistaken – that that whole hillside is honeycombed with old lead mine workings."

Roberts noticed Reggie's demeanour change slightly. "Oh yeah? And how does that fit in?"

"Look, if we had information that would stop the sale, the Albrights would not be happy to say the least, so they pay us to help it go away."

"Pay us what you frigging numbnuts? You just said they didn't have any money."

"No – but they do have land."

Reggie smiled. "Go on."

"When we tell Turnbull about these mine workings, he gives us a cut from whatever he's getting out of this to keep it quiet. And here's the best part – I will make sure the planning consent goes through, and when the work to convert the property is almost complete, we approach the developers with these documents and get a big fat pay-off for losing them somewhere."

"And if they don't?" said Reggie.

"The building will be condemned, and even if it proves that the mine shafts exist – and I believe they do – and that they are no real threat, it would still be enough to put people off from buying the apartments, and as a consequence the developers will have lost a fortune."

Roberts waited for a reply but received none. "Is there something wrong?" he asked.

Carlyle carefully placed his wine glass onto the table and massaged his chin with his thumb and forefinger. "There might be," he said.

"Well – let me have it."

"Well if you cast your mind back twenty odd years to the Commonwealth Games Project, you'll remember that my sister – your wife – and I had some dealings with its construction. Part of this involved getting rid of thousands of tons of waste material which we got paid handsomely for.

"So?" said Roberts, none the wiser.

Reggie sighed. "Think about it."

"Sorry, I'm still not with you."

"Most of it went down those bloody mine shafts of yours and I'm not keen on drawing attention to them."

Roberts laughed.

"What's so funny?"

"No-one's going to start digging the bloody things up, this is fool proof."

"So how much do you reckon we stand to gain in total?" asked Reggie, greed being his second nature.

"Well from the Albrights there's that five acres that the new by-pass will go through – if you know what I mean – thus opening it up for development. There's also funding in the pipeline for a business park. As for Turnbull, I reckon we could squeeze out £40k – maybe more. The developers – twenty percent of whatever they're going to make, which if I'm not mistaken could be worth 150 grand each. And the beauty of it is, without any risk to us whatsoever."

"You reckon they're going to make in excess of £1.5million from the conversion of the old Sanatorium? A little optimistic don't you think?"

"Well it was only a guestimate. I haven't gone into it in any great detail but whatever way you look at it, it's got to be a good earner."

Although Reggie was always one to make a few quid when the opportunity arose – especially if he didn't have to do anything for it – he had his doubts as to whether the old place was really worth the trouble. He eased gently back into his chair. "So why are you telling me this? You could keep the lot for yourself."

"The thing is; someone in my position would need to keep their distance – if you see what I mean. I'll leave all the arrangements to you, plus you have the facility to launder the money and my share will come from a fortuitous win at your dog track."

"60/40," said Reggie.

"Sorry?"

"60/40 if I'm going to take all the risk."

"There won't be any," replied Roberts indignantly. "I just can't be seen to be too close to these people, that's all."

"It's 60/40 or I'm not interested."

Roberts exhaled and slumped back into his seat. "60/40 it is," he said.

—⁓—

Philip woke up with a start as Catherine came into the sitting room carrying a tray bearing two mugs of hot chocolate and an assortment of biscuits. She placed the tray onto the small coffee table that sat pride of place in the centre of this large room, its furnishings and décor a legacy from his childhood. He had considered getting rid of his parents' furniture and redecorating but for some reason these familiar things, although outdated, made him feel secure in a world that always seemed to be changing.

She sat opposite him, a plate with two digestive biscuits balanced on her knees, the mug with its sweet liquid cupped in her hands. He could hardly bring himself to look at her, let alone talk.

"No chocolate ones?" he asked.

"No, you had the last one the other day."

This was not a raucous house by any means, but even by their standards, this silence was oppressive. Philip suddenly dropped to his knees in front of her. "Look I don't know what came over me. Please, you must forgive me."

She reached out and placed her hand gently against his face. "I know," she said, "but you must understand it's hard for me after what happened. However, I am getting over it and I'm sure it won't be long before we can be back to normal."

"Not sure what normal is to be honest."

"Just being ourselves, I guess – like things used to be," replied Catherine, taking a biscuit from her plate.

He got up off his knees, picked up his cup from the table and sat back down onto the sofa. "That has taken a great weight off my mind."

"There's just one thing. What happened earlier? You would not consider that normal, would you?"

"Oh goodness no," he replied, "I would never do that again."

—⁂—

Fortunately for Margaret, thanks to Solley's insistence aided by several bottles of bubbly, everyone had agreed to scampi and chips and his sultry tones could now be heard reverberating through from the bar; Margaret's guests, fuelled on Champagne, willingly singing the chorus at the top of their voices. Everything was fine as long as she didn't get a visit from the local constabulary as she wasn't yet licensed for music – if that what this was.

Solley looked over at Paul who was joining in with the others in a second verse of *Roll Out The Barrel* and felt somewhat relieved as he seemed to be having fun, but he knew he would not be his old self until Kim was fully recovered.

The proceedings were brought to an abrupt halt by Margaret announcing that their evening meal would shortly be served in the Dining Room.

—⁂—

Kim thanked the nurse as she placed a glass of fresh fruit juice and a feta cheese salad on a tray in front of her.

"I wasn't sure if you were hungry or not, but you must really eat something. The bread is baked here and all the food is prepared on site. Our chef is really very good."

At first Kim found this hard to comprehend – a chef of this quality in a hospital? But she did have to admit the food looked very good. The variety of salad leaves mixed with pine nuts, olives, feta and passion fruit looked very appetising.

"I looked at your menu sheet," continued the nurse. "I didn't see anything there that suggested you had any allergies."

"No," replied Kim, "this is just fine."

"In that case, I'll leave you to your meal. Just call me when you have finished. Oh, by the way," she added as she was just about to leave the room, "the sticky toffee pudding is to die for."

This statement brought about an awkward silence before both women started to laugh at this somewhat inappropriate euphemism.

"Oh, one more thing," said the nurse, "have it with the custard, it's the real thing. You can always order anything you like by using the phone."

"Room Service?"

"Only the best for our patients."

With that the nurse smiled and closed the door behind her. This encounter had lifted Kim's spirits, she would make a full recovery, she just knew it. But the phone also offered something else that was not as trivial as dessert. It gave her the opportunity to speak to her children.

Toby wouldn't even notice if she did not speak to him for a month as long as there was nothing he needed, and on the odd occasion when there was, it was difficult to decipher the grunts that came in the way of a reply. And as for a full coherent sentence, she hadn't had one of those from him since puberty raised its ugly head.

However, Jenny was very different, she would become suspicious if she did not phone. Not only that, what would happen if she phoned her mobile or Paul's for that matter? This whole idea of sending them to Margate with Derek was ludicrous. And why had Julie not said anything? She must have realised. It was obvious that no-one had gone into any form of detail for they were in as much shock as she was, especially Julie as they were inseparable. Although they were not identical twins they shared so much. Julie was acting on impulse just as much as she was.

She picked up the phone, dialled nine for an external line and stared at the receiver – could she do this without breaking down? Either way she had no choice. Perhaps she could leave a message with Derek but that would only raise suspicion. She listened intently to the dialling tone hoping that it would not be answered, thus letting her off the hook, if only temporarily.

"Hello?"

"Oh, hello Jenny, it's Mum here," she said, holding the phone slightly away from her.

"Where are you phoning from?"

"Oh, a friends."

"I can hardly hear you."

"Nor I you," replied Kim, "it must be the connection; anyway, did you have a nice day dear?"

"Yeah, went down onto the beach this afternoon."

"What about your brother?"

"Oh, he went out somewhere with that Nathan boy."

"I thought he was in prison?"

"Apparently not," answered Jenny, "suspended sentence. That kid is a bloody menace if you ask me."

"Look Jenny, you must tell him I want him to stay away from that boy. Is your Uncle there?"

"No, he's over at the hotel."

"Never mind, I'll speak to him later. Look darling, have a nice time, I love you."

There was a slight pause.

"I love you too," said Jenny. "Is everything ok?"

"Of course it is darling, why shouldn't it be?"

"Oh nothing, you just sound a bit, you know, lonely."

"Don't be silly now and don't forget what I told you, and if you get any bull tell him I will stop his allowance."

"Mum?"

"Yes darling."

"If you do, can I have it?"

"Of course not."

Jenny laughed. "Only joking, can't blame me for trying."

"I'm going to phone your Uncle, I'll see you in a couple of days."

Kim replaced the receiver. That was all she needed. If she had known that little shit Nathan Turner was at large she would never have sent them down there. Still, maybe the thought of Toby losing his allowance would be enough to put a stop to anything.

She dialled Derek's number. "Hi Derek, it's Kim here."

"Hello babe, how are you?"

"Ok thanks, things seem to have gone well."

"I thought it might be Julie, I wasn't expecting you to phone so soon. Is everything all right?"

"I have just spoken to Jenny."

"Jenny? Have you told her?"

"No, I'll do that when they're back, but she tells me that Nathan Turner is still about."

"You sure?" asked Derek. "I thought he was found guilty of that car theft that led to that accident. Nasty business."

"Well it seems he got a suspended sentence and what's more, Jenny tells me Toby's with him."

"Leave it with me babe. I'll go and find him right now."

"Oh, and when you do, tell him from me that if he goes anywhere near that little bastard, I'll cut his allowance off for six months."

"Ok sweetheart. As I say, leave it with me."

—◊—

Paul made his way into the kitchen to find Margaret loading the dishwasher. He had come to apologise for Solley's boisterous

86

behaviour but he just stood there watching her, being totally oblivious to his presence. It then dawned on him he would be doing exactly the same if he caught Kim bending over the dishwasher without her knowing he was there.

"Hello."

"Oh, you surprised me," she answered, standing up and removing her rubber gloves then wiping her hair from her face.

"Look, I just wanted to say sorry."

"For what?" said Margaret, tossing the gloves onto the counter.

"For Solley, he's not everyone's cup of tea."

"Oh there's no need, really. I haven't enjoyed myself so much since…" Margaret paused. "And anyway, he's a big hit with the rest of the guests."

Paul picked up a tea towel and started to dry some of the glasses that had been put on the side to drain.

Margaret stepped forward. "No really, I can't have that," she protested.

Paul smiled, "Make some coffee while I see to these then we'd better get Solley off that piano."

"Fair enough," she replied, making her way over to a large pot containing coffee beans.

As she poured them into the grinder, again Paul found himself spellbound by this exceptional woman, but the sudden and harsh sound of hundreds of rock-hard coffee beans being ground into a fine powder brought him back to his senses. What the hell was he doing? However, he knew full well he was falling for her.

It was then he found himself asking her an inappropriate question, which even he found difficult to understand why he had done so. "What did Mike die of?"

At first Margaret did not answer.

"I am so sorry; I have no right to ask you that, it was totally out of order."

"No that's ok, it's no secret. It was cancer, one minute he was fine, the next thing we knew he had been diagnosed with this terrible disease. Even then it did not seem possible, there were no signs but six months later he passed away."

Hearing this made Paul feel very uncomfortable; just by asking this question he felt he had betrayed Kim in her darkest hour. And why did he want to know anyway? It shouldn't be of any importance to him but for some unknown reason, he felt it was. This coincidence seemed unreal – would this be him in a year's time? Was he subconsciously trying to replace Kim already? Surely he could not be that cold-hearted, plus he had always loved his wife and the thought of life without her was unbearable.

"There you are!" announced Solley, bursting into the kitchen. "There's been a disaster," he slurred, using the doorframe for support."

"What's happened?" asked Margaret looking across at him, more than a note of concern in her voice.

Waving his arms in the air to dramatic effect he announced to all the world that they were now out of champers.

Margaret glanced across at Paul, an incredulous look on her face.

"I'll deal with this," he said, "come on, we'd better get some coffee in you."

"Vy?" slurred Solley.

"Because we have an early start tomorrow and you're pissed as a newt!" explained Paul, taking him firmly by the arm.

"Me? Don't be ridiculous," he slurred again, slowly sliding down the doorframe despite Paul's effort to keep him upright.

It was then that two of the women hikers came looking for their new and exciting companion only to find him now sitting on the floor. Immediately they tried to get him to his feet but their efforts were in vain. The combination of Solley's size and their own state of inebriation inevitably resulted in them joining him on the floor in a giggling pile.

Paul, now exasperated with his partner's behaviour, stepped over Solley's long legs followed by Margaret. They made their way to the bar to find the other guests in what could only be described as a state of partial undress, with one of the women trying to relieve the gentleman of his trousers, while his wife – now in bra and pants – was sitting on his chest doing her best to rouse him.

"Shall I throw a bucket of water over them?" he suggested.

"Well we can't leave them like this. I'll lock the doors, if you would be so kind as to deal with it."

"Of course," he replied. After all, this fiasco was partly his fault.

Paul took hold of the woman who had now succeeded in removing the man's trousers – although she seemed a little perplexed as to what she was supposed to do with them.

"Come on," he said, helping her to her feet.

This offer of assistance was received with indignation. "And who exactly do you think you are?" she slurred, just moments before passing out.

He turned his head to see Margaret entering the bar, "What room?"

"Number seven."

"Ok, I'll get her upstairs."

He lifted the woman over his shoulder in a Firefighter's carry and followed Margaret up to the room. After a little effort she opened the door and he laid the woman out on the bed in the recovery position.

"One down, five to go!" he remarked with a hint of a smile.

8

Frank woke to the sound of his alarm. He unzipped his sleeping bag and rolled out onto the lino-covered floor, its cold and unfriendly surface a stark reminder of how low he had fallen, and even this poky office would soon offer no shelter from the elements as the rent was due in a week's time and he could not afford to renew it.

He hitched up his underpants and filled the kettle, dropping in two teabags before placing it on the single ring electric cooker, holding his hands out to capture every vestige of residual heat escaping from it. Unshaven and dejected he looked about him – although this place was just one wipe away from a shithole, it was his lifeline. No office – no business.

However, in a strange way, it was what people kind of expected when they came calling for his services – something seedy and depressing, as if the premises should somehow reflect his occupation, one that was despised by all, including those that benefitted from it. Even the prostitutes that paraded themselves up and down the streets in front of his office got more respect than he did.

"Shit fuck!" he exclaimed, pulling his hands away from the now boiling kettle and examining his wrist. "Fucking idiot!" he said to himself as he rinsed it under the cold tap.

He poured the hot tea carefully into his Union Jack mug and

picked up the box of sugar cubes. There were five left and he tipped them into his drink, spilling tea over the side, causing brown streaks to run down, washing away previous stains while creating new ones in their wake. He then unhooked the yellow and green bungee cord that kept the fridge door shut and held the milk bottle up to the light before removing the foil lid, sniffing and then discarding its contents down the sink.

With mug in hand, he crossed over to the only thing he had left of any value that he could truly call his own – a genuine Edwardian wing-backed leather chair.

Frank eased himself into what he once referred to as his throne, the cold clammy leather sticking to his bare skin. He placed his drink on the table and opened the left-hand drawer, pulling out an assortment of wires with bits of old sticking plaster hanging from them. *Wiring people for sound never failed,* he thought.

If these guys said anything that might be to Ian's advantage, he would capture it on the miniature recorder. But the real trick in a situation like this was not to incriminate oneself. This could be a double-edged sword when it came to both parties wanting to hide something.

—⚈—

Paul knocked firmly on Solley's door and waited for a few moments before trying again but there was still no answer. He tried the handle but it was locked so he placed his face against the door. "Solley, Solley," he called. "Wake up you stupid bastard."

"Good morning."

He turned to see one of the lady hikers, looking very much the worse for wear, making her way across the landing before pausing at the top of the stairs. She reached out and took hold of the newel post while he watched nervously as she composed herself for the descent. The last thing he wanted was for her to tumble down and break her bleeding neck; that would be all Margaret needed.

Paul rapped on Solley's door one more time, with one eye still on the woman until he could bear it no longer.

"Allow me," he said, taking her by the elbow.

"Migraine."

"Sorry?" he said, keeping a close eye on his unsteady charge.

"Migraine – you see I get it sometimes."

"Yes of course," he replied with a smile.

"One loses their balance and it's also difficult to focus properly."

"One step at a time," he said, helping the woman to the foot of the stairs.

"That was most kind of you."

"No problem," said Paul as he walked with her to the breakfast room, relieved to find her companions already seated. "Catching is it?" he asked.

"What is?" she said.

"Migraine."

"Oh, I don't think so. Why do you ask?"

"No reason," he replied, smiling and looking at her companions. As he left the room he saw Margaret making her way from the kitchen with two plates covered in an assortment of fried goodies.

"I could murder one of those!"

"If you care to take a seat, I shan't be a moment," she replied.

"Before I have breakfast, there is just one thing."

"Ok, let me take these through and I'll be right with you."

Paul watched as Margaret delivered the breakfasts to their waiting recipients, her effortless grace and deportment captivating him.

"Now what is it?" she asked on her return.

"It's Solley – I can't raise him."

"I'm not surprised after last night," she replied with a churlish smile on her face.

"I was wondering if you could unlock the door."

"Well it's against protocol but under the circumstances…"

Paul followed her up the stairs, unable to remove his eyes from her curvaceous form as it moved rhythmically from side to side with every footfall. It was then he noticed her muscular calves – like the rest of this impressive woman, they were perfectly formed.

Auntie Doreen, he thought, *that's who it was.* He could still see her with her sticky-out petticoats and stiletto heels gliding over the parquet floor of the Palais Ballroom with exactly the same muscle structure.

"Do you by any chance dance?" he asked as they reached the landing.

"Pardon?" she replied, turning to face him with a broad smile.

"No, I was just wondering if you danced, that's all."

"I heard you first time – it just seemed a strange thing to ask."

"It's your legs – they remind me of my Auntie Doreen."

"Oh really, how intriguing."

Paul was starting to feel a little embarrassed at his sudden and unexpected outburst. "In the nicest possible way of course," he continued. "She was a ballroom champion, got to the finals at Liverpool in 1968. I couldn't help but notice the similarity in your legs."

"Well Sherlock, as it happens I do – or rather I used to until… Well, you know… And you, do you dance?" she enquired.

"Oh yes," he replied, "It runs in the family – no pun intended!"

"And your wife?"

"Oh Kim – no, two left feet that one."

She knocked on Solley's door, "Mr Solomon."

"It's no use; I've tried at least a dozen times."

Margaret placed the key in the lock but it wouldn't fit. "That's strange," she said, trying it again. "It's no use, there's something in the way." She knelt down and looked into the keyhole, "The key's in the other side. It's these old locks you see."

"Sorry," said Paul, somewhat distracted by Margaret's posture.

"Solley's left his key in the lock, I can't undo it," she explained.

"What about in emergencies?"

"Don't tell me – tell English National Heritage! Look, I have to finish breakfast – go out the back and try the fire escape. If the window's shut, you can flip the catch back with a knife."

"Yes, I know what you mean, these old sash windows are easy to open."

"Come on," she said, heading for the stairs, "I have just the thing."

Paul followed Margaret dutifully to the kitchen where she opened one of the drawers and handed him a breadknife.

"I find this best," she said, "its blade is long and thin enough."

He took charge of the knife and made his way to the old Victorian fire escape, treading lightly on the cast iron, not wanting to disturb the gentleman and his randy wife. Pausing outside Solley's window, he slipped the long blade up between the glazing bars and tapped the brass catch back on itself, then carefully eased the sash open and placed first one leg, then the other, inside. The screams could be heard downstairs.

What the frigging hell's going on? thought Margaret. "Please stay here," she said to the guests, placing the coffee pot on the table.

"Shall we phone the police?" asked one of the women.

"No!" snapped Margaret. "That will not be necessary, I am sure everything's fine. Please help yourselves to more coffee."

She walked to the bottom of the stairs just out of sight of her guests then ran up as fast as she could and began hammering on Solley's door. To her surprise it was opened by a rather bleary-eyed Mr Solomon.

"Where's Paul?" she asked.

"Sorry?"

"Oh shit," she said as she went to knock on the door next to Solley's, only to have a rather irate Mr Fuller open it to reveal Paul with knife in hand pleading his innocence and Mrs Fuller with chair raised in defence.

—◊—

Philip placed his breakfast dish into the sink as Catherine brushed tiny flakes of dandruff from his collar.

"Will you be late tonight?" she asked.

"Not sure, I'll ring about five if I think I might be."

"It's for the best. If you leave it any longer, who knows what might happen."

"I think it might heal on its own eventually."

"Now come on, we have been through this, you promised."

"Ok" replied Philip. "I'll keep my appointment with Dr Patel."

He kissed Catherine on the forehead and picked up his case.

—∞—

"Good morning Councillor," said Hunter.

"Well?"

"Sorry Councillor?"

"Have you seen Townsend about that assault yesterday?"

"He's not in his office."

"Oh really?" With that, Roberts made his way over to Mrs Grayson. "Where's Townsend?" he demanded.

"Doctor," she replied.

"Why?"

"To get his face looked at I would imagine."

"Yes, of course. Tell him…" the Councillor paused.

Mrs Grayson sat poised with pencil and paper at the ready, as instructed by Philip – all messages to be written down.

"Never mind," he said, turning his back on her and going over to Nigel's desk. "I want you to get over to HR," he said to Hunter. "Tell them what happened yesterday and remember – *he* pushed *you*."

—∞—

Frank hitched up his trousers. "Look at me," he said to himself, "fucking wasting away." He removed his belt and placed it on the desk and using his pocket knife, forced the tiny blade against the hard leather, twisting it from side to side. Finally, he fashioned a hole big enough to put the metal prong of the belt buckle through.

Trousers now firmly in place he slipped on his shoes and jacket, and with the tools of his trade safely ensconced in a black case with chrome edging, he made his way down the dimly lit stairway and out onto the pavement.

The traffic at this time of day was always busy, the still morning air allowing the fumes from the slow-moving vehicles to accumulate. It was nowadays not uncommon to see people with facemasks, especially Japanese tourists who for some reason frequented this area, a trend which he always felt somewhat peculiar as apart from the market, he could not see any other meaningful attraction.

He placed a cigarette between his lips and made his way into a side street to find his car covered in pigeon waste – something which normally would have sent him into a rage, cursing every avian creature that had ever flown. But what did he care now? He hadn't made the last payment and he couldn't afford the next. If they were going to repossess it, they could have the fucking bird shit too.

—m—

"I'm not sure quite what you're referring to Councillor Roberts" said Mrs Grayson warily.

"So, you're saying Mr Hunter has just made this up for his own entertainment?"

"No, but I don't think it was that bad."

"You saw the altercation?"

"Yes."

"And Townsend acted in an aggressive manner?"

"Well…"

"Well?" said Roberts, towering over her.

"I guess it might have looked that way."

"And did Mr Townsend touch Mr Hunter?"

"I… I… think so."

"Well you had better get your facts right, because if they think you're trying to protect Townsend and hinder the course of justice, you could find yourself out of a job."

Roberts handed her a sheet of paper. "Now this is Mr Hunter's account of what happened which I believe to be the truth."

Mrs Grayson took the note and read it carefully.

"Can you remember that?" he asked.

"Yes."

"Good," said Roberts, retrieving the sheet of paper from her hand. "I'll take that," he added, placing it into the shredder. "Congratulations Mrs Grayson, I think you may have just saved your job. Oh, and when Mr Townsend deigns to grace us with his presence, tell him I was looking for him."

—⁊⁊—

Paul now found himself in Margaret's small office with the Fullers in full swing and Margaret trying her best to calm the situation, with Solley sitting in one corner nursing a sore head, mug of strong black coffee in his right hand.

"I don't care if you offer us a whole year free," said Mr Fuller, "you could not pay me to stay another night in this shamble of a place. Not only do I not expect to pay for what you call hospitality, you will be hearing from my solicitor. My dear wife has a delicate disposition."

Paul had heard of stretching the imagination, but nobody's was elastic enough to ever consider Mrs Fuller of anything other than the proverbial brick shithouse! And the way she was wielding that chair about, she could have fended off a herd of bloody rhino.

"No," continued Mr Fuller, "we will collect our things and be on our way. I do not wish to spend another minute in this place."

"Err, before you go," said Paul, "perhaps you would care to take a look at this." He showed him his phone.

Margaret watched in amazement as the colour drained from Mr Fuller's face. The somewhat delicate Mrs Fuller then elbowed her husband out of the way in order to see what had brought her irate husband to a standstill.

"Give that to me!" she said, reaching out with her podgy hand, the fat under her arm jiggling about as if somehow it had a life all of its own.

Paul snatched the phone out of her reach but what happened next, he could not have foreseen as Mrs Fuller's podgy hand turned itself into a fist of iron that smashed into his nose with such force it sent him tumbling backwards over Solley's outstretched legs. No sooner had he hit the floor, then she was astride him, twisting his right arm in such a fashion that it sent an unbearable pain along its full length, culminating in his shoulder with what could only be described as sheer agony.

The involuntary screams of pain were too much for the lady hikers to ignore as they left the breakfast room and rushed across the hall to the office, with Isabelle the first to reach it. She threw the office door open but to her surprise its motion was arrested by something hard and heavy on the floor which happened to be Paul's head.

Each of the women, now eager to see what on earth was unfolding in the small room, vied with each other to see through the half-open door. Solley now joined in the fray as he tried to lift this massively heavy woman off his friend; this assault on his wife galvanising Mr Fuller into action as he in turn put Solley into a headlock.

This surreal scene was brought to a sudden and dramatic halt as the small office filled with a cloud of freezing vapour as Margaret plied the fire extinguisher directly over the antagonists, but not before she had taken Paul's phone from him containing the compromising pictures of Mr Fuller with his wife in a state of semi-undress, and one of the lady hikers removing his trousers.

However, the only person truly identifiable was Mr Fuller – unless you were unfortunate enough to be familiar with Mrs Fuller's backside with its accompanying tattoo of a naked man wielding what looked like a large hammer, the word *Thor* just visible.

Margaret told the ladies in no uncertain terms to return to the breakfast room, fortunate that none of them had had the foresight to record this unbelievable event on their phones. She then shut and locked the door, the mist from the extinguisher now dissipated. All that remained evident of its deployment were beads of condensation running down the window pane.

"Mr and Mrs Fuller," she announced. "You are to collect your belongings and leave. I will not charge you."

Mr Fuller was just about to protest when she brought him up short. "You will do as I ask and these photos will remain with me," she said, putting Paul's phone in the small safe.

Reluctantly the Fullers complied with her request, knowing that in this instance they had little choice in the matter, so she unlocked the door to the office as Solley helped Paul to his feet and the defeated Fullers made their way up to their room, watched by the four lady hikers.

"Are you ok?" they asked in unison as Margaret emerged from her office, a faint mist just visible surrounding her.

"Yes ladies, everything is fine."

She turned to see Paul being helped out by Solley.

"What the hell?" he said. "That woman's like a bloody gorilla."

"Beverly the Bull you mean," said Isabelle.

"Sorry?" he replied, nursing his arm.

"That was her stage name."

"Stage name?" asked Solley.

"Yes, she was a professional wrestler in her day, although that must have been nearly twenty years ago now."

This unexpected news went a small way to restoring Paul's male ego, although he knew he had been totally at her mercy.

—⁜—

Philip removed the bandage from his face.

"Well Mr Townsend, this is indeed a fine wound you have,"

said Dr Patel as he got out of his chair in order to take a closer look. "Exactly how did you come by it?"

Philip remained silent, reluctant to lie again.

Dr Patel leaned in a little closer. "This I would hasten to guess was caused by a sharp implement – a knife I would say."

"Yes," replied Philip, looking down at the floor.

"I take it this was a result of an assault?"

"Yes."

"Have you reported it to the authorities?"

"No."

"Oh, and why not?"

Philip refused to reply and just continued to stare at the floor.

"Ok then. Let's see what we can do with this."

Dr Patel examined the cut with great care. "Fortunately, it is free from infection, though more through luck than judgement I would say. Unfortunately though, it is too late to suture it together, it will have to heal naturally, though this will leave a rather messy scar. I will prescribe you antibiotics and you are to change the dressing daily. I want you to call into the Health Centre every other day for the next two weeks."

"T... t... two weeks?" mumbled Philip.

"Yes of course, it is vitally important that you do not get an infection. Now I will dress the wound." Having done so, he then handed him a prescription.

Philip took the form and made his way to the door.

"Oh Mr Townsend, remember to make your follow-up appointments."

—※—

Frank glanced down at the fuel gauge – the thin white needle was hovering tentatively above the red empty demarcation line. *It will have to do,* he thought. He had already scoured the car for change the other day in order to put a gallon and a bit into the tank but in just a few minutes time he would have the rest of the money he owed Carlyle. If it wasn't for the threat to Maureen, he would just fuck off somewhere and let Carlyle find him – if he could.

He pulled into the layby and checked his watch – 09.36. *Strange,* he thought, *Ian was a stickler for punctuality.* Just then he lunged back from his window. "Jesus, where the bloody hell did you come from?" he demanded, opening the passenger door.

"I parked further down the road, thought it might rouse suspicion if we're parked together."

"Yeah, too early for dogging."

"What?"

"Never mind, but try not to make a habit of that, it's not good for my blood pressure."

"Do you have it?" asked Ian, looking about furtively.

"The wire, yes of course; and…?"

Ian did not answer.

"My money?"

"Yeah, well that's something I was coming to."

Frank's stomach sank. "Don't tell me you haven't got it?"

"Yes, of course I do. Just not here, that's all."

"Well what fucking good is that to me?"

"Look, I'll have it by the end of the week I promise."

"In that case; no money – no wire."

"Don't be daft," replied Ian. "If this thing goes tits up how's that going to help either of us? You must realise that."

Frank knew he had no choice. He was just a pawn in a game he had no control over, but then maybe not…

"Fuck you!" he said. "Get out of my car."

"Look, I said you can have the money, you'll just have to wait that's all."

"I won't tell you again."

"You lost your fucking mind?" said Ian, looking at the pistol now in Frank's hand. "Ok, ok, I'll get the money tonight."

"Now."

"Now? That's out of the question; I would have to go to my house."

"Ok then, that's what we'll do." He turned the key in the ignition.

"Wait!" said Ian, reaching across and turning the engine off. "Take this." Frank looked down as he removed his wrist watch. "It's worth more than six grand easy, we'll call it insurance. I'll give you your money at the end of the week and I get my watch back."

Frank had had plenty of experience with fake goods but this was kosher, worth at least ten big ones.

"Fair enough," he said, placing the watch into his pocket before turning to the back seat to retrieve his suitcase which he unzipped and told Ian to remove his jacket.

"Where did you get that thing?" asked Ian.

"What thing?" replied Frank, untangling the wires in the case.

"The fucking gun, numbnuts!"

"Oh that? Not hard to come by if you know the wrong people, and unfortunately in my line of work I have met quite a few."

"Well I don't like it, it worries me."

"Relax; I wasn't going to shoot you. As far as this is concerned," he added, placing the gun into his pocket, "you won't see it again."

Frank told Ian to ease himself forward and in what seemed no time at all, the recorder and the small microphone were in place.

"Keep your jacket done up at all times," instructed Frank. "All you have to do is press this button, it will record for ten minutes."

"Is that all?" asked Ian, looking at the small device.

"It's enough. Just don't get caught up in a load of meaningless banter. Oh, and when you ask a leading question, try not to make it too obvious."

—⁓—

Paul led Solley up to his room and unceremoniously dumped him in the shower.

"I'll be back in five," he said. "You'd better be ready."

"Of course, I'm not going to mess this one up."

"Well from where I'm standing, it looks very much like it."

He made his way back downstairs, passing the four lady hikers consumed with the morning's events, and found Margaret clearing away the breakfast things, announcing his presence with a small cough.

"Look, I'm so sorry for what happened. If there's any way I can make it up to you – and of course I'll pay for any damage, loss of earnings, that sort of thing."

Margaret placed the tray of dirty dishes on the sideboard. "Look, you have nothing to worry about and to be brutally honest, I haven't had so much fun in… well I can't remember. Not since Michael passed away anyway. And as far as damage – well, one empty fire extinguisher and a little tidying up, that's all."

"What about the Fullers?"

She placed her hand into her apron pocked and pulled out a bundle of notes. "They left this in their room. It seems as though those photos really scared them."

Paul smiled, "By today's standards they're really very tame and talking of photos, can I have my phone back?"

"Of course."

He followed Margaret into the office where she opened the small cupboard and got down on her knees to open the safe.

"Before I give you this," she said, "I want you to make me a promise."

"Oh, and what would that be?"

"Delete those photos. The last thing I want is them getting on the Internet. People might get the wrong impression of this hotel."

"Better than that," he replied; "I'll let you delete them."

With great speed and dexterity, she deleted the pictures.

"Wow, that's impressive. It took me two weeks to work that out!"

"Oh, as part of my previous life I worked for an IT company and was involved with phone technology."

He sat down on the edge of the small desk which was covered in various pieces of paper waiting to be filed. "There's something I was going to ask you," he began. "We were due to leave today as you know, but I don't think Solley's going to be in a fit state to drive so I wondered if we could stay an extra night?"

Margaret looked about her, "Well as you can see we're awfully busy," she laughed, "but I'll see what I can do."

"Well that's settled then, I'd better get His Lordship sorted."

"Paul?"

"Yes."

"Forgive me for prying but why don't you drive?"

"I'm not insured on his car."

"Oh, right. So how is it you are going to get to wherever you need to?"

"Taxi," he answered. "Hopefully he'll know where it is."

"Where what is?"

"The old Sanatorium."

"You mean Highgate?"

"Yes, that's the place. Shouldn't be telling you this but now we have to get a taxi it won't be a secret for much longer."

"What won't be?"

"Two London wide boys wanting a ride out to the old hospital in the middle of bleeding nowhere has to raise some questions, and you know what taxi drivers are like?"

She smiled. "It will probably be Sam Ryder, he's the local guy round here and you're right – it will be all over the place by tomorrow. There is one problem," she added.

"Oh, what's that?"

"You will have to walk the last mile and a half."

"Why?" he asked, sounding somewhat dismayed.

"The track up to the old Sanatorium is too rough for anything but a 4x4, although you might be able to negotiate the first half mile by picking your way around the potholes. But there is no way you'll get Sam to do that."

"Don't get me wrong, Solley's my best friend – a real diamond geezer as they say where I come from – but he can be a right pain in the arse sometimes."

"Look," she said, picking up the tray of dishes, "I could run you out there."

"You?"

"Yes, I still have the Land Rover. I was going to get rid of it but it was Mike's pride and joy, plus it's so handy in the winter. The only trouble is, it's petrol and very thirsty."

"Well if you really don't mind," said Paul, "that would be just perfect. I'll go and get Solley."

—⁓—

"I'll see you tonight," said Ian.

"I thought you couldn't get the money until the end of the week?"

"I want my fucking watch back before you pawn it," he replied, opening the door. "Not only that; if Frances finds it missing there'll be hell to pay! Oh, and a word of advice, lose that gun."

Ian slammed the car door and climbed over the old stile to make his way across the muddy field to his vehicle.

9

"Ah Mrs Goodman, how are you this morning?" said Mr Rathbone, "I'm glad to tell you that everything has gone according to plan. I trust you have had your breakfast?"

"Yes," replied Kim.

"And do you have any questions for me?"

"Only one really," she said, adjusting her pillow. "How long will it be before I know everything is ok?"

"It should be no more than a few weeks. By then we will know."

Kim hesitated. "And if things aren't good?"

"I will be honest with you, there is always the possibility with any form of cancer that treatment will not be successful but in your case, I am very confident that you will make a full recovery. I may not be able to see you personally on all of your visits but I will make sure that I have time available to meet any concerns you may have regarding your treatment and recovery.

"The nurse will change your dressing for something a little more practical. Now if there's nothing else, would you please excuse me Mrs Goodman."

Kim felt as though there was so much she wanted to say but at this present time she was lost for words. She picked up her phone, it was Derek.

"Hello?"

"Kim? Sorry to bother you but I think you should know."

"Know what?"

"Look, don't get yourself all worked up but Toby's in hospital."

"Hospital? What's happened?"

"Nothing too serious, he had to have his stomach pumped out."

"Why?"

"He had been drinking tequila. He passed out on the beach and fortunately one of the group he was with phoned for an ambulance – a girl called Amber Watson."

"Yes, I know her. Her father runs The Happy Crab Restaurant; we go there quite often when we're down that way. So how is he?"

"Oh, sick as the proverbial dog," replied Derek, "but he will make a full recovery. No real harm done."

"This is all I bloody need," she said. "That Nathan Turner wasn't there by any chance?"

"Not sure, it's quite possible. Most of the local kids were on the beach last night. Nothing unusual in that, it's been that way since I can remember – summer holidays, good weather. Mind you, it's changed since our day; things seem to be getting out of hand over the past few years. I wouldn't mind betting the local authority will try to put a stop to these beach parties. Julie's picking you up?"

"Yes."

"What time?"

"About 12."

"You're staying with Julie I take it?" asked Derek.

"Oh no, I'm going home."

"Is that wise with Paul being away?"

"I'm quite capable of looking after myself," she retorted.

"Of course, but if there's anything you need – and I mean anything at all – just phone, we're only a couple of hours away."

"Don't worry about me," said Kim, "I'll be fine."

—⁓—

"That's it," said Margaret, pointing up a long track that seemed to wind its way into total obscurity.

"You can't see the Sanatorium," observed Paul.

"False summit," she replied, putting the Land Rover into gear.

Solley craned his neck to get a better look, "You mean that's not the top?"

Paul unfastened his seatbelt and opened his door.

"Where are you going?" asked Solley.

"Nowhere in particular," he replied, stepping down from the battered 4x4 and making his way along the narrow road for some 50 metres or so. He stood there, listening, but apart from some birds, there was nothing. Even the wind that seemed to be ever present, did not feel so inhospitable out here. There was something about this place that captivated him.

"When you're finished, let's get on with it," shouted Solley, half leaning out of the Land Rover.

Paul acknowledged this remark with a gesture of his hand.

"Well that's nice!" he remarked, hauling himself back into the vehicle.

"I know this is none of my business but I think there's something on his mind," said Margaret, turning off the engine. "I've seen that look before."

Solley glanced in the side mirror to see Paul still gazing across the stone wall. "Look," he said, "promise me you won't say anything?"

"No, of course not, if you don't want me too."

"I wouldn't normally tell – well a stranger – this but you're different somehow and I know I can trust you. The thing is; it's Paul's wife. She has recently been diagnosed with cancer."

That word cut through Margaret like a hot knife.

"Paul told me about your husband so I know you'll understand."

"What kind is it?"

"Melanoma."

"How serious?"

"Not sure really," said Solley, "but most people recover, don't they? From that type I mean?"

"Yes, yes," she replied as Paul approached the vehicle, making him out in the rear-view mirror, his shoulders rounded, head slightly bowed.

Last night he was so vibrant, she thought, *but there were times that gave him away. Every now and again he would appear distant, as if his thoughts were somewhere else.* She had seen that look before in her husband's eyes. Telling her, he had said, was the hardest thing he had ever had to do but it was when he said he felt guilty, and that he had let her down, and for that he was truly sorry. No matter how hard she had tried to convince him otherwise, he could not shake this ridiculous thought from his mind.

Margaret was shaken from her thoughts as a large black Range Rover flew past them. Paul looked up, quickly stepping onto the verge, its long, wet grass soaking his very expensive St. Antonio's.

"Fucking moron," he shouted as the vehicles brake lights burst into crimson life, throwing the vehicle's rear end out into the middle of the road as the 4x4 system fought to control this massive vehicle and bring it back into line. But before it had the chance, it swerved violently to the left and charged up the track sending mud and stones flying in every direction.

"He's in a hurry," said Paul, climbing back into the cab of the Land Rover.

"Well he's heading in the same direction as us," observed Solley.

"Perhaps it's your man?" suggested Margaret.

"Most likely," answered Solley, "at least he seems enthusiastic."

"Well there's one thing for certain," remarked Paul, "he owes me a new pair of shoes."

Margaret had noticed the inappropriate footwear but decided not to mention anything on the assumption they had no alternatives. "Shall we go?" she said.

"No, we'll wait," replied Solley.

Margaret noticed a change in their demeanour as they sat and waited. Their light-hearted and carefree attitudes had evaporated like the early mist and she was starting to feel uncomfortable. She glanced at her watch, "I can't wait too long, I must get back."

"Of course," they apologised.

She stamped her foot on the clutch pedal and taking hold of the gear stick with her left hand, she lifted herself off her seat slightly to gain more purchase before forcing the reluctant transmission to accept first gear. This exercise successfully executed, she followed the Range Rover up the track as it disappeared over the horizon.

"What time do you want me to pick you up?" she asked as the Land Rover bounced and wobbled its way up the pot-hole strewn track.

Paul looked at his phone. "Pick us up at 1pm, if that's ok with you?"

"That shouldn't be a problem. I have to go into Little Gaddeston but I should be back in time to get you."

He handed her a note. "It's my number," he explained. "You do what you have to. If you can't make 1pm, just call."

Margaret snatched the note from him as if she was frightened of losing control of her vehicle. With it screwed up in her hand and with a firm grip on the steering wheel, she started to negotiate the most difficult part of their ascent.

She had not been up here since last summer but the deterioration of the track due to the severe winter they had recently experienced had certainly taken its toll. The ruts had now become mini ravines, but despite the enormity of the task, the plucky little 40-year-old Land Rover just kept on plugging its way steadily up to the summit where there to greet them, some 100 metres away, stood the imposing structure.

Immediately both men could see the potential of this building as she drew up alongside Turnbull's Range Rover.

"I'm glad you were driving," said Solley. "Ok, we'll see you about 1pm."

"Do you mind if I hang around and wait for you?" she replied.

"No; why?"

"Oh, I just don't fancy going down there and back again."

Paul felt guilty at the imposition he had caused her and felt that she should be reimbursed for her trouble, but he knew she would refuse straightforward compensation.

"Look," he said. "How are you at dictation?"

"My shorthand used to be pretty good, although it's been a while. Why?"

"Would you take notes for us?"

"Yes, if you like."

"Good. We will pay you of course."

"Oh, there's no need for that."

"Of course there is," insisted Solley. "This is business."

Paul looked up as a figure emerged from the side of the building.

"That must be Turnbull," said Solley.

Margaret looked thoughtful. "He looks familiar."

"His name's Ian Turnbull if that's any help," said Paul, opening his door as Ian approached the Land Rover.

"Ian Turnbull at your service," said the man, reaching out to shake Solley's hand.

"Solley Solomon and this is my partner, Paul Goodman."

"And this is our secretary," offered Paul, "she will be taking notes."

"Yes, yes of course," said Turnbull. "Well if you would care to follow me." *Fuck,* he thought, *I wasn't expecting that!* "By the way," he added, "perhaps you should lock your car."

"Why?" asked Margaret, looking about her.

"Can't be too careful, that's what I always say. Now if you would be so kind as to follow me."

They followed Ian around the side of the old Sanatorium with Solley stopping every so often to check the exterior of the building and record notes into his phone.

This made Margaret wonder as to why Paul had asked her to

accompany them if they were going to dictate to their phones. Somehow, she felt as though there might be some other reason for her presence, but what exactly it might be eluded her.

Ian rallied his entourage, "I must ask you to stay close to me. Although the property is structurally sound, there is rather a lot of discarded material lying around."

Sitting next to the rear doors was a holdall from which he retrieved a large torch. "I'm sorry I don't have one for you," he said, "but if you stay close to me I'm sure this will be fine."

With effort he forced open the somewhat reluctant doors.

"Rats?" asked Solley.

"Sorry?"

"Are there any rats?" he repeated.

"Not to my knowledge," replied Ian, looking a little disconsolate as this thought had not crossed his mind.

"Well I hope not, I can't stand rats!"

For a moment Ian was hoping that this mention of vermin might discourage their secretary from accompanying them but to his annoyance and disappointment she seemed unperturbed. The question now was how was he supposed to broach the subject of a pay-off if she was present? After all, he didn't know if she could be trusted and it would be too risky to take a chance.

There was something else too. For some reason she seemed familiar, but despite racking his brain he could not place her. Then again, if they were from London, it would be very unlikely that he would have seen her before.

With Ian in the vanguard, they made their way into the depths of this once magnificent building.

—m—

"Good morning Mrs Grayson," announced Philip.

But instead of her usual overenthusiastic welcome, he was met with a somewhat subdued response. Immediately he knew something was wrong as she did not even make eye contact but continued scrolling through a list of accounts.

He decided not to press the matter as he had a good idea as to what, or rather who, was behind this uncharacteristic behaviour, so he went into his office, closed the door, placed his case next to his desk and hung his jacket in its usual place. His morning ritual was interrupted by a knock on the door and he opened it to see Linda standing there, which he had to admit was a little unexpected. However, what made this encounter with the Head of Human Resources so unusual was the sight of Barry standing behind her, both with solemn expressions.

"May we come in?" she asked.

"Of course, please take a seat."

He went to close the door but as he did so he caught a glimpse of Mrs Grayson looking in his direction. This in itself was not unexpected, as a visit from the Head of HR, let alone her deputy as well, was bound to arouse suspicion, but it was the way she looked away as she caught sight of him – it was most unnatural and the manner in which she started to rearrange her desk made him suspicious.

"Now," said Philip, sitting down at his desk, "of what service can I be to you?"

Linda placed a small recorder on the table. "Do you have any objections to us recording this conversation?"

"No, none at all. P… p… please go on."

"Well Mr Townsend," she began.

This use of his surname did not bode well he thought as he tried to appear as relaxed as possible.

"We have had a report from a member of staff," she continued, "that you approached them in an aggressive manner and then physically assaulted them by means of pushing them in the chest with both hands. Is this true?"

Philip was lost for words, he knew what Linda was referring to but it was nothing like she had suggested. Or maybe he *had* overstepped the mark and thinking about it, he may have touched Hunter, but it could no way be described as an assault.

She raised a hand to stop him as he was about to speak.

"I must warn you Mr Townsend," she said, "We have a witness to these events."

He took a deep breath. "I know what you are referring to. I did have a heated discussion with Mr Hunter after he said inappropriate things about my wife."

"What exactly were these inappropriate things?" asked Barry.

Philip cleared his throat, "He said 'was it my wife that cut my face and was it because I would not stop shagging her, because if he was in my position, that's he would do.'"

Barry and Linda looked at each other.

"Are you sure that's exactly what he said to you?" she asked.

"Yes, word for word."

"Well if what you are telling us is true, it puts a slightly different light on things. Do you have anyone that can verify your account of events and what was said between you?"

"No."

"Did you remove your bandage and force your face into Mr Hunter's?" asked Barry.

Once again Philip hesitated. He knew lying was not his forte but maybe he had changed. "No, that's a lie too," he said. "I did remove the bandage but only because Mr Hunter accused me of faking my injury for attention."

"Was this before or after the alleged remarks he made about your wife?" asked Barry.

"Before," answered Philip, holding eye contact with him.

"Well thank you for that," said Linda, "but I am afraid that we are going to have to suspend you until further notice."

"Suspend me, why?"

"If it was just your word against the accuser that would be one thing," explained Linda, "but there is a witness that verifies the accuser's statement so you must see, until we have a clear idea of what exactly happened, you are barred from these premises until further notice with effect from now. If you would be so kind as to collect your personal items, Barry will escort you from the building."

At first, he did not respond.

"Philip, did you hear me?"

"Err, yeah, yes."

Linda got to her feet. "You will be hearing from me in due course. Barry will stay here."

Philip placed his case onto the desk, flipped the catches and opened it slowly before methodically placing the picture of Catherine and his paperweight inside it.

"Is that it?" asked Barry.

"Yes," he replied, sounding rather pathetic.

"Ok, follow me."

This ignominious exit in full view of everyone was excruciating. The only people not to look at him were Mrs Grayson and Hunter.

"Just one minute," he said as he passed Mrs Grayson. "The Anderson files are incomplete."

Mrs Grayson looked up at him as he fixed her with a pleading look.

"I'm sure you will put things right," he said.

Philip now found himself out on the High Street. What the hell was he going to tell Catherine? Then it dawned him – if this wasn't bad enough, supposing his successor discovered the missing files? Somehow, he would have to get them back. But how?

He could not bring himself to go home, not until after 6pm at least, so he made his way down the High Street and turned right into Meadow Park where he found a bench next to the boating pond and sat down in the sun. He opened his case and removed a greaseproof bag containing four cheese and pickle sandwiches. It was rather early but he had to do something to pass the time and it would certainly take time to eat these in his condition – if he could at all. Perhaps he should have listened to Catherine but he had never been a fan of hummus, or yoghurt for that matter.

—⁓—

"Well gentlemen, what do you think?" asked Ian.

"It's too early to be certain of anything until we get our surveyor to give us more information," said Paul, "but from what we have seen I think I can say for myself and my colleague that we are most definitely interested."

"Good," replied Ian, "but I must warn you that there are other parties interested."

"Do you mind if I talk to Mr Turnbull alone for a moment?" said Solley.

"No, be my guest," said Paul.

Solley placed his large arm across Ian's shoulder and shepherded him back to the building.

"What do you mean *other parties?*" he asked. "You told me that you would make sure there was no other competition."

"Did I?" replied Turnbull.

"You know fucking full well you did, that's what the money was for."

Ian turned off the recorder. "I think there has been a misunderstanding. That money was to make sure my client accepted your offer but there have been developments since then."

"What developments?" asked Solley, trying to contain his temper.

"It appears just yesterday; my clients were approached by a potential buyer. A Russian gentleman I believe."

"Bloody Russians!" he exclaimed, "muscling in on every bloody thing."

"But there may be a way round this," said Ian.

"Oh? And what might that be?"

"You just leave that for me to worry about. But of course, I will need some more funding."

Solley was not happy but what could he do? This place had the potential to be a big earner with the new railway line to be announced next year.

"Look," he said, "I'll give you another £10k if you make our Russian friend disappear as it were."

"£20k," replied Ian.

Solley looked over his shoulder before wrapping his large hand around Ian's throat and shoved him hard against the cold stone wall. "£10k and that's my final offer!"

Ian knew he was pushing his luck. "Ok, I'll do my best but I can't make any promises. You can't do this kind of thing on the cheap."

"Now you listen to me – you'll be well taken care of but I need some results. My partner is not happy with this situation; I have to give him something," he said before releasing Ian from his iron grip.

—⁓—

Philip folded the empty sandwich bag and as he looked about for a rubbish bin, he noticed two young men in the distance walking towards him. His stomach turned over, *Surely not?* he thought. But it was – two of the gang that had scarred his face forever.

He felt an almost overwhelming sense of panic, like the proverbial rabbit trapped in the headlights, unable to move. He then decided he would make a run for it. But surely that would only draw their attention? Instead, he opened his empty case and pretended to rummage through it as though he was looking for a mislaid item.

The pair were now almost upon him and Philip could feel the case shaking as it rested on his trembling knees. *Please, please just go by,* he thought. His prayers were answered as the two men walked past, both deep in conversation, and a sense of relief washed over him.

It was then he noticed the paperweight he had taken from his desk. He took it into his right hand, its weight somehow feeling reassuring, its smooth round surface fitting into the palm of his hand as though it had been specifically made to do so.

Philip now found himself some 50 yards behind his assailants as they crossed the grass into the trees. The shortest one went down with the first blow, the other took two. Philip returned to where he had been sitting and tossed the paperweight into the boating lake.

—⚭—

Frank pushed his way through the crowded bar filled with lunchtime office-wallahs quaffing prawn sandwiches and knocking back pints of real ale. Even the women were downing this strong beer as though it was nothing more than spring water.

He looked about but there was no sign of Billy Quinn.

"Looking for someone?"

He turned to see Billy standing behind him.

"Over here," said Frank.

"What about a drink first?" asked Billy, looking longingly at the bar.

Frank knew he was on thin ice for there was no way Billy would hand over the documents without payment. It was then he remembered the watch, but how would he settle things with Ian? Not only that, Billy would only accept cash, plus the watch was worth ten times what he owed him. Frank shepherded him to the far end of the pub.

"I texted you to call it off," he said.

"When?" asked Billy, half an eye still on the bar.

"When you were in the fucking Sanatorium, that's when."

"Oh, I didn't get anything, probably no signal. Those walls must be three feet thick I reckon."

"And that's another thing; I told you to take the documents not his fucking car as well."

"It seemed like a good opportunity as the keys were still in the ignition. Not only that, it would have looked suspicious just taking the files."

"Ok, maybe you have a point. Look," said Frank, "let's go back to my office."

"What, leave a perfectly good pub without a drink?"

"You want this bloody money don't you?"

"Yes of course but I'm sure we have time for a quick one."

"Just do as I fucking say," he hissed.

"All right," replied Billy. "No need to get your knickers in a twist."

—m—

As Margaret pulled into the car park it dawned on Paul that the hotel had been left unattended for some time.

"Who's been looking after the place?" he asked.

"Oh that will be Alan; he does the garden for me and the occasional odd job."

"You mean the young man that was here yesterday when we arrived?"

"That's him, he's a nice lad, plus he works for next to nothing. Not sure why?" she added thoughtfully, easing herself down from the Land Rover, her skirt rucking up in the process.

I know why, thought Paul, catching a glimpse of her upper thigh.

"Thought you had to go into town," said Solley as the two men followed Margaret into the hotel.

"I do," she replied, "I was just going to tell Alan he can go."

"Would it be all right if we helped ourselves to a drink?" he asked as she made her way to the kitchen.

"Of course, I trust you," she replied, opening the door.

They went into the empty bar.

"I'll be mother," announced Solley as he grabbed a bottle of

12-year-old malt by the neck, lifting it off the shelf and pouring two large measures then writing down what he'd had on a small note pad Margaret kept behind the bar.

"So?" said Paul.

"So?" repeated Solley.

"What was all that cloak and dagger stuff about?"

"Sorry about that, hope Margaret didn't think I was too rude." He hesitated and looked about to see if anyone was around. "I didn't want Margaret to hear," he said in a low voice. "Not that I don't trust her."

"But?" asked Paul.

"Well it appears that our friend…"

"*Your* friend," corrected Paul.

"Whatever! Apparently, he's been informed by his client that they have had another offer."

"I thought he'd convinced the vendor to sell to us? Wasn't that what the money was for?"

"Of course – well some of it – but this offer comes from a Russian Mafia boss trying to launder some of his ill-gotten gains."

"Are you seriously telling me that the Russian Mafia are interested in a dilapidated old hospital in the middle of fucking nowhere? After all, its true value lies in the fact that the new Northern line will pass within a mile of this place and we are the only people that know that – unless your Uncle…?"

"Steady on," protested Solley, "careful what you say. I know he's a bit of a wide-boy but he wouldn't stitch his family and friends up."

"You're right, that was wrong of me. Anyway, what makes you think he's Russian Mafia?"

"Because every bloody rich Russian is a bloody crook and as such is a member of the Mafia."

"Ok, not so loud," hissed Paul, "do you want everyone to hear you? You never know who might be about!"

Solley turned around arms open wide. "Who?" he said, "there's nobody here. Look," he added, leaning across the bar and dropping his voice to a whisper in case Paul might be right, "this place is going to make us a fortune when the railway line comes through."

"And that's another thing."

Solley gestured with his hands for him to lower his voice.

"How do we know for certain that this railway's definitely coming this way?" Paul continued.

"You know as well as I do," he replied, sounding somewhat indignant.

"Your Uncle?"

"Yes, he's part of the committee."

"But these things change all the time. We could put the best part of £1.5million into this and get seriously burned."

"That's not going to happen," said Solley reassuringly, refilling his glass at the same time. "Anyway, nothing's guaranteed but that's just life. We did not get where we are today without taking a few risks."

"Ok, fair enough. But that still leaves our Russian friend."

"Fuck 'em," he replied. "Let's get one over on them for a change."

He raised his glass. Paul took a deep breath and brought his to meet it.

"To the Oligarchs – fuck 'em," they said in unison.

—⚍—

Billy followed Frank up the dark staircase. "You should get this craphole painted sometime," he said, running his fingers across the wall.

"I like it this way," replied Frank. "It adds atmosphere."

He opened the door to his office and offered Billy a seat.

"Phew, I thought it was bad out there!" said Billy. "And what's that smell, something die in here?"

"Never mind that, let's have a look at what you have for me," replied Frank, holding out his hand.

"No way, I wasn't born yesterday, I want my money first."

"How do I know they're what I want?"

"Whether you want it or not, you're paying for it! I've carried out my part of the bargain."

"Ok, how do I know that you haven't read them, seen their value and fobbed me off with some shit ripped out of a magazine?"

"I wouldn't do that to an old friend."

"Piss off Billy; you would sell your grandmother if she were worth anything."

"No need to get personal," he replied. "Ok, you can have a look but I'm not handing them over until I get what I'm owed."

Billy removed the pink folder from his dirty coat and untied the ribbon holding the documents in place. He opened the file, and with Frank at a safe distance on the other side of his desk, removed one of the documents and allowed him to read the heading.

Frank knew this was valuable – very valuable. "Ok, come back tonight, 10.30 sharp. Your money will be here waiting for you."

"Why do I have to wait until tonight?" he asked, raising his voice.

Frank put his hand into his pocket and pulled out Ian's watch, holding it under Billy's nose.

"Bloody hell!" he exclaimed. "Where did you get that?"

He dropped the watch back into his pocket. "That's not your concern. The only thing you need to worry about is that this watch is going to pay you and maybe, just maybe, add a little bonus."

"How much?" he asked greedily.

Frank eased back into his leather chair. "Twenty percent."

Twenty percent of £1,000 certainly is worth the wait, Billy thought. "Ok," he said, getting to his feet. "I'll be here, 10.30pm sharp."

Frank knew it was worth the promise of the extra money to make sure Billy came back.

—◦◦◦—

Philip glanced at his watch. *"It can't be,"* he said to himself as he looked twice – the hour or so he imagined had elapsed was little more than twenty minutes. His mind kept switching from the files he had taken to the two thugs he had just poleaxed, reassuring himself with the fact they were still moving when he left. He was just about to cross the main road when he found himself outside *Frank's Private Detective Agency – All work undertaken, Divorce a Speciality.*

Why not? he thought. *What did he have to lose?*

Just as he was about to enter the building, the door burst open and what he could only describe as a vagrant, pushed past him with the words, "Mind where you're going pal."

Ok, maybe this is not such a good idea, thought Philip, his doubts growing the further he climbed the dingy stairway. But then again, if the proprietor was as seedy as the premises he occupied, he might be just the right person for this type of job. Ask no questions – that sort of thing.

"Come," said Frank, knowing full well it wasn't Billy; but the last person he expected to walk into his office was the Town Clerk, Philip Townsend.

"You must be Frank," said Philip, holding out his hand.

"Yeah," he replied, getting to his feet.

"Private detective?"

"That's me," he said, feeling a sense of relief. It was obvious he had no idea who he was or what he had done – or maybe he did and he was just being clever. "What can I do for you?"

"My name is…" Philip hesitated, "Anthony Banks."

"Well Mr Banks, how can I be of service?"

"I'm afraid it's rather a delicate matter. I need your reassurance that whatever transpires between us remains strictly confidential."

"I can assure you Mr Banks, you have my word. As long as it isn't murder," added Frank, jokingly.

"No, no, of course not," he replied hastily.

"Ok then, what is it you need me to do?"

Philip cleared his throat, "Some important files have gone missing and I was responsible for them. I know you are not going to believe this but I left them on the bus."

Although Frank knew this was a lie, it was not uncommon for

valuable documents to be left on public transport. "Can you tell me which bus, what time and when?" he asked.

"It was two days ago. It was the 18.20 from the Town Hall, no. 78 to Harpenden."

"I trust you have contacted lost property?"

"Oh, of course."

"Ok, what exactly is in these files?"

"I would rather not say," replied Philip.

"I will need some idea of their importance and what they contain, Mr Banks. If I am to make enquiries, I need to make them in the right place and for that I would need to know of what value they would be and to whom."

Philip knew that what this man had said made sense, and that he would have no choice but to divulge their contents.

He took a deep breath. "They concern various transactions relating to payments from the Local Authority to certain construction companies dating back over twenty-five years."

"I see," said Frank. "Leave it with me, I have lots of contacts. If they are out there I will find them. Of course, I will need a retainer up front but seeing as it's – let's say a public service – I'll settle for a small amount of cash, just for immediate expenses."

"How much?"

"£1,500," replied Frank.

"I d...d... don't have that kind of money on me. I'll have to go to the bank."

"That's fine; I'll wait here for you."

Philip made his way back down the grimy stairway and out into the bright afternoon sun. He crossed the High Street and into a conveniently placed branch of his bank.

"Yes Sir, how can I help you?" asked the young lady.

Bundling the money into his briefcase, he scurried back across the road.

"That will do nicely," said Frank, taking the money and thanking Mr Banks over the sound of his rumbling stomach.

He opened his notepad and pressed the top of his pen with his thumb. "Right Mr Banks, I'm going to need a little more information."

10

"Oh, Councillor Roberts," said Nigel, looking up from Philip's desk.

"I see you are settling in nicely."

"Yes, but whether I'll get the position has to be seen."

"You scratch my back," he said, tapping his nose. "Now when can you get me those files I mentioned?"

"First thing tomorrow."

"Really Nigel? I am disappointed in you," replied Roberts, looking at his very expensive watch. "You have two hours plus – well let's say goodwill."

Nigel knew exactly what would be required of him – he was to be Roberts' personal *gofer* – that is, if he wanted this job (and he did).

Townsend was only a few years older than him; it could be a decade or more before he got the chance of promotion and who knows, five years or so from now, he might even be Director of Finance. If kowtowing to Roberts was the price he would have to pay, so be it.

"Very good Councillor, I'll see to it right away."

"That's more like it young man. I can see you going a long way with that kind of attitude." He turned to see Linda standing in the doorway. "Ah Linda, what can I do for you?"

"It's actually Mr Hunter that I'm looking for."

"Well in that case I'll be on my way."

"Oh, Councillor?"

"Yes Linda?"

"I would like a quick word with you before you go this evening. About 5pm, my office?"

"Of course, it will be a pleasure," he answered. *That's all I fucking need,* he thought as he made his way to the chamber for the afternoon's session. *I just hope the bitch didn't hear too much.*

"I guess you know why I'm here Nigel?" said Linda.

"Is it about what happened the other day?"

"Yes, it is, and there's something that bothers me a little."

"Oh?" said Nigel, feeling his arse tighten. Had he made a mistake or had that cow Grayson lost her nerve? "And what might that be?" he asked as innocently as possible.

"Well in your account of things you said that Mr Townsend pushed you with both hands."

"Yes, that's right."

"Well according to Mrs Grayson, she said it was one."

"No, it was definitely two."

Linda turned in her chair, as there was a knock at the door.

"That will be Barry I daresay. Come in," she called. "Ah Barry, I want you to assist us in clearing up a little misunderstanding. Nigel, will you please follow us."

Nigel looked at his watch. "I have some rather urgent papers to find for the Councillor before 5pm."

"Not to worry," she replied, "this won't take long."

Reluctantly Nigel followed them out into the open area that housed four desks. One was his –hopefully – old desk, one Mrs Grayson's, then Rachel's and Amy's – although at this present time, Mrs Grayson's desk was unoccupied.

"Nigel, would you please go and stand exactly where you were when the alleged confrontation with Mr Townsend took place."

"Yeah, ok."

"Now, are you sure that's where you were standing at the time?"

"Yes, quite sure – positive."

"Good," said Linda. "Now Barry, I want you to stand in front of Nigel. A little closer I think – that will do." She then made her way to Mrs Grayson's desk. "Now Nigel, would it be ok if Barry places his hands on your chest?"

"I don't see how this will help," he protested.

"Please bear with me if you would be so kind. Ok?"

Barry placed his hands against Nigel. "That's fine," she said. "You can return to your duties now Nigel."

Linda watched as he made his way back to his office.

"Any the wiser?" asked Barry.

"Well from this angle – and that's if you were standing in exactly the right place – it would be hard to see if Mr Townsend had placed his hands on Mr Hunter."

"Well she did say that he pushed him. Maybe she saw his outstretched arms?"

"That's possible, except for one thing – the screen."

"I'm not quite with you," said Barry, feeling a little awkward.

"Ok, go and stand exactly where Mr Hunter was just standing." She positioned herself directly in front of Barry. "Now, as I push my arms out, you move back."

Barry did so and clattered into the screen that separated Mrs Grayson's desk from Rachel's. "Right, I see what you mean. In order for Mrs Grayson to have seen Mr Townsend push Mr Hunter, he would have fallen into the screen."

"That would seem to be the case," she confirmed. "But when I asked Mrs Grayson if that's what happened, she was adamant that at no time did Mr Hunter touch the screen."

—⁓—

"Billy, it's Frank here… How many fucking Franks do you know…? Look there's been a slight change of plan, be round at my office by 9.30pm. I'll have your money."

"You sure you don't want me to stay?" asked Julie.

"No, I'll be fine," said Kim, placing her overnight bag onto the hall table.

"Look, I think I should stay – for tonight at least."

"It's ok, I'll be fine, don't worry."

"But I do. It wouldn't be normal if I didn't, I am your twin sister after all."

"I know it's just…" Kim hesitated.

"Just what?" asked Julie.

"Look – if I get desperate I'll call."

"Ok, have it your way. What time's your appointment tomorrow?"

"At 10am."

"I'll pick you up at 8.30am – give us time to find somewhere to park. And that's another thing – you would think they would have a car park for their patients – especially with what they charge."

"It's ok, I'll get the bus."

"No, no, I wasn't suggesting it's too much trouble. I was just saying…"

"No, you're right," confirmed Kim. "It's a nightmare trying to find somewhere to park and I don't know how long I'll be."

"So you'll get the bus?" said Julie sarcastically.

"Why not?"

"When was the last time you were on a bus?"

"What's that got to do with it?"

"Well go on – tell me," she insisted.

"Oh I don't know, twenty years ago."

"Quiet; it's not a place for someone in your condition."

"My condition?" said Kim, sounding a little indignant.

"Yes, you have cancer, remember."

"Thanks for reminding me."

Julie took her sister by the hand. "Listen, you have to take care of yourself and the stress of negotiating public transport – especially at that time in the morning – when you don't have to, suggests to me that you have not given your recovery proper consideration."

Maybe Julie was right, thought Kim. *Perhaps she was not being realistic. Or was she subconsciously pretending that none of this was actually happening to her?*

"Look," said Julie, "I'm here for you and in a selfish way it helps me to help you." She pulled Kim to her in a tight embrace and broke down in tears. "I don't know what I would do if anything happened to you," she sobbed.

"Nothing's going to happen to me, I'll be fine. And you're right, I do need your help," she added, realising that what was happening to her had wider implications. She had never been a selfish person and this was certainly not the time to start. "Look," she said, "stay the night."

"No, it's ok if you want to be by yourself."

"No, that was stupid of me. The last thing I want is to be here on my own. I guess I was feeling sorry for myself that's all. Come on, there's a bottle of bubbly in the fridge."

"Should you be drinking?"

"Oh, probably not, but one can't hurt, then we'll order some pizza and put on a movie, how's that?"

Although Kim was some five minutes younger than her sister, she had always acted the eldest and had taken care of her older sister. Why should this be any different? Plus, it gave her a sense of purpose and would help to take her mind off things, if only temporarily. If she was to beat this she would need support from her friends and family.

—m—

Philip's feet were starting to ache, he had not walked this much since he was in the Scouts and his footwear was far from appropriate for long distances. He could feel that the back of his heels were already blistered – this was something he would have to hide from Catherine.

Despite the pain emanating from his feet, it was not enough to distract him from his present plight. Losing his job was bad enough, especially if he were to be dismissed for improper conduct concerning an assault, or even an alleged assault, but all that seemed to pale into insignificance compared to the loss of the files he had illegally removed.

But then again, what choice did he have? If what had happened to his wife that night nearly two years ago became public knowledge, it would destroy her. And what the hell was he thinking going to a private detective? For all he knew he could go straight to the authorities. The whole situation was a complete and utter mess.

It then dawned on him that the blackmailer's promise to return the files immediately after he had done what he needed to do was probably a lie as well. He felt a wave of despondency wash over him – what could he do? His only hope would be Frank Hibbard.

It was hard to believe that his life just a few days ago seemed perfectly normal. All he could do now was to let things run their sordid course.

Philip paused at the gate and looked at the double-fronted house that had once been his parent's and his childhood home. He made his way slowly up the path and inserted his key into the lock, as he had done countless times, but before he could open the door he was met by Catherine. At first, he could not quite believe what he was looking at.

"You… you… you look different," he stammered.

"I'm so glad you noticed."

It would be hard not to, he thought, observing her tight top, short skirt and new hairdo. This came as a complete surprise to him as Catherine, given the choice, would often dress down.

She grabbed him by the hand and pulled him into the hallway. "What do you think?" she asked, doing a twirl.

"It's really nice," he answered, trying to sound as positive as he could.

"And that's not all," she said proudly. "Guess what I've done?"

He did not answer but dropped his head and raised his eyes in anticipation of whatever it might be.

"I have booked a table for two at Mario's," she announced.

"Mario's?" he repeated.

"Yes, we used to go there, remember?"

"I kn… kn… know but…"

"Look it's time, time to put the past behind us. We're still young, we have all our lives ahead of us and I know how hard these last few years must have been for you, but now things will be different. I actually feel free for the first time.

"At first I wasn't sure how to react after what happened the other day but I then realised that for you to behave like that was totally out of character and that you must have been near breaking point. The last thing I want is to lose you."

"L… l… lose me?" said Philip. "That would n…n…never happen."

"Well then, that's settled," she said. "We have a new beginning starting from today. Now you go and get ready, the table's booked for 7.30pm."

As he made his way upstairs, the irony had not escaped him. How normal had his life actually been? What had happened that night, when Catherine was pulled from her car on that lonely back road? She never said, and although Philip had given strict instructions not to hurt her in any way, he could never be certain about what exactly happened, but he always felt as though her reluctance to talk about it might be an indication of something he could not bring himself to even consider.

But now, after all this time, she had finally overcome her fear to the extent that for the first time since the assault she had actually left the house unaccompanied, although recently she had got into the habit of gardening and this at least got her talking

132

to the neighbours. And now there was this major breakthrough –
just in time for him to be sacked for violent conduct and possible
prosecution for removing sensitive files and handing them over to
an unauthorised party!

"Julie's staying the night," said Kim.

Paul felt a sense of relief at this news. "It's for the best; you never
know."

"Know what?"

"Well it might all of a sudden hit you, and having someone
there might help."

"I guess you're right."

"You sound a little down but I guess that's to be expected."

"Well to be truthful," said Kim, "I got off to a good start this
morning, better than I thought I would, but..."

"But what?" asked Paul, a sinking feeling in the pit of his
stomach; had they found something else?

"It's Toby."

"Toby; why, what's wrong?"

"He was taken to hospital to have his stomach pumped out
after a drinking session on the beach last night," she explained.

"Is he ok?"

"Oh yeah, sick as a dog according to Derek!" she laughed.

"And where was *he*?" asked Paul.

"He was over at the hotel."

"I thought he was looking after them?"

"Toby's 18, he's not a child. Anyway, I don't think it was entirely
Toby's fault."

"Oh, so someone force fed him alcohol then?"

"No, I think he might have been with that Nathan Turner."

"I thought he got banged up for that crash he caused when he
stole that car?"

"Apparently he got a suspended sentence. Can you believe it? I would never have sent them down there if I had known he was still at large. That boy has always been a bad influence on Toby. So, what time are you back? I don't suppose it will be until late?"

"Well actually I was going to come to that. You see last night…"

"Don't tell me, this has something to do with Solley."

"How did you guess?"

"Ok, what's he done this time? Is he in the local nick for breach of the peace?"

"Not quite. He had a skin-full last night and managed to get the rest of the guests legless as well," said Paul with a laugh. "You know what he's like – showing off as usual, got his hands on a piano and one thing led to another. The end result is that he can't drive, not until he's sobered up properly, and the last thing I want to do is to head down the motorway with soppy bollocks at the wheel still half-cut."

"No, of course not," she agreed.

"Anyway, we're staying the night, plus this hair-brained scheme of Solley's might not be so daft after all. I wish you were here to see the place, it has so much potential. It's magnificent, it really is. And if we can get it for the right price, and well – if things pan out as he seems certain they will, this could make us a tidy little sum. The other thing is I want to have another look round the place on my own."

"And exactly how are you going to do that?" asked Kim.

"I'll get up early. You know what Solley's like, never up before lunch at the best of times. I'll be gone and back before he even knows."

"Why on your own?"

"There's… I don't know, there's something I can't quite put my finger on, and if I go with Solley he will only distract me, plus I have a feeling about the vendor's agent."

"You mean he's not kosher?"

Paul never made any statements over the phone that might

incriminate himself or anyone he might be connected with. "I wouldn't go that far," he said, knowing full well that Turnbull was as bent as a paper clip, "but what harm can it do?"

"And how are you going to get there unless Solley drives? Come to that how did you get there today?"

Paul was just about to say 'taxi' as the thought of him cavorting about the countryside with a beautiful widow would not sit well with Kim, but then again, she was not to know that.

"The owner of the hotel kindly ran us over there in their 4x4," he said.

"That was kind of them; would they be willing to do that tomorrow as well?"

"I'm sure Margaret won't mind."

"Oh, *Margaret* is it?" she teased.

"Oh, it's not what you're thinking, she's… really old," he lied. *Fuck it,* he thought. *Why did I say that?*

"Ok, see you tomorrow."

—⁓—

Philip watched from a slight distance as the waiter led his wife to their table, catching the eye of every man in the restaurant. He knew she was extraordinarily beautiful but after all these years of being a virtual recluse and the way she always used to dress down, he had forgotten just what a stunner she was. Even the women could not help but notice her.

Apart from her perfect figure, excellent deportment and classic good looks, she carried with her a presence that seemed to totally overwhelm any room she entered, and to top it all she had a first in English from Manchester. And she was his, to the total disbelief of everyone he knew. He had even experienced outright hostility from some as if he, Philip Townsend, had no right to such a creature.

However, he knew why he was so fortunate, it was quite simply the fact that Catherine was an only child of older parents.

Although he was staid and old fashioned, she seemed to find this familiar and reassuring. But things started to change, especially after Nick Tobin and that tart of a wife of his moved in next door with her so-called coffee mornings. He could hear them when he was in the garden, squawking and giggling, and whenever Catherine returned from one of Beverley's get-togethers she would be distant, less content; 'Why don't we do this and why don't we do that?'

And as for him, Philip knew exactly what he was after – and in his own home! Can you believe it? There he was as large as life with Catherine in her swimsuit and him in his shorts lounging in the garden with cocktails. Ok, there were three sun loungers and drinks for three, but when he made his presence known Nick made out that Beverley had just conveniently gone on an errand of mercy for her sick mother. Sick? There was nothing wrong with the old cow with her four ton of make-up and short skirt. Really, at her age! But you know what they say – like mother, like daughter.

However, things resolved themselves after the break-in. Still, the upside was that Catherine seemed to have reverted to her old self until about six months later when she got a phone call from Beverley – they were having a house-warming. Of course, she wanted to go. He told her there was no way he would set foot in that house and that they were leading her astray but would she listen? Inevitably she came back full of it and the next thing it becomes a regular event, every Wednesday. He'd told her that no good would come of it.

But now after all this time it was hard for him to accept this more outward going side that had been suppressed in her by overbearing parents. Philip knew that once she had found her self-confidence she would undoubtedly see him for what he really was – an unattractive, boring stick-in-the-mud with a boring stick-in-the-mud job. Life had so much more to offer someone like Catherine and he knew he could not provide it.

As the waiter pulled back her chair, Philip could tell that the eye of every man was on her curvaceous backside as she placed it tentatively on the seat and that every man there was wishing it was them she was easing herself onto. However, his concerns for Catherine's propensity towards a more dynamic way of life and its consequences for him would have to wait – getting those files back was his first priority. Who knew, this whole thing might work out to his advantage.

—ɷ—

Frank looked at his watch, it was now 10.15pm. *That stupid bastard Billy, where the hell is he?* he thought to himself, looking through the dirt smeared window of his first-floor office. Apart from the regular street walkers and the occasional taxi dropping off clients, there was no sign of him. He reached into his pocket and retrieved his phone.

"Billy, is that you? … What? Speak up; I can hardly hear you… Where? Hold on." Frank grabbed a pen. "The Water Mill, south side of Easham. What the fuck are you doing out there? …. Ok, stay where you are, I'll be over in 30 minutes and don't go anywhere."

Franks car coughed and spluttered its way onto the forecourt of the filling station and with the help of a van driver; he pushed the vehicle to the nearest pump.

"Thank goodness for that money from Mr Banks" he smiled to himself. Not only had it filled his empty stomach but it had filled his all-important car. He pulled out of the filling station and turned left at the first roundabout. As he flipped the wiper switch the half-worn blades juddered across the rain-splattered screen, leaving an oily smear in their wake, turning the red tail lights and beams of oncoming traffic into a kaleidoscope of distorted rainbows. He pressed the wash-wipe button but to no avail. He tried again, this time pressing harder as if this extra effort would somehow conjure up a hidden reserve of water.

"Shit," he leaned forwards, and using the sleeve of his raincoat, ran his hand over the inside of the screen in a vain attempt at improving his vision. "Who the fuck?" he said, fumbling for his phone while trying to keep his steel charge on the road. "Ian? What can I do you for?"

"If you have pawned that watch I'll…"

"You'll what?" said Frank.

"Where the hell are you, your money's here and I want that watch back?"

"Look I can't talk now but I have some good news on those missing documents, just be patient."

"You know where they are?"

"I put out a few feelers and I had a call from this bloke. I'm heading off to meet him right now. The thing is, he wants five grand."

"Don't you give him that fucking watch."

"I wasn't going to. I'll pay him from what you gave me earlier," said Frank, knowing full well he had already given it to Carlyle. But then again Turnbull was not to know that. "The only problem is; you now owe me eleven grand."

Ian was not happy, but it was still very much worth his while. "Ok, I'll get you the extra."

"Good," he replied, "I'll phone you when the deal's done. Oh, by the way, I'll keep the watch until I get the rest of my money."

Frank knew that after paying off Billy and Reggie he would only come out with about three grand. He realised the documents were worth much more than that but it wasn't worth getting too greedy, after all, just 24 hours ago he was twelve grand in debt to someone who would not think twice about cutting his hands off.

He pulled into the half-empty car park of the Water Mill pub, got out of his car and just as he was about to lock it, felt a presence behind him.

"Hello Frankie, fancy seeing you here."

"Reggie!" he said, his heart beating nineteen to the dozen. "What are you doing here?"

"I could ask you the same thing but we both know the answer to that one don't we Frankie?"

Reggie moved back slightly as a black Range Rover drew up alongside them. The rear window opened and Frank stepped forwards to see Billy wedged between two heavies. Reggie opened the front passenger door.

"Please," he said, indicating for Frank to get in the vehicle.

His first instinct was to do a runner but then again, what was the point? He slipped obediently onto the front seat.

"I will see you shortly; we can have a nice cup of tea and a little chat. Oh, and fasten your seatbelt," said Reggie, slamming the door.

The Range Rover swept out of the car park at high speed and disappeared amongst the traffic.

—m—

"Another one?" asked Solley.

"No and neither should you. After last night, I want to get home tomorrow," said Paul, removing Solley's empty glass.

"I told you we could have gone home today."

"Are you bleeding serious? You could hardly stand this morning."

"That was this morning. My rate of recovery is legendary."

"Yeah, that's as may be, but I'm not a fan of your driving at the best of times, let alone when you're still half-pissed."

"Oh, look who's talking; at least I still have my licence," he retorted.

"Yeah, and that's something that's always puzzled me. How is that even possible?"

"I'm a good driver," he said defensively.

"More like a lucky one," replied Paul, turning to see Margaret standing behind him. "Sorry, didn't see you there."

"Well I'm off to bed," announced Solley, removing the glass from Paul's hand and draining the last drop as a show of defiance.

Margaret and Paul wished him good night.

"I hope you don't mind me asking," she began, "but curiosity has got the better of me."

"Well you know what they say about that?"

She ignored the remark, eased herself onto one of the bar stools next to him and tided some of the beer mats into a small pile.

"So, what is it you want to know?" he asked.

"I was just curious as to what you are planning to do with the old Sanatorium, that's if you don't mind me asking."

"Well to answer your second question no I don't mind you asking, and I'll give to you the answer to your first question but only if you would do something for me."

"Oh, and what's that?" enquired Margaret, looking a little defensive.

"Look, if we take this project on, we'll need someone here we can trust – to oversee things if you like – and I was thinking that someone could be you."

"Oh," she said, a little surprised, "I wasn't expecting that. And exactly what would you expect of me?"

"Well a project of this nature involves a lot of administration, mostly dealing with local contractors and the planning authority – making sure invoices are paid and contractors honour their obligations."

"Won't you have a site manager for that?"

"Yes of course, but he won't be able to handle everything. He will need a secretary on a job of this nature, plus – and this is a big plus – I need someone here I can trust. Someone who knows what's going on and won't give me any bullshit. So, what do you say?"

"Well I can't deny that the money wouldn't come in handy and speaking of money, what's the going rate?"

"I was thinking of £20 an hour plus a cash bonus of ten percent of your gross pay."

"And how many hours a week would I be expected to do, bearing in mind I have this place to run?"

"Well it would probably be four hours a day, including weekends."

"And ten percent of my gross pay when the job's finished?"

"Yep."

"Ok," said Margaret. "You have yourself a secretary."

"Good, I'll run it by Solley tomorrow. I'm sure he will be as glad to have you on board as me. Oh, and speaking of Solley, I wonder if you could do me a little favour?"

"Depends."

"The thing is I want to have another look round the old hospital tomorrow, first thing. I wonder if you could take me out there."

"What time?" she asked.

Paul hesitated. "About 5.30am."

"Oh, right."

"That way we can be back by 7.30am in time for you to get breakfast, plus this is strictly between us – Solley's not to know."

"And exactly how are you going to get in?"

"Oh, I'm not going inside, that would be illegal. No, I just want to have another look round the outside. You can get a better idea of the buildings structural condition than you can from inside more often than not."

"Ok," replied Margaret, "as long as we're not breaking any laws."

"Mrs McIntyre, I am surprised you would ever suggest such a thing!" he smiled. "And the answer to your first question is we plan to turn the building into luxury apartments."

"Paul?"

"Yes."

"Why do you want to go without your partner?"

"Oh, nothing untoward I can assure you. Solley has an eye for a good deal but sometimes he's a little headstrong. I want time by myself – get the feel of the place, you know? And not only that, it's a long way to just pop back."

"Especially if you can't drive," she remarked with a smile.

"You heard?"

"Yes, but don't worry, I wasn't eavesdropping. I couldn't help but overhear."

"Well that doesn't surprise me; he's got some gob on him that's for sure. Look, I told you I wasn't insured on Solley's car because if you tell people you're banned from driving, they get the wrong idea."

"Oh? And what idea would that be?"

"That you're a menace to the public or that you were drinking and driving. You know; that sort of thing."

"And you?"

"Speeding on the motorway," he explained. "I already had six points but I had just taken delivery of a new Aston and I was late for an important meeting. You know what's it's like with these cars?"

"No, not really."

"Well, they're so well-made and powerful, you have to keep your eye on the speed at all times. They got me at 118mph and consequently a year's ban."

"Ok I'll meet you down here at 5am," she said, picking up the empty glasses.

11

The brightly lit houses that had lined the roadside now gave way to industrial buildings – the type that take no time to erect, all girders and corrugated sheeting. The Range Rover pulled onto a patch of wasteland between two large warehouses and came to a stop at the rear of one of them and waited. A few moments later Reggie's car drew up alongside and the driver got out.

Frank gave him the once over. *Big fucker,* he thought. *Well over 6ft and a good 18 stone easily, Eastern European by appearance, probably Russian.*

It was fashionable to have a Russian bodyguard and Reggie was no exception. Frankie was only too aware of their formidable reputation, one that was justly deserved – hard as nails and devoid of emotion.

Frank watched as this monster of a man approached and opened his door. His first instinct was to make a run for it but even if he were to put some distance between himself and his new friend, there was nowhere to escape to. Plus, from what he could tell, as was the norm with these places, apart from the way in, everywhere was surrounded by high security fencing topped with razor wire and the last thing he wanted to do was to piss this guy off by giving him the run-around.

He stepped out into the warm damp air to the sound of car

doors opening as Billy was hauled unceremoniously from the back seat of their vehicle and led, with Frank, to a small side door. Once inside the massive building they were taken to a partitioned area that doubled up as an office of sorts. They were seated with Reggie standing in front of them.

"Now gentlemen," he said. "I think we all know why we are here?"

Billy dropped his head onto his chest.

"I'm afraid you have the advantage," said Frank, eyeing up his surroundings.

"You're right on at least two accounts," replied Reggie. "I do have the advantage and you have every right to be afraid because if I don't get what I want, things could turn messy."

"And what exactly is it that you want?" he asked, trying to sound ignorant.

Reggie sighed. "Well, if you insist. Our friend Billy here came to me. It seems you employed him to steal a car and in that car were certain documents that you were willing to pay more than ten grand for."

Ten grand? thought Frank as he glowered at Billy who lowered his eyes.

"But Billy, being Billy, got greedy and thought he could do better and came to me, but for some reason it seems that he has lost his memory and can't seem to recall where he put them – isn't that so Billy? That's if they ever existed in the first place – or could it be they are just a figment of an alcohol-induced imagination."

Billy did not answer but just remained motionless, a blank stare on his face.

"Now," continued Reggie, "why would that be I asked myself? Could it be that Billy has got all entrepreneurial all of a sudden and thinks he could do better elsewhere? Or perhaps there's another reason? Now there's two ways we can sort this little dilemma out: either Billy can co-operate or you can tell me what's in these documents that's so important that he would risk messing me about, and for we all know what the consequences of that would be?"

Frank was totally perplexed. If Reggie was going to give Billy more money why had he backed out? After all, Reggie had a reputation for coaxing information out of people – normally with the aid of a pair of pliers. It then dawned on him that Billy must have somehow stayed sober long enough to read them.

Despite his appearance, Billy had had an excellent education and had reached the dizzy heights of a Senior Civil Servant with Customs & Excise until his wife left him. He had always struggled with drink and after she left, he turned full-time to the bottle. Less than a year later, he was divorced, out of home and job, living in a cardboard box under the flyover. Billy was no idiot, just an alcoholic.

But here lies the dilemma, he thought. *If Billy won't tell Reggie, or for some reason he can't, fuck knows where that would lead?*

Reggie drew a chair up in front of Frank and sat down. "There's something that's been troubling me Frankie boy. Where the hell did you get your hands on ten grand?"

"He's got the money," said Billy, "look in his right pocket."

Reggie looked over at his Russian heavy.

"No, I'll save you the trouble," said Frankie, retrieving the watch from his coat.

Reggie took the watch and examined it carefully. "My my, Frankie, you are a dark horse. Trying to cheat your wife out of her rightful settlement? Or did she say you could keep it? But you and I know it's neither, is it, for there's no way you could keep this secret and if I know Maureen, she would strip you down to your underpants and even think twice about taking those as well."

Reggie leaned forward slowly until his face was just inches from Frankie's. "So? Whose is it and how did you come by it?"

"I bought it years ago as a form of insurance. Maureen never knew anything about it."

"Oh please, please Frankie! You know as well as I do…" Reggie dangled the watch in front of Frank, "… that you pawned every last thing you had so you could bet on the dogs. If it wasn't for the fact Maureen had the house signed over to her, you would have lost that as well. So Frankie, for the last time, who does it belong to?"

"Look," he pleaded, "it's mine, it's the only thing I have and the only reason I didn't pawn it is that it's my father's. It means the world to me."

Frank did not get the response he half expected. Instead of the back of a hand across the face for such a blatant lie, Reggie showed him the back of the watch. Inscribed on it were the words *"To my darling Ian, for 25 wonderful years, love Frances."*

"Now if I recall," said Reggie, "your father's name was Edward?"

Frank had been in some tight spots before but this had to rank up there with the best of them.

"Cat got your tongue Frankie? Maybe my colleague here can loosen it a little? You know whose watch this is? *I* do but I want to hear it from you. No? Cat still got your tongue then? Ok, I'm a reasonable man, now either you tell me how you came by Ian Turnbull's watch or…"

Reggie turned to one of the two men standing either side of Billy and gave a nod. The smaller of the two smashed Billy in the face, breaking his already twice broken nose.

"That, Frankie boy, is just for starters."

"Ok," he said. "I'll come clean. I stole it."

"Really Frankie, that does surprise me. I never took you for a thief, a little tax evasion maybe."

"Ian had a job for me."

"Oh, and what sort of job? It wouldn't have something to do with the old hospital?"

"Kind of."

"Well I'm all ears."

Frankie cleared his throat. "You know it's up for sale and there have been a few break-ins?"

"What, up there?"

"Believe it or not, kids mostly – out for a cheap thrill. I was desperate for work – as you know I'm short of money – so Ian asked me to keep an eye on the place until it's sold. The last thing he wants is some crack-head burning the place down. When I was round at his house the other day discussing things, I checked out the security. I went back the next day – I knew the place would be empty as Ian had told me that they were off to Leeds – antiques – quite a collector is our Ian – so I broke in and took the most valuable thing I could find that was easy to move and sell."

"That's bullshit," exclaimed Reggie as he dropped the watch into his pocket. "I'll keep this I think, can't trust you with it. Don't worry Frankie; I'll make sure Mr Turnbull gets his property back. So, these documents, what's in them and does our mutual friend Ian Turnbull have something to do with them?"

Frank knew Reggie was a nasty bastard but what made him so dangerous was his intelligence. Rumours had it that he was tossed out of Oxford for running a vice ring.

Oh what the fuck? he thought. The barrel smashed into Reggie's forehead, ripping a chunk of flesh from the top of his right eye. "Nobody fucking move," he screamed, the pistol held firmly in both hands. "Ok Billy," he said, "get the car keys."

Billy did as instructed as Reggie got to his feet, his hand stemming the flow of blood.

"You have overstepped the line this time Frankie boy," he spat, wiping the blood from his face.

"Yeah, well that's my problem."

"None of us here are armed," said Reggie, "so why don't you put that thing down and we can discuss things like adults."

"I wasn't fucking born yesterday," answered Frank.

"Look, if you don't do as I say, then we know what will happen don't we?"

"You mean Maureen don't you."

"Well Frankie," said Reggie, "it does make you vulnerable."

"You know Reggie, I always thought of you as an intelligent man but it seems as though I was mistaken."

"Oh? And why would that be?"

"Because you have left me three choices: one – hand over this gun and get fed to the pigs, two – make a run for it and have you get to Maureen…"

"And the third?" asked Reggie.

Frank's finger squeezed the trigger.

"No!" screamed Billy, "I'll tell him what's in them. These documents contain details of business transactions between certain construction companies and the local authorities. One of these companies listed was Marshalls Aggregates that delivered materials for the new by-pass to the tune of £2.8million but its parent company was Carlyle Construction. It was then I realised the potential consequences to myself if I handed these over to you."

Reggie was fully aware of Billy's past occupation and what he could do with this information. "So why would I pay for these documents telling me what I already knew?" he asked. "It was all above board."

"Not quite," replied Billy. "Your brother-in-law is a Mr Roberts – or should I say Councillor Roberts – and has several hats; one of them being Head of Planning."

"So?"

"Cast your mind back twenty years."

"I'm afraid you'll have to be more specific," said Reggie.

"Your company won the contract to build the Commonwealth Village, worth an estimated £8.5million."

"So? As I told you, all this is legit."

"Well so it seems at first," continued Billy. "I found a payment from the local authority for £1.8million paid to your company for construction work. Now it so happens that Councillor Roberts' wife is a director of Landfill Management. They get a contract from Marshalls to dump thousands of tons of waste to the tune of £50 a ton, less £20 dumping fee, and according to Landfill Management and Marshalls they took delivery of 110,000 tons which was paid for. However, according to Knight Bridge Surveyors, they estimated that only 30,000 tons was dumped at the site. And that's just for starters."

Reggie started to look rather uncomfortable, "You work fast Billy, for an alcoholic."

"I can do when I'm motivated, but this information is locked up in here," he added, tapping his head. "I went to see my superior shortly after I became suspicious. I was told to leave this matter to him and was never to mention it again."

"Why would that be?" asked Frank, gun still levelled at Reggie.

"It would have been too controversial to raise this matter just before the Queen arrived to open the Commonwealth Games, so I guess it was swept under the carpet. However, times have changed. As you are aware – with what I know, coupled with these documents (which quite frankly I thought would have found their way into the shredder by now), they are if you like – and please pardon the pun – the proverbial smoking gun."

"I'm feeling a little dizzy," said Reggie, "do you mind if I sit down?"

"Be my guest," said Frank, "but no funny business."

Reggie perched on the edge of an old plastic chair and made himself as comfortable as possible.

"So where are they now?" he asked.

"They're quite safe," replied Billy. "In fact, from your point of view it's a good thing."

"Oh, and how do you come to that conclusion?" said a rather irate Reggie.

"Well at least this way you don't have to worry about these papers turning up unexpectedly. And of course, it's insurance for us. I don't need to tell you how this works do I?"

"But how do I know I can trust you?"

"You'll just have to. Now I think for keeping our little secret, a small retainer would be in order – say forty grand a year each?"

Reggie was not used to being on the receiving end of these kinds of transactions but he was fully aware of what the consequences would be if these documents got into the hands of the authorities, coupled with what Billy knew.

"Ok," he agreed. "But I'll tell you both this for nothing – if either of you ask for any more, or by some way or another I get a visit from the Fraud Office, I don't need to spell out the consequences for you and your loved ones."

Both Frank and Billy knew this threat was not an idle one and that they could only push him so far.

"Now go on, get out of my sight before I changed my mind," said Reggie.

"There's one more thing," said Frank, "give me the watch."

Billy and Frank left the warehouse and emerged into the warm damp evening air.

"What now?" asked Billy.

"Fucked if I know, I thought you were the brains behind this outfit," said Frank, tossing the car keys over the embankment.

—◊—

"You must be tired."

"Yes and no," replied Kim, easing her feet off the sofa.

"You must rest."

"What do you think this is?" retorted her sister rather curtly.

"You know full well what I mean," said Julie gently.

"Sorry, I didn't mean to be short with you. I'm a little on edge, that's why I thought it might be best if I was on my own."

"That's perfectly understandable."

"Is it?"

"Of course," replied Julie, picking up the empty coffee cups.

"I don't know – it's as if…" Kim hesitated. "It's as if…"

"What?" asked Julie, placing the cups back down and sitting next to her sister.

"Oh, just lately – and I know what you're going to say, it's this melanoma nonsense – but there's more to it than that. If you want to really know – I feel redundant."

"That's just stupid what on earth makes you say that?"

Kim took a deep breath. "We're not getting any younger, the kids have grown up, we have a nice home plus the apartment in France and the holiday cottage in Cornwall – we have achieved all there is to achieve. There doesn't seem to be anything to aim for now."

"Grandkids?"

"I would like to think so," replied Kim, "but I'm not sure."

"Well I don't know about you but I intend to enjoy myself while I can," replied Julie, brightly.

"I know all that. But where's the cut and thrust, the excitement of taking a risk, buying your first home, children?"

Julie knew exactly what Kim was talking about. She had wondered the same herself as one shopping spree turned into another, one holiday in the sun became merged with all the others. However, this was not the time for unjustified mutual self-pity. She was here to keep her sister's spirits up.

"Where are you going?" asked Kim.

"Two secs," she answered as she made her way to the study, only to return a few moments later with an arm full of photo albums.

"What on earth are they for?"

"Press flowers, what do you think?" she replied sarcastically. "Look, this one dates to 1972."

Julie opened the cover with great reverence and lifted back the thin sheets of yellowed tissue that separated each page.

"Oh my goodness!" exclaimed Kim, looking at herself and Julie on Southend Pier with their polka-dot summer dresses and ankle socks to match.

"I think we look sweet. You're lucky to have a daughter; it's hard having three boys. They're just so… insensitive."

"Oh come on, the boys are lovely."

"In short doses maybe," agreed Julie. "Don't get me wrong, I love them to bits, but sometimes you just want a break from a house with four men in it – and Derek's no better – if anything, I think he encourages them."

"In what way?"

"Well take last week we went over to Dougie's."

"Oh yeah, it was their silver. Shit, I forgot to send a card."

"Don't worry too much."

"Why?"

"Well after Pauline got drunk and fell into Dougie's Koi pond with half a bottle of brandy in her hand, it all got a little surreal. You should have seen it. There's me and Derek trying to get her out, while Dougie's running around with a big net telling everyone to fill buckets with water so he can save his precious fish. I ask you – as if a bit of cognac is going to harm them; the bloody pond's nearly the size of our pool.

"I very much doubt whether they're even talking to each other, let alone wondering why you forgot to send them a card. Anyway, I digress. While we were away, Derek told the boys they could have some friends over to stay the night – no more than five, tops."

"You're brave" said Kim.

"You've changed your tune all of a sudden – two minutes ago butter wouldn't melt in their mouths. As I was saying – we stayed over, not that I wanted to after that fiasco, but by then both of us had had too much to drink and there was no way I could get Derek to fork out for a taxi from Cheltenham. So, to cut a long story short, we got back about 12ish the next day. As you can imagine the kitchen was a complete shamble – I grant you, that I half expected. Also, the house reeked of air freshener."

"At least they had made some effort."

"I thought the same at first but it wasn't until I opened the bin to put the rubbish in that I could smell it."

"Smell what?" asked Kim.

"What the bloody hell do you think? Weed. Oh, and not just a puff or two, there must have been a dozen or so tabs in there. So I storm upstairs and drag them out of bed and start reading them the riot act when Derek shows himself and wants to know what's going on. I tell him what I found and do you know what he said?"

"No."

"Where's mine? Can you frigging believe it?"

"Well come on," said Kim. "Everyone's at it nowadays. It's reckoned that at least half the judges in the country use it."

"I don't care – not in my house. But it's always been the same, even when they were kids. I would tell them to do something and when they didn't, instead of backing me up, Derek would do it for them. They're spoilt."

Kim could not deny that their kids had had it easy compared to them. But wasn't that what it was all about? Give your kids the best you can afford. But then again, maybe it wasn't – her and her sister's childhood had been an extremely happy one although money had been tight. There were so many more pressures on kids today.

"I guess you're right," she said.

"You're damn well right I am," replied Julie. "Oh, listen to me, I'm supposed to be the one cheering you up and all I've done is complain about my husband and kids."

"Here, look at this," said Kim, leafing over another page.

"That's never Uncle Sam surely?"

"Yep."

"And who's that with him?"

"Don't you recognise her?"

She took the book and took a closer look. "No, it can't be; is that Auntie Helen?"

"Yes," smiled Kim.

Julie studied the photo carefully, "No way, she was so beautiful."

"Mum said she could have been a model back then."

"I wonder what happened."

"You know, surely?" said Kim, looking a little surprised.

"No?" she replied, eager to learn more.

"So Mum didn't tell you?"

"Come on, you know you were always her golden girl."

"I guess that's true," said Kim thoughtfully. "You were always a bit of a tomboy, even in your teens. In fact, you were a right feminist rebel without a cause."

"What happened?"

"She found out apparently she could not have kids so she just gave up on herself."

"Oh, that's so sad, I had no idea. I wonder why Mum never told me."

"Probably thought you wouldn't be interested, it was a long time ago now."

Julie looked wistful. "I wish I had been closer to Mum."

"I don't know what you're complaining about; you were the apple of Dad's eye."

"You really think so?"

"I know so. Do you remember that time you got in at three in the morning?"

Julie looked a little vague.

"Don't tell me you've forgotten Teddy Rogers? Took you to Brighton on the back of his Vespa?"

"Oh god yeah. It broke down on the way home."

"And Dad chased him down the High Street with that cricket bat?"

Julie placed her hand to her mouth, "Oh, I felt so sorry for him," she said. "He had been the perfect gentleman. It was three days before he summed up the courage to come back for his bike."

"I know; Mum stopped Dad from dumping it in the canal on more than one occasion. I wonder whatever happened to Teddy."

"Moved up North somewhere I heard."

"You had a real crush on him, didn't you?"

"Guess I did now you come to mention it."

"What?" exclaimed Kim. "Of course you did, you sulked around the house for nearly two weeks."

"That's only because Dad grounded me," replied Julie defensively.

"Did you ever think about trying to get in touch with him?"

"Yes, but two weeks is a long time when you're seventeen. He was with someone else by then and who could blame him? Who would want a girlfriend whose father was a psychopath?"

Kim laughed, "That's a bit harsh, he was just overprotective, that's all."

"I know; funny thing is he mentioned that night to me a couple of years before he passed away."

"Oh? What did he say?"

"Just that he was sorry for over-reacting. Why he waited 22 years to say anything, I'll never know."

—◊◊—

Billy and Frank made their way into the night.

"Where the hell do you think you're going?" asked Frank.

"Night bus," explained Billy.

"No you fucking don't, you're coming with me, you have some explaining to do."

"How far is it to your place?"

"First I'll have to get my car," said Frank.

"And where's that?"

"You know where it is – it's back at the Water Mill."

"That's miles away," complained Billy, disconsolately.

"You reckon? Look, take my coat, we'll see if there's a cab round here."

Frank found the name of a local firm of taxis stuck to the wall of the telephone kiosk with a piece of chewing gum.

"What's the name of that street?" he asked Billy, screwing his eyes up.

"Trent Street," he replied.

Frank repeated the name of the street to the taxi company. "Just come off late shift and my car's packed up," he explained. "That's really good of you, cheers." He replaced the receiver.

"What was all that about?" asked Billy.

"Wanted to know why we were out here this time of night."

"Don't blame them, after all, who the fuck would be?"

The light drizzle had now turned into thundery rain.

"This must be it," said Frank as a pair of headlights turned the corner. "Fuck," he said, "that's all we need."

"What?" said Billy, staring in the direction of their potential saviours.

"Just let me do the talking, ok?"

The police car drew up in front of them and the officer in the passenger seat lowered his window.

"May I ask what you are doing here at this time of night Sir?" he said.

It always amused Frank how the police always used the word *Sir* as if it was some kind of insult. "Apart from getting soaking wet officer, we're waiting for a taxi," he replied.

"And what's your business here?"

Billy stepped a little closer to the car, his collar turned up. "We work for Larson's Containers. Just finished late shift, my cars packed up – the battery I think, any chance of a lift into town?"

The officer ignored this remark.

By now, the rain had reached what could only be described as monsoon in nature with big fat raindrops finding their way into the patrol car. Just then their taxi arrived.

"Well that's us officer, we'll be on our way if that's ok," said Frank.

"ID."

"Sorry?"

"I want some ID or proof of where you work."

"Oh, of course officer," said Frank, as a knot tightened in his stomach.

"Echo-Two-Zero. Officer in need of assistance. Cromwell Street; outside the cinema." Without another word, the patrol car sped away leaving Frank and Billy at the kerbside.

"You waiting for a taxi?" called the driver.

"Yes, that's us," confirmed Frank, crossing the road with Billy following.

—〜〜—

"What's the matter darling? You've been tossing and turning for the last hour."

"Oh nothing," replied Ian. "Can't sleep, that's all."

"Not like you," said Frances, easing herself up on her pillow. "Would you like one of these?" she offered, leaning out of bed, opening her bedside drawer and removing a box of sleeping pills.

"No, I'll go down and make a cup of tea. Would you like one?" he added, slipping on his dressing gown.

"Oh why not, I'm awake now."

Ian made his way downstairs and opened the cupboard to reveal a selection of herbal and fruit teas.

"Where's the bloody regular tea?" he said to himself as he shuffled the boxes about the cupboard.

"What you looking for?"

This sudden and unexpected intervention startled him, causing him to knock several of the boxes onto the floor.

"Oh, you startled me," he said, bending down to retrieve the spilt items.

"You are on edge," said Frances, joining Ian on the floor. "Is it this hospital thing?"

"No – well, kind of."

"Look you sit down, I'll see to this."

Ian sat by the Aga and watched as Frances stacked the boxes neatly back into the cupboard. She closed the door just as the kettle came to the boil, then poured the water into the teapot, sending a woody aroma out into the kitchen.

"What's that?" he asked.

"Lapsang Souchong."

"Smells like compost to me."

"It's good for you. It might even help you sleep."

Frances handed him his drink. "Where's your watch?" she asked as she sipped at her tea.

"Sorry?"

"Your watch; it's not on your bedside and you're not wearing it."

"Oh it stopped," he replied hurriedly.

She sounded surprised. "Stopped?"

"Yes, I took it to the jewellers – Makepeace & Son, on South Street. Should get it back tomorrow."

"It's still under warranty."

"Is it?"

"Yes, I'll get it back first thing. I'm surprised they didn't ask you."

"Err, well, probably thought it had run out. And there's no need for you to bother, I'll get it."

"It's no bother," she said, "I'm going into town early tomorrow anyway."

"I said I'll get it" snapped Ian.

"Ok, keep your shirt on!"

"Look, I'm sorry. As I said earlier, I'm a bit on edge at the moment. You're right about the hospital thing; it is playing on my mind. We'll drink this and then get back to bed."

—〰—

Frank handed over £30 to the taxi driver who drove off into the night.

"Get in," he said, opening the car door. "I have some questions for you, Billy my friend."

Billy eased onto the passenger seat and closed the door. A few seconds later he was joined by Frank.

"So what is it you want to know?" asked Billy, as if what had just happened had slipped his mind.

"First, have you gone fucking mad, going to a nutcase like Reggie Carlyle for money?"

"Look, I'll be honest with you, I'm desperate for cash."

"Not that fucking desperate. No-one's that fucking desperate!"

"Look, it's not for me – my daughter's husband lost his job when Corneal Steel closed last month. It seems as though they might lose their house and they have two kids. Anyway, once I had an idea as to what was in these documents, I knew how useful they could be to Carlyle – he could use them to blackmail his competitors and that could be worth a lot to him – and me. A sort of business transaction if you like."

"Oh, so you thought you could branch out into the criminal underworld by doing business with Reggie Carlyle?"

"As I said, it would be in his interest. But after contacting him I read the remainder of the files and it was then that I realised they were as incriminating for Carlyle as for his competitors. At first I thought he would be glad to have them to do whatever he wanted, just pay me a lump sum, but it then dawned on me the position I was in – with my previous occupation and what I knew – I could be a permanent threat to him. And we know what happens to people like that? I got cold feet and tried to make a run for it but they collared me at the bus station."

"So where are the papers now?"

"They're in the post, second class."

"Who did you send them to?"

"You."

"Me?" Frank exclaimed.

"You wanted them remember, and where's my £1,200?"

"Yeah, err, I guess you're right. Second class you say, today?"

"Yes," replied Billy.

"Ok, so that will take two or three days to get to my place."

"Is there a problem?" asked Billy.

"You could say that. My tenancy runs out at the end of the week, they'd better arrive by then. Well?"

"Well what?" asked Billy.

"Get out."

"Where am I supposed to go?" he complained.

"That's not my problem."

"What about my money? Not only that," he added, "We're partners now."

"You nearly got us both killed and you want me to give you money?"

"Yes," replied Billy. "I got us a good deal."

"You don't for a minute think that Reggie is going to pay us, do you?"

"Why not?"

"As far as Reggie is concerned, you still have your legs and to him that's a good deal. The best thing we can do is to get rid of these documents as soon as possible and hopefully that will be an end to it. Now get out."

"I'm not going anywhere, I want my £1,200. I got you those documents remember?"

"No Billy – you haven't."

"Yeah, but they're in the post."

"I only have your word, and after that little fiasco, how can I be expected to trust you? I'll tell you what, when I get my hands on them, then you can have your money. Now clear off!"

12

Paul picked up his phone from the bedside and turned off the alarm, threw back the duvet and made his way into the en-suite. Ten minutes later he was downstairs but there was no sign of Margaret. Should he try to wake her? No, he would give it a minute. He moved over to the window and looked out. The sun was just nudging above the horizon, underlining the grey streaks of cloud with a pale pink tinge.

Red sky at morn, shepherds warn, he thought.

"Sorry, didn't mean to startle you," said Margaret, holding two mugs of steaming tea. "Thought you might need this," she added, handing him one of the mugs.

He sipped at the golden nectar. "Oh, you're a real life-saver, that's for sure"

"Is it rain or dry, I can never remember?" she asked, indicating the sky.

"Rain, if you believe that sort of thing. My mother was a great one for old wives' tales; she seemed to have one to fit every occasion. Still, that's enough of that," he said, placing his empty mug on the table. "I guess we should make a move if that's still ok with you?"

Margaret finished the last of her tea. "Fine by me," she said.

As they made their way out into the chill morning air, he could not help but notice how clean and fresh it tasted as he took a deep breath, filling his lungs.

"Nothing quite like it is there?"

"No," he replied. "You forget just how good it is when you live in the centre of the city."

They crossed the gravel drive tentatively to the waiting Land Rover.

"Fingers crossed," said Margaret as she opened her door.

Paul waited with bated breath. The last thing he wanted to do was to wake Solley whose room looked directly over the car park.

"Here goes," she said turning the ignition key.

If ever one wanted to define the sound of indifference, this was surely it as the engine reluctantly turned over. "She's not an early bird," she explained. "I think the points might be damp."

Margaret tried again and this time the murmurings from under the bonnet seemed more encouraging. "Don't want to flood her," she said, voice slightly raised as she feathered the gas pedal, finally coaxing the V8 monster into life.

The early pink tinge had turned into a violent blood red.

"You know, I don't think I have ever seen a sunrise like this before. It reminds me of a painting in the National Gallery, not sure who it was by."

"Turner?" suggested Margaret.

"Yes, I think it was now you mention it. Kim knows them all – she drags me round the galleries every now and again."

"Do you know why the light in his paintings is so luminous?"

"Because he liked it that way?"

"Not quite. It's for the same reason this sunrise is so intense – it's to do with particles thrown up into the higher atmosphere by volcanic activity. It so happened that Turner's most productive period occurred when there had been major eruptions, most notably Tambora."

"Really," he replied, "you are a mine of information."

Margaret smiled. "What time are you leaving today?"

"Oh, keen to get rid of us then?"

"Oh no, just wondered if you would like lunch that's all."

"Probably not. Look, you are ok with this idea of working for us? If you're not, just say so."

"Sounds like you're having second thoughts."

"Me? No, that's the last thing I want you to think. I was so pleased yesterday when you said you would join our little team."

"The answer to your question is no – I am not having second thoughts. I actually feel quite excited at the prospect. To be totally honest with you, this hotel idea was really Michael's. No – that doesn't sound right – we both liked the idea, but I guess his heart was in it more than mine and now he's gone and what with all the problems with the fire escape, plus the everyday running of the place..." Margaret paused.

"The romance has gone out of it?"

"I could not have put it better myself."

"Stop the car," said Paul suddenly.

"Sorry?"

"Stop the car – now."

Margaret pulled in next to an old rusty gate held in place with several pieces of baling twine. "What's the matter?" she asked, turning off the engine.

"Look," he began, "if we are going to be honest about everything, there's something I should tell you."

But before he could continue, they turned around to the sound of a loud horn. Taking up the entire lane behind them was a massive tractor with a baler attached to the rear.

"Amazing," said Margaret. "Pull over for just one second and you obstruct someone's access. Probably thinks we're townies who don't know any better."

Margaret fired up the Land Rover and trundled down the narrow lane. "Whatever it is you need to tell me," she said, "will have to wait until we turn off. There's nowhere to pull in along here and the last thing I want to do is block the lane again, just in case he comes this way. He looked pissed off enough as it was. Mind you – can't blame him, you get townies parking their cars in all manner of inappropriate places, especially this time of year. Probably thought we spent the night there."

She fed the large steering wheel through her delicate hands as they turned off the lane and up the track.

—m—

Kim slipped on her dressing gown and made her way downstairs to the kitchen, her throat burning with thirst. She opened the fridge door and reached in, taking hold of an ice-cold bottle of lemonade. Just the thought of this effervescent lemon flavoured liquid on the back of her parched throat made her feel better.

"Shit!"

The glass bottle exploded as it hit the travertine floor, sending its carbonated contents with its accompanying shards, in all directions. She just stood there surrounded by a sea of foaming lemonade with its mini icebergs of glass just waiting to puncture the soft underside of one's foot.

"Don't move," said Julie, "I'll get you something to put on."

A few seconds later she returned armed with a pair of Paul's green wellies. She tiptoed around the larger pieces of broken bottle, her slippers affording some protection from the smaller ones.

"Here," she said, taking Kim by the elbow, "put these on," placing the boots just in front of her.

It was then Julie noticed the big fat teardrops rolling down Kim's face, leaving a thin black trail in their wake. She removed a tissue from her sleeve and dabbed at her mascara stained cheeks.

"Fancy not taking your make-up off before bed," she said, trying to make light of things.

Kim turned slightly and placed her head onto Julie's shoulder.

The two women stood there, holding one another, bathed in the light from the open fridge.

—◊—

Margaret eased the Land Rover to one side.

"Can you manage?" she asked, as Paul tried to open his door. The wire of the nearby fence restricted its ability to open fully and in addition, the vehicle was at a precarious angle, making what would normally be a mundane task somewhat of an ordeal.

"Hold on, I'll get out and you can climb out this side," said Margaret, opening her door.

"No, wait. Back there I wanted to tell you something."

"Ok," she answered, pulling her door to.

"Normally I would have asked my wife Kim to see to things." Paul hesitated, trying to find the right words, but no matter how you said it, cancer was cancer and he knew it would hit a raw nerve with Margaret.

"The thing is," he continued, "she's undergoing treatment for melanoma."

Margaret did not reply. Although Solley had told her, hearing it from Paul was very different. It had somehow become personal, even more so now she had been offered this position that would normally have been taken by his wife.

Paul noticed her knuckles turning white as she gripped the large steering wheel tightly.

"I know," she said quietly.

"You know, how?"

She hesitated, the last thing she wanted to do was to betray a confidence. "Solley told me."

"Solley?" replied Paul, his voice raised.

She placed her hand on his arm. "Don't be too harsh with him; he thought it best I knew."

"When was this?" he asked, looking straight ahead through the windscreen to avoid eye contact.

"Yesterday, she answered.

"He told you this in confidence I trust?"

"I would never have told anyone except yourself, but I feel under the circumstances I should be honest with you."

"I appreciate that, I thought it best to let you know the situation as it stands, especially as... well... your husband and all. At least that's cleared the air," he added, looking at Margaret. "Now come on, we're burning daylight."

—⚍—

"No leave it," said Julie, "I'll see to it."

"I don't know what happened. It just fell out of my hand."

"Easily done, it was probably wet."

"Maybe," replied Kim, taking her hand as the pair of them negotiated their way around the broken glass. "I think the last few days have taken more out of me than I thought."

"Do you want to go back to bed?"

"No, I would like to stay down here."

"Ok, I'll get your duvet."

—⚍—

Margaret watched Paul make his way around the building, dictating into his phone.

"One of the things you have to look for," he called, pausing at the base of a broken downpipe, "are the windows. If they're lined up properly then there shouldn't be any substantial settlement."

"And these?" asked Margaret, raising her voice against the ever-present wind.

"Well the glazing bars are all parallel with each other, and apart from those panes that have been deliberately broken, the others are all in good condition," he replied as he slowly scoured the surrounding area. "Of course, there'll be no main sewerage;

the waste water will have been carried off to a large soakaway somewhere. We'll have to fit a treatment system of our own."

"Is that difficult?" she asked, making her way over to him.

"No, not especially, just depends on how pedantic the Environment Agency is. It's like a lot of things nowadays; the biggest hurdle is getting round the red tape."

"Tell me about it; just running a small hotel is like negotiating a minefield of bureaucracy."

"Still it keeps our friends in Brussels busy," laughed Paul, trying one of the side doors.

"I thought you didn't need to get inside," she remarked, turning up her collar.

"I don't, just seeing if it's stuck – another sign of settlement. Come on," he said, making his way over to a low dry-stone wall and climbing up. He held out his hand, "Coming?"

Margaret hitched up her skirt and took hold of Paul's outstretched hand. In one swift movement she was on top of the wall with him.

"Well?" she said.

"Sorry?"

"What now?"

This brief physical contact had sent a shock wave through Paul. What the hell was happening to him? He had experienced that feeling before – but when? It was so long ago. It then dawned on him – it was his first kiss. He could still remember it now, behind the bike sheds with Caroline Thompson. She had dragged him round there initially against his will and shoved her firm breasts against his chest. It was like no other experience he had had.

But here he was, nearly forty years later, reliving that extraordinary moment.

"I'm waiting," she said.

"Oh yeah," he replied, turning and starting to climb the steep bank at the rear of the Sanatorium.

Margaret followed until they had reached the top.

"This will do," he said, out of breath.

She soon joined him, her breathing measured and gentle as he retrieved a small pair of field glasses from his jacket.

"What are you looking for?"

"Want to see if there are any dips or hollows in the roof," he explained, "also the state of the slates."

"How's it looking?"

"Well it all looks fine. Of course, we'll have to check for woodworm."

"No new roof then?"

"Not if we can help it, although to be honest it's quicker and easier to rip it off sometimes and start afresh, but because of its age we will have to use the same materials, however, if these are sound that would save us a lot of time and money. National Heritage are a stickler for... what am I saying? There's no need to tell you what they're like."

Paul lowered the field glasses to see that Margaret now had her back to him and was looking down the valley, her tweed skirt and green wellies suiting her so well.

"Penny for them?" he asked.

"Oh, I was just admiring the view. It's wonderful up here; I wouldn't mind a luxury apartment of my own."

"I'll put you down as our first client then," he said with a wry smile.

"I wish!"

It was then she noticed something had caught his attention.

"Found a problem?" she asked.

Paul didn't answer.

She looked at his face, the colour having drained from it. "Are you ok? Only you just look as though you've seen a ghost."

"Yeah, of course I am, and I don't believe in ghosts," he replied curtly. "Not sure if that chimney stack is out of true, it will need looking at. Come on, we'd better get back down."

"Those chimney stacks," she said, following him down the bank, "wouldn't you get rid of them?"

"I would very much like to," he replied, watching each footfall as he negotiated the slippery bank. "Doubt we would be allowed to though."

"Wouldn't that be a bit risky, all those open fires?"

"Not really, they would be converted to gas."

"Oh, I know the type. They look pretty authentic."

"Yes, and from National Heritage's point of view, the essential character of the building will be maintained."

"Goodness me," she exclaimed looking at her watch, "it's 6.45. I should really be getting back now."

"Yes of course," he replied as he stopped at the wall and waited for her to join him, but to his surprise she leapt down with the grace and ease of a feline, then held out her hand to assist him.

"That will not be necessary," he said haughtily. "I am quite capable of breaking my own neck thank you," and with that he jumped down. Although the wall was not over high, for some reason unbeknown to him, his knees were reluctant to accommodate this sudden and unexpected manoeuvre, and they locked as he impacted the ground, sending him tumbling forwards across the wet and muddy ground.

Margaret tried desperately not to laugh but her efforts were in vain. "Are you all right?" she asked, bending down to assist him.

"What does it look like?"

"My, you are in a mess," she laughed, in-between bouts of giggles, as she helped him to his feet.

"Great, just great – look at the state of me," he said, examining the grass stains on his trousers. "How the hell am I going to explain that to Solley?"

"Haven't you got another pair?"

"No, we were only going to be here one night remember."

"Come on," she laughed, "I'll put them through the wash."

—⁂—

Julie woke from an uneasy sleep, her neck stiff from being wedged up against the arm of the sofa and looked across the coffee table to her sister curled up in a tight ball, the king size duvet covering her completely. She slowly sat up, not wanting to disturb Kim, and sat there for a moment looking at the pile of bedclothes that housed her twin sister, the only sign that there was someone in residence was a slight movement caused by Kim's gentle breathing.

For some reason, this reminded her of those wet days when they were children and could not – or were not allowed to – play outside. Their mother would allow them to strip their beds of the sheets and drape them across the furniture, constructing what seemed to them to be a tented city with a labyrinth of endless passageways and adjoining rooms.

Apart from themselves, their private domain was inhabited by their dolls and teddy bears. It felt so safe under those flimsy sheets as the rain crashed against the parlour window. In some ways it was like life itself – everything feels safe and secure but we are all just one tug away from disaster.

—m—

"Are you ok?" asked Margaret.

"Yes, why?" replied Paul, examining his trousers again.

"Oh, just that you seem very quiet that's all." She then realised that he was probably thinking about his wife and how she was coping. "That was thoughtless of me, of course, you have a lot on your mind," she added apologetically.

Paul patted her hand gently and gave a slight smile. "Tell me," he said, "What do you know of the old hospital?"

This question surprised her a little. "Not that much really, we have… sorry, I keep saying that… *I* have only been here eighteen months. Mind you, you do get to hear things in the bar, it gets quite busy on a Friday night and at weekends with locals and of course your day-trippers."

"What sort of things?" asked Paul, totally focused on Margaret.

This sudden change in his demeanour, from distant to her now being the centre of his attention made her feel quite uncomfortable, a little nervous even.

"Err, let me think," she began. "Of course, you must understand that most of it's hearsay and nonsense."

"Go on, I'm all ears."

"Well the most common piece of folklore relating to the Sanatorium goes back to the 1950s or early 60s. Previous to that the hospital was used by the military in the 2nd World War. Well, when I say used, it was commissioned by the Ministry of Defence for the duration of the war to treat potential gas victims – I guess on the account of its history for treating TB. But as you know, gas was never used. The hospital was too isolated for it to be taken over by the new National Health Service after the war, that's when it was last officially used."

"You mean it's been empty all that time," said Paul, somewhat surprised.

"Yeah, sixty odd years at a guess. You look a little perplexed?" she added, half an eye on the narrow lane.

"No, it's just that the building doesn't look as though it's been abandoned that long. If you had asked me, I would have said twenty years at the most."

"It's funny you should say that," she said, slowing down for a sharp bend.

"Why?"

"Well some people reckon it was never abandoned after the war but used for experiments."

"Of what kind?"

"Genetics, it's rumoured that the place was filled with Nazi scientists captured at the end of the war."

"Well the least said about that the better," he remarked as they drew up outside the hotel.

"Well it's still here," she said, getting out of the Land Rover.

"Why, what were you expecting?" he asked, forcing his door open.

"Oh, nothing really; just a figure of speech."

He followed Margaret into the hotel and started to make his way upstairs.

"Do you want me to wash those for you?" she called.

"Are you sure you don't mind?"

"Not at all."

He looked about, slipped off his shoes and undid his belt, then tossed the soiled trousers down to her.

"They shouldn't take long," she called up, "I'll put them through the dryer."

Paul turned on the landing to be confronted by a familiar face. It was that of Isabelle. He knew he should offer some explanation but his mind had gone blank. The look on her face was a mixture of embarrassment and 'I know what you have been up to'. She lowered her head and made her way past with a curt, "Good Morning."

He returned the greeting, trying to sound as though standing in a public place in his underpants was perfectly normal. Closing the door to his room he couldn't decide whether to grab an hour or two or have a shower and shave. His deliberations were interrupted by a knock on his door. He opened it, half expecting to see Margaret but to his surprise it was Solley.

"Ah, that's good, you're up I see."

"What do you want this early?"

"Thought we could get away as soon as possible," he said as he entered the room. "Breakfast is from 07.30. Well?" he added, making himself comfortable on the edge of the bed.

The last thing Paul had been expecting was to see Solley much before 10am. "Look," he said, "You go down; I'll be with you shortly."

As he closed the door he realised his mistake. *Shit,* he thought, *I can hardly have breakfast in my boxers.* It was then he remembered room service.

"Ah, Margaret, have you put those trousers in the wash…? Oh, right I see. Just that Solley's down for early breakfast… That would be perfect if you don't mind."

A few moments later he opened his bedroom door to find Margaret standing there, a pair of grey trousers neatly folded over her arm.

"Try these," she said, "hopefully they'll fit."

"Thanks," he said, taking the trousers and shutting the door. Unfortunately, they were a little too big – to say the least – but what choice did he have? *I don't suppose Solley will notice anyway,* he thought.

Solley looked up from the breakfast menu as Paul entered the dining room, "I'm having the full…" he paused in mid-sentence. "What the frig are those?"

"What?" replied Paul, trying to sound indignant, knowing full well what he was referring to.

"Those things hanging from your waist?"

"Oh these," he laughed, "I packed them by mistake. Should have listened to Kim, let her do it for me but I didn't want to trouble her."

Solley got to his feet and placed his hands on his hips. "Since when did you lose that much weight? Come to that, when did you put that much weight on?"

"These have always been a little bit big. Got the wrong size and couldn't be bothered to take them back."

"Take them back? I would have stuck them in the bin or recovered the sofa with them! And that's another thing, what's wrong with the ones you had on yesterday?"

Paul had to think fast, he knew any delay would give the game away. "Last night after you went to bed, I spilt coffee on them."

"Oh I see," said Solley, sitting back down again. "You stayed up to enjoy the company of our extremely beautiful hostess without Solley to keep an eye on you?"

"Ah, gentlemen," said Margaret, looking a little harassed. "I'm sorry; I wasn't expecting anybody quite this early. What can I get you?"

"I'll have the full English," announced Solley, "with extra bacon."

Margaret turned to Paul. "I think I'll just have some cereal and toast," he said.

The two men watched as she made her way back to the kitchen.

"There's something I wanted to talk to you about, concerning Margaret."

"Oh yeah?" replied Solley, a twinkle in his eye.

"Nothing like that. The thing is I have asked her to work for us."

"Oh really, I wasn't expecting that. In exactly what capacity?" he asked. "And there's another thing, why didn't you mention this to me first?"

"Look, we need someone this end we can trust."

They stopped talking as Margaret returned to the table with two large glasses of ice-cold orange juice. "Your breakfast won't be long," she said, placing the glasses in front of them.

Solley waited for her to get out of earshot then leaned forward and said in a low voice, "So you reckon you can trust her?"

"I know you do," answered Paul.

"What's that supposed to mean?" he asked, taking a sip from his juice.

"You told her about Kim."

"That was in strict confidence."

"The only reason I know you told her is because I thought she ought to know the situation before taking on this particular task. I could tell from her demeanour that she knew something. It was then that she told me what you had said to her," explained Paul. "Well?"

"Well what?"

"Do you agree with me that Margaret would be ideal for the position?"

"As it happens I do," he answered. "And a similar thought had been going through my mind but in future as far as this project goes, we make decisions together – everything up front."

Paul had a pang of guilt about his early morning visit to the

Sanatorium but he felt his secret was safe and it would be in everyone's interest to keep it that way.

—⁊⁊—

"It's quarter to eight," said Catherine, surprised that Philip was not already up.

"Oh, I forgot to tell you that I was signed off for a couple of… weeks."

"See," she said throwing back the covers, "I told you it was serious. Daresay they will be lost without you," she added, making her way to the en-suite."

"Daresay," he replied, pulling back the covers.

Catherine paused and turned to face him. "Not getting up?"

"Why?"

"Well it's not like you to lie in. You're always up at 7.30, even at weekends."

"Well it's about time I treated myself to a lie-in."

A few moments later she made her way back to the bed and removed her dressing gown, tossing it over the Indian style wicker chair before resting her right knee on the edge of the bed. As Philip turned to face her she eased the straps of her nightie off her shoulders, the satin-like material cascading down her body and settling round her slim waist.

He moved forward and ran his hand up over her perfectly shaped breasts. Catherine tossed back her raven hair as he knelt in front of her, caressing her curvaceous thighs, at the same time circling her nipple with his tongue.

—⁊⁊—

"What?"

"That's no way to answer your phone. I might have been a potential client," said Ian.

"Yeah, bit of a long night," said Frank. "Anyway, what do you want at this time in the morning?"

"So?"

"So what?" he repeated, trying to wipe the sleep from his eyes.

"This good news you have for me."

"Oh that. Hold on," he rolled off his half-inflated mattress, got to his feet and tossed a teabag into his mug.

"Well I'm waiting," said Ian impatiently.

"Those papers you lost."

"Had stolen you mean," he corrected.

"Yeah, whatever. I might be able to help you with that."

"You know who's got them then?"

"Possibly," yawned Frank.

"Look, don't play stupid games with me. If you know who's got them – and judging by this I guess you do – for goodness sake tell me!"

Frank poured the steaming water into his mug, casually stirring the teabag. He then used the spoon to squeeze it against the side of the mug in order to get every last vestige of flavour from it. He was enjoying having Ian on a piece of string and he intended to toy with him for as long as was practical.

"Let's say we're in negotiations for them," he said.

"These negotiations – how advanced are they?"

"Things were going quite well…" he paused.

"What the fuck do you mean – *were* going quite well?"

"Money."

"Money?" repeated Ian.

"Yep – that's the hold-up – ten grands' worth."

"Fucking hell – I thought you said it was five?"

"Do you want these documents or not?"

"Yes."

"Well, you can bring it round with the rest of my money this morning – and in case your maths is not up to scratch – that's sixteen big ones you owe me. You still there?"

"I'll be round at 10am," answered Ian curtly.

"That suits me," said Frank, sipping from his mug.

"Oh, and you'd better have my watch. Frances has already given me the third degree about it."

—⁓—

Solley rubbed his hands with glee as Margaret placed what could only be described as a homage to fried food in front of him.

"That does look good, I'm beginning to wish I'd had the same," said Paul as his friend began to tuck in with gusto.

"The bacon and sausages are all local," explained Margaret over her shoulder as she made her way back to the kitchen.

"Well if she can keep accounts as well as she can cook," said Solley, reaching for the tomato ketchup, "we won't go far wrong." He paused, "What's the matter? It's not like you to turn down a fry-up, especially one as good as this. Not hungry?"

"Yes and no."

He placed his knife and fork on his plate. "Have you spoken to Kim yet?" he asked gently.

"No, not yet; I had a text from Julie though, just before I came down."

"What did she have to say?"

"Thought a bunch of flowers would cheer her up."

Solley took his phone from his jacket.

"What are you doing?"

"Flowers," he explained. "I know this guy, he's a friend of mine – well a little more than that really. Anyway, he's a florist; I'll get him to send round the biggest and best bunch of flowers she's ever seen."

"No that won't be necessary, I think what Julie means is for me to take them."

"Oh, of course. Tell you what, I'll get Jeremy to take them round to my place, we'll pick them up before I drop you off."

"Ok, that's fine; but make it tasteful!"

"Paul Goodman, what do you take me for!" he exclaimed. "I'll have you know I am the epitome of good taste – well Jeremy is – they'll be just fine."

He then set about demolishing the remainder of the pile of fried food on his plate as Paul nibbled at his toast. Finally, he patted his stomach, "That will do me for a while."

"How is it you never stop bloody eating and never put on any more weight?" asked Paul, finishing the last of his juice.

"Active lifestyle," he smiled.

"You – active?"

"Yeah, of course – I'm always on the go."

"That's news to me," said Paul, pouring his tea.

"That's because I am a doyenne of the night. When you're all tucked up in bed fast asleep, I'm on that dance floor shaking my stuff 'till the early hours."

This he then demonstrated with a wiggle of the shoulders.

"I hope you enjoyed that?" asked Margaret as she came to clear the table.

"First class," said Solley. "If you would be kind enough to make up our bill now please?"

"Of course," replied Margaret, picking up the plates.

13

Councillor Roberts scoured his desk. "Suzie!" he shouted. "Did Hunter bring some files over for me?"

"No Councillor."

"Right!" He made his way through the council chamber and up the magnificent marble stairway, straight to Nigel's office.

"Good Morning Councillor," said Mrs Grayson as he approached.

He grunted a begrudging acknowledgement as he swept past her desk then, without knocking, burst into Nigel's office.

"Ah, Councillor," said Nigel, getting to his feet.

"I want those files," he barked.

"I was just on my way."

"You better had be."

"But first…" Nigel hesitated and leaned to his left slightly, looking through the half-open door to see Mrs Grayson give a nervous smile. "Would you be so kind as to close the door Councillor?"

Roberts duly did so. "Well man, what is it?"

Nigel cleared his throat. "Yesterday afternoon Linda collared me and started asking all sorts of questions. I have to admit I got a little flustered – I'm not sure whether she actually believes our side of things."

"Don't you mean *your* side of things?"

He cleared his throat for a second time. "The thing is Councillor, I don't know if we can totally trust Grayson."

"She will tell things as they are, don't you worry about her. Now get those bloody files."

Nigel flinched as Roberts slammed the door behind him as he left. This was a job that might need some assistance he thought as he left his office and crossed over to Mrs Grayson's desk. If anyone knew of these files and their location, it would be Philip Townsend's trusted assistant – or former – he thought as he greeted Mrs Grayson.

"I need to find some files dating back to around 1850 regarding the area around the old Sanatorium at High Gate."

"What sort of files Mr Hunter?"

"Please, let's keep it at Nigel, shall we? After all, we don't even know if my position will be permanent and as to your question, surely there can't be many files from that period and that specific area?"

"You will be surprised Mr... sorry, Nigel... the Victorian's were sticklers for paperwork."

"Tell you what, why don't you accompany me to the Records Department and we'll see what we can find."

Mrs Grayson, followed by Nigel, made their way to the lift that would take then down to the basement where all the local authority's records were housed. The descent in this confined space being carried out in silence. The stainless-steel doors opened to reveal rows of grey filing cabinets.

As she led the way, Nigel watched her intently as she made her way down the narrow passages that separated the serried ranks of floor to ceiling cabinets. He could not help but notice that she was rather fit for her age, her walk was precise but elegant, and he could not keep his eyes off her buttocks as they rose and fell with every footstep – evidently still firm. He did not know what it was about this place but he felt aroused to the point of getting an erection.

"What's the matter with you?" he muttered to himself.

"Sorry?" she said, turning to face him.

"Oh nothing," he replied angling himself away from her slightly; hand in his left trouser pocket doing his best to hide his arousal.

"Not far now," she explained. "Did you know this used to be the old nuclear bunker? This lot was moved down here in the early 1990s, just after the Cold War ended."

She stopped at one of the identical cabinets, the only thing distinguishing one from another was a letter followed by several numbers.

"You will have to step back slightly," she informed Nigel, removing a key from her pocket. "Do you have yours?" she asked.

"Oh yes, of course." It was in his left pocket. There was nothing he could do; just hope she didn't notice. *To hell with it,* he thought.

"Thank you, Nigel. I don't know about you but I find it rather stimulating down here, must be all this history wouldn't you say?"

"Ah, yes, err it's very interesting."

Mrs Grayson opened one of the cabinet drawers and drew it out to its full length in front of her. She stepped back slightly towards Nigel and bent over the outstretched tray of files in a somewhat exaggerated manner, her firm backside raised.

Before Nigel realised what he was doing, he found his right hand on her bottom.

"Oh Mr Hunter, you are a naughty one," she said, at the same time taking hold of the hem of her skirt and pulling it up over her hips.

Hunter could not quite believe his eyes – she was wearing stockings and suspenders. He fumbled at his belt, no thought as to what the consequences might be, his animalistic instincts taking complete control of his rational mind. No sooner than he had entered her than he ejaculated, almost tipping her over the outstretched tray of files.

"What are you doing?" he exclaimed.

"Oh, let's call it a little souvenir shall we," she replied, as she took two photos of him with his trousers down around his ankles and a semi erect penis for all to see.

"Give that to me you old bitch!" he screamed as he reached out to grab the phone from her but before he could do so, she dropped it into the filing cabinet along with her key and shoved it closed with her knees.

"Now Nigel, it seems as though you might have made a mistake. What would HR think if they saw those photos of you exposing yourself to me?"

"What do you want?" he hissed.

"Me? Now let's see, what do I want? Well for a start, I want to keep my job."

"I don't quite understand."

"You don't? Well maybe I should explain. The altercation you had with Mr Townsend?"

"Yes, what of it?"

"You know as well as I do that it was not as you made out, plus for some reason, Councillor Roberts wants me to back up your side of events at the risk of losing my job. But why, I asked myself? I have spent the last couple of days racking my brains but it was when you asked me to come down here…"

"What does that have to do with anything?"

"I don't know; I was rather hoping you would tell me."

"I have no idea what the bloody hell you are talking about."

"Ok, let's try this. These files, as far as I know, haven't been touched since they were put here nearly twenty years ago and I helped with the transfer of all of these documents, but late last week, the caretaker told me that Mr Townsend was down there at these very same filing cabinets and this morning Suzie phoned me to see if I knew of any files, and tells me that Roberts bit her head off because you had not left them for him. Then ten minutes later we are down here at the very same cabinet. I would hazard a guess that you and Councillor Roberts are up to something, and getting rid of Philip is a crucial part of it."

"Look," he pleaded, "I have no idea what he's up to, all I know is that Roberts asked Philip several times for a certain file regarding the Sanatorium at High Gate but he seemed reluctant to get it for him. It was when Roberts found out about our little confrontation that he forced me to exaggerate what happened in an attempt to get rid of Townsend, and my reward for this would be his job. That's why I'm down here now – to get whatever it is he wanted."

"Which is what?"

"I'm not sure, all I have is this number," he said, holding out a piece of paper.

"Give it here," said Mrs Grayson.

"Is it the file Townsend took?"

"I have no idea but I think there could be a connection."

"And what would that be?"

"That would be telling lover boy."

"Well, what am I going to do? Councillor Roberts won't take no for an answer."

"He could make an official request for them," she suggested.

"I doubt it."

"Why?"

"Because it doesn't make sense to go to all this trouble to get them," Nigel said. "Whatever he wants, he doesn't want anybody to know about it. Ok, so Roberts has us over a barrel but what about Townsend – he's as straight as a die."

"So am I," she answered indignantly, "but he managed to find a way of getting to me. I would not put anything past that man."

"The thing is; what happens to me? You'll have to back me up – you've made a statement confirming my side of things."

"Well maybe, maybe not?"

"I'm not quite with you?"

"These compromising photos I have of you could be just as damaging for Councillor Roberts."

"How do you make that out?"

"Well, simply through association. If I were to say that you were both conspiring against me, he would have no choice but to resign. Imagine the publicity if he didn't?"

"I don't see how that would work," queried Nigel, "he could just deny everything you say."

"You're forgetting one important thing. He's already backed you up to the hilt on the assault accusation which we both know is complete nonsense."

—⁓—

"Fancy a coffee? We're making good time and it won't take long, there's a services just up here."

Paul glanced at his watch. "Yeah, I suppose we have time."

Solley pulled off the motorway and up the slip road at speed, Paul pressing his right foot hard into the floor. He parked in the one remaining spot just metres from the entrance.

"Award-winning," he announced, opening his door.

"How do you know that?" asked Paul as they made their way towards the stone-clad building.

"Bloody great sign outside that's how! Look, be a love and get me a large latte and a slice of chocolate cake along with whatever you fancy. I'm going for a leak," he added, handing him a £20 note.

He went to the counter where a round-faced cheery redhead enquired as to what he would like.

"Err, large latte and…"

The young lady waited patiently. "Sir?"

"Oh yeah, some chocolate cake and a tea please," he continued. Paul took the tray.

"Sir, your change," called the girl.

"Keep it." He found a table next to the large tinted plate glass window and sat down, placing the tray on the table.

"No cake?" enquired Solley as he returned from the men's Room.

"Yeah – look" replied Paul.

"No, idiot – for you; it's home-baked."

"What?"

"Home-baked, there's…."

"Don't tell me" he interrupted, "there's a sign."

Solley sat down. "Are you ok mate? This won't take long and had to stop for a piss anyway."

"No, that's ok, I could do with a cuppa myself" he answered, taking hold of the cardboard tab and lifting it out of the teapot. "There's something I should tell you."

"Oh yeah," dark brown cake crumbs tumbling from his lips. "You should have some," he mumbled, "It really is good."

"Maybe next time we're this way."

"Ok, let's have it then."

"You know earlier we agreed that we would keep each other informed – no secrets."

"Yeah," he answered, taking another large bite from his slice of cake.

"Well I have a bit of a confession to make."

Solley's interest in the chocolate cake seemed to diminish somewhat. "You have my undivided attention."

Paul cleared his throat. "First thing this morning I had a trip up to the old Sanatorium."

"When did you say?"

"This morning," he repeated.

"What time? I was up just after 7am and you were in your room at 7.30am."

"I had just got back," he explained.

"And how did you get there? Don't tell me you took the Merc and pranged it?"

"Don't be so bloody stupid, Margaret took me over."

"But why?" asked Solley.

"I just wanted to have another look, get a second feel of the place on my own. If we are going to put the best part of £2million into this project, I want to make sure it feels right. After all, it's not like it's just up the road."

Solley leaned back slightly in his chair and puffed out his chest. "Oh well, I'm glad you told me. Is that it?"

"Yeah, that's all."

"So what does your gut tell you?"

"This will sound…"

"Oh, don't tell me," he interrupted, "you've got cold feet. It's that Margaret isn't it?"

"Margaret?" exclaimed Paul, not quite knowing what he was getting at. "She has nothing to do with it."

"I know what happened. You went up there and somehow she talked you out of it, I bet."

"No," he replied. "Anyway, why should she do that, it's nothing to her?"

"It's what women do."

"Kim's not like that. She's up for it, even with things as… well, you know."

"Maybe," he shrugged.

"There's no maybe about it, that's why I'm sitting here with you right now."

Solley raised his hands, "Ok, fair enough. But there's something else isn't there?"

Paul looked a little furtive, almost unsure of himself, something that Solley was not accustomed to. "It's… it's just, there might be a problem."

"Oh? What kind of problem?"

"One of the reasons I went up there was to have another look at the outside, see if I could spot any signs of settlement, that kind of thing – you know."

"And?" he enquired, leaning forward slightly.

"It looks fairly good, even the roof looks sound."

"So then, what's the problem?"

Paul paused and poured the remainder of his tea. "I don't know if you noticed but the place seemed to be in very good order for its age."

"In what way?"

"I know there was a lot of stuff lying around but the paintwork and just the feel of the place, it all seemed to be in such good order – especially as it's supposed to have been empty for nearly sixty years."

Solley licked his fingers after finishing the last piece of his cake. "Now you come to mention it, you're right. Apart from all that crap scattered about, you would think it was still in use."

"The thing is," continued Paul, "there's this rumour that after the war ended it was kept by the MOD for experiments, employing captured Nazi scientists."

"Where the fuck did you get that from?" he asked, to the obvious annoyance of two women sitting at the opposite table.

"Margaret," he replied in a low voice.

"See – I knew I was bloody right. Solley's always right; she has scared you off with all this nonsense."

Paul indicated for him to keep his voice down. "No, she's done nothing of the sort, but it could have an influence when it comes to selling the apartments. You know what people can be like when it comes to a property's history."

"It might be a selling point," he said thoughtfully.

"What? .Ex-concentration camp Nazi's experimenting on all those poor bastards! After all, you should know what I'm talking about."

"Why me?" he replied indignantly.

"Because you're Jewish – or had you forgotten?"

"No I haven't, but I think you're just looking for a flimsy excuse to pull out."

"Look – I've told you already – as far as I'm concerned, I'm still in, ok?"

"We'd better be on our way," he said, finishing his coffee.

"There is one more thing, and don't lose your rag."

"Go on," said Solley impatiently, sitting back down in his chair, arms folded tightly across his chest.

"I took my field glasses with me. It was when I was looking at the roof, I'm sure I saw someone looking at me from one of the attic windows."

"Bollocks – who the hell would be up there?"

The two women opposite tutted and left their table.

"Anyway," he continued, turning his attention back to Paul. "The windows are all boarded up."

"No, not the ones in the attic, or hadn't you noticed?"

"Ha, it's just your imagination. You were bricking it just walking round inside the place the other day."

"No I wasn't," he replied defensively. "It was you who was bricking it. '*Is that a rat – oh what's that over there?*'" he added, taking the piss.

"That's rats and that's different, but you have always been scared of that sort of thing," teased Solley. "Your imagination's too fertile, all those comic books you read as a kid. I could never see what you saw in them."

"I'm not scared of…"

"Ghosts?" he interrupted.

"Yeah… ghosts."

"What about the time we were all round at Lester Fairchild's house and we were all telling ghost stories; and his cat climbed through the bedroom window? You were out of that place quicker than a stabbed rat!"

"Can't say I remember," replied Paul dismissively.

"Bollocks – of course you do. Lester's mother made you pay for that vase you broke on the way down the stairs. Anyway, all I am trying to say is these few days have been well, stressful to say the least, and what you saw was just a figment of your imagination – or maybe even a trick of the light, that's all."

However, Solley could tell that his attempts at trying to persuade Paul it was just an overactive mind playing tricks on him had failed. The look on his face told a very different story.

"Come on old man," he said, "let's get you home."

—⚡—

Frank picked up his phone and took one last look around his office.

"It's Frank, Frank Hibbard... Yes, yes, I'll be out today... What you talking about? You should fucking pay me for this stuff; it's worth at least £500 of anyone's money. Anyway, you know I'm skint and I had to hand the car back today so there's no way I can get rid of it. Now listen up, I want you to do me a favour. I'm expecting a very important package tomorrow; can I collect it from your office...? Oh, you'll be here tomorrow...? Ok, about 12, that's fine, I'll get it then... Cheers Raj, you're a diamond."

—◊—

Nigel looked up from his desk as the door burst open to reveal – as he had expected – Councillor Roberts' extensive frame, a broad smile across his face.

"You look pleased Councillor."

"Of course I am, the Three Rivers Project has got the all clear," he said, closing the door behind him. "Now, let's make it a perfect day, shall we?" he continued, leaning on his desk with all of his substantial weight.

"I know what you're referring to Councillor, but I am afraid I am going to have to disappoint you."

Roberts eased himself slowly up to his full height, chest puffed out like some kind of giant blow fish.

"Oh, and why might that be I ask?"

Nigel's pretence at calmness had evaporated in the shadow of this imposing man. "They're not there," he blurted out.

"Not there? What do you mean *not there*?"

"I went down to the Records Department with Mrs Grayson – she helped move all the documents to the basement over twenty years ago. Did you know it was once a nuclear bunker?" he added in a desperate attempt at trying to change the subject.

"Yes, I fucking did," replied Roberts, his voice held in check. "You need two keys to access the files, is that correct?"

"Yes Councillor."

"You have one? And…?"

"Sorry Councillor?"

"Don't play stupid games with me boy! Who has the other?"

"Oh – Mrs Grayson."

"Quite, so I want you to go out there and find out when it was taken and who took it."

"She doesn't know."

"You reckon she's telling the truth?" said Roberts thoughtfully.

"Oh yes."

"I don't believe you, you're lying to me, I can tell a liar a mile off. I don't know what your game is Hunter but you're messing with the wrong man. Now get your key and you and I and Mrs Grayson are going to take a little trip down to Records and we will have a good look, just in case you have – let's say – overlooked them."

"I can't do that," protested Nigel, "not without the chairman's approval. Some of these documents are still restricted, it would be highly irregular."

"I'll tell you what's highly irregular Hunter, and that's you and that silly old cow out there stealing official documents for your own personal gain."

"That's not true," said Hunter, getting to his feet.

"Sit down if you know what's good for you," snapped Roberts. "Now you listen to me and you listen carefully, it's your word and hers against mine. And don't forget, you have both lied to HR already which has resulted in the suspension of a senior and very much respected member of staff."

Nigel now found himself between the proverbial rock and a hard place. He would have no choice but to do as Councillor Roberts requested, but how could he? There was the phone with the compromising pictures – once Roberts had hold of them, his life would not be worth living.

He looked up from his desk and studied the towering edifice to overindulgence, wondering what it would take to kill such a man.

"Well," barked Roberts, "I am waiting."

"Yes of course," he replied, taking his key from his desk.

—⁂—

Well at least this last transaction would be a reasonable one, thought Frank, looking at his watch as the hand moved closer to ten. "It's open," he called.

Ian tossed a brown envelope onto the table which landed with a satisfying thump. He then picked his watch up and slipped it on to his wrist.

"Don't mind if I count it?"

"No, it's all in £50s," said Ian as he sat down opposite Frank and watched him studiously count the cash, note for note, finally taking a deep breath and putting the money into his pocket.

"Well that's us I think," he said.

"Not quite. Those papers – I need them soon, and I mean like right now."

"I'm picking them up tomorrow at 12. I'll meet you in the layby, let's say 1pm? No, better make it 1.30pm to be on the safe side."

"So who's got them?" asked Ian, "and where are you collecting them from?"

"Well the answer to your first question is that's my business, and the answer to your second question is the same. And don't think about putting a tab on me, I'll spot them a mile off and you could ruin everything."

"The only reason I asked, Frankie, is that I thought you might be glad of a little support. I mean, you don't know who you're dealing with."

"Don't worry about me; I can take care of myself. Oh, and how's the sale going?" he asked, lighting up the remains of a cigar.

"So, so," coughed Ian. "Bloody hell, that's a bit strong."

He smiled and blew a greyish cloud of smoke into the small room.

"Well my answer to your question is…"

"Don't tell me," Frank interrupted, holding his hand up, "that's your business."

"Funny enough," replied Ian, waving the pungent smoke from his face, "that's not what I was going to say."

"Oh," he said, a little surprised.

"No, I might need your help," he continued.

Frank dropped the remains of his cigar into his empty mug. "Go on," he said, his eyes wide at the thought of another possibly lucrative deal.

"The two wide boys that came up here from London seem very – and I mean *very* – interested, which surprises me a little."

"Why?"

"They seemed like the type that would keep their cards close to their chests so I decided that a little competition might spice things up a bit."

"Hold on, I thought you said they were the only ones interested?"

"Yeah, they are."

"So where's this competition coming from?"

"You."

"Me?" he exclaimed. "I'm afraid you will have to be a little more precise."

"For all intents and purposes," he explained, "you are now Alex Pintov, a Russian billionaire and you are going to increase the price."

"Well it's not as if I wouldn't appreciate the money, but don't you stand the risk of frightening them off?"

"Not if we are careful."

"Ok, so how is this going to work?"

"Well," said Ian, "I have already told them that you – or should I say Alex – has made an offer, some of it in cash and my client is willing to accept this offer, but if my client should find out about his background as an ex-KGB and now Russian Mafia, he would not accept the offer."

"Ok," said Frank, "but how do I fit into this?"

"I want you, as Alex Pintov, to make some enquiries about our Mr Solomon and Mr Goodman."

"What sort of enquiries?"

"Nothing too heavy, just what their property portfolio's like, what kind of rent they're charging. I want it to look as though you're sizing up the competition – and of course I don't need to say they have to think you're Russian."

"Ok, if I agree to this, what's in it for me?"

"Well, that depends if you're successful or not."

"Well let's suppose I am."

"Two big ones," replied Ian. "Not bad for a few phone calls."

Frank picked his cigar out of his mug and drew on it several times but to no avail.

"Do you have to light that stinking thing up again?" he said as Frank was just about to strike a red tipped match on his desk.

"They're Cuban," he replied indignantly as the friction from the lacquered surface of the desk brought the match into life, its pale-yellow flame being sucked into the black cold ash of the cigar stub, once again returning it to a pungent eye-watering wad of South American tobacco.

"Ok," he said, "you can count me in."

"Good," said Ian, handing over another envelope. "In there you will find details of the purchasers. Remember, nothing too heavy, I just want them to know they have some competition that's all."

"You can trust me," said Frank through his Cuban smoke screen.

—◊—

"How was it?" asked Julie, getting up from one of the identical seats that lined the clinic waiting room.

"Not too bad," replied Kim, "just a little tired that's all."

"Well that's to be expected. Do you want me to take that?"

"Sorry?"

"Your bag, do you want me to take it?"

"Oh no, it's fine. Don't know why I brought it to be honest, just habit I guess."

"A girl should never be without her bag," laughed Julie, opening the door for her sister.

Kim shielded her eyes as they made their way out into the bright early afternoon sunshine. "Did you manage to get parked OK?" she asked, scouring the street for Julie's car.

"Yeah, eventually," replied Julie, stepping into the road slightly, arm outstretched.

"What are you doing; I thought you had the car?"

"I'm getting us a taxi."

"No, I want to walk."

"Just a moment," said Julie to the taxi driver.

"It's too far on a hot day like this, you'll wear yourself out."

"No, it will do me good."

"I haven't got all day love," said the driver, "do you want this cab or not?"

"Yes," replied Julie.

"No," said Kim.

"Well make up your bleeding minds, I haven't got all day," grunted the driver.

Kim took hold of Julie's arm, pulling her back. "We'll walk thank you."

With that the less than courteous driver closed his window and drove off down the road.

"I really think you should reconsider Kim, you're supposed to be resting. You need all of your strength."

"Look, if it's too much for me we'll get a taxi then OK?"

Julie begrudgingly accepted defeat. "I'll take that," she said, relieving Kim of her handbag. "What the bloody hell have you got in here?"

"Purse, phone – you know – the usual, and I bet it's no heavier than yours. Anyway, where are you parked?"

"Green Lane."

"That's not too far."

"It's a good twenty minutes at least," replied Julie.

"No, fifteen tops."

"Look Miss Know-it-all, I know what time I bought my ticket and I know what time I got to the clinic."

"Well in that case you could not have come through the park."

"Surely it's not quicker?" countered Julie.

"Of course it is." Kim rolled her eyes.

"When was the last time you walked somewhere?"

"Maybe from today I will walk more – after all it is supposed to be good for you. Not only that, London is such a beautiful city. You lose touch with the place."

"You know you're right I guess. We've lived here all our lives and just take it for granted. Listen to me," she paused, "and that's another thing – who made you all green all of a sudden?"

"Helen; every time we come into town she insists on public transport. At first I was horrified at the idea but it's actually not that bad if you avoid the rush hour."

"I thought you said you hadn't been on a bus for twenty years," remarked Julie.

"I haven't, but taxis are public, aren't they?" smiled Kim. They paused. "See, through here," she indicated, "and Green Lane's on the other side of the park."

"Oh, so it is," Julie exclaimed, sounding surprised. "You know I used to bring the boys down here to feed the ducks."

Suddenly she lurched violently to one side, dragging Kim with her. At first, she couldn't quite comprehend what was happening as there was this young man directly in front of them; then it dawned on her that he had hold of their bags and was pulling them towards the trees.

From the corner of her eye she noticed Kim lunge at their assailant, who responded with a blow from the back of his right hand, sending her crashing to the ground. Julie released her tenuous hold on the bags, allowing their attacker to make a run for it as she bent down to aid her sister.

"Are you OK?" she asked but Kim did not reply, and she noticed a thin dark red line making its way from underneath her head.

Julie looked up as a young man on a bicycle skidded to a halt, dropping his bike to the ground.

"I'm a doctor," he said, "have you phoned for an ambulance?"

"No." It was then she remembered their phones were in the bags. "They were stolen."

"They're on their way," said another voice from behind her. Within minutes the police and an ambulance were there and Julie watched helplessly as her sister was stretchered into the back of the ambulance accompanied by the young doctor and a paramedic.

"Where are you taking her?" she shouted.

"St. Michael's," answered the paramedic.

"If you would care to come with me," said one of the officers.

"I can't," she protested, "that's my sister."

"That's ok," replied the officer kindly, "we'll take you to the hospital and you can give us a statement at the same time."

The officer followed Julie into A&E. "Wait here," he said, "I will inform them who you are so they can tell you what's happening."

She sat down in a corner opposite a rather battered table with a liberal covering of out-of-date magazines.

"Now madam," said the officer. "If I can start by asking you your full name and address and phone number, including mobile."

Julie gave the information. "Thank you, now if you could do the same for your sister… That's fine, now if you can tell me exactly what happened."

"I can't remember much, it all seemed to happen so quickly."

"Don't worry, just start by telling me what you can."

"Well, we were walking along arm in arm. I was carrying both our bags over my left shoulder."

"Both bags?" enquired the officer.

"Yes, you see my sister had just left Lime Tree Clinic."

"Oh, I know, the private surgery."

"Yes, she's being treated for cancer."

"I'm sorry to hear that," he replied gently.

"As I said, we were just minding our own business when I felt this tug on my arm. There was this young man trying to rip the bags from me, but like an idiot I held on. Instinct I guess."

"Quiet," he agreed, taking notes. "Can you describe him for me?"

"Err, let me see. He was fairly ordinary."

"How tall would you say, about my height?"

"No, no shorter than you."

"5'8," would you say?"

"Yes, yes, I guess about 5'8."

"What else can you remember of him?"

"He had short black hair, and deep-set eyes – very dark."

"Did he have any distinguishing marks – tattoos, earrings, piercings, scars?" asked the officer.

"No, I don't think… yes, wait a minute, he had a scar over his top lip, quite pronounced."

"Can you describe what he was wearing?"

"Err, white t-shirt – there was something written on the front but I can't remember what. Oh, and green baggy trousers," she added, "the type with lots of pockets."

"Cargo pants?" suggested the officer.

"Yes, that's them."

"And did you notice his feet?"

"Orange stripes. Yes, he had orange stripes on his trainers."

"Excuse me a moment Madam." The officer spoke into his radio, "Yeah, go on… scar over his top lip… t-shirt, green cargo pants and orange trainers. Yep, that sounds like him."

"Well Madam, I may have some good news. It looks as though we have detained the man responsible for assaulting and robbing you and your sister."

"Gosh, that was quick!"

"Can't even fart around here without us knowing about it. Oh, sorry," he apologised, "you'll have to excuse my French."

"No, that's ok officer, I've heard much worse."

"Here are my details," he said, "report to this station and hopefully you'll get your belongings back. You will then be asked to make a formal identification."

"Can't we just get our stuff back?"

"Charges will be brought if this is indeed the man that assaulted you. We can't have people like that running around, this is a very serious matter – especially as we don't know the condition of your sister."

"No, quiet," she apologised, "how stupid of me. When do I have to go to the station?"

The officer looked at his watch. "It will have to be this evening. Say, if you could do it within the next 2 hours?"

"Of course, I'll go over as soon as I have news of my sister."

"As I said, if you could do it within the next two hours, I'll be at the station."

14

"Mrs Grayson?"

"Yes, Councillor Roberts?"

He was taken aback slightly by the defiant tone in her voice. "I need you and Hunter to accompany me to the Records Department. I believe that the cabinets are dual locked?"

"Yes Councillor, that is correct."

"Well what are you waiting for?" he snapped.

"I will need to know which files you are wishing to access."

"Does it matter?"

"Of course Councillor, some of them are still restricted and would need authorisation from the committee."

"This is outrageous. I am an elected member of the Council and you're telling me you have access to these so-called restricted documents and I don't?"

"Yes, that is correct Councillor," she replied. "The reason is, is that councillors can change every few years. The position of trust if you like, is given to long-term members of staff who have undergone the necessary security checks."

"Have you undergone these checks?" Roberts asked, turning on Hunter, once again using his massive frame to intimidate.

Nigel looked blank, he had never heard of them. "I… I…"

"Well man?"

"I don't know."

"What the hell do you mean you don't know – you must know?"

"I guess not Councillor."

"Well I am afraid I cannot be of assistance to you Councillor," said Mrs Grayson, "until either Mr Hunter has the appropriate clearance or you get a form 1475."

"A what?"

"A form 1475," she repeated. "It gives you permission to access specific information."

"And how does one get one of those?"

"From the committee, Councillor."

Roberts had never heard of a form 1475, but then again, he had never needed access to restricted files. Sometimes in his job, the least you knew the better.

However, he could smell a rat, but then again, at no time did the timid Mrs Grayson appear to be lying and as far as going to the committee – that was totally out of the question. They were the last people he wanted to be involved.

He would make some discreet enquiries, see if there was such a thing as a form 1475, and if there wasn't, and these two were playing games with him, then the gloves would be well and truly off.

Nigel and Mrs Grayson watched him storm off.

"You never told me I needed security clearance?" whispered Nigel.

"You don't – only one of the key holders has to have it."

"Do you know what you have done?" he said in a low voice. "When he finds out he will go frigging mental."

"How's your libido?"

"Sorry?" he replied, taken aback slightly.

"Fancy another trip down to records?"

He could not quite believe his ears. "Have you lost your mind?"

Mrs Grayson tossed the spare key into the air and caught it

deftly on its return, dropping her right hip and leaning her head slightly to one side at the same time.

"Oh, to hell with it, why not?" he said.

—w—

"You must be Mrs Goodman's sister. I am Mr Kahn."

"How is she?" Julie asked.

"She's going for a routine brain scan," said the doctor.

"A brain scan?"

"Don't worry, as I say it's just routine, you can't be too careful with head injuries. Once we have the results I will be able to make a better-informed diagnosis. Your sister is being treated for cancer I understand."

"Yes Doctor."

Mr Kahn looked at his notes. "At Lime Tree Clinic I see, and her physician is Mr Rathbone."

"Yes."

"Good, she will stay here tonight. Call this number tomorrow, about 10.30am, and I will be able to advise you then as to what you should do from there."

"Mr Kahn, I would like a private room for my sister."

"I understand. I believe that can be arranged."

Julie made her way across the car park which seemed to stretch for miles. The sea of multi-coloured vehicle roofs shimmered and danced in the late afternoon sun. As she picked her way carefully around the thin ribbons of melting tar, the smell of them combined with that of thousands of rubber tyres felt for some inexplicable reason, reassuring. It had taken her back to those hot childhood days when they would go to the coast and picnic from the back of their father's Ford Zephyr estate because Grandad hated the thought of sand in his sandwiches.

Finally, she negotiated her way to the main road but despite the number of people going about their business, it did little to reassure her. It was as if the events earlier that day were forming a graphic picture in her head – all she could see was his face, expressionless, his eyes fixed on her bag, totally unaware that it belonged to another conscious being. It was almost as if he was ripping fruit from a tree, oblivious of his actions or their consequences.

"Green Lane Police Station" she said to the taxi driver.

"Your friend decided to get the bus then?"

"Sorry?"

"Earlier today – you and your friend stopped me" explained the driver. "She wanted to walk."

"Oh, it was you."

"Yep, never forget a face. Most of my colleagues are the same. You need a good memory to pass *The Knowledge*."

"Sorry?" she replied, not sure what he was talking about.

"The Knowledge, it's what we London Cabbies call the test you have to take to get your licence."

The journey went by in a blur of unrecognisable faces as they passed by on the adjacent pavement until she was brought out of her trance by the taxi driver.

"Here we are Madam. That'll be £9.50."

Julie handed over a £10 note and crossed the street, up several steps and through a security screen, the type you find at airports.

"Yes Madam, how can I help you?" said the prim young woman from behind a glass screen.

"My name's Julie Fowler. My sister and I were mugged in Green Lane Park earlier today. PC Thomas told me to report to this station."

"Ah yes," replied the young woman, "I believe he's still here. If you would like to take a seat, he won't be long."

Once again Julie found herself in a sterile environment – the smell of disinfectant hanging heavily in the air."

"Mrs Fowler?"

She looked up to see PC Thomas and a middle-aged woman, her long mousy hair tied back, the two-piece suit she was wearing looking a little worn around the edges. She stepped forward and held out her hand to introduce herself.

"I'm DCI Blackett; would you please come with us to the Interview Room?"

"There's one thing I have to do," said Julie, "and that's phone my sister's husband. He's on his way home from a business trip and I can't allow him to return with her missing."

"Of course," replied DCI Blackett. "Use mine," she added, handing Julie her phone.

"Hello?" said Paul, not sure as to who was phoning him as he didn't recognise the number.

"It's Julie here."

"Everything ok? You sound a little worried."

"Yes and no," she replied. "It's Kim."

"What's wrong?"

"There's no easy way to put this but she – or should I say we – were mugged earlier today."

"Mugged?" exclaimed Paul, raising his voice. "What the hell are you talking about?"

"We were on our way to the car from the clinic when this man grabbed our bags. Kim was knocked to the ground in the fracas."

"Is she hurt?"

"I'm afraid so," she replied in a low voice.

"How serious?" he asked, trying to sound calm, as he was now aware that Solley knew something was wrong and seemed to be paying more attention to the phone conversation than his driving.

"I'm not sure, she was unconscious," explained Julie. "She's in St. Michael's."

"Ok, we'll go straight there. Are you all right?"

"Yes, I'm fine. I'm at Green Lane Police Station at the moment. They think they might have caught the person responsible."

"Ok, I'll see you later," he replied, hanging up.

"What the hell was all that about?" asked Solley.

"Kim and Julie have been mugged."

"When?"

"This afternoon," said Paul. "It appears Kim has been hurt, we need to get to St. Michael's. Whoa, steady on!" he added as the car surged forward.

"What are you talking about," he replied, "this is an emergency."

"I know, but I want to get there in one piece. Plus, I don't want us to get stopped by the police for speeding and waste time."

Solley eased off the accelerator to just under 95mph but it wasn't long before this speed was reduced to a steadier 60mph as the traffic built up on their approach to London.

"It might take some time," said Solley. "It's Friday evening, the traffic will be murder."

Just the sound of this word sent a cold shiver down Paul's spine. After all, he had no idea as to Kim's condition.

—ᘏᘏ—

Julie stepped into the sparsely furnished interview room followed by the police officers.

"Please take a seat," said DCI Blackett. "We'll try and be as brief as possible. PC Thomas has told me of your circumstances. This interview will be recorded." She started by giving the time and name of the person being interviewed. "May I start by asking you how Mrs Goodman is, and do you have any details of her condition?"

"Err, well, I don't know really," replied Julie. "The doctor told me she will need a brain scan, he said it was routine with head injuries."

"We will of course get a detailed report of her injuries," said Blackett. "It is these that will largely dictate how we approach this offence."

"Sorry, I'm not quite with you?"

"Quite simply Mrs Fowler, at the moment we have a charge of assault and robbery. I'm not trying to sound trivial but it is the assault that is the more serious of the two offences. It will depend on the severity of the injuries as to the charge."

"I see."

"Now if you could tell me exactly what happened," continued DCI Blackett. "Take your time, there's no rush. We will of course have to interview your sister when she is able."

Julie took a deep breath. "Well, as I said to PC Thomas…"

—m—

The question for Roberts was how to approach this delicate situation. Originally, he thought a simple request to Townsend would provide him with what he wanted, however, that was obviously not the case. But why had he prevaricated over this seemingly straightforward demand? And there was another thing too, why had he not mentioned this form 1475?

He was starting to feel uneasy. Townsend must know something – but what? After all, the only thing Philip knew was that he wanted historical files regarding the old Sanatorium, and why shouldn't he? After all, he *was* Head of the Planning Committee. And that was another thing – why were these files restricted? They were over one hundred years old.

It then occurred to him that the information he wanted regarding the possible mine workings under the old hospital pre-dated its construction by at least sixty years. The hospital's post-war history may link them together in some way. He had been aware of the rumours that surrounded the place but he had never heard of anything official or otherwise to suggest that these stories of Nazi scientists carrying out weird experiments were nothing more than that.

Roberts had his own theory as to what lay behind these rumours. He believed it was because a Dr Heinrich Muller had helped with the decommissioning of the place in the 1950s and it was this that kick-started the stories, even though Muller was Swiss.

However, none of this answered the question as to what interest Townsend could possibly have in these files.

Of course, he suddenly thought. *That was it – Carlyle!*" Apart from Roberts, the only other person to know of his intentions was his brother-in-law.

It all now started to make sense – it was obvious Carlyle had got to Townsend. That cut on his face would have been Reggie's work no doubt because Townsend being Townsend had refused to hand them over and reckoned he had threatened to do the same to that pretty little wife of his. That's why he didn't want to go to the police!

The question now was where to go from here. Was Reggie pulling a fast one? Ok, he was a devious lying bastard and a dangerous one at that, but why two-time his own brother-in-law? He would have no choice but to confront him. But then again – maybe he should wait – after all, Reggie might not have got around to telling him about the files yet.

However, if he was trying to pull a fast one, he was messing with the wrong person this time. "And I don't care what kind of fucking psychopath he is," he said, "nobody rips me off!"

—✽—

"You can spend a few moments with her," said the nurse. "As a precautionary measure your wife's head movement has been restricted by means of a head brace. It looks rather dramatic but there's nothing to be too concerned about."

"Hello love," said Paul, taking Kim's hand gently and kissing it. "I don't know if you can hear me or not…" He paused, for some reason he could not think of anything to say, his emotions getting the better of him. Seeing his wife in this state due to someone else's criminal behaviour left him lost for words. All he wanted to do was get hold of whoever was responsible and smash their head repeatedly into the ground.

"Mr Goodman, may I have a quick word?"

Paul turned to see a tall, young fresh-faced man – white coat and ubiquitous stethoscope round his neck – standing in the doorway.

"I'll be back in a minute love," he said, kissing Kim's hand gently once again and placing it by her side.

"I am Dr Williams – Mr Kahn's number two if you like," explained the young man. "Earlier today your wife had a brain scan – it's routine with head injuries."

"Has she… you know… been damaged?"

"The blow to her head was sufficient to render her unconscious and there's quite a lot of swelling, therefore we felt it necessary to sedate her. She is also being treated with analgesics and we will carry out another scan first thing tomorrow. Do you have any questions Mr Goodman?"

Paul felt slightly ashamed of himself for he felt surely there was something he should ask but for the life of him he couldn't think of anything.

"Well if that's all Mr Goodman, I'll bid you goodnight."

Paul made his way slowly back to Kim's room and stood there in the doorway for a few moments just looking at her immobilised in that hideous contraption. Although he knew she was unaware of his presence he felt he had to say something. He crossed the room to the bed and taking her hand, gave it a squeeze. But as before, there was no response.

"I must admit," he laughed, trying to sound as light-hearted as possible, "you gave me one hell of a fright when I saw you in this thing but they tell me it's just precautionary – can't be too careful in these situations. Apparently, I can't stay too long, it's vital that you rest."

Now lost for words, he kissed her gently one more time before leaving and made his way through the maze of corridors with their brightly coloured suspended signs directing one to various wards and departments. Finally, he emerged into the busy foyer, at the far end of which seemed to be some kind of disturbance – a drunk or irate patient. Whatever it was, it was only the appearance of two police officers that seemed to quell the situation.

Feeling a tug on his arm, his immediate thought was that it was Julie, but on turning he was confronted by a wizened old woman, a green and red scarf round her head, her hand outstretched.

"Bloody hell!" he said, pushing past her. "Is nowhere sacred nowadays?"

It was then he noticed Solley talking to someone.

"Steady on mate, look where you're going."

Paul apologised to the man on crutches who seemed indifferent to his words.

Julie turned to see him approaching, his eyes bloodshot. It was if he had aged ten years in just two days. "How is she?" she asked.

"Not here," replied Paul. "We'll talk later."

—⚏—

"Are you ok darling?"

"Err yes of course. Why?"

"That's the second time I've asked you for the garden twine. Not the whole thing; cut me off a piece."

"How long?" asked Philip.

"As long as the last piece you cut."

He did as instructed and cut a piece of green string about a foot long then handed it up to Catherine.

"We might need some new trellis," she said.

"New what?"

Catherine climbed down from the steps. "There's something on your mind I can tell," she said.

"It's nothing really; just wondering how they're getting on without me."

"They will just have to manage, that's all," she replied, removing her gloves. "So, first thing tomorrow, a trip to the garden centre," she continued.

"Why?" enquired Philip.

"New trellis; haven't you been listening to a word I've said? I told you, this is half rotten – another windy day and the whole thing will come down and that could damage the clematis."

"N… n… no, not tomorrow. I have something I need to do."

"Ok, I'll come with you. We can pick it up on the way back."

"No, look," he replied, taking her by the arm. "I have a few things I need to sort out."

"What sort of things?" she asked, placing the twine and gloves into her apron, a concerned expression on her face.

"It's nothing to worry about."

"If you say so."

"Come on," he said. "Let's tie this clematis back and I'll make us some tea."

"It's only early," she pointed out, "and there's so much to do."

"Such as?" he asked, looking about.

"For a start there's the box hedge, and those reeds in the pond need thinning."

"Can't say I fancy that, not after all this warm weather," remarked Philip. "I know what, why don't we go to the Three Feathers? We can get a table outside and get supper there," he added, taking the shears from her.

"But we were out last night," she answered, as if this kind of indulgence was verging on the obscene. "Anyway, how are you going to manage with your mouth?"

"I managed last night."

"I know – that's only because I knew you could have the pasta and shellfish. You need a hammer and chisel to get through the food at the Three Feathers."

"Oh it's changed a lot in the last few years," he protested. "It's a proper gastro pub now with all sorts of fancy dishes."

"Oh really?" queried Catherine. "And how do you know so much about it?"

"Christmas lunch last year; you should really have come."

"No, I didn't feel like it, not after the Christmas Party."

"No, that was a bit much," he agreed. "I don't know what happened to be honest; it's never been like that before."

"Too much alcohol," she said, taking the shears back from Philip.

"Anyway, what do you say?"

"I'm not sure, two nights in a row."

"I don't see why not. We used to go out several times a week until they moved in next door and brought all that trouble with them."

Catherine did not reply but looked away, her head slightly lowered.

"Oh, I'm so sorry," he said, "and you're doing so well. Please forgive me; that was so insensitive. If you would rather stay in we can. I know, what about a Chinese takeaway?"

"No, you're right," she announced, heading to the shed with the shears. "We'll go to the Three Feathers."

—ᵐ—

Roberts stared at the phone. He picked up the receiver and placed it down again. Maybe it would be best to wait, but for how long? If he's got the files and he was going to tell him, he would surely have done it by now. No, he would sound him out.

He picked up the phone again and punched in the number.

"Hello?"

"Reggie, it's John here."

"About time, look I can't talk long; I'll meet you at the pub, around seven."

"That's good for me."

Roberts replaced the receiver. *I'll have to play it cagey,* he thought to himself. *I'll see how he reacts when I tell him about the delay, I'll know then if he has them or not.*

—ᵐ—

"This will do," said Philip, leading Catherine to a large corner table. "Not too busy tonight," he observed. "I'll get a menu, or would you rather sit outside?"

"No, it's quite cool now."

"Maybe you're right, and it looks like rain."

He crossed to the bar and ordered two large colas.

"The special's clam chowder," said the barman as Philip picked up the menus.

Catherine's people-watching was interrupted as he returned with two glasses brimming with cola and the menus tucked under his left arm. She watched him intently as he negotiated several of the patrons, finally arriving at their table without spilling a drop.

That was Philip all over, she thought. *Every act, no matter how menial, always carried out with due diligence.*

"The special's clam chowder," he said, placing the drinks down on the coasters with great deference.

"That sounds very American."

"Now you come to mention it, I think the owner might be from the States."

"What makes you say that?" she asked, looking about her to see if he had spotted something to support his assumption. But to all intents and purposes, it looked like any other English pub.

Philip sipped at his drink. "When we were here last Christmas someone mentioned it was owned by two brothers from L.A. They came over here some years ago looking for their ancestors or some such, and fell in love with the village. It just so happened that the pub was up for sale at the time so they made an offer and took it over. Not many free houses left now, nearly all owned by multinationals."

"I'll tell you what's really nice about this place," she said, leaning forward slightly. "No games machines. I'm sure there used to be some over by the door."

"I know, I think it's that and the real ale, plus the amazing food, that makes it so popular, although tonight may be an exception. Have you made up your mind?"

211

"I think I'll have the steak and ale pie."

"What about a starter?" replied Philip, still studying the menu.

"No, I think I'll just have a main, the portions look awfully large."

"Very good," he said, taking the menus back to the bar and placing their order.

—◊—

Roberts pulled into the car park but there was no sign of Reggie's 4x4. He decided rather than wait in his car, he would go inside, it would be less suspicious he thought. He locked his car and turned to make his way across the now almost full car park.

"Oh Jesus!" he exclaimed.

"You do have a nervous disposition Councillor," said Reggie. "I would get that looked at if I were you."

"Sorry, you… Hey, what happened to your eye?"

Carlyle knew this would draw Roberts' attention. He had considered telling him about what had transpired earlier but thought better of it. Maybe the least he knew the better for now, not only that it would be a loss of face, a sign of weakness even, and that would never do. He would let things run their natural course and intervene when it was most appropriate.

—◊—

Catherine looked up to see a very slim and attractive young waitress dressed in black top and short, tight black skirt bring their respective meals.

"That does look good!" she said.

"And it tastes as good as it looks," answered Philip.

She watched the girl weave her way back past the tables, every man following her every move until her cute bottom disappeared behind the bar. Well, except the couple farthest from them and Philip that was. He was busy tucking into his crab salad.

Philip was right, she thought. *They should get out more. After all, what could happen if she was with him and they came to places like this?*

It was then that she noticed that he had stopped eating, his attention being drawn to two men as they approached the bar, their backs to them now. She had not seen them come in – she had been too interested in the waitress, but for some reason the taller one seemed familiar.

"Are you ok?" she asked.

"Err, yeah. You know, I think it would be nice to eat outside, plus it's getting very crowded in here."

"I thought you said it looked like rain?"

Philip did not answer but picked up his plate and drink and without another word, left the table and made for the rear exit that led to the beer garden. This sudden and unexpected departure left her feeling exposed and vulnerable. How could he just leave her there? After all, he knew how difficult just leaving the house was for her, let alone being deserted in such a busy place.

It was then that the taller of the two men Catherine had spotted turned in her direction, his gaze immediately fixed on her. It was Councillor Roberts – she had met him at the Christmas Party and had taken an instant dislike to him.

"Oh don't come over here, please, please," she said to herself. But it was too late to do anything now.

"Mrs Townsend – what an unexpected pleasure. May I introduce you to my brother-in-law?"

"Pleased to meet you," said Reggie, hand outstretched, his eyes undressing her. "All on your own?"

"Err, no, Philip's outside."

"Not fallen out I hope," said Roberts, a broad smile cutting across his face.

"He must be mad," said Reggie, sitting down next to her, "leaving such a beautiful woman all on her own. You never know what might happen. But there's no need to be concerned now we're here, isn't that true John?"

"Of course," smiled Roberts.

Philip found a table at the far end of the beer garden, its surface covered in a light film of green moss interspersed with blotches of yellow lichen, its thin tendrils radiating out across the slats of wood giving the illusion of being covered in tiny spiders.

He sat down in the shady spot, oblivious to the fact he had just ruined his second-best pair of trousers and looked up expecting to see Catherine but she was nowhere to be seen. He felt a sense of panic well up inside him. Supposing Roberts had recognised her? But surely not, they had only met in passing and he was drunk at the time.

He then remembered what Roberts had said about his *pretty little wife*. He would have no choice but to go back inside and face him and if that wasn't bad enough, if he was not mistaken, the person with him was that obnoxious brother-in-law of his, Reggie Carlyle. Although they had only met on two occasions, and then only briefly, the man had terrified him. It was no use, he would have to go back and confront them. Hopefully Roberts had not mentioned his suspension.

His worst nightmare was confirmed as he entered the now busy pub to see Catherine hemmed in on both sides by Roberts and Carlyle. She looked so small and frightened, like a tiny bird trapped by two large cats waiting to pounce. As he cleared his throat, Roberts and Carlyle looked up.

"Ah, Philip, there you are," said Roberts. "I think Catherine here was beginning to think you had deserted her."

Carlyle said nothing but just stared at Philip with his dark, cold eyes, almost lifeless.

"No, n… n… n… no, just a slight misunderstanding that's all," he answered. "I have found a nice table outside next to the field," he added, addressing Catherine.

She went to get up but was prevented from leaving, Reggie's large hand firmly pressed against her thigh. Roberts stood up.

"There's something I would like to talk to you about." He then turned to Catherine. "Please, if you would excuse us for a moment this is council business. I won't keep him long."

Roberts placed his large arm around Philip's shoulder and led him towards the bar. "Your wife doesn't know you have been suspended, does she?"

"N… n… no Councillor."

"Good, there's no reason for her to know but you have to help me."

"Help you, how?"

"You know what I'm talking about."

Philip did not reply to this leading question.

"Those files I asked you for," continued Roberts, "you have them, don't you?"

"No," he protested.

"Look, I am sick and tired of this little game of yours. If you think I'm a nasty bastard then you want to get to know my brother-in-law better, which you will do if I don't get those files."

"The files you requested are still there."

"I have warned you once, there is not going to be a second time."

Philip glanced back over his shoulder to where Catherine and Reggie were sitting. "Ok, let's go outside," he said.

"That's better," said Roberts.

—❦—

"Would you like me to stay tonight?" asked Paul, taking the glass of untouched brandy from Julie. "Tell you what, I'll order some food, Indian ok?"

"I'm not hungry," she replied, getting up and walking over to the French doors, looking out over the large terraced gardens with its immaculate lawns and perfectly shaped cypresses.

"Everyone that sees the garden thinks we have people in to keep it this way," she said. "But it's all Derek's work you know. Except the design, that was Kim's of course. Do you remember what a state this place was in when we bought it, and how much I was against the idea? But she insisted that with a little hard work it would be a fantastic bargain."

"Yes," he replied, now standing just behind her.

"I'll let you into a little secret," she continued. "See those roses by the pond?"

"Yes."

"Kim planted the bright red one. I wanted them all to be the same pale yellow. I think she did it for a joke. I took the first flower and pressed it, I still have it. That was twenty-five years ago almost to the day."

Paul looked at the single scarlet rose surrounded by a sea of yellow.

—∞—

Roberts followed Philip into the car park and to the corner furthest from the pub.

"Look," explained Philip, "those files are still there. The reason I didn't get them for you straightaway was because I was stalling."

"Oh, and why might that be?" said Roberts, now just inches from him.

"I did take files from that particular cabinet and gave them to unauthorised persons."

"Are you fucking winding me up Townsend?"

"No, it's true."

"But why?" asked Roberts, "and you of all people?"

"I had no choice," he explained. "I was the subject of blackmail."

"Who blackmailed you?"

"I don't know," he answered, "they just told me to put the files into a dumpster. As I said, these files you requested were stored together. When you asked for them it seemed to be too much of a coincidence and the other thing was – why would you want files dating back over 200 years? It was then that I realised it must have been the files that had been stored with them that you wanted –

the ones I had taken – so I was hoping to stall you long enough for me to get them back as promised and return them with nobody the wiser."

"These documents, what exactly did they refer to?"

Philip took a deep breath, "They relate to transactions involving the construction of the Commonwealth Games Village."

"Are you sure?" asked Roberts, looking a little uneasy, as it would appear that they had been deliberately hidden.

"Of course I am."

"Look, this is no place for this kind of conversation. You'd better come with us."

"Err, ok. I'll just tell Catherine I have some council business to discuss with you."

"No, she's coming too."

"There's no need for that," he protested.

"I'll decide what's necessary. You my boy are in deep shit and if you want to stay out of prison, you'll do exactly as I say. Think of all those long lonely nights your pretty little wife would have to spend on her own. But then again, it might not be too bad for you, knowing Reggie and I would be there to look after her and see to her needs," added Roberts, that broad grin spreading remorselessly across his fat face.

Philip grabbed his arm as he turned to head back to the pub. This show of defiance caught the Councillor by surprise; not only that, his grip was strong.

Roberts turned on him, "Unhand me," he demanded, "or I will…"

"Or you'll what? Don't forget I know what's contained in those files and some of it's pretty damning, if you get my meaning."

Roberts demeanour changed, "Come on," he said, "Let's not get all confrontational, I'm sure we can work something out to our mutual benefit."

Philip released the Councillor and followed him back to the pub.

15

As Solley made his way into the kitchen from the adjoining double garage, the red light on the phone was flashing. He picked up the receiver and listened to the message then scribbled it down on a scrap of paper. It read *'A Mr Pintov – Russian I think – phoned today asking about the number of properties we own and in what areas.'*

He dialled Jackie's home number. "Hi, it's Solley here, I got your message. What's all this about a Russian?"

"Sorry I couldn't be more precise, his accent was hard to understand, but he seemed to want to know how…"

"Yeah, I got that in your message," he interrupted. "Did he leave a contact number?"

"No; I dialled 1471 but it came back as a withheld number."

"Ok, if he phones back, get his number and contact details but don't tell him anything."

"No of course not," she replied, a note of indignation in her voice.

"No, of course you wouldn't. Sorry for phoning you at home so late."

Solley replaced the receiver. He was just about to phone Paul and tell him what Jackie had just said but decided against it; he would ring in the morning.

"No, I would rather go home," protested Catherine as Philip encouraged her up from her seat. "And what about our food?" she added, hoping that this excuse would put a stop to whatever this was.

"It won't take long," he said.

Reluctantly, with Philip holding her arm, she followed Roberts and Carlyle to their car. Roberts opened the rear door to the large black 4x4 allowing her to climb in, doing her best to keep her knees together and preserve her dignity. However, this seemingly simple exercise was made somewhat difficult on account of her rather short skirt; she would have changed into something a little longer but Philip had seemed happy for her to wear it. This look had always pleased him but it made her feel slightly self-conscious, her preferred choice of clothes always displeased him. He would look for a moment or two and then say, "Isn't that a little old for you."

She could feel Roberts' eyes staring at her long slim legs accentuated by her high heels. "Now Mrs Townsend – or may I call you Catherine?"

"Err, Catherine."

"Good to be on first name terms. We are all friends here aren't we Philip? It was bad manners of us to drag you away from your meal but not to worry; we'll more than make it up to you."

—⁂—

Frank sat on the edge of the bed and bounced up and down a couple of times then without removing his shoes, he flopped back onto the soft mattress. It felt strange, for the last three weeks he had slept on the floor on a leaky airbed that by the early hours had deflated to the point of almost non-existence leaving him with two options – get up and spend five minutes re-inflating it or lay there on the hard floor, trying to find some support from the vestiges of air still trapped in the corrugated vinyl envelope.

At first the former option won out but as time went by, he became used to the hard floor and as a consequence he found the soft mattress uncomfortable. Despite his desire for much-needed sleep, he could not settle. He would go for a walk, try out his new shoes.

He grabbed the black plastic bag containing his old clothes and made his way downstairs to find Mrs Brown on the phone.

"Just a minute Doris," she said before addressing him. "You have your key Mr Smith?"

At first Frank did not register. "Oh please, call me Frank."

Mrs Brown looked a little coy.

"Yes, thank you," he continued, "and by the way, the room's lovely."

Mrs Brown continued to hold her hand over the mouthpiece as she watched Frank leave. "Oh, he's such a nice man, so well dressed. He's an architect you know… well that's what I thought but he said he preferred the homely touch…oh Doris, you are awful. Mind you, given half the chance, I would let him go over my foundations any day."

—⁓—

The late evening traffic had died away to a steady stream of well-interspersed vehicles. Frank looked across the road at Mario's – it had been a long time since he had been somewhere that posh.

To hell with it, why not, you only live once, he thought, and he had the money – he might as well spend it. If he didn't then that toad of a solicitor of hers fucking would, not to mention what he owed Reggie.

He spotted a gap in the traffic and made a dash for the other side of the road, placing the plastic bag containing his old clothes into a litter bin. As he entered the restaurant, stepping into its warm confines, he was immediately enveloped in the most divine smell of Sicilian cuisine.

"Does Sir have a reservation?"

"No," he replied.

"Well in that case Sir, I'm not sure if I can be of help to you."

Frank stuffed £20 into the Maître d's top pocket.

"I think Sir might be lucky, if you would care to follow me."

Frank followed him to a small table near the kitchen. Not his preferred choice but the restaurant did seem to be busy. He made himself comfortable.

"Would Sir care to see the wine list?"

"No, just bring me a bottle of your finest red."

This was more like it, he thought, looking forward to the first decent food he could remember having for a long time. He looked up as the wine waiter stood before him.

"Would Sir care to try the wine?"

"No, just pour," he replied. "And to save time, I'll have the lobster starter and the ribeye steak."

"Very good Sir," said the wine waiter, one eyebrow slightly raised.

—◊—

Paul answered the door to a spotty youth, his red and yellow moped phut-phutting behind him at the kerb.

"Two kormas and rice," he announced.

Paul handed over the exact money and a fiver as a tip.

"Thanks mate," said the young man as he returned to his metal steed.

He watched as the youth sped off down the private road and paused to allow the electric gates to open, then closed the front door and made his way into the kitchen, the smell of curry making him feel hungry but somehow this felt wrong. How could he eat while Kim was lying in hospital? But then again, he would need something and for that matter so would Julie. Kim would need all the support she could get and they would, as difficult as it may seem, have to try and behave as normally as possible. Thank goodness she had sent the kids down to stay with Derek.

"Ah Julie," he said as she entered the kitchen. "The famous Bengal Star korma brought you out I see."

She gave a half smile. "No, I came to make some tea."

"Yeah, of course," he replied, "but at least try to eat something – it's important for you to keep your strength up. The last thing Kim's going to want is to see you looking unwell."

"I guess you're right."

"Of course I am, I'm always right!"

He peeled the foil lid off one of the containers and divided some of its contents onto two plates, then did the same with the rice.

"There's plenty more if you want it," he said.

"No, that's more than enough," replied Julie, pushing the food about her plate before placing a small forkful into her mouth.

—⁓—

Frank looked up as the waiter placed the lobster with its accompanying sauce in front of him.

"Bon Appetit," he said before leaving him to his meal.

Frank wasted no time; he ripped into the crustacean with gusto. It tasted incredible. *No more messing about with second rate takeaways for me,* he thought. He picked up the wine bottle and was just about to pour another glass when he saw Councillor Roberts enter the restaurant.

"Bollocks, that's all I fucking need."

But then his stomach turned over a second time as none other than Philip Townsend and his wife, accompanied by Reggie Carlyle, followed him in.

Within seconds he was careering through the kitchen to the

bewilderment and dismay of the staff. The door to the rear of the kitchen was open and he found himself in a small courtyard, a high fence on all sides, the only exit being a wooden gate firmly padlocked.

"No you fucking don't!"

He turned to see the biggest Italian he had ever laid eyes on, baseball bat in hand.

"Come here!" he screamed. "You pay."

Fuck that, thought Frank, leaping up onto one of the two metal dumpsters, removing his leg just in time as the baseball bat smashed with great force onto the top of the bin where it had been. From his new vantage point, he wasted no time in leaping over the fence, regardless of the consequences. Fortunately, his fall was broken by several black rubbish bags piled up on the other side, the force of his landing causing several of them to split, covering his new suit with half-rotten food waste and ripping his trousers to boot.

But that was the least of his problems – something had cut deep into his leg and blood was literally pouring out all over the place. He placed as much pressure onto the wound as he could to stem the flow, then became aware of the padlock to the gate being unlocked. If this wasn't bad enough, the last thing he needed was a broken arm.

Hauling himself to his feet he hobbled across the street hoping his pursuer would have second thoughts about smashing his brains out in public. This assumption proved right as he looked over his shoulder to see the irate restaurateur gesticulating for all he was worth from the other side of the road.

—⁂—

"Ah Councillor Roberts, nice to see you again," said the waiter. "Please, Mr Carlyle, come, your usual table is ready."

Philip knew he was now in serious trouble. He also knew what those files he took contained and what that could mean for Roberts and his brother-in-law. Although on the surface everything seemed legitimate, he was fully aware that with some digging around, a whole can of worms would soon rise to the surface – most of them with Roberts and Reggie Carlyle's names on.

His only hope was that this so-called private detective could find them in time, but the thing was, how much pressure would Roberts and Carlyle put on him if they thought he was lying, and he was only too aware he would have to hand the documents over, making him an accessory – as if things weren't bad enough already. He knew full well that Catherine was his weak point, although to some that might sound a contradiction in terms – surely he was, and always had been, the weak one.

However, this vicious unprovoked attacked on him had changed something inside. Sure, he was scared of Roberts and terrified of Carlyle, but if that greasy bastard Carlyle laid another hand on his wife, so help him, he would shove this steak knife right through his eyeball.

It was at this very moment their eyes met but instead of averting his gaze, Philip met him head on. For some reason he had never felt this alive and he knew that Carlyle knew it too. It was the only thing a man like him understood.

The top right-hand side of Carlyle's lip rose slightly before he returned to his menu.

—◊—

There was no way round it – he would have to seek medical help. Frank ripped his new shirt and, using his belt, fastened the wad of soft cotton to his inner thigh. But how the hell was he going to get to the hospital without drawing attention to himself? A half-naked middle-aged man covered in blood would have the first cop to see him asking all sorts of awkward questions.

He retrieved his phone from his pocket, wiping the dark sticky blood from its surface.

"Come on, come on," he said. "Ian – it's Frank here, I have those files you wanted."

"Where are you?" asked Ian, relieved at this unexpected good news. "Where?" he repeated.

"I'm at the back of the old Victoria Theatre, Grosvenor Road. Do you know it?"

"Yeah I know where it is. What the hell are you doing there?"

"Look, do you want these fucking files or not?" he grimaced.

"Of course, keep your shirt on."

Even Frank could not escape the irony of this last remark. "Ok then," he said, "get your arse over here as fast as you can."

"I'll see to that," said Paul, "you get to bed."

"Paul?"

"Yes Julie."

"Kim's lucky to have you."

He smiled and put the remains of the takeaway in the fridge before placing the plates into the dishwasher. But only Paul knew his loyalties were divided. No matter how he tried, he could not get Margaret out of his mind. This selfish infatuation for another woman while his own wife was lying in hospital with melanoma and a head injury after being mugged tore at his innards. Could it be that the earlier thoughts he had so readily dismissed were not so far from the truth after all?

And that was another thing, what if this project did take off and he got to see Margaret on a fairly regular basis? Not only that, he would be 250 miles from home. It was inevitable he would have to stay overnight on occasions, maybe longer at times, and of course the nearest place that made any sense was Margaret's hotel. Maybe Solley was right? But the $64,000 question was could he trust himself?

But then again, he was running before he could walk. Even if he were stupid enough, there was no reason for Margaret to feel the same as he did. He knew she was not the type to break up a perfectly good marriage and especially under the circumstances, but he also knew deep down that Margaret had feelings for him – the way she took his hand the other day, her eyes lingering on his fractionally longer than they needed to. There was definitely a connection between them despite the fact he was 52 and she was only 35.

But hey – what the hell did age have to do with it? His mother was 12 years older than his father and they were still happily married. But it would break their hearts – and then there were the kids. Ok, they were technically adults but they would always be his children. The whole idea was ludicrous.

He closed the door to the dishwasher and made his way back into the sitting room, the bottle of brandy still on the table. He looked at it for some time before placing it back inside the drinks cabinet. It had been over fifteen years since he had modified his behaviour towards alcohol, although recently he sometimes wondered whether he was returning to his old ways. He had tried abstaining but this only led to bouts of over-consumption. Maybe it was time to seek professional advice once again?

Throughout that terrible time Kim had never complained or given up on him – and goodness knows, she had had plenty of reason to. She had persevered with his drink problem for more than a decade before that night.

Even after all this time it still made him feel ashamed. But Kim had always maintained that it was the *man* she had married, not the drink. Her lies regarding the bruising to her face in order to protect him almost convinced him it had been an accident. The only good thing to come out of it was getting professional help. The last thing he needed at a time like this was a relapse. But the temptation to wash all these thoughts from his mind with copious amounts of alcohol was still strong.

—m—

Reggie handed over a wad of cash to the waiter who seemed beside himself with gratitude. This show of subservience was almost to the point of grovelling but then again, these people had been brought up to respect power in whatever form it took, and Reggie's power was one they were all too familiar with.

"I daresay you two have had enough of us by now," Roberts addressed Catherine.

She tried her best to sound positive, but at first the words failed her. "It's b… b… been lovely," she stammered unconvincingly.

"Well we'd better get you home then," he continued.

Philip took a deep breath of cool night air as they stepped out onto the pavement. Reggie's chauffeur-driven car drew up in front of the restaurant and Catherine was the first to get in followed by Philip. Reggie slammed the door shut and jumped into the front passenger seat before the vehicle sped off down the now empty street. Philip felt uneasy, for sitting the other side of Catherine was another one of Reggie's so-called employees.

"I think you need to turn here," he said, but his advice went unheeded. "I don't think you can get to the Three Feathers this way," he continued anxiously.

Finally, the yellow street lights that had accompanied them on their journey so far faded into the distance as they headed out into the blackness of the countryside.

"Where are we going?" he demanded.

Reggie turned and placed the barrel of a 9mm pistol to Philip's forehead.

"Be quiet," he said.

Catherine placed her hands on the seat in front of her to steady herself as the 4x4 bounced and jostled itself down what could only have been a track. Finally, after what seemed to be ages, the vehicle came to a halt and Philip tried his door but it would not open. Reggie got out, opened the rear door, and using his gun he indicated for Philip to get out. No sooner had Philip done so, then Reggie slammed the door shut.

"Stay here and don't move," he growled as he got back into the vehicle. "If you want to see your wife again you do exactly as you're told!"

Philip watched helplessly as the 4x4 drew off into the night, taking his wife with it.

The silence was almost overpowering, broken every so often with the piercing cry of a vixen. Philip turned to face the sound of an approaching vehicle which slowly drew up next to him, the only occupant being the driver who lowered his window.

"Get in," he said.

Philip did as instructed.

—w—

Ian walked up the steps of the theatre and peered through the heavy glass doors but there was no sign of Frank – or anyone for that matter. Had he heard him right? He then made his way down the narrow alleyway that separated the theatre from the Art Deco flats so beloved by the makers of period programmes, but there was still no sign of him.

What the bloody hell was he playing at? he thought.

"Down here."

"What the fuck?" he exclaimed, stepping back in fright. At first Ian could not make sense of what was happening.

"Don't just fucking stand there, help me up."

He bent down and hauled Frank to his feet. "What the hell's happened to you?"

"No time for that; I need a hospital. No not like this, give me your jacket."

Reluctantly Ian did so.

"Now help me to the end of the alley and get your car. If anyone sees us, I'm drunk OK?"

With one arm around Ian's shoulder, they managed to reach the road where he propped Frank against the wall.

"Do you have those files?" he asked.

"Yes."

"Where, I can't see them."

"Look, I'm fucking bleeding to death here. If you don't get me some help, you'll never see them."

Ian then noticed that his breathing had become more laboured and knew this was a bad sign – a very bad sign. Frank could no longer keep himself upright and slowly slumped to the ground. Hurrying to where he had parked his car, half walking, half running, he could not afford to waste time but on the other hand he didn't want to draw too much attention to himself – or more specifically to Frank.

He pulled up to the rear of the old theatre opposite the narrow alleyway and made his way into its dark recesses.

"Frank… Frank! That's all I fucking need," Ian said as he bent to lift him off the ground.

To his surprise he was quite light and felt bony – almost malnourished. With Frank on the backseat Ian headed for the hospital, pulled up outside A & E and opened the rear door.

"Come on, we're here," he said. "Frank – we're here."

He leaned in and tried to pull him out but for some unknown reason he had all of a sudden become heavy. "Frank – you're going to have to help me. Frank?"

He placed his fingers against the side of his neck, carefully adjusting them, feeling for a pulse. "Oh fucking hell; no, no, this can't be happening!"

Ian called for help and a man with a gauze patch over his eye came to his assistance. Between them they carried Frank into the hospital where the woman behind the glass screen picked up her phone and a few moments later a young doctor came bursting through the double doors to assess Frank.

"He's lost a lot of blood," said Ian.

The doctor did not reply to this observation but called for assistance. Within minutes Frank was on his way for a blood transfusion.

The car containing Philip pulled into the car park of the Three Feathers.

"You're to go home and wait there," said the driver. "We'll be in touch."

Roberts poured himself a glass of 12-year-old malt whisky and eased back into his favourite armchair. At least he now knew his brother-in-law was not trying to two-time him. However, he was less than happy with the way things had turned out. He only hoped – contrary to instinct – that Reggie would show some restraint, but if what he had told him earlier was true, and these documents that Philip had taken had information that could somehow tie Reggie and his wife together in what he knew to be less than above-board financial dealings, then what choice did he have but to go along with his plan?

And that was another thing, if Reggie knew so much about their content, who told him and how did they know? It was obvious that whoever got Philip to place those files into the dumpster was turning the screw on his brother-in-law.

Philip opened the door to his car and sat there for a few moments before driving off. Suddenly the car lurched to one side.

"You're very nervous," said Reggie, emerging from the back seat. "Just keep driving nice and steady. This is comfy," he added, making himself at home on the rear seat, "just the two of us – man to man so to speak. I know a few things that you don't and more importantly – that my brother-in-law is unaware of – and for your sake, and your wife's, it must stay that way.

"Now, I had an interesting conversation with a Mr Frank Hibbard and that low-life wino friend of his, Billy Quinn. It seems as though they have some documents – I wonder if these could be the same ones you took from the council offices. Do you know anything about this?"

"No," replied Philip. It then dawned on him that maybe Frank had told Carlyle that he had paid him to find them. It now seemed as though he had been successful – but wait a minute, how did he know it was him? He gave a false name and address. Of course – he must have had them all along. It was him – the voice on the phone. Why hadn't he realised before? Hibbard… he was the blackmailer.

"I don't have to tell you that lying to me would be a mistake." Reggie held his mobile phone next to Philip's ear.

"Catherine, is that you?"

But before he could say anything more than her name, they were cut off.

"Now listen very carefully Philip; I am, as you may know, a man of little patience. I want you to tell me who gave the documents to Billy."

"All I know is I was told to put them into a dumpster at the back of a kebab shop."

"And how much did you receive for this?"

"Nothing."

"I find that hard to believe. You risk your career – not to mention a possible criminal record – for nothing? No-one does that."

Philip realised he had no choice but to tell Carlyle what he had told Roberts.

"Ok," he said. "I'll tell you why I did it for nothing. I was blackmailed."

"You, blackmailed?" repeated Carlyle. "And what could somebody possible blackmail you with?"

"Somehow – and believe me I don't know how – he found out about something that happened to my wife nearly two years ago.

It caused her to have a nervous breakdown which she has only just recovered from."

Reggie eased himself back slightly. "Ok, as a gentleman, I won't ask you about this terrible event that befell your wife, but it is starting to make sense. I believe I know who blackmailed you, would you care to know?"

"Yes of course," replied Philip.

"But I think you know already don't you?" he continued. "By the way, have you had any dealings with a man called Ian Turnbull?"

"The estate agent you mean?"

"Of sorts you might say."

"Not personally, although he did apply to have the parking area increased outside his agency," he replied. *Of course,* he thought, *the old Sanatorium – the sale was being handled by Turnbull. Could this have something to do with those documents?*

"Now you don't need me to tell you how much trouble you're in but there may be a way out if you co-operate. I know who has these documents and I want you to get them for me."

"But how?"

"By giving the person that blackmailed you a taste of his own medicine so to speak."

Philip braked hard, he was losing concentration.

"That was close," said Reggie. "Don't want to jump a red light and draw attention to ourselves, do we?"

"N… n… no, it's just…"

"I know. You can drop me off shortly but first I will tell you who blackmailed you and what you are to do. The person that got that information on your wife was Frank Hibbard – so-called private detective. You're to go to his office and tell him that you know it was he who blackmailed you and that if he doesn't give you the documents you will go to the police – and remind him that blackmail is a serious offence."

"But I would get into as much trouble for taking the documents," said Philip. "Not only that; it would be my word against his."

"You had them legitimately – you were taking them to Councillor Roberts, he will back you up. Also, who's going to believe the word of a low-life like Frank Hibbard – a man in debt, part-time alcoholic and a disgraced police officer – against that of a highly respected and devoted town clerk who, and you may not know this, is in line to become the next Director of Finance. I don't need to remind you that the well-being of your wife will depend on your success in retrieving these documents. I have great faith in you Philip, I am sure things will work out just fine."

"What if he refuses to co-operate?"

"Pull over here," demanded Reggie.

Philip checked his rear-view mirror, indicated and pulled over to the kerb.

"Then you hand him this."

He took the envelope and opened it. Inside was a photograph of a young woman leaving a terraced house. "Who's this?"

"It's Hibbard's daughter. You'll make it quite clear to him as to what will happen to her if he doesn't co-operate."

"I c… c… could n… n… never do something like that."

"I take it you wish to see your wife again?"

"Y… y… yes of course."

"Well then my dear friend, I think you might be surprised as to what you are capable of – or maybe you already know. Your wife will remain in our care until this little matter is resolved," said Reggie reaching for the door handle. "Oh, and by the way, Hibbard is not to know I sent you." With that he slipped off the back seat and disappeared into the night.

—၈၈—

Margaret turned off the vacuum cleaner and ran into the office, grabbing the receiver.

"Hello, High Gate Hotel," she said, slightly out of breath.

"It's Solley here."

"Oh hi – sorry about the nuisance caller voice, what can I do for you?" she asked, taking a couple of deep breaths.

"You know the other day I confided in you about Paul's wife?"

"Yes."

"It seems events have taken a turn for the worse."

"Oh, I'm sorry to hear that."

"Well, what I'm trying to say is that the project is off."

"It's very kind of you to have phoned me," said Margaret, trying to hide a note of disappointment, "but I totally understand."

"We shouldn't have mentioned anything in the first place," continued Solley, "but what is done is done. If you are ever down this way, you have my number. No point in wasting good money on expensive hotels, not only that, it would be nice to see you again."

"Thank you for the offer and I hope everything turns out for the best."

Margaret replaced the receiver and looked about her. It seemed selfish but without the extra money she would have to sell the hotel. But who in their right mind would want something like this stuck in the middle of bloody nowhere? And look at the state it was still in, despite all time and money they had ploughed into it; it would need thousands more spent on it to bring it up to an acceptable standard.

—m—

"You did what?" shouted Paul.

"I told her it's off," replied Solley.

"What about Turnbull – have you spoken to him yet?"

"No, that's why I'm calling you now – before I tell him."

"I wish you had spoken to me first," said Paul. "After all, it was you that said all decisions had to be mutual."

"I know but this is different."

"In what way?" he asked, his voice slightly raised.

"Do you really need me to spell it out for you? Your wife is lying in hospital unconscious and is being treated for cancer; your duty is to her and her alone. This was a non-starter to begin with and I know it's all my fault but you can't start gallivanting up and down the country at a time like this."

"I told you – Kim was adamant. She wanted me to go ahead with the High Gate project."

"Yes I know, but that was before all this."

"Well you could have waited until I had spoken to her and hear what she has to say."

"Ok, have it your own way. I won't contact Turnbull until you have spoken to Kim."

"Wait a minute," said Paul, just as Solley was about to hang up, "are you getting cold feet and using Kim's condition as an excuse to get out?"

He waited for some moments before Solley replied.

"I can't believe you said that! We have been friends for over forty years. I looked out for you, helped you with your first property. You're like a brother to me, how could you ever think such a thing, let alone say it out loud?"

"Look, I've been… Solley? Solley? Fuck it!" Paul slammed the phone back into its holder. What the hell was he thinking? Not only that but Solley was right, how could he even think of embarking on such a project – especially one of this nature and so far away – at a time like this? It was totally selfish, even if Kim wanted him to go ahead with it. And that could all change. Solley was right – it was just a non-starter.

However, he knew there was something else that made this so hard to let go – Margaret. No matter how he tried to convince himself that it was just his imagination, he knew there was more to it. But why could he not just forget her? Put her out of his mind?

He loved Kim, he always had – or did he? There had never really been anyone else in his life. His feelings for her were real and strong but did he really love her? And what was love come to that? All he knew for sure was that Margaret made him feel alive in a way he had never felt before.

Making his way upstairs he stood in the doorway of their bedroom. The thought that they may never sleep together again was too much for him. He turned the light off and made his way to the guest room, he would sleep there until Kim was back where she belonged.

16

Philip looked at his watch for the umpteenth time that morning. *Would he be there?* he thought, *what if he couldn't find him? No, he will be there; Carlyle seemed to think he would be and he seemed to know what was going on. But could he really threaten him in the way Carlyle wanted and what if this Frank dug his heels in and refused to play ball, what would happen to Catherine?*

One more glance at his watch told him it was time to go. Thirty or so minutes from now, he would find out.

—⁓—

Paul eased the half-eaten bowl of cereal to one side. He was exhausted from a fretful night thinking of Kim and now this unfortunate business with Solley, how could he ever have said such a hurtful thing, and one he knew to be untrue? However, this was not the time for self-pity.

You made your bed Paul Goodman, he thought, *you'll just have to lie in it.* Still at least he would get to see Kim shortly.

—⁓—

Philip parked some 100 metres or so from Frank's office, pressed the *Lock* button on his key fob, and watched the indicator lights flash twice accompanied by two high-pitched beeps. However, even this did not satisfy him so he tried the door then, now convinced his car was secure, he made his way along the High Street.

This part of town had seen better days, most of the shops he knew as a child had long gone, replaced with takeaways, betting shops and loan shops. He passed one showing a happy couple with a fistful of cash, above them a neon sign displayed the words *Your Future's Bright with Lend Right. We're the ones you can trust.*

He paused at the edge of the road, the traffic being heavy. Not so heavy as to make one's way across in the hope that the slow-moving vehicles would succumb to this audacious trespass on their hallowed ground and allow him free passage, but just a steady stream of fast-moving metal waiting to devour anyone foolish enough to toy with it. Finally, his patience was rewarded and he made a dash for the other side.

He had always hated crossing roads ever since he could remember. His mother had put the fear of God into him and even now, as a grown man, he could hear her voice warning him of the consequences of not heeding her advice.

Trying the door, to his relief it was open and he made his way up the staircase to Frank's office to find a tall Asian man and what Philip took to be his wife.

"Yes, can I help you?" the man said.

It was all too obvious that Frank's Detective Agency was no more.

For some reason Philip felt he needed an excuse for this intrusion "Err, no. I just came to collect some papers, that's all," he said, turning to leave.

"Oh yes, Frank mentioned them. He was supposed to be here over an hour ago. I take it you have come to collect them on his behalf?"

"Yes," he replied instinctively.

The stranger handed him a large brown envelope. He thanked him and was about to leave for a second time when the man spoke.

"Just one moment."

Philip felt a sense of panic, was he going to ask for them back? After all, this seemed too easy. But then again, these could be anything.

"When you see Frank would you please give him this," the man added, handing him a small trophy.

"I'll make sure he gets it," he said, taking hold of the tiny silver cup inscribed with the words '*World's Best Dad*'.

Philip wasted no time, stuffing the large brown envelope inside his coat, he took off down the stairs as fast as he could and without making it look too obvious, out onto the sun-bleached pavement. This time he crossed the road almost without thinking, causing a black 4x4 to plough into the back of a blue delivery van as it screeched to a halt. Ignoring this accident, he continued to his waiting car and once inside, ripped the envelope open to reveal the missing documents.

The sense of relief was almost too much to bear but this elation was immediately replaced with a sense of foreboding. What happens when Frank turns up and finds them missing? He only had to ask for a description of who had taken them and Frank would know it was him. After all, how many people had a four-inch gash on the left side of their face? And not only that, what lengths would he go to get them back? He placed the papers on the passenger seat next to him and pulled out into the stream of traffic.

—◊◊◊—

Reggie was now losing his patience with the van driver's protestations but this was not the place for a scene. He pulled out a wad of cash.

"This is twice what that piece of shit is worth," he said. "Now move it out of my way."

"I might have whiplash," protested the van driver.

Reggie turned to his vehicle and beckoned with his left hand. The van driver's jaw dropped as three of the biggest and most terrifying men he had ever seen emerged from the Range Rover.

"If you don't get this out of my way now, my friends will do it for you!" snarled Reggie.

A few moments later he and his crew were back on the move.

"Hey Boss."

"Yes Keith?"

"If Frankie had them in his office why didn't we just go there and get them?"

"Two reasons – one, Frankie does not have them, and two, if he did, he's not an idiot like you. That would be the last place he would keep them," he explained.

"What's this Philip Townsend doing here?"

Reggie looked to the heavens, "For the love of… Now Keith, are you listening?"

"All ears boss."

"Why am I doing this?" he muttered. "Townsend is here to put pressure on Frankie to get the documents I want from that low-life Billy Quinn, ok?"

"Oh yeah, right boss," replied Keith, none the wiser.

Reggie turned to see Joe with his hand in the air, "What's this, bloody twenty questions?" he asked.

"No boss, but if this Townsend bloke is going to give you these papers, why go to all the trouble to follow him here?"

"Because," he explained; "as with everyone else, I don't trust him. He's not stupid, if he thinks there's a way of getting his wife back and us off of his case, he will try it."

"And what about Frank, boss, are we just going to let him go?" asked Keith.

"Don't you worry your pretty little head about Mr Hibbard; we'll be paying him a visit shortly."

—⁓—

Paul and Julie were surprised at how quickly Kim had recovered from her ordeal. She was calm to the point of nonchalance. This show of indifference to what would have been a devastating ordeal, especially under the circumstances, was reassuring.

For some reason he was feeling a little uncomfortable as he decided to tell Kim of his intentions to withdraw from the High Gate project. This news was not well received and the fact that he had intimated she was responsible for this decision, upset her considerably.

"Under no circumstances is this project to be terminated on my behalf, is that quite clear?" She reached across to her bedside and picked up the phone. There was a moment of awkward silence.

"Solley?"

"Oh Kim, I wasn't expecting to hear from you so soon. How are you feeling?"

"Fine," she replied. "Now listen to me. Paul has told me that he's pulling out of the High Gate deal and that you were part of his decision. I've told him he's not to do anything of the sort. I will get better so unless there is another reason that this refurbishment can't go ahead, then you both have my blessing. This is just what I need to help me through this, crazy as it may seem. I just know that if this is a success then I will be ok. Don't ask why but I do."

"Ok," he said, "if that's the way you feel then we'll go for it."

—⁓—

Ian placed the bottle of brandy on the table and replaced the stopper. He would need a clear head when the police turned up asking questions as to how Frank had got into such a state. But why should they? He hadn't given anybody his name or address. However, Frank had been delirious before he passed out, he could say anything and give the game away.

Still there was nothing he could have done except leave him to bleed to death, which he might well have done had he got the documents. And to top it all, there was still the sale of the old

Sanatorium to consider. The Albrights would be waiting for him, but there was still no news from Goodman or Solomon.

Just then his phone rang. He looked at the number, it was Solomon. Ian took a deep breath and waited for a few more seconds.

"Hello, Ian Turnbull speaking."

"It's Solley Solomon here."

"Ah Mr Solomon, how can I help you?"

"My partner and I are going to make an offer tomorrow morning."

"Well that is good news. I am sure Lord Albright will be looking forward to hearing from you. However, I must warn you that there is a slight fly in the ointment so to speak."

"Oh, what kind of fly?"

"The Russian one we spoke of earlier to be exact," replied Turnbull.

Solley did not mention the conversation his secretary had had with a Russian, asking questions about his dealings.

"Now you know where we stand on this one," he said. "You'd better not let me down."

"The thing is Mr Solomon; I have a feeling that this Russian gentleman is going to make a significant offer despite my best efforts. One that I think will most certainly beat yours. However, there may be a way round this little problem of ours."

"Oh, and what might that be?" he asked, feeling as though he was about to get shafted.

"Well Lord Albright is – how shall I put this – slightly old fashioned. I believe that this interested new party is buying the old Sanatorium as part of a money-laundering operation."

"What makes you say that?"

"Nothing – I just made it up but if I were to tell Lord Albright that I had my suspicions, he would drop their offer like a hot potato."

"I'm not paying you any fucking more."

"Oh Mr Solomon, what do you take me for?" answered

Turnbull. "I think we should meet to discuss things properly – say tomorrow?"

"Tomorrow?" exclaimed Solley. "I only got back yesterday."

"Time is of the essence Mr Solomon."

"Ok, 6pm tomorrow."

—⁂—

Philip pulled in to the open space that looked out over the distant town. His mum and dad used to bring him up here along with his little sister at weekends. In the summer it had been ice cream and in the winter – when the weather would allow – it would be fish and chips. But what he loved most were the long walks that they would undertake across the windswept moors. The sense of freedom and the total isolation from everything that troubled him – here he felt safe with the people he most loved.

However, this was the first time he had been back here since the accident that so tragically killed his parents some eight years ago. He had driven past the very bend in the road where it had happened. It had been a late winter's afternoon – it seems the road had been icy after a heavy shower and his father lost control of their car just as a lorry came around the corner. The impact was so great that his parents' car was split in two, spinning them both out onto the cold black tarmac along with their still warm fish and chips.

He removed the large brown envelope addressed to F. Hibbard from the front passenger seat and began to read the documents that Reggie Carlyle was so desperate to get his hands on. It soon became apparent why and he was surprised that they still existed, for if what he suspected was true, then there would be a lot of embarrassed people – and a lot more than just embarrassment for some.

This was his chance to free himself and to make some money to boot but the question was how? Reggie still had Catherine. He was – as he had made quite clear – not a patient man and he would no

243

doubt be waiting impatiently for Frank to hand these papers over. If he pushed him too far there was no telling what he might do.

He sat there staring out over the patchwork of fields that lay spread out beneath him, with the town he had lived in all his life forming a dark uneven line on the horizon.

Of course; Turnbull, he thought.

— ∞ —

Ian opened his front door half expecting to find the local constabulary there. "Who the hell are you?" he said.

"You know who I am," replied Philip.

"I've no idea who you are; I've never set eyes on you before!"

"I believe you know a Frank Hibbard?"

Ian's anger at this stranger's intrusion evaporated on the sound of Frank's name. "You'd better come in."

Philip followed him into a large and ornately furnished sitting room.

"Ok," said Ian, "what do you have in common with Frank?"

"Let me introduce myself, my name is Philip Townsend."

Ian did not reply but slowly lowered himself onto the sofa, grabbing the bottle of brandy from the onyx coffee table as he did so. "What do you want?"

Philip took a glass from the silver tray that sat on top of a handsome sideboard and handed it to Turnbull.

"What do I want?" he said. "Now that is a leading question. Where do I begin? Oh, I know where – how silly of me. It was you who hired Frank Hibbard to blackmail me into removing certain documents. These documents you were going to use to twist Councillor Roberts' arm regarding planning permission, not to mention his brother-in-law."

"Whoa – hold on, I had no intention of involving Carlyle."

"Well it's too late for that, you already have, big time and he's not a happy man! Plus, he knows it was you who wanted these

244

documents. That's how I found out it was you who paid Frank to blackmail me."

"Look, all I wanted to do was turn the heat up a little on Roberts so as to make sure the planning application for the conversion of the old Sanatorium into luxury apartments went through without any problems. He carries a lot of influence round here but I don't have to tell you that. I only needed them for a day or two but my car was stolen and the papers went missing."

Philip took his glass of brandy and sat opposite Ian. "The thing I can't quite work out," he said, "is how did you know about these papers in the first place, and their significance regarding Roberts?"

"You might find this hard to believe but it was pure chance," explained Turnbull. "I was clearing out the attic when I found some old newspapers put up there to wrap things in. It was one of these that caught my eye – you know how it is, lift up a carpet and find some old newspapers – you can't just help but read them?

"Anyway, to cut a long story short, this was a local rag – out of print now for all of, well it must be fifteen years. Its front page covered the construction of the Commonwealth Games Village and how it should be built in such a way that it could be used as council housing afterwards. There was this small piece, quite insignificant really, about a local firm and how it was the only one involved in the construction and all the others were from outside the area."

"You mean Carlyle Construction?" asked Philip.

"Yes, they were the only local company involved. Oh, and of course, Hadway Aggregates, which in effect is a subsidiary of Carlyle Construction. The thing is that all the local companies were overlooked except for Carlyle Construction and Hadway Aggregates. It seems on the surface that Carlyle and his sister played only a small part in the construction work. But what a lot of people didn't know was that they had sub-contracted out the rest of the work for a very large sum of money to outside firms."

"How do you know all this?"

245

"Through Frank," replied Turnbull. "After I read the paper I contacted Frank to see if he knew anything. Apparently he did, he had a contact in Customs & Excise who had become suspicious and started an investigation which was immediately curtailed by his superiors."

Philip wondered if this could be the Billy Quinn Reggie mentioned, but then surely not, not from Carlyle's description.

Ian continued, "Of course this got me thinking, so I paid a visit on the off chance to one of your predecessors – William North – a name I recognised from a house I sold some years ago and who was also mentioned in the paper. Fortunately for me he was in need of money. I asked him if there were any documents relating to the construction of the Games Village, he said there were and where I could find them. The reason they had not been destroyed, or come to light until this present day, was because he had hidden them away among some old documents – only he knew where they were.

The problem was how to access them without Roberts finding out – that's where you came in. The question was – how to get you to get them for me. That's where Frank came into his own. I want you to know I am truly sorry for what happened to your wife."

"Speaking of my wife, do you have any idea as to where she is now?"

"No," he replied, looking a little guilty.

"She's with Carlyle," said Philip. "He's holding her until he gets these documents. He's waiting for them as we speak. And do you know where these documents are?"

"No," said Ian, eager to learn of their whereabouts.

"I have them."

"And how the hell did you get hold of them?"

"That is not of your concern."

"You came here for a reason – you could have taken these documents straight to Carlyle but there's something else on your mind – money."

"That's why I'm here," confirmed Philip. "I wanted to know why these documents were so important to you and what you were going to do with them?"

"You know full well what I was going to do with them. I wanted them to put pressure on Roberts."

"So this is related to the sale of the old Sanatorium?"

"So now you know – what's your price?"

Philip did not answer straight away but handed his glass to Ian for a refill.

"You don't seem to be in a rush to save your wife," he said, taking the glass from Philip.

"I see it this way – I could give Carlyle the documents and get my wife back but then what would I have? No job and with my record blemished by Roberts and his lies, little prospects of one. So this is what I propose. You will give me fifty percent of whatever you stand to make from this deal and I want £150,000 from both Carlyle and Roberts. After all they would have little or no choice, I haven't had the chance to read these documents fully but from what you have told me they seem pretty damning. But first, we need to find this contact of Frank's – keep him safe. Do you know where we can find him?"

"No idea," replied Ian. "As far as I know, he lives on the streets. Hard to imagine really – one minute you're someone high up in Customs & Excise, the next you're eating out of a bin. Wait a minute, what about your wife?"

"As long as we, or should I say I, have these documents, she will be safe."

"I wouldn't count on it, he's a crazy bastard. I think the best thing you could do is hand over these papers and get your wife back and draw a line under the whole thing."

"That would suit you would it not? After all, Roberts would no doubt make sure this application your client's want will go through just to keep a lid on things and you would make a tidy profit. When I get what I want then they can have the documents."

"You're stark raving mad, Carlyle will never agree to that. You would risk your wife for a few grand?"

"You see, that's where Carlyle has made a mistake. He thinks I would do anything to get her back but I'll tell you this – she's nothing but a slag. I know what she was doing next door with that Nick Tobin and that tart of a wife of his. He was taking turns in fucking both of them at these so-called coffee mornings. Oh she was clever mind you, said I should come over some times and that they were really nice. What did she take me for? Of course, they would be when I was there but as soon as my back was turned they would be at it again. So you know what I did?"

"No?" said Ian, stepping back slightly as Philip got to his feet. This seemingly placid non-descript man had taken on a new demeanour. His eyes were wide, his movements sharp and agitated. Turnbull was frightened of upsetting him in his present state – there was no telling what he might do.

"I broke into their house, smashed the place up and pinned that fucking yapping mutt of theirs to the kitchen door with a carving knife. After that she could not stand to be in the place so they moved over to Long Meadows. And do you know what that conniving wife of mine did?

"No," said Ian, feeling extremely uncomfortable.

"Drove over there once a week to get a good seeing-to, that's what she did. All that I had done for her and that's how she repaid me. But I put a stop to that. Do you know Sheepcot Lane?"

"Yes."

"Well that's the way she used to come home after her visits to them. I hired three men to attack her. You know the sharp bend before the turn to Wendover?"

Turnbull nodded.

Philip continued, "I covered my face and stepped out into the road as she was slowing for the bend. When she stopped, the men I had hired dragged her from her car and off into the woods. I drove her car into a deserted parking area and left her with them.

So if you think you or anyone can use her to get at me, you're wrong!"

"So how come you agreed to take the documents if Catherine means so little to you?"

"My career – that's what matters to me – and being happily married to a normal woman and not some kind of nympho-whack-job is an important part of that. If they found out what had happened to her, then I'll be bypassed for promotion. You know something? I feel a weight has been taken off my mind. I have never told anyone that story before so you see how much I trust you," he smiled.

—m—

"Oh, and that's another thing" said Joe to Keith as he handed him a cup of coffee, "You stay away from her unless Mr Carlyle says otherwise."

"Ok," he replied, "but it is tempting knowing she's just through that door. Don't tell me you wouldn't want to yourself. I mean, how often do you get to meet a woman like that? Maybe this husband of hers won't co-operate. Do you think Reggie…?"

"Mr Carlyle to you," said Joe.

"Ok, but do you think he will let us loose on her?"

"Maybe, hard to tell, you never know with Mr Carlyle. He might let her go or cut her up and feed her to the pigs."

"Don't say that," replied Keith. "What a waste."

—m—

"Hi, Solley, I have been trying to get you all afternoon."

"I've been busy, make it brief."

"Look I shouldn't have spoken to you like that earlier, it was wrong of me. I know you would never use Kim as an excuse – or anyone for that matter – that's why I respect you so much. You say what's on your mind, no nonsense."

"I take it this is an apology," replied Solley curtly.

"Of course it's a bloody apology, what I said was inexcusable."

"I accept your apology. I know you have been under a lot of pressure recently but it still came as a shock."

"Tell you what, after I've seen Kim tomorrow, I'll take you out to lunch – anywhere you fancy, I'll leave it up to you to book a place. Make it for three; it would be nice for Julie to come too."

"I can't do that."

"Oh come on, I'm trying to make amends here."

"I know, it's a nice gesture but I have a meeting tomorrow at 6pm with Ian Turnbull."

"So soon?" asked Paul. "What's it about?"

"Sounds as though he's fishing for another hand-out."

"Well you know what I think – nothing in the way of sweeteners until we have planning and the deal is signed."

"That's what I told him but it seems as though there's another hand in the ring."

"Oh, who?"

"Not too sure, but it seems as though a Russian is trying to offload some cash."

"Do you reckon it's kosher?"

"Could be, the other day Jackie spoke to this bloke, he was asking all sorts of questions and she reckoned he had a Russian accent."

"Hold on," he said as Kim entered the room from the en-suite before making her way back to bed, aided by her sister.

"Is that Solley?" she asked.

"Yeah."

"Good, I hope you two have made up."

"You make us sound like a couple of schoolkids."

"You are most of the time and what's this I hear about a Russian?"

"Hold on a sec Solley," he said before addressing her. "Solley's got to go up North tomorrow. It seems there's another player involved."

"Does he know who?"

"No, just that he thinks he's Russian."

"You'd better go with him."

"No, I don't think that's a good idea, I've only just got back."

Kim dropped her eyes, "Do as I tell you, I'm in good hands, there's nothing you can do here unless you fancy spring cleaning the house for when I get home?"

He smiled, "Solley, it looks as though you'll have me for company tomorrow."

"That's fine by me but what about Kim?"

"She won't have it any other way."

"Ok, I'll phone Margaret, see if she has room."

"No, leave that to me."

"Ok, please yourself, I'll see you about 12ish; that should give us plenty of time to get there."

—⁂—

Philip moved a little closer to Ian, his eyes now narrowed to tiny slits. "You are to arrange a meeting with Carlyle and Roberts," he said, "somewhere quiet but public. They are to bring Catherine with them and hand her over with the money. In return I will give them the documents."

"Carlyle will never go for that."

"Then he can keep the bitch and I'll make these documents public knowledge with evidence to back them up. After all, what do I have to lose?"

"You're on your own with this," said Ian, "I want nothing to do with it."

"It's too late for that my friend, and if you don't do as I tell you then I'll go to the police. No, better still, I'll tell Reggie that you have the documents. But of course, you won't will you? But then again, Mr Carlyle is a reasonable man wouldn't you say? I'm sure as soon as you explain to him that it is really me that has them, he will believe you and forget all about it."

Philip paused and placed his finger to his bottom lip. "But then again, he might not and why should I lie? All I want is my beloved wife back. Remember, it was you that got Frank Hibbard to blackmail me for the documents in the first place and he knows that. No, I think if it comes to my word against yours, I am pretty confident he will believe me – after all he knows you're involved with the sale."

He looked over Ian's shoulder to the onyx mantelpiece, "I take it that's a picture of your daughter," he said.

"You leave her out of this."

"It's a nasty world we live in – you only have to look at what's happened to my poor wife."

Ian lunged forward and grabbed Philip by the throat but to his surprise he was immediately overpowered and thrust back against the wall.

"Ok, ok, I'll do it," said Ian.

He eased back from Turnbull, "Of course you will. As I said, you have no choice."

—⁜—

Paul looked up to a sound of a knock on the door. A young and very attractive Filipino woman entered and placed a tray of food on the table, turning it so it sat across the bed in front of Kim.

"Thank you," said Kim.

The young woman smiled and left.

"The room might be as good as the clinic but the food – well, look for yourself!"

"It looks ok to me," replied Paul, taking a spoon from the tray and helping himself to some potato and gravy.

"That's because you grew up eating your mother's cooking," she retorted.

"She wasn't that bad," said Paul in his mother's defence.

Kim lowered her head and glowered at him.

"Ok, so she was no fancy cook," he admitted, "but we all survived."

"That's as maybe, but I want to do more than that."

"Made your mind up?" he asked, shovelling into his mouth more of the congealed glutinous mess that covered the plate in a brown sticky pool, with only the half-cooked broccoli stalk tenuous enough to break the surface. Whatever else lay underneath remained a mystery; one that Kim had no intentions of uncovering.

"What do you think Sherlock?"

"Thought as much, I told Mr Kahn that you would probably rather go back to the clinic."

Once again, Paul and Kim were interrupted, but this time it was Mr Kahn himself.

"I just called by to let you know that I have sent Mr Rathbone the details of our findings," he said, "and that he is happy for you to return tomorrow."

—⚊—

Catherine looked at the stale bread, its corners turned up revealing the crudely sliced cheese, and the glass of water next to it with tiny bubbles of oxygen clinging to its sides. She watched as occasionally one would break free and rise to the surface. She had no idea as to what all this was about, but it was no game that was for sure and she knew she would have to eat something.

She picked up the bread and closed her eyes; its rough dry texture grating the roof of her mouth. Reaching across the table she took hold of the glass and gulped at its tepid contents, forcing the mouthful of stale sandwich down her throat, then forced herself to repeat the process until she had finished.

Apart from a soiled mattress, the room was devoid of furnishings. It was then, for the first time, she noticed that there were no windows, the only light came from a naked 40-watt lightbulb. The room was nothing more than a large cupboard.

Catherine tensed as she heard the sound of a key being placed in the lock. The door opened slowly to reveal a black void and she tried to make out who was shrouded by its shadow.

17

"What time is it?"

"6.30am."

"What?"

"Do you want coffee?" asked Solley.

"Does it look like I want coffee?" said Marco as he pulled the duvet over his head.

"You should try getting up early now and again, it's quite rewarding," said Solley, making his way to the en-suite bathroom.

Marco threw back the duvet and slumped out of bed.

Solley looked over his shoulder, "Where are you going?" he asked, mouth full of toothbrush.

"To make some breakfast."

"I was only pulling your leg."

"No, you're right. I was just thinking the other day it was time I did more."

"You pay your share."

"I don't mean that," he said, pushing his feet into his fluffy slippers. "I have become lazy and you don't help."

"Oh that's right, blame me."

"I'm not blaming you for anything, it's just you encourage my lazy side by doing everything from the shopping to the washing."

"Well I wouldn't let that unsettle your conscience. The

shopping's on-line – well most of it – and apart from a few bits, Clara does the rest."

"Look, when was the last time I sold anything?"

"Err, not sure."

"See – you can't remember."

"Why, are you short of money?"

"Hell no; I sold all my work from the previous year and the prints and photos are selling like there's no tomorrow but I've not touched a brush for nearly ten months. I am worried I have lost my edge."

Solley came out of the bathroom, toothbrush in hand. "Oh, I see, is this your way of telling me it's over between us?"

"Where the hell did that come from? Of course fucking not but I know we need to do something and I believe I know what it is," confessed Marco as he followed him.

Solley returned to the bathroom and rinsed his mouth before sitting on the edge of the Edwardian bathtub. "Go on then, enlighten me," he said.

"We have plenty of money and time."

"Speak for yourself!" he interrupted.

"Oh don't give me that – you're rolling in it, not to mention your property portfolio – what's it worth now, £8million; £9million?"

"Not quite," replied Solley quietly.

"Ok, so it's £7million," said Marco dismissively.

"That's all very well but I don't have any spare time."

"That's bollocks too. You have a great team and from what I've seen of things, if anything, you get in their way."

"Oh, thanks for your vote of confidence."

"Don't you recognise a compliment when you hear one?"

"Ok, fair enough. Now let's hear what it is you have on your mind."

"Charity work," announced Marco.

"Sorry?"

"We take a year off," he continued, "and travel to Africa and help with a building or water project."

"Now I'm regretting that I ever suggested you get up early, it obviously doesn't agree with your brain," remarked Solley, turning on the bath taps.

"I'm serious and I want you to take it seriously too."

He turned off the taps. "Ok, let me give it some thought, it's such a monumental decision plus now I have this big new project on the go."

"What new project?" asked Marco, raising his eyebrows quizzically.

"The hospital conversion up North."

"You told me last night that that was off because of Paul's wife. Has she all of a sudden made a miraculous recovery?"

"No, of course not, I jumped the gun," he explained. "I naturally thought after this mugging business, the whole thing would have to be called off but I spoke to Kim just after you went out last night, and she was adamant for it to go ahead."

"Well you could have told me."

"I would have done but I took a sleeping pill, I was restless after the drive. And that's another thing," he added, "what time did you get in last night?"

"3.30am," replied Marco somewhat guiltily.

"Well then, I couldn't have told you until now. Anyway, I'm going to have a shower."

"I thought you were having a bath?"

"I've changed my mind; it happens you know."

Marco made his way out of the bathroom to the sound of a high-pitched yelp.

"Do you need it so hot?" shouted Solley from under the cascade of steaming water as he fumbled for the controls.

—m—

Reggie stepped into the windowless room. "I trust you are being taken care of," he said in a low voice.

"Please let me go," pleaded Catherine. "I won't tell anyone."

"Tell anyone what? You have not been mistreated in my absence, have you?"

"No, but you have no right to hold me here against my will."

"I think there's been a misunderstanding. Nobody's holding you here against your will, you're quite free to go," he said stepping back from the unlit doorway to reveal two of his heavies. "However, I must warn you that we are a little isolated here and my assistants tell me that a couple of the attack dogs have gone missing – isn't that right boys?"

"Yes boss," replied the taller of the two.

"You could wait until we find them or let us take you to your husband."

"Yes, yes, I would like that," she replied.

"Good, I must say your husband has turned out to be somewhat of a surprise, it seems he's quite a gambler, also I think there's something you should know about him – or rather about his past. But before I tell you, I think it's only fair that my assistants here have a little fun, after all they have been working very hard recently," said Reggie, removing his phone from his pocket.

The two men moved into the room pulling black ski masks on over their heads, then took hold of Catherine and threw her down onto the soiled mattress. Reggie switched his phone on to camera and, with a smile on his face, started to film the sordid events as they unfolded.

—⚬—

"Ian, it's Frank. You have to get me out of here right now."

His wife looked across at him. "Who's that darling?"

"No-one you know," replied Ian as she poured the boiling water into the teapot. "Yes, I will see to it straight away," he said, returning his attention to the phone.

"What the hell are you talking about?" said Frank.

"The day after tomorrow will be fine."

It was then that Frank realised Ian could not talk freely. "Ok, I got it," he said. "Now listen, I need you to come to the hospital to collect me. They say I can't leave unless there's someone to look after me. I must get out of here, those documents you lost – I know where they are."

"Hold on, I think that was someone at the door," said Ian. "Would you be a dear and get it," he said to his wife, "I'm expecting something important."

He watched as his wife left the kitchen. "What the hell are you talking about?" he said. "I had that Philip Townsend round here last night. He told me he had the documents."

"Well he doesn't, they were posted to my office the other day."

"But you don't have an office anymore."

"I fucking know that but I asked Mr Bhutan to look after them for me. Now get the hell over here now."

"Hold on a sec, you told me you were in negotiations for them, how the fuck did they end up in the post?"

"Quite simply, I handed them over an envelope with my office address on it and watched them place the documents in the envelope. It was posted as I handed the money over."

"So you're telling me you handed over ten fucking grand of my money and you have nothing to show for it... Oh, hello dear, I won't be a minute."

"Look it'll be ok," said Frank, "you'll have to just wait a little bit longer, that's all."

"You must be hearing things darling," said Ian's wife, "there's no-one there."

"Sorry?" he replied, grabbing his car keys.

"You asked me to check the door."

"Did I? Right."

"Where are you going off to in such a hurry?" she asked. "You haven't touched your breakfast."

"Something's come up," he explained, making his way down the hall followed by his wife.

"Well you just make sure you're back by noon," she said. "Don't forget we're meeting Jane and Malcolm over at The Three Feathers."

Ian closed the door abruptly in her face without the slightest acknowledgement of her concerns. "Well that's nice!" she remarked.

He pressed the button on his key fob and waited impatiently for the garage doors to open. Before they were fully raised he ducked under the metal shutter, ignoring his neighbour's cheery good morning. He placed the key into the ignition and paused.

What the fuck was going on? he thought. *Why on earth would Townsend tell him he had the documents if he didn't? He must have them or why would he set up a meeting with that nutcase Carlyle? But then again, how the hell did he get his hands on them if what Frank had told him was true – and there seemed to be no advantage in lying? There was only one way to find out, he would have to see things through. He was up to his neck in it and the murky waters were rising fast!"*

—⁓—

"I have to say, this feels somewhat strange," said Solley as he eased off the slip road and merged with the fast-moving traffic, heading North for the second time in two days.

"How do you mean?" asked Paul nervously, eyeing the stream of vehicles as Solley edged his way across to the overtaking lane where they would no doubt stay until their exit some 240 miles later.

"Us doing this while Kim's – you know, in hospital," he explained. "This mugging business after what she's gone through. I just feel guilty, that's all."

"And you think I don't?"

"That's not what I mean."

"No I know; I'm sorry. But you heard what she said and God

knows how I'm going to concentrate on anything but this is not about what *I* want."

"I know, but somehow it just doesn't seem right."

"Ok, you tell me what I should do."

Solley now found himself on the spot without a reply, after all, who could possibly know what was the right thing to do in such circumstances? However, this time he was spared the embarrassment of trying to answer an impossible question as his hands-free phone rang.

"Solley here, what can I do for you?"

It was Margaret. "I know this sounds very unprofessional but I was wondering if you and Paul would mind sharing the bridal suite. You see, I seem to have a bit of a rush on, and I really need the money."

"Well it's fine by me but I will have to consult my partner."

He looked across at Paul who had heard every word. Paul shrugged his shoulders. "What the hell," he said.

"The bridal suite you say?"

"Don't worry," said Margaret, "I'll only charge you for the singles. Alan's up there now separating the beds."

"That sounds a little odd. Who wants separate beds in a bridal suite?"

"Oh you'd be surprised. Most couples have lived with each other for years nowadays before tying the knot and sometimes we get older couples that are having a second honeymoon," she explained.

"Ok, then the bridal suite it is."

—⚬⚬⚬—

"I don't like this one bit," said Roberts as Reggie sipped the last few drops of Earl Grey from his bone china cup. "And where's Townsend's wife now?"

"She's outside with Keith and Joe."

"What!" he exclaimed, getting to his feet.

"Sit down," said Reggie. "No-one can see her, and as to whether you like it or not, that's the way it is. These documents could see us go down for a long stretch."

"Hold on a minute, I had nothing to do with any of this; this whole scam was set up by you and Sylvia."

"You are a miserable, spineless pile of lard at times."

Roberts looked over to the doorway to see his wife standing there. "Come on, fair's fair," he said.

"I'll tell you what's fair," said Sylvia, "you sticking up for me – that's fair. Just look around you, this house, the swimming pool, the cars, not to mention the holidays and everything fucking else I have paid for! You owe me and don't think for one minute you can worm your way out of this one because I'm going to make it quite clear that you knew everything that was happening."

"Ok, but kidnapping and holding her hostage, that's in a different league altogether."

"And it's a league, that like it or not, you're now in," added Reggie, "so we have no choice but to work together."

Roberts took a deep breath and resigned himself to his fate. "So when are we meeting Turnbull?" he asked. "And there's another thing, how did Townsend get hold of the documents if Billy Quinn had them?"

"That I can't say but Turnbull would not have arranged this meeting unless he had something for us," answered Reggie. "We're to meet this evening at a small hotel in the middle of nowhere called the High Gate."

"I know the place but I have a better idea."

"Oh, what's that?" asked Sylvia.

"The old Sanatorium – we could all meet there; sort this mess out and go our separate ways. It's only a few miles from the hotel."

"Turnbull would never go for that," said Reggie. "He wants the security of somewhere public but also somewhere we can have a modicum of privacy."

"You know, it still might be for the best if I don't come with you," said Roberts. "After all, I am a public figure and the owner of that hotel had applied for planning permission which I refused, so it might be awkward."

"No, I disagree; I think it would give us a sense of legitimacy having Councillor Roberts with us – a respected public figure. I'll get Keith to bring our new friend in for a bath and some clean clothes."

"You lost your bloody mind? I can't have her in this house."

"And why not, she's already sitting in your driveway. As I have said, it's too late to try and hide from this, plus you're starting to worry me and that makes me nervous. And when that happens, I can't think rationally and sometimes I do things to people that afterwards, even I find somewhat disturbing."

Roberts looked at his wife for some show of support but none was forthcoming. In spite of having been married for over twenty years, she was – and always would be – a Carlyle first. Defeated, he slumped back into the sofa.

"Have it your way," he said simply.

"I always do," replied Reggie, retrieving his phone from his jacket pocket. "Bring the girl in."

Sylvia left the room and opened the front door but despite her hard nature even she felt empathy for this poor creature that now stood forlorn on her doorstep.

"Leave her with me," she said, taking Catherine's hand and leading her to the staircase.

"Well then," said Reggie, "now we have that sorted, I'll see you at 7pm sharp. And don't let me down."

"There's just one thing before you go," said Roberts.

"Oh, and what's that?"

"What am I supposed to do with her?"

"Quite simply take her with you tonight. Oh, of course, along with your share of the money. I'll see myself out."

Sylvia escorted Catherine to the large, marble tiled bathroom. "Well, what are you waiting for?" she said, standing in the doorway.

"Sorry?" she replied in a pathetically low voice.

"Get your clothes off. I'll wash them and put them through the dryer."

Catherine started to unbutton her blouse. "Look, you'll have to help me" she pleaded.

Sylvia stepped into the bathroom, locked the door and started to unbutton the blouse. It was then, without warning, Catherine grabbed her. She tried to pull herself free of Catherine's grip but found it impossible to break her hold.

For the first time since her ordeal had started, Catherine felt as though she had gained some sort of control, but what surprised her most was this strength that seemed to have appeared from nowhere.

—⁙—

Roberts made his way into the garden and along the cobbled path to what he liked to think of as his sanctuary which consisted of little more than a modest 10foot x 8foot shed. It was the only place where he felt comfortable. Despite his brash and overbearing personality, he was a lonely man. He had never really had what one could call real friends, he always felt it was this inability to get on with others socially that had made him so determined to succeed, at whatever cost. However, it seemed as though he would now have to pay the price. But then again, he always knew that someday he would.

He removed the padlock and closed the door behind him as he entered the shed. Along one side was a bench with his tools carefully arranged but what made this place so special to him, was an old armchair. Sylvia had been on to him for ages to throw it out and she had even threatened to get someone in, but one afternoon while she was out shopping, he manhandled the decaying piece of furniture to his place of refuge.

—⁙—

The more Sylvia tried to free herself, the more Catherine's vice like grip tightened around her arms and she now felt that she was losing control and started to panic – a situation she was not accustomed to – finally submitting and calling out for her husband.

—◊—

Roberts closed his eyes as the sound of a string quartet filled his ears.

—◊—

The two women crashed to the floor with Catherine on top, legs either side. Scattered about them were items from the bathroom cabinet which had been ripped from the wall by Sylvia as she fought to stay on her feet. There, just inches from her finger tips, lay a pair of scissors.

Now fearing for her life as Catherine's powerful hands compressed the flabby flesh around her windpipe, Sylvia grabbed the scissors and stabbed her in the upper thigh. But to her consternation she was not released, instead she felt herself being hoisted to her feet, turned around towards the sink and having her head smashed against it.

Catherine then started to shake her violently from side to side and Sylvia now knew she had no choice but to kill this deranged woman. Suddenly she felt herself being released and instinctively made for the bathroom door. Fumbling with the bolt she could not free it in time as she felt her head twist as Catherine took hold of her peroxide blonde hair and swung her across the bathroom, hitting her face on the edge of the free-standing Edwardian bath. This sickening blow made Sylvia nauseous, causing her to puke. Desperately, she tried to regain her feet, but with the floor now lubricated with her vomit and the blood from Catherine's wound, she could not gain purchase on the slippery tiles.

Catherine could feel her opponent getting weaker. However,

this did not manifest itself into any form of sympathy on her part whatsoever but acted as a form of encouragement. Not wanting to lose her hard-won advantage, she repeatedly smashed Sylvia's face on the edge of the bath, her broken teeth pinging off the shiny enamel then settling into the growing pool of blood that had now formed a sticky conveyor belt carrying the pieces of shattered enamel inexorably towards the plughole.

—❦—

Roberts punched the air in time with Beethoven's 5th Symphony.

—❦—

Catherine suddenly became aware that Sylvia had become extremely heavy, almost a dead weight. As she released her, she watched her face slip down the side of the bath, leaving a crimson smear. Wasting no time, she made her way out onto the landing and down the stairs to find the front door locked.

—❦—

Roberts placed the padlock back with great reverence and turned to see Catherine just feet from him, spade in hand.

—❦—

She climbed the back fence and made her way into the woods that adjoined the property but the question was what to do now? She could not go to the police, not after what she had done. *So what next?* she thought. Could anyone connect her to what had just happened? After all, she had been taken there against her will. She needed to find Philip. She could get home cross-country only having to negotiate a couple of minor roads for the last thing she wanted was anyone to see her in this state. She would get rid of these clothes and shower off. Philip would know what to do, he always did.

—⁓—

Frank signed the release form and limped his way along the corridor with the assistance of Ian.

"So why did Townsend come round to my house and give me all that bullshit about his neighbours, and that it was him who stopped his wife's car the night she was attacked, and say that he has the documents if he hasn't?"

"It's obvious," replied Frank, "he wants his wife back and there's only one way he knows how – make everyone think he has the files."

"And then what?"

"He's desperate; he's hoping he will think of something. It's his only hope, poor bastard."

"I'm not so sure," replied Ian. "He seemed very convincing."

"Look, I told you, he can't possibly have them. Ok – did he show them to you?"

"Err, no, not exactly."

"What do you mean *not exactly?*" asked Frank, holding tight to Ian's arm.

"He does have a summary sheet."

"So, he probably kept that when he removed the files. You know what his kind of people are like – need to keep something back."

"Look, I have…" Ian paused. He was just about to tell Frank of the meeting he had arranged this evening with Carlyle but at the last second decided not to.

"What is it?"

"Oh, nothing," he replied. *Maybe it would be best if this meeting did go ahead,* he thought, *bring everything out into the open as it were. This thing would have to resolve itself one way or another.*

He looked across at Frank, "So where do you want me to take you?"

"To my sister's, she's away for a couple of weeks, I'll organise things from there."

"Are you sure that's a good idea? The last thing you want is Reggie turning up on your sister's doorstep."

"Yeah, you're right. You could always put me up in a hotel?" he added.

Ian turned his head and looked him in the eye.

"What do you think I am – made of fucking money?"

"Ok, it was just a suggestion."

"No wait a minute, do you know what, that's not such a bad idea and funnily enough, I know just the right place."

Frank stopped, "Are you stupid or something, how the fuck am I going to get down there?"

"Oh, of course," Ian turned him away from the stairway and helped him towards the elevator.

—※—

Catherine hid herself at the edge of the road as a white builder's van sped past, lowering her head as pieces of small stone and mud shot in her direction. She waited for the vehicle to disappear round the bend before making a dash for the other side but as she got to her feet, she felt a sharp pain rip through her upper leg. The stab wound Sylvia had inflicted on her had gone mostly un-noticed but now she was almost home the adrenalin had started to wear off. It was all too apparent that the injury might be more substantial than she first thought.

Every step was met with agony as she limped through the densely packed trees that bordered the back of their house, but her ordeal would soon be over. It then dawned on her that she might be seen by her neighbours so she did her best to try and smarten herself as much as circumstances would allow, took a deep breath, stepped out of the wood and made her way to the back gate where she lifted the latch.

"Shit, please, please no," she said.

She tried again but it was no use, the gate was bolted from the inside. Why this had come as such a surprise to her was odd to say the least, the gate had always been locked. Why the hell did she even try to get in this way in the first place? She looked along the line of almost identical fences – they seemed to stretch for ever in both directions.

It was then she heard a noise. "Philip, is that you?" She stepped back slightly, holding her right hand to her chest. "Oh, Mr Brown, you startled me."

"I am sorry my dear, I didn't know you were there. I was just about to trim the Leylandii; Dorothy has been on at me to do something with it for ages. Mind you, if it was down to her, she would get rid of the thing altogether, but as I told her, the blackbirds like to nest in it. You have to look out for nature nowadays you know."

"Yes, quite; I seem to be in a bit of a fix" she added.

"Oh, how come?"

"I came out through the front door and forgot my key. The back's open but this gate is bolted from the inside. Seeing as you have your step ladder, I wonder if you could lean over and undo it for me."

"Shall I call Philip?" he asked.

"No, he's not in."

"Oh, that's strange, the car's there and I'm sure I saw him only ten minutes ago."

"He's in the loft," she replied hastily. "Laying some boards, he won't hear the doorbell."

"I thought you said he was out?"

"Please, could you just lean over and undo the gate?"

"Oh very well." Henry did as requested, and she pushed her way through and up to the house. Philip looked up from the kitchen sink, at first not registering what he was seeing and she fell against the back door just as he opened it. He pulled her inside and closed the door but as he did so, he saw Mr Brown peering over the fence, a look of bewilderment written across his face.

Catherine slumped to the kitchen floor, her arms tight around his legs, her sobbing becoming almost hysterical. It was then that he noticed her blood-stained leg and the state of her hair. He lifted her to her feet and started to strip off her clothes.

"What are you doing?" she cried.

But he didn't answer as he tipped her over onto her back and pulled off her skirt and tights. She now found herself naked on the cold kitchen floor as he shoved her clothes into a plastic bag then grabbed a tea towel, ripping it almost in half, and tied it round her leg to stem the flow of blood. He pulled her to her feet, hoisted her over his shoulder and carried her upstairs to the bathroom, dumping her unceremoniously into the bath tub.

Philip turned the shower on to maximum and she squealed as the jet of cold water smashed against her naked body. He opened a bottle of shampoo and poured the entire contents over her head. Fortunately, the water was now warm, almost hot and she closed her eyes as he rubbed the shampoo into her hair. Despite his less than gentle manner, she felt a great sense of relief as the soapy water cascaded over her skin.

He then removed the blood-soaked rag and put it in the bin for sanitary wear and examined the wound. Fortunately, the bleeding had now started to ease.

"Stay there," he said. "I'll get you some hot sweet tea."

Catherine sat motionless in the bath, the hot shower streaming over her, and watched the water, tinged pink by the blood from the small but deep wound in her upper thigh, as it drifted down between her legs and then swirled around the plughole before disappearing from sight. She was no fool, she knew this ordeal was far from over but she was home, in her own house, with Philip, safe for now.

19

Alan looked up as Margaret entered the kitchen, "How did you get on with those beds?" she asked.

"Fine; one of the legs is loose but I think I managed to fix it."

"I hope so," she replied, "the last thing I want is for it to collapse in the middle of the night. Sit down a minute, I'll make some coffee, I've been meaning to talk to you."

Alan's stomach turned over, he knew the place had been struggling and this was obviously it. Ok, so the money wasn't great but it was better than nothing and what's more, he liked working for Margaret.

"I don't think I can manage this place without you," she continued, "how would you like to work here full time?"

"Are you serious?"

"Of course I am. I won't be able to increase your hourly rate – not until things pick up. And that's the dilemma – I have two choices – make a go of this place, which is where I need you – or give up. What do you say?"

Alan hesitated for a moment. "Ok, I'll give it a shot."

"Good, that's a great weight off my mind. Do you have a suit? Don't worry; you won't have to wear it often. When you've finished with the wood pile I want you to go home, get changed and come back this afternoon. What are you like at cooking?"

"Err, not sure, not really tried."

"Well ok then, this afternoon you will have your first cooking lesson."

—⁂—

As Roberts opened his eyes, it felt as though there was a heavy weight resting across the back of his neck. He tried getting to his feet but no sooner had he lifted his head, than he felt a wave of nausea wash over him. Finally, after several more attempts, he managed to get to his feet and stagger up the garden path.

The back door was wide open and he reached the kitchen just in time to throw up in the sink. Grasping the counter top with both hands he retched several times before sitting on one of the chrome and black leather chairs that stood sentinel around the large smoked glass dining table.

He desperately tried to recount events but everything seemed to be a blur. Sylvia had told him to get someone in to fix that section of loose cobbles. *I must have tripped and hit my head on the wall,* he thought.

He made his way into the hall and shouted for Sylvia, wincing each time, but his plaintive cries for assistance went unheeded. Still unsteady, he went along the hall. At first it didn't register but on closer examination he could make out what looked like specks of blood on the ivory carpet. He followed the crimson trail up the stairs to the bathroom, its door slightly ajar.

"Sylvia, are you in there?" he called.

Placing an unsteady hand on the handle he eased the door open. The sight that met him beggared belief. There in the middle of the floor lay Sylvia, her body curled tight, blood splattered over the travertine floor and white sanitary wear giving the impression of some kind of high-class abattoir. He felt for her pulse – she was still alive. Roberts retrieved his phone.

"Reggie, it's me. Get over here now and bring Dr Hussein with you."

He went back downstairs to the fridge and grabbed a bag of ice and large packet of frozen peas before returning upstairs then using a towel he wrapped them around Sylvia's head.

Dr Hussein had proved useful in the past; Reggie had helped smuggle his brother over from Iran – for a fee of course – but he also knew that having a doctor in his debt would be very useful. Now Roberts would benefit from his brother-in-law's foresight, as if he turned up to A&E with his wife in this state, he would face some very awkward questions – the kind he wanted to avoid at all costs – after all, what excuse could he possibly give for the type of injuries his wife had sustained? Domestic violence would be the first port of call for anyone's imagination.

Still unsteady he made his way downstairs to answer the front door.

"What's all this about?" demanded Reggie.

"Where's Dr Hussein?" asked Roberts, looking over his shoulder.

"He's on his way. Do you mind telling me what's going on?"

Roberts led him up to the scene of carnage.

"What the bloody hell happened here?" exclaimed Reggie.

"That fucking bitch that's what."

"She did this?"

"No, I fucking did," he replied sarcastically.

"So what happened and where were you?"

"Sylvia brought her up here to get cleaned up. I was outside in the shed."

"That must be Hussein," said Reggie as the doorbell rang. "I'll go and let him in, you get something to clean this mess up. Do you have any plastic sheets?"

"What?"

"Oh never mind, there might be one in the car," he replied as he went downstairs to answer the door.

After what seemed to be a whole bath tub of water and cleaning agent, the bathroom was almost back to normal. Roberts went into the bedroom to find Sylvia lain out on the bed, a plastic sheet stretched out under her.

"Will she be ok?" he asked.

"From what I can tell, she should be all right," replied Dr Hussein. "But it's not possible to be absolutely sure unless she has a brain scan."

"No hospitals," said Reggie. "She'll be fine, Sylvia's a tough cookie."

"That's as maybe, but she will need extensive dental surgery."

"Leave that to me, I know someone who can see to that discreetly."

Dr Hussein gave Roberts a list of things to look out for and said to contact him if he noticed anything untoward. He placed some painkillers on the bedside. "I'll be back tomorrow, 7.30am."

Roberts sat on the edge of the bed and held his wife's hand. Her face was almost unrecognisable from the massive amount of swelling; her lips were puffed and split. Despite their differences he had always loved her, although he could never be sure if it was reciprocal. But she was still here after all these years.

He looked up to see Reggie standing in the doorway, his face contorted with rage.

"I think you have some explaining to do."

"I told you what happened," he said, "and that's an end to it."

"No it's not, and where the hell were you while my sister was getting her brains bashed out on the edge of the bath tub?"

At first Roberts felt defensive, but then how could he possibly defend himself? Reggie was right. "As I told you, I was outside in the shed."

"And what the hell were you doing in there while your wife was fighting for her life?"

"I go there sometimes to listen to music – unwind, relieve the stress," he explained. "I'm just as upset as you – she is my wife after all. But honestly, who would have thought someone like that was capable of something so violent?"

Even Reggie had to admit to himself this was the last thing he would have expected, but he was not going to tell Roberts that, he wasn't going to let him off the hook that lightly. "Ok, so where do we go from here?"

"Sorry?"

"Where do we go from here?" repeated Reggie. "Are you deaf as well as incompetent?"

"No, I heard you first time."

"Ok, so let's hear it."

"I… I… don't know."

"No, of course you don't, because my friend, there is nowhere to go. Not only is my sister half-dead, but we have lost our only means of putting pressure on Townsend for those documents – if he actually has them."

"Still, I guess we are 300 grand better off," remarked Roberts, hoping this statement might take some of the heat off him.

Reggie remembered that look in Philip's eyes at Mario's. "Don't under-estimate him," he said, "he's a devious bastard, mark my words – and as they say, it takes one to know one."

"I might need to get this," said Roberts somewhat sheepishly as his phone rang.

"Yeah, whatever," replied Reggie, plonking himself down on the end of the bed.

"Ok… Right… We'll be there." He put his mobile back into his jacket pocket. "You won't believe who that was."

"No, don't tell me – Father Christmas?"

"You might say that. It was Townsend."

"Are you winding me up; because I'm not in the mood for that kind of nonsense?"

"And what's more," he continued, "he wants to keep the meeting for tonight."

"You serious?" said Reggie, raising himself up on the sofa.

"Yep," he replied proudly, as if he had somehow organised this strange turn of events.

"I don't know why you're so upbeat."

"Well I guess he wants to negotiate for the documents."

"Of course he does," replied Reggie.

"But at what cost to us? Remember, we have nothing to negotiate with. On the other hand, he could just have gone to the police, or the press even."

"No, he's not stupid," replied Reggie. "He's got his wife back and he still wants to cash in – and who could blame him? When's the next chance someone like him is going to get the opportunity to lay his hands on 300 grand? And that could only be for starters."

—⁓—

"Look, before we go to the hotel, let's take a wander up to the Sanatorium," suggested Paul as they turned off the motorway and onto the 'A' road that would lead them eventually to the narrow road that snaked its way over the moors.

"Ok, if you want," replied Solley. "There's a couple of pairs of boots in the back, thought we might end up there."

Finally, after what seemed like ages, they turned off the 'A' road and onto a narrow strip of tarmac known locally as the Ghost Road from a time when the corpses of highwaymen and vagabonds would be strung up along the roadside as a warning to whoever might be tempted to take advantage of those travelling this high and lonely moorland pass.

"There's something I ought to tell you," began Paul, looking across at Solley.

"Oh, what's that," he replied, slowing down for a quad bike taking up the middle of the road, ahead of about thirty sheep, while two mud-splattered dogs darted about, encouraging any stragglers to keep pace with the main flock.

"Looks like we could be here for some time," he remarked, keeping a reasonable distance. "So then, what's on your mind?"

"You know the other day I went to see the place while you were asleep?"

"I don't think that day's going to get pushed back to the recesses of my mind any time soon."

"Well there's something I think I ought to mention before we give the final ok to this project," he continued.

Solley lifted himself slightly out of his seat in order to see if there was any sign of a gate into which this son of the soil would lead his trusty flock. "Oh, and what's that?"

"I know you're going to tell me I'm losing it…"

"Go on, try me."

"You know I took my field glasses with me so as I could get a better look at the roof…"

"And you saw your phantom staring back at you," he quipped.

Paul ignored the remark and continued, "The thing is I was a little concerned with the hospital's past."

"Look that Nazi scientist stuff – it's just local bullshit. People out in places like this make up stories all the time. I mean what the bloody hell else is there to do round here?"

"Well anyway, I've been doing a little research."

"What?" he replied, a hint of incredulity in his voice. "When the hell did you get time for that?"

"I couldn't sleep so I started to trawl through various stuff on the Internet. I found this…"

He handed him a print off – it was a photograph of a young German soldier dressed in full SS regalia.

"That's Dr Herman Klost," he said. "The thing is; he went missing from the French sector just before his trial at Nuremburg."

"What had he done?" asked Solley, fully expecting Paul to give details of his part in the extermination of the Jewish people.

"Well that's the odd thing, not much by all accounts. His rank was – it seems – purely honorary, he was involved in food production; early genetics, bit like Mendel.

"Who?"

"You must have heard of Mendel and his peas?"

"Oh yeah – the flowering type."

"Yeah, that's him. Anyway, it was thought that he was brought to the UK secretly so as to help with the British food shortages after the war. It seems as though he discovered this bacterium that increased the nutrient value of bread and cheese – two of the nation's staples."

"Ok, so what?" doing his best to look at the photo and keep to the narrow road.

"Well this is where it gets a bit weird," he continued, "because that's the person I saw at the window."

Solley stopped the car suddenly and looked across at Paul. "Are you feeling ok?"

"Yes of course – well not really, but that has nothing to do with this and before you say anything else, I know what I saw. Remember, I had my field glasses and this face is the same one I saw early that morning."

"Don't be so bloody daft man. Ok let's assume – and I mean assume – there was someone there, that in itself would be strange enough, but one thing I can do and that's assure you that it's not some 100-year-old Nazi scientist that has somehow defied the aging process!"

"Ok, I agree with you, but it might be his grandson."

"What? You really are trying my patience; it was nothing more than a trick of the light."

"But if you think about it, it makes sense."

"No it bloody doesn't. You have a lot on your mind – you are just worried about Kim. It's funny how the mind can play tricks when you're concerned about something."

"Let's just imagine these rumours are true." Paul saw the look of disdain on his face. "Look, just humour me for a few seconds, that's all I'm asking."

Solley shrugged, "Ok," he said, "but I must warn you you're wasting your time."

"It's not impossible that he married a local girl and they had children – or perhaps he even got some poor girl in the club."

"Well, let's just say – and I'm only doing this to humour you – if that did happen, why on earth would he be there at that particular time and at six o'clock in the morning? None of it makes any sense whatsoever."

"I don't know," replied Paul quietly.

"Of course you don't. Look, I don't mean to sound obtuse or anything, but remember you accused me of trying to get out of this deal. If this is some kind of way of telling me you're not interested, you don't have to make up fantastical stories about 100-year-old Nazis or their possible descendants – I fully understand."

"No, I want this for Kim but believe me, I know what I saw."

This conviction of Paul's made Solley feel somewhat uncomfortable as he eased his foot on the accelerator as the last of the sheep disappeared off the road and into a nearby field, their canine minders in hot pursuit, and acknowledged the young lad on the quad bike, his cap low over his forehead, as they passed.

Solley pulled over onto the grass verge opposite the track that led up to the Sanatorium. He got out and carefully made his way round to the back of his car where he opened the boot, removed a pair of black wellingtons with yellow tips, placed them on the ground and sat on the edge of the trunk. He then removed one of his shoes and cautiously leaned forward to place his right foot into the boot.

Paul, now impatient, decided to see what was taking so long but as he got out of the car the shift in weight was enough to make Solley lose his balance at the crucial moment sending him head first into the sticky red mud.

"Bloody Nora!" he shouted as he made his way to the back of the vehicle to find his friend with one shoe on and one wellington half on floundering about on the wet grass like a fish on the river bank, cursing for all he was worth.

"The boots were a good idea," he said, retrieving his pair and slipping them on.

"Don't say another fucking word!" answered Solley, trying to get to his feet to find Paul resting on the rear nearside of the vehicle, arms folded and a look of incredulity written across his face.

"Me, what would I say?"

"That's two coats ruined in two days," he complained. "If I keep this up I'll be broke before we've finished."

"Well maybe you should wear something a little more appropriate for the countryside instead of a three grand camel hair coat."

Solley did not answer but slammed the boot with such force it made the car bounce on its suspension. "Ok?" he said, brushing mud from his jacket.

"I'm ok," he replied, his tight-lipped expression breaking into a broad grin as he surveyed his companion standing there covered in a mixture of soil and what one could only assume was sheep shit. In addition, his boots were not only far too big for him, but were also on the wrong feet.

Paul's attempts at discretion, now totally undermined by this comical appearance, meant that he could no longer contain himself and despite Solley's determination to maintain his displeasure, his laughter – now verging on hysterical – was so infectious, even he in his present state could not help but see the funny side and what the fuck? It was only a coat and in the scheme of things it was of no real importance.

Taking hold of Solley's left arm in order to help balance him while he changed his wellingtons to the correct feet they then made their way up the rutted track, rivulets of water running down the indentations.

"This'll cost a few grand to make up into a decent road."

But Paul did not answer, his attention being drawn to the horizon.

"What you looking at?"

"Up there," he pointed.

"What, I can't see anything?"

"No, it's gone now."

"What's gone?" asked Solley, screwing his eyes up in an attempt at catching a glimpse of this mysterious object. "You're not seeing things again are you?"

"Maybe, but it definitely looked like someone – might have been that bloke on his quad."

"I didn't hear anything."

"I don't suppose you would with this wind, and it's a long way away."

"Well if it was our sheep farmer friend having a nose, who could blame him – two city types turn up in a limousine and start trudging about the countryside – it's bound to raise suspicion."

"I guess you're right," he answered as he started to make his way up the track.

—⁂—

Philip opened what used to be his father's drinks cabinet and took out an unopened bottle of malt whisky and placed it with some reverence in the centre of the table. He then retrieved a crystal tumbler and sat it next to the bottle. It would be there waiting for him when he returned, just like his mother had done for his father every Friday evening.

But this bottle was special; it had been presented to his father for his part in the construction and maintenance of the massive Kariba Dam in Africa. He had always maintained that he would open it on his retirement but their unfortunate car accident had interceded this modest promise to himself.

However, this would indeed be a time for celebration, thought Philip. His wife was back, and after this ordeal she would be his forever. His fears that she might stray were now gone, plus the prospects of promotion, not to say a very large sum of money and the best thing of all – he would not have to compromise himself. Ok, there was the little matter of the confession he had made to Turnbull, but that was just Ian's word against his.

He eased his sleeve back from his watch – it was nearly time. He ran over his demands once again – £150,000 from each, plus his old job and then promotion. It then occurred to him that his wife's miraculous escape could not surely have been down to ineptitude on her captor's part. Reggie Carlyle was a professional – it would take more than someone like Catherine to evade their clutches.

But then again, there were her injuries – surely they were not sustained by accident but must have been the result of confrontation. What if by some miracle she had overpowered them with force, using a utensil such as a knife? Surprise would no doubt be on her side – after all, who would think someone like her would be capable of such a thing? However, what had she been subjected to? Whatever it was it had probably been a major factor in her obvious determination to escape.

Philip sat bolt upright. *What if she had killed Carlyle?* he thought. He told himself to calm down and took another glance at his watch. *Go to the meeting, you will soon find out.* As he made his way upstairs, he was tempted to question Catherine on her miraculous escape but then thought better of it.

—m—

They stood in front of the magnificent statement to Victorian self-confidence.

"Well there's no sign of Turnbull," said Paul, "what time did he say he'd meet us?"

"Around 6ish," replied Solley.

Paul looked at his watch, "Well it's quarter past now. I hope that bastard hasn't stood us up for any reason."

"I very much doubt it, he's earning well out of this. Hold on a sec, I'll just get this," he added, retrieving his phone from his soiled coat.

"What do you mean you can't make it? We've been standing here like a couple of lemons for the last twenty minutes," lied Solley, so as to emphasise his point. "Ok then, 11am tomorrow – and you'd better bloody well be here."

"What was all that about?"

"Turnbull," he replied. "Apparently something very urgent has turned up and he can't meet us."

"What's happening then?"

"He said he'd be here tomorrow, 11am sharp."

Paul sighed, looking at the building, "I don't know about you but it looks even more impressive a second time."

"I know what you mean," said Solley as he walked away. "That's odd…"

"What?" asked Paul, making his way over to where he was standing, pointing at the ground.

"What do you make of those?"

"Tyre tracks – fairly recent I would say."

"Yeah, but I don't know if you've noticed or not, there were no signs of any vehicle coming up the track."

"Quad bike," suggested Paul, "I told you I saw something."

"Ok, so where did he go?"

The two men circumnavigated the building looking for signs of where the quad had come from but they couldn't find any tyre tracks leading to or away from the Sanatorium. Paul hunkered down and examined the deep marks from whatever had passed this way.

"You know, they don't look like quad tracks."

"All right Sherlock – how would you know what quad bike tracks would look like?"

"Toby and I went over to Marsden a couple of months back on one of these quad bike safaris. There were quad bike tracks all over the place but none of them looked like this."

"Fair enough," replied Solley. "So what do you think made them?"

"Well for a start there are no tread marks," explained Paul. "You know if I didn't know better, I would say they're from a fork-lift truck."

"Piss off! What the hell would a fork-lift truck be doing up here?"

"Ok, so what do you suggest?" he replied with a note of indignation in his voice.

Solley looked at his watch. "A large brandy and some of Margaret's excellent cooking," was his answer, and with that he strode off down the hill, leaving Paul looking at the mysterious marks. "Are you coming?" he shouted over his shoulder.

"Yep, won't be a sec," taking a photo of the smooth indentations.

—◦—

"Is that the best you can do?" said Reggie as Roberts entered the room.

"I can't hide it; after all, I was hit with a spade."

"Your memory's come back then? So much for tripping over – or were you just too embarrassed to admit the truth?"

"I was concussed," he replied in his defence.

"Ok, let's make a move."

The two men made their way to the large 4x4, its engine running.

"You know I said that Philip held all the aces?"

"Yes," replied Roberts, buttoning up his coat.

"Well that's not entirely true." Reggie retrieved his phone from his jacket and showed Roberts the film he had taken of Catherine. "Well – what do you think?"

Even Roberts, who was hardened to such things, felt a little uncomfortable as he watched Reggie's heavies rape this defenceless woman.

"The last thing either of them would want is this all over the Internet."

"I have to hand it to you Reggie," replied Roberts, patting him on the shoulder, "you are nothing if not resourceful."

—◦—

"I won't be long," said Philip.

"Don't leave me here on my own," pleaded Catherine.

"Look you will be safe here; the house is locked and I'll be no time at all. Before you know it, I'll be back, I promise. I'll even have my phone on all the time if you should need me."

He took hold of her wrist and pulled her hand from his arm, "You will be fine."

—⁓—

"Where are you off to this time?" asked Frances as she placed a casserole into the Aga.

"You know I have a lot on with this hospital deal and everything."

"I know, you told me, but there's more to it than that."

"What the hell are you talking about?"

"Your behaviour – you've been acting strangely lately."

"No I haven't, it's your imagination," replied Ian.

"Oh come on – you were over an hour late the other day. I felt so embarrassed, I ran out of things to say and what's more Jane and Malcolm are really your friends, and when I asked where you'd been you hesitated and made up that excuse about a flat tyre. I took the liberty of having a look – the spare's fine."

"That's because I had it changed this morning," he answered quickly.

Frances sighed. "Ok, so it's none of my business and maybe I'm better off not knowing. So what time should I expect you back tonight?"

Ian kissed her on the forehead gently. "Don't wait up," he said, "and don't worry."

"What makes you think I'm worried? Is there something I should be worried about?"

"No of course not, it's you that seems to think there's something untoward going on."

Frances took his hand. "Look if there's something – and I

mean anything – I want to know, after all, I might be able to help."

"For the last time everything is fine," he answered as he picked his car keys up from the small mahogany side table.

—ⁿⁿ—

"It's funny," said Paul as they pulled off the narrow road into the car park of the High Gate Hotel, "I feel as though I've known this place for years."

"We've been spending too much time together – I was just thinking the same thing," replied Solley, applying the handbrake. "Well at least it won't be as interesting as last time I hope."

"Interesting? That woman was lethal – my back still hurts," he added, raising himself in his seat as if to emphasise the fact. "Oh, by the way, what was in that box in the boot? It looked pretty impressive – I meant to ask you earlier but those mysterious tyre tracks took my mind off it."

"For the last time, there is nothing mysterious about anything – it's an old building we are going to renovate and make a small fortune from."

"So?"

"So what?" he replied, raising his hands.

"The box in the back – what's in there?"

"Guess," said Solley, turning in his seat to face him.

"I don't know."

"Go on – have a guess."

"Err – dynamite?"

"What the hell would I be doing with dynamite?"

"I don't know – it's the first thing that came into my head."

"Well it's not dynamite, it's two pairs of night vision goggles."

"What?"

"Yep," he replied proudly, "they're state of the art. This means we can explore the whole place without relying on torches. And these – I'm telling you – are fucking brilliant! I'm not kidding you – it's like day only just a bit green."

"Where the hell did you get them from?"

"Podgy Mitchell."

"What the fuck does Podgy know about night vision goggles?"

"Look, I tried them out already and they're kosher."

"Ok, I just don't want us ending up in possession of some stolen military equipment that's all."

"You worry too much," he replied dismissively, getting out of the car.

Paul waited for a few minutes as Solley retrieved their overnight bags from the boot. He needed a few seconds to collect himself – his heart was already racing at the thought of seeing Margaret again, especially as he had convinced himself that after the news of Kim's attack, he would never see her again. He knew in his heart of hearts there was no future for them but just to have some contact – even if it was only now and again, would do.

Solley stopped halfway between the hotel and his car and turned – raising both bags slightly as if to say 'What are you waiting for?' Paul took a deep breath and followed him into the hotel.

"I thought Margaret said she had a rush on?" said Solley. "It seems quiet to me."

"Tell you what though, I don't know what she's cooking but it smells divine."

Just then Alan burst into the hallway donned in Margaret's husband's chef's jacket and striped blue trousers.

"I see you're multi-talented," observed Solley.

"Sorry," he replied looking a little quizzical.

"Landscaping to haute cuisine."

Alan looked a little bemused.

"He means cooking," said Paul.

"Oh, yeah, Margaret's teaching me. I'll go and tell her you're here."

—∞—

Ian was just about to start the car when his phone rang.

"About bloody time; have you got the documents?"

"No," replied Frank.

"Why the hell not?" asked Ian, impatiently looking at the time.

"Because he's on his way to Pakistan."

"Who the fuck is on their way to Pakistan?"

"The guy I rent – or used to rent – my office from. He said he would keep any post for me, I was going to collect it only I ended up in hospital, remember?"

"Who told you that?"

"His son," replied Frank, trying to alleviate the pain in his leg with another pillow.

"Well get him to give you his father's phone number."

"I have his bloody phone number numbnuts! I've been trying to get him all bloody day on it. I've only just managed to get his house number as it was ex-directory. It was his son who told me that he's on a flight out of the country."

"Does his son know anything about the documents?"

"No, I asked if he knew if his father had been over to the office and he said he had, earlier today, but he knew nothing about any papers."

"Maybe they didn't arrive today?" suggested Ian hopefully.

"They should have been there Friday morning at the latest so they would definitely have been there the following day."

"So why does this Mr Bhutan not answer his phone?"

"Because he's on a pilgrimage," explained Frank, "and apparently he won't answer his phone for another seven days."

"That's all we fucking need," replied Ian as he turned the key in the ignition. "And Frank – stay in your room. I don't want anyone to know you're at the hotel. What room are you in?"

"Number eight," he said. "But why this place?"

"It's nice and out of the way," Ian explained. "And Carlyle would never think of looking for you there."

"I fucking well hope not."

"Ok then, sit tight – the last thing I want is for you to end up as pig feed – not until I have my hands on those documents anyway."

"Well that's nice I must say," he answered and hung up.

Ian pulled out of his driveway. *Maybe Townsend did have them after all,* he thought, *but how?*

—ɱ—

Margaret made her way out to greet Paul and Solley. "I'll take you up to your room," she said, bending down to take their bags.

"That won't be necessary," said Paul, "we can manage those."

"Ok, if you insist."

The two men followed her up the wide staircase.

"These rises are shallow," said Solley, "funny; I didn't notice them last time."

"They were made this way," she explained, "so the Victorian ladies would not have to lift their skirts and show their ankles."

"Is that so?" said Paul, his eyes fixed on her long slender legs. "How times change," he continued in a low voice to himself.

"Sorry, I didn't catch that?" she said as they reached the landing.

"Oh it was nothing, I was just muttering to myself that's all. It's an age thing," he added with a smile.

Margaret opened the door to the bridal suite revealing, as promised, two separate beds with ample space between them.

"My," observed Solley, looking about him, "this is rather exquisite."

"I know," she replied, sounding a little downbeat. "We rather went overboard on this one, it was our first renovation."

"Well, I must say you have made a wonderful job of it."

"I'll leave you two to get settled, dinner is served from 7pm."

"Margaret?"

"Yes Paul?"

"I thought you said you were busy."

289

"We are," replied Margaret, "but they don't arrive for another hour. Is there a problem?"

"Oh no, not at all, just being nosey that's all."

"Look, I do really appreciate this, as I said I really need the money. The thing is I'm expecting ten members of the Leeds Murder Mystery Society and if they like the place and recommend it to their fellow members, it could prove to be quite lucrative."

"We don't mind sharing," said Solley, "it's not the first time we've had to do so, and seeing as you're part of our team now so to speak, you scratch my back and I'll scratch yours. Oh, by the way, before you go, is Alan now your cook? I saw him kitted out in his full regalia in the hallway earlier."

"No, no," she laughed, "I was just teaching him the basics. The thing is I have two choices – give up or give it a go – and to make this place work I need an assistant, and Alan has kindly agreed to work full-time as gardener, head cook and bottle washer, and I have promised him if things take off, then a post as manager."

"Is Alan cooking tonight?" asked Solley, a little apprehensively.

"Oh goodness me no, but I believe he has great potential, that's for sure. Now you must excuse me," she added, leaving the room.

"You know," he said, looking around the room, "I think our idea of bringing Margaret on board was a good one, I have a feeling she will turn out to be a real asset."

"Well just remember it was my idea," answered Paul, unzipping his bag.

20

Philip looked at the address, this was it all right. He rang the bell and waited until finally the door was answered by a tall, thin, willowy woman and an even taller, thinner man.

"What is it you want?" she asked.

"I wonder if you could help me."

"I'm afraid if you're looking for a room we're fully booked."

"Oh no, you misunderstand, I'm not looking for a room but for someone who might be staying here," he explained.

"We don't give information of that sort to anyone," said the man, presumably her husband.

"I know it's out of office hours but I'm here on council business," continued Philip.

"And who exactly might you be?" asked the woman.

He showed them an out-of-date ID due to his present one being taken by HR.

"Ok Mr Townsend," said the man, "who is it you're looking for?"

"I need – and this is quite urgent – to speak to a Mr William Quinn," said Philip, hoping his assumption that Frank's Customs & Excise contact Ian had spoken of, and Billy Quinn, were one and the same.

"Oh, Billy you mean," replied the woman to her husband's annoyance at her unwelcome interjection. "He's not with us."

"Oh, really; any idea where I might find him?"

"He could be anywhere," said the man, stepping slightly in front of his wife. We don't allow people in if they've been consuming alcohol you see. My bet would be the Arches over by the breaker's yard by Market Street – it's as good a place as any," he added, handing back his ID.

Philip looked at his watch; *It's worth the effort,* he thought to himself.

—◊◊—

"What time is it?" shouted Solley as he turned himself around in the shower, allowing the powerful stream of hot water from the large copper shower head to pummel his body.

"Half six," shouted back Paul through the open door. "Why?"

"Just thought we could have an aperitif."

"Ok, but only the one – I don't want a repeat of what happened last time."

The sound of the cascading water stopped as abruptly as it had started and Solley stepped out of the shower cubicle in a cloud of steam. Paul turned to leave the bathroom.

"Don't go," said Solley, reaching for one of the large white fluffy towels.

"What the hell do you want me for?"

"Oh, don't flatter yourself; see that bottle over there?"

"Yes."

"Pour just a few drops on your hands and rub it into my shoulders and back."

Reluctantly Paul did as instructed. "Bloody hell fire – what's in this stuff?" he exclaimed.

"You've heard of frankincense and myrrh?"

"Yeah."

"Well it's not that but it is an ancient Egyptian equivalent. It's extracted from what is now a rare plant that only grows on certain sections of the Nile."

"How much did you pay for this crap?" asked Paul, looking at the bottle.

"You do exasperate me sometimes Paul Goodman; you're such a Philistine. £1500 if you must know."

"And you're a bloody fool Solley Solomon" he replied as he slapped him hard across his backside.

"Ow; and there's me thinking all this time that you didn't care!"

—⁓—

Philip stopped his car some 50 metres from the aqueduct that carried the Manchester to Leeds canal. There were several brick arches, some of which had their entrances boarded up with double doors used for storage or cheap car repairs, but two were still open to the elements. It was in one of these that he hoped would house the man he was seeking.

He approached with caution as it was obvious that several of the people ensconced among their dark recesses, were either drunk or out of their minds on drugs. He would need his wits about him, find this Billy Quinn, and get out.

It was then that two men caught his attention, sitting on the ground with their backs against the cold damp brickwork. Philip decided he would ask them if they had seen Billy. He cleared his throat and one of the men looked up from the cheap bottle of wine he was clutching in his left hand.

"I wonder if you gentlemen can help me. I'm looking for a Mr Billy Quinn; do you know where I could find him?"

"Maybe," said the man with the bottle, nudging his companion and handing it to him. "What's in it for us?"

Philip pulled out a £20 note and the man reached out greedily for the money.

"Not so quick, I want to know where Billy is first."

"That's him over there, next to the fire."

Philip duly handed over the cash which was snatched from

his grasp immediately. The vagrant's companion, who had seemed oblivious to the transaction that had just taken place, made a lunge for the money, smashing one of the bottles of cheap wine in the process. Turning his back on the ensuing alcohol-induced confrontation, he made his way deeper into the void, approaching the men huddled around a small fire.

"One of you Mr Quinn?" he asked.

"And who might you be?"

He turned to see the owner of this crisp and well-educated voice standing directly behind him. "That is of no importance to you at this juncture but I believe you have been recently acquainted with a Mr Carlyle."

He noticed the man's expression change from one of cautious curiosity to that of fear. "I see you know who I am talking about then," he added.

"We can't talk here," replied Billy in a low voice.

"Ok, I have a car but first I want to make sure I have the right person. Tell me what you know."

"What I know – not too sure where to begin."

"Well start by recounting your dealings with Carlyle."

"You're referring to the documents regarding the construction of the Commonwealth Games Village?"

Philip grabbed his arm.

"Where are we going?"

"To find you somewhere safe to stay until this is sorted. That's my car over there, now go and wait for me." As he handed over the keys, this demonstration of trust gave Billy the confidence he needed to go along with his new acquaintance's instructions.

Philip removed his phone from his jacket. "Turnbull? It's Townsend here; I have some interesting news for you."

"Oh, what's that?" replied Ian, hoping he had heard the last of Townsend.

"I have located Frank's little helper. We're going to need somewhere to keep him out of harm's way."

"And what the fuck do you expect me to do about it?"

"You're an estate agent, aren't you?"

"Yeah, so?"

"Well you must have empty properties you're trying to sell."

"Look…"

"No, you look," he replied, "you're in this up to your neck like it or not."

"Ok," sighed Turnbull. "There's this property – the owners are in Spain – we can keep him there for a day or two. Go to my house, my wife will expect you. All you have to do is ask her for the Brookside keys and tell her I sent you. The water's turned off from under the utility room sink. Oh, and when you get some food for him, don't forget a couple of bottles of cheap brandy – we don't want him going walkabout in search of alcohol."

—◊—

Billy looked up as Philip got into the car. "What now?" he asked.

"I am taking you somewhere safe for a couple of days. Take this," he added, handing him a mobile phone.

"I already have one."

"Never mind that – this one's fully charged. You are not to use it but keep it on at all times. Now this is vitally important – you are not to leave the house and for goodness sake keep the noise down ok?"

Billy nodded.

"Listen," continued Philip, "the only reason you're breathing is because Reggie believes you have those documents." He turned and reached over to the rear seat. "But as you can see, I have them."

"How the hell did you get those?" he asked, wide-eyed.

"That is of no concern to you but if you don't do exactly as I say…"

Billy reached out to grab the papers but as he did so he felt an agonising pain rush up his right arm.

"You fucking bastard," he screamed. "You've broken my arm!"

Philip eased the hammer back down next to his seat. "It's not broken but if Carlyle knows you don't have these documents tucked away somewhere safe; that will be but a taster of what you can expect. Now stop making such a fuss and put your seatbelt on."

———

Ian turned into the car park of the hotel. It was indeed isolated and windswept but he was not alone. He watched as about ten people tumbled out of a red minibus and sat there for a few moments, observing this merry group as they made their way into the hotel before following them. The scene that met him a few moments later was almost comical as everyone was talking at once. The woman behind the reception desk was trying her best to make order of a group of middle-aged old farts trying to out vie one another for attention.

He went over to the bar.

"Yes Sir?" said Alan, "what can I get you?"

"I guess it will have to be orange juice."

"Very good Sir."

"Tell me, what's going on out there?" he said, nodding towards the reception, "some kind of reunion?"

"Oh no," replied Alan, opening the bottle of juice, "they're members of the Leeds Murder Mystery Club. They're looking for hotels with atmosphere."

Ian took a cursory glance around. "Well this place certainly has it in spades," he said.

"I know what you mean," smiled Alan, handing Ian his drink. "That will be £1.60. Can I get you anything else?"

He handed over a £5 note, "Have one yourself," he said.

"That's very kind of you. I'll have the same if that's all right."

Ian took his drink and sat in the corner near the window. He knew Councillor Roberts quite well and Carlyle by reputation.

Ian was not a hard man but he was not scared of them either. His attention was then drawn to a black Range Rover as it pulled into the car park next to his car. He watched intently but it was some time before the front passenger door opened and a mountain of a man prised himself out of the 4x4 and opened the rear door.

That must be Carlyle, he thought.

His suppositions were confirmed as Roberts emerged from behind the vehicle accompanied by what could only be described as a walking Panzer tank. Ian could feel his heart racing, he had not been scared but he was now. He knew these guys would rip your arms and legs off just for the fun of it.

"Mr Turnbull?"

Ian almost jumped out of his seat.

"We weren't expecting to see you until tomorrow," said Solley. "I was just saying to my partner I was going to phone you later to confirm the time for our meeting in the morning but I guess that won't be necessary now."

"Wh… wh… what are you doing here?" he stammered.

"You know what we're doing here."

"No, I mean *here* – why this dump of all places?"

"It's not that bad," said Paul in Margaret's defence. "Some of the rooms have been refurbished to the highest quality I'll have you know."

"Well look gentlemen; this is a bit awkward."

"Are you ok?" asked Solley, noticing his furtive glances towards the entrance.

"Look – that Russian I told you about – he's here."

"Where?" asked Paul, inquisitively, looking over his shoulder.

"No, don't do that," he said, getting to his feet. "They're on their way in, it's important they don't know who you are."

"Ok," said Paul, "I get you. Come on Solley, we'll get that drink you so desperately wanted," he added, steering him towards the bar.

"What the hell was that all about?" asked Solley. "Does it matter if that Russian knows who we are? I'm not afraid of some bloody jumped-up peasant."

Paul was no great fan of the Russians either but Solley's family had suffered at their hands, albeit a long time ago, and his feelings towards them were tarnished by the stories he had heard from his grandparents.

"Two large brandies please Alan, oh and a couple of packets of peanuts."

"I thought we were supposed to be on the wagon, and you're ordering doubles?"

"Well things change."

"There you are gentlemen," said Alan, "I'll put this on your tab."

"And one for yourself while you're at it," said Paul, opening the packet of peanuts, spilling several in the process.

"I think this could be them," said Solley.

"Don't look, let's just do as Ian asked. I think it might be to our advantage for them not to know who we are – not just yet anyway."

"Ah, Councillor Roberts," said Ian, holding out his hand.

Roberts acknowledged this gesture of friendship and introduced Reggie. Ian offered his hand but this time it was rejected.

"Can I get you gentlemen a drink?" he asked.

"Two large single malts," replied Roberts.

"And no ice for me," said Reggie as he made himself comfortable.

"Where are you going?" enquired Paul.

"I need a piss," replied Solley in a low voice.

"What? You only had one a couple of minutes ago."

As Solley made his way out of the bar, he was watched by Carlyle, his dark beady eyes following his every move.

It was obvious that these two men were not your average locals but must be the owners of that ninety grand Merc sitting out in the car park, thought Reggie. His curiosity now raised, he would now make it his business to find out who these two out-of-place characters were.

Ian returned and placed the respective drinks on the table. "I hope we can…"

But he was cut short. "Sit down and listen to me – you my friend, have caused me and my brother-in-law a lot of anguish and that is something I am not happy about. We know you are mixed up with that pile of shit Frank Hibbard – the question is how mixed up? For your own sake, you had better tell us all you know about the missing documents and where that low-life Frank is – as despite my best efforts – he seems to have disappeared. That is, if you want your family to prosper. Do you understand what I am saying?"

"Look you have it all wrong," began Ian. "As far as I know Frank hasn't even laid his hands on these documents."

Reggie leaned forward. "Do you really take me for an idiot? I know full well that you and your sidekick have the papers and I am willing to be reasonable and come to a fair price for them but if you start to mess with me, I'm sure your daughter will have a very unpleasant surprise waiting for her when she gets back to her apartment."

"Look," he pleaded, "what I told you is true, Townsend has them."

Reggie eased back into his chair and sipped his whisky. "You really believe that?"

"Yes, or I wouldn't be here."

Reggie laughed, "Do you really think I'm that stupid? It was him that gave them to Frank. Surely a man of your intellect can do better than that and if this turns out to be some kind of false errand, I won't be very pleased."

"How the fuck did *he* get hold of them?" asked Roberts trying to distance himself, already knowing of Philip's involvement regarding the missing papers.

"I have no idea but as you know it was him who asked me to organise this meeting. He should be here any minute. He gave me this," answered Ian.

Roberts took the single sheet of paper and handed it to Reggie. "What's this?" he asked.

"It's the introduction sheet," explained Roberts. "There's one with every file, it gives a brief outline of the contents."

"How do we know he did not just keep this with him before handing over the documents to Frank?" asked Reggie.

"Look, you must believe me," said Ian, "I have never seen these papers – all I know of them is from this."

"Ok, but how is it Billy Quinn knows so much about them if, as you say, Townsend has them?" asked Roberts.

"Billy Quinn, who the fuck is Billy Quinn?" asked Ian, doing his best to look genuinely bewildered but at the same time eager to find out whether he had a connection to Frank and the disappearance of his car and its all-important contents.

"So," said Reggie, "you have not heard of the infamous Billy Quinn and his recent exploits with a certain friend of yours?"

"Honestly," he replied, "I have no bloody idea as to who or what you are talking about."

"Now that is interesting don't you think Councillor?"

"Err, ah, yes," replied Roberts, "I guess you can't trust anyone nowadays," not quite sure what Reggie meant.

"Well gentleman," said Reggie. "If, as you say, Townsend has the files and we conclude our business in an amical manner, then that will be the end of it."

Ian was sorely tempted to ask what would happen if things did not go Reggie's way but of course, he knew the answer to that question.

—◊—

Solley returned to the bar, at the same time observing the two men with Turnbull. "Tell you one thing for nothing," he said, sitting back on his bar stool.

"What's that?" asked Paul.

"If those two are Russian, my uncle's a Dutchman!"

"He is," retorted Paul.

Solley glowered, "You know very well what I mean."

"Sorry, I couldn't resist it."

"The one with his back slightly towards us is trouble – I know his sort a mile off, gangster if ever I saw one."

"Oh come on, you can't go around accusing people of being gangsters, not without some evidence."

"No? Well I took a look outside, and in the car park is our car, a minibus that would belong to the Mystery Murder lot, Alan's old crate, Turnbull's Lexus and two blacked-out Range Rovers."

"So? Just because he has a blacked-out Range Rover and looks a bit dodgy, doesn't mean he's a gangster."

Solley handed Paul his phone. "Take a look at this – I took it while they weren't looking."

"Bloody hell, are they out there?" he asked.

"Yep – heavies if ever I saw one."

"What the hell do you think Turnbull is mixed up in?" asked Paul in a low voice, trying to look as though he was taking a general interest in things as several of the Murder Mystery party came into the lounge.

"I don't know but I sure as fuck don't want it to involve us."

"Hold on – you know what I reckon's happening?"

"No; what?"

"I reckon these two with Turnbull are negotiating terms, you know what recluses some of these Russian oligarchs can be, you only have to look at Stamford Street – half of it is owned by one and nobody has ever seen him."

"That's true," replied Solley, sipping the last few dregs from his glass. "Tell you what; I wonder if Margaret knows them?"

"I very much doubt it; they hardly look to be the type she would frequent with."

"I don't mean that – but if they're from around here, she might know who they are."

Before Paul could reply, Solley was easing his way through the chatty group that had taken up residence at the far end of the bar and made his way across the hallway. Now confident he was out of sight, he burst into the kitchen.

"Oh Solley," said Margaret, "if you're wondering about dinner it will be a bit delayed I'm afraid – Pauline's only just got here, something to do with her new washing machine."

"No that's fine," he replied, "but can you spare me a minute?"

"I really am rather busy at the moment," she replied, holding the lid to a massive tureen in one hand and a ladle in the other.

"Look, it will only take two seconds, I promise and it is really quite important."

"Err, ok," she replied, removing her apron.

"Now I want you to go into the bar and have a word with Alan."

"I thought you said this would only take two seconds?"

"Please, just bear with me."

"Ok then, what do you want me to ask him?"

"Oh, I don't know, just make something up. In the corner by the window are three men. Now you must remember to be discreet – they're not to notice you looking at them. I want you to see if you recognise any of them."

Margaret sighed and muttered something before leaving him in the doorway and making her way into the noisy bar, where she asked Alan to put two bottles of Champagne on ice.

"They're quite a lively bunch," said Paul.

"Who?" replied Margaret as she tried to get a look at the men Solley was so interested in.

"Your Murder Mystery group."

"Yes, they are," she replied curtly as she turned away from him and headed back out into the hallway.

This brush-off attitude left him feeling somewhat confused. Had he said something? She seemed ok earlier. Or had he been kidding himself all along? Why would such a woman like Margaret have any interest in a man of his age – and a married one at that?

It then dawned on him that he had not given Kim a moment's thought until then – he had been totally obsessed with Margaret. What a complete idiot he had been – was this as Solley had said – the real reason for being here? An obsession with a woman he could never be with, and if that was so and this had clouded his judgement, was this project with all its baggage, really a good idea?

Solley stepped forward from his hiding place "Did you recognise any of them?" he asked eagerly.

"Yes," she replied in a low voice as she took him by the arm and led him back into the kitchen. "The one in the far corner facing the bar is a Councillor Roberts, he's Head of the Planning Committee – it was he who led the opposition to my renovation plans. My husband felt he was fishing for a backhander."

"Oh really," said Solley, "now that is interesting. What about the others?"

"Nobody really – except Turnbull of course, but you already know him."

"And what about the ugly bastard – please excuse my French?"

"Not sure, he kind of looks familiar but I can't put a name to the face."

―〜―

Reggie looked at his watch, "Where's Townsend?" he barked.

"He won't be long," said a nervous Turnbull. "He said he had something to do before coming over."

"Oh did he? The thing is, I don't like to be kept waiting, I make rash decisions when I get impatient and we don't want that do we?"

"No," replied Turnbull, praying that Townsend would arrive soon.

"What do you know of those two?" asked Reggie, nodding towards the bar.

"Sorry?" replied Ian, trying to sound uninterested.

"Don't mess with me Turnbull, you know who I'm talking about."

"Oh, those two you mean. No idea – tourists?"

Reggie glowered at him, "You'd better not be planning anything."

"Of course not," he replied, "why would I do that? All I want to do is get this over with and get out of here."

"Excuse me gentlemen," said Reggie as he got up and went outside.

—⁂—

"Cheer up," said Solley as he plonked himself back down next to Paul.

"You look pleased with yourself."

"I might have reason to be, you see the big bloke in the corner? No… don't look."

"Ok, ok, yeah I know who you mean."

"His name is Roberts, Councillor Roberts to be precise."

"How does Margaret know him?"

"Well it seems he's on the Planning Committee and it would appear that since Margaret's husband would not drop him a few quid, he refused planning permission for the rest of the work to be carried out."

"Well if that is the case I think our Mr Turnbull will have a few questions to answer."

"Yes and no," replied Solley. "After all, it might work in our favour – in fact, thinking about it, it will," he added, ordering two more brandies.

—⁂—

"I want you to go to this address," said Reggie, handing a piece of paper to the heavies minding one of the 4x4s. "When Turnbull's wife answers the door, tell her that you have come to collect some documents regarding the sale of the High Gate Hospital and when you're inside phone me."

"Do you think she'll let me in boss?"

"She will if you tell her her husband sent you. She's bound to know about the sale of the old Sanatorium."

—∭—

Margaret cleared her throat, "Ladies and gentlemen, I'm very sorry for the delay but if you would care to come through to the dining room now, dinner will be served. Thank you for your patience."

Reggie returned to the bar to find it now devoid of the noisy society group and the two mysterious men.

"Give me your phone," he ordered.

"Sorry?" replied Ian.

"You heard me first time."

"Look this is no place to make a scene."

Reggie moved a little closer to Ian and looked behind him, they were alone. He grabbed Ian's left arm with his powerful hands and before he could react, Reggie had snapped his little finger. Ian let out a shriek of pain.

"Now, give me that phone!"

Ian fumbled in his jacket and handed it to Reggie.

"Give it to Roberts," he said.

He did as instructed and returned to nursing his damaged finger.

"Everything ok gentlemen?" asked Alan as he returned to the bar with two bottles of Champagne.

"Everything's fine here," replied Roberts.

"Are they cold?" asked Reggie, nodding towards the bottles.

"No, they need half an hour in the chiller first; I've only just brought them up from the cellar."

"In that case we'll settle for a bottle of your finest red."

"Right, what type would you prefer?"

"Oh, I'll leave that to your good judgement young man," said Reggie with a half-smile.

"Ok, I won't be long," replied Alan as he left the bar and made his way into the kitchen.

"What is it?" asked Margaret with two plates of asparagus soup precariously balanced.

"One of the men in the bar has asked for a bottle of our finest red," explained Alan.

"What type?"

"That's the thing – he left the choice to me."

"Err, ok, the claret is very good."

21

Philip was now getting anxious as he pressed the intercom.

"Yes?"

"I have come to collect a key for Brookside."

"Oh yes," replied the voice, "Ian said you would be round."

Frances opened the door and handed him the key. "Oh my, what happened to your face?"

"Horse-riding accident," he replied.

"Oh, now that is interesting," she said, "I remember when…"

But before she could say another word Philip had turned his back on her and was for all intents and purposes, running down the driveway.

How rude! she thought, closing the door then making her way into the kitchen where she removed a half empty bottle of vodka from the back of the fridge. She sliced a lemon and placed some into a tall tumbler with ice. It was then she noticed they were out of tonic.

Kicking off her slippers she slipped on her shoes and grabbed her purse from the counter. "Oh for goodness sake," she said as the doorbell rang again, "Who can that be now?"

"Yes," she said impatiently to the intercom, hoping to get rid of this unwelcome visitor as quickly as possible.

"My name is Mr Jackman," came the reply. "Your husband is

negotiating with my boss regarding the old High Gate Hospital. He left some documents here – I've come to collect them."

"Oh of course," she said, opening the front door.

No sooner had she done so than she was bundled into the sitting room.

"Sit down and be quiet," said Joe sharply. "Do exactly as you're told and you will not come to any harm."

"What the hell's the meaning of this and who the hell are you?" demanded Frances

"That is of no concern to you," replied Joe.

—⁓—

"Ah, gentlemen – this looks like our wine," said Reggie, glancing up.

"I hope you'll be pleased with the choice," said Alan, showing him the bottle.

Reggie placed his hand into his top pocket and removed his reading glasses. "Ah, fine choice young man."

"Would you like me to pour?"

"No that will not be necessary, just bring one glass – my friends are driving – don't want them to break the law now do we?"

"No," replied Alan rather nervously as he went to fetch the wine glass.

It was then that Ian's phone started to ring.

"Give it here," said Reggie.

"Why?" replied Roberts.

"Don't argue, just give it here."

Reggie took it then handed it to Turnbull. "Well go on, answer it."

Ian tentatively took the phone and answered the call. He listened carefully to his wife.

"That's enough," said Reggie, snatching the phone back.

"Look, she has nothing to do with any of this," said Ian.

"Oh, but she does my dear friend," answered Reggie, "she is your wife and that makes her connected – and that goes for the rest of your family. Ah, thank you young man," he added as Alan placed the glass on the table and removed the cork from the bottle.

"Is there anything else I can get you gentlemen?"

"No, that will be all, now run along."

"Now I want you to listen," said Reggie as he carefully poured the wine into his glass. "I want those documents and I don't care who I hurt to get them. As I have already said, I am a reasonable man and I and Councillor Roberts are quite happy to pay a reasonable price for them – that's business. But what you and your jumped-up clerk are doing is very, very different – you are taking me on at my own game and believe me, you will lose."

—⁓—

Philip grabbed items at random off the shelves until his basket was full.

"That will be £42.75 please," said the youth behind the till.

"Two seconds," he replied as he made a dash for the end of the shop that housed a selection of beer and cheap wine.

"Brandy, brandy," he muttered, "where the hell …? Ah, there it is." He grabbed a couple of bottles of cheap brandy and returned to the till, pushing past the next in line, apologising as he did so.

"That will be £61.40."

Philip handed over two £50 notes.

"Do you have anything smaller?" asked the young man.

"What? No."

"Only I don't have enough change at the moment. If I serve these people first…"

"Never mind," he said, grabbing his groceries and the bottles.

"What about your change?" called the youth as he rushed out of the shop.

Ten minutes later he pulled into the long drive of a detached house and headed to the front door with Billy in tow.

"Right," he said, making his way to the kitchen and dumping the food and brandy on the counter. Opening the cupboard doors below the sink in the utility room, he turned the stop-cock to ON and immediately there was a familiar sound of toilet cisterns filling.

"Now listen to me," he began, "the electric's off and you're not to turn it on under any circumstances ok? There's enough food there to last you a couple of days – remember your life depends on nobody knowing you're here."

"You can trust me," replied Billy, eyeing up the bottles of brandy.

Philip did not reply to this statement of trust. "I'm going to leave you now – remember what I said." He paused halfway out of the kitchen then returned, grabbing one of the bottles.

"Hey, what are you doing?"

"One bottle will be enough," he replied as he made his way down the hall and slammed the front door behind him.

Philip looked at the time indicated on the dashboard of his car, it was 7.20pm. If he got a move on he should be at the High Gate by 8pm at least; ok a little late but the thought of that rat Turnbull sweating it out in the company of Reggie Carlyle brought a warm glow to the pit of his stomach. He was now keen to get this over with. *But would it ever really be over?* he thought, *and what if they would not accept his terms? No, they would have no choice, he held all the aces.*

But he did regret telling Turnbull about Catherine. Was it really true? What if she had just been friends with the Tobins after all and all those terrible things he had done were unnecessary. No, he must not think like that – he was not at fault, he wasn't stupid, he knew exactly what had been going on over there. You only had to look at the way Nick looked at her – his eyes were all over her backside. It had to be done, for her sake, she was easily led. Catherine needed him as much as he needed her.

He gave a slight shudder at the thought of Nick's hands

groping his wife's naked body. She deserved what she got, so did they, but what he had told Turnbull about him not caring for her was a lie – she was the centre of his universe and now she was truly back there where she belonged, nothing could separate them now.

—ᴍ—

"That was truly amazing," said Solley as Margaret removed their plates.

"How was it for you?" she asked Paul, full of anticipation.

"Ok," he replied in a low voice.

"Oh, right. I'll get you the sweet menu then."

"What's the matter with you? That chicken chasseur was bloody fantastic, even Connelly's of Leicester Square would struggle to do better. Sorry, I forgot, you're worried about Kim, I'm sure Margaret realises that too."

Paul looked up from his glass, "You're a good man Solley Solomon."

"Now you do have me worried. That's the second time in the last two days."

"No, it's true. There's something…" Paul stopped in mid-sentence as Pauline arrived at their table with the sweet menu. Without looking, Solley said he would have the Tiramisu

"And for you Sir?" asked Pauline.

"Oh, no not for me, I'll pass."

"What," said Solley, "that's not like you?"

"What about a selection from our cheeseboard, it includes a local award-winning speciality, Moorland Blue?" she suggested.

"Very good, I'll have the cheese and biscuits," said Paul, not really paying attention.

Solley waited for her to leave the table and head back to the kitchen. "Since when the bloody hell have you had cheese and biscuits? There's something else on your mind isn't there? It's Margaret isn't it?"

"No."

"Come on – you were like a love-sick schoolkid when we arrived, you couldn't keep your eyes off her."

"Ok, so I admit it – I can't help myself but you must understand that I would never betray Kim."

"I know," he replied, pouring the last of the wine into Paul's glass. "Look, Margaret is an amazing woman, even I can see that. If there were anybody out there that could convert me – and that's saying something – it would be her. She's beautiful, determined, kind and good fun, well-educated. What straight guy would not fall in love with her? But you are married to an equally beautiful woman with all the same attributes. What you see in Margaret is what you did in Kim all those years ago; you're just trying to wind the clock back and believe me my friend, that is a mistake."

Paul knew that these words of wisdom from Solley were true but he could not help his feelings.

"I must say this," he continued, "and I want you to be honest with me. Do you think that your feelings for Margaret will – now or in the future – interfere with this project? Because if you do, I want out, do you understand?"

"Yes of course, my behaviour towards her will be totally professional," he replied, moving his glass as Pauline placed a varied selection of organic cheeses and water biscuits in front of him.

Solley looked at the variety of cheeses with envious eyes, "Now I'm wishing I'd chosen that," he remarked.

Paul pushed the platter to the centre of the table, "Help yourself."

"I don't mind if I do, but you're not having any of mine."

—◌—

Where is he; where the fuck is he? thought Ian as he felt a sense of panic take hold of him. It was then that his phone received a text message.

Roberts read it as it came through, "It's Townsend," he said. "He'll be here in ten minutes."

Ian felt a sense of relief flood through his veins only to be replaced by a sickening feeling in the pit of his stomach. *What if Frank should phone him?* he thought. Ian knew he would have no choice but to go up and see him.

"Excuse me gentlemen, I need to use the little boys' room."

"So does Roberts," said Reggie.

"Err, oh, yeah, of course."

Ian, accompanied by Roberts, made his way to the toilet. On their way back, he noticed Paul and Solley in the dining room. "Excuse me," he said to Roberts.

"Hold on, you're not going anywhere without me," replied Roberts.

"Look, I'm just going over there to speak to those two gentlemen. You can watch me from here, there's no way out of the dining room as you can see."

"Ok, but no funny business – remember I'll be watching you."

Roberts was as keen as Reggie to know more about these two out-of-place characters and if Turnbull knew them – as it seemed he did – this could be a good opportunity to find out who exactly they were.

"Oh, hi," said Paul, "I thought you didn't want to be seen with us."

"Look, I can't talk long, you must go to room eight and knock on the door and say Turnbull said don't use your phone."

"Well that is good of you," said Ian, shaking Paul's hand. "You're most understanding, here's my address."

Ian wrote down what he had just told them on a piece of paper. "If anyone asks, I caught your car on the way in and we've settled it with cash."

With that, he re-joined Roberts. "What was all that about?" he demanded, "and who are those men?"

"No idea, bit of an odd couple don't you think?" replied Ian, "but I caught their car on the way in and felt I should give them my details. They said they would settle for cash."

"Since when have you been so honest?" asked Roberts.

"Don't worry, it's just that kid."

"What kid?"

"The one behind the bar," he explained. "I think he saw me as I came in, he had been looking over this way when those two were buying their drinks. I guess he was telling them what he had seen."

"And?" asked Roberts.

"And what?"

"What did they say to you when you went over?"

"That it was honest of me to…"

Reggie raised his hand and beckoned them over, he then pointed to the doorway. They looked across to see Philip approaching. Reggie offered him a seat and turned to Ian.

"Why don't you make yourself useful and go and order some coffee?"

Turnbull made his way across to the bar.

"Now we're all together, that's nice isn't it?" said Reggie. "So let's get this over with," he added, noticing that Philip had arrived empty-handed. *This might not be his forte,* he thought, *but he was no fool.*

"I have the money," he said to him, "where are the documents?"

"Err, could you excuse me, I really need to use the gents," said Townsend.

"Must be the cold," he remarked, "Feel free."

Roberts got up to accompany him but Reggie indicated with his hand for him to sit down. "He's not going anywhere, not with 300 grand at stake. And not only that," he added, "you might get a reputation accompanying strange men to the toilet."

Philip left the bar and went across the hallway.

"Careful!" exclaimed Solley.

"Please forgive me," said Philip, "I didn't see you."

"What do you mean, *didn't see me*? I'm 6 foot bloody 4 inches tall and weigh 18 stone! How the frig could you *not* see me? And look at my jacket, it's ruined," he added, looking at the spilt brandy.

Reggie nudged Roberts and nodded towards the hallway where Paul, Solley and Townsend seemed to be deep in conversation.

"What do you make of that?" he asked.

"Do you reckon it's some kind of set-up?" replied Roberts, looking decidedly nervous.

"They're not police if that's what you're thinking. I know them all round here and I've never seen them before."

"They could be up from London?" suggested Roberts.

"No – for two reasons – one, what would Scotland Yard want with us, and two, if they were police they would be more discreet about it. But there's something not right – that's for sure – first Turnbull, then our friend."

—⁓—

"I'll pay to have it cleaned," said Philip apologetically.

"You're damn right you will," replied Solley. "400 quid it cost me."

Philip took out his wallet but he had used all his cash at the convenience store. "I am really very sorry," he said, "but I don't have any money on me."

"Look," said Paul, now getting a little impatient, "give us your address and we'll send you the bill."

"Oh that's right…" Solley began.

But Paul held up his hand, "Just do as I say, I've had enough of this fiasco."

"Ok," grumbled Solley, "but don't think you can get away with it."

Philip took a card from his wallet and handed it to him before excusing himself.

Solley made his way to the foot of the stairs, "I'll need to change this," he said.

"I'll come with you," said Paul, "I want to phone and see how Kim is."

—◆—

Philip closed the cubicle door and locked it, *300 grand*. The thought of all that money. For some reason it all seemed too easy, he would have to be careful. After all, what was stopping them from taking back the money once he had handed over the documents? Still it was too late to get cold feet now. Of course, there was always his job and that promotion – should he make that part of the deal? Why not, what did he have to lose?

—◆—

"Hold on a sec," said Paul, pausing outside room eight. "What about this?" he added nodding towards the door.

"There's certainly something going on," replied Solley, "Turnbull looked like a rabbit caught in the headlights. And as I said, those two downstairs – or one of them anyway – is definitely a gangster."

Paul knocked hard on the door but there was no reply.

Inside, Frank froze, looking at the door.

"I have a message for you from Ian Turnbull," came a voice from the other side.

Frank was puzzled – who did they know that had a London accent? Whoever it was, they weren't going away so he eased slowly off the bed and made his way over to the door.

Solley was just about to say something but Paul stopped him with a raised hand. "There's someone in there," he mouthed.

"It's important, I need to speak to you," he called.

Frank's curiosity had got the better of him and anyway – if it was Carlyle it made no difference now they knew he was there.

Paul stepped back from the door slightly as the handle started to turn.

"Who the hell are you?" asked Frank, peering through the gap.

"Can we come in?" said Solley.

Frank opened the door, allowing the two men in and then checked the corridor. He closed and locked the door behind him. "What is it Turnbull wants you to tell me?"

"He has a message regarding a Mr Roberts."

On hearing this news Frank stepped back slightly, losing his balance in the process.

"You ok?" asked Solley, "you look a little pale."

"Don't you worry about me, I'm fine."

"What's your name?" asked Paul.

"Frank."

"Now Frank, before we tell you what it is that Turnbull wants you to know, you can tell us something. Who are you and what is your connection to him?"

"Nothing really, just a friend."

"Oh, just a friend?" repeated Solley. "So why didn't he just come up here and give you the message himself?"

"Tell you what," he said, "if you tell me who the fuck you are, I'll tell you who I am."

"I'm afraid it doesn't work that way," said Paul.

"Seems as though our friend will have to find out the hard way," added Solley.

"Seems so," replied Paul, making for the door.

"Ok, ok, I'm a private detective and I do some work for Turnbull now and again."

"That sounds feasible," said Solley.

"What is it Turnbull wants me to know?"

"Not so fast, this Roberts – describe him to me."

"Why, you obviously know who it is."

"Don't mess me about, just describe him to me," he repeated.

"Ok, if I must. He's a big fat ugly bastard."

Solley looked at Paul, who nodded. "Fair description wouldn't you say?"

He turned his attention back to Frank. "He has a friend with him – a short stocky man, well-spoken, red curly hair. Goes about with a couple of gorillas, and drives a black Range Rover with a private number plate RC3."

Frank sat down on the edge of the bed and exhaled. "That's Reggie Carlyle – he's a bad sort."

"Gangster?" asked Paul.

"Yep – a very bad man," he confirmed.

"See I told you, didn't I?" said Solley, addressing Paul. "Ok, so what is it Turnbull has to do with them?"

"Wait a minute – you're the two developers up from the smoke."

"Who we are is of no concern to you," replied Paul.

"Oh yes it fucking is – I could be very useful to you."

"Let's – and I say let's – just pretend we are who you think we are, how could you help us?"

Frank beckoned the two men closer, "There are these documents relating to the construction of the Commonwealth Games."

"What the hell are you talking about?" retorted Solley. "That must be nearly twenty bloody years ago."

"Look, just listen. Turnbull used me to persuade the town clerk to hand over these documents regarding the construction of the Games Village. It appears that things were not – how shall I put it – done with the best interest of the public at heart. Contracts were not awarded to the most competitive companies and not only that, Carlyle and his sister – Councillor Roberts' wife – were submitting false invoices for work they had not carried out properly as they were dumping thousands of tons of waste materials down some old mine workings.

"But this whole thing was swept under the carpet so to speak. However, by pure chance, Turnbull found out about them. He went to visit a retired senior civil servant who had fallen on hard times and was quite willing to divulge all he knew for a price."

Solley put his hand into his pocket and looked at the card the stranger had given him. "I take it this Roberts and Carlyle are mixed up in these dodgy dealings?"

"Right up to their fat little chinny chin chins!"

"Does Philip Townsend ring a bell?"

Frank stared at Solley, his mouth open.

"Thought as much," he said, sitting down on the bed next to him.

"How do you know that?" he asked in a low voice.

"Oh, we have our sources. Ok, we'll talk tomorrow morning," he added, making for the door. "By the way – don't call Turnbull, Roberts has his phone."

"How the hell did you know about this Townsend bloke?" asked Paul as they made their way into their room.

Solley placed his soiled jacket over the back of one of the chairs and removed the business card Philip had given him earlier, handing it to him. "Get that would you?" he said as he made his way to the bathroom.

Paul answered the door. "It's Frank," he called.

Solley came into the room from the en-suite, naked to the waist. "I thought you were supposed to be hiding? What is it we can do for you?"

"How do you know Philip Townsend?" he asked.

Paul looked across to Solley who nodded his approval and he gave Frank the card.

"Where did you get this from?" he asked.

"Our Mr Townsend," replied Solley.

"When?"

"Oh, about ten minutes ago."

"What, you can't have!"

"Well I can assure you I did."

"You mean he's downstairs?" asked Frank.

"Yes, and he was coming from the bar where Turnbull was talking to your friends Carlyle and Roberts."

"I have to find out what's happening."

"I think we would all like that, but short of walking up to them and asking, I really don't see how," said Solley.

"Hold on a sec," said Paul, "I might have an idea. You two wait here."

"Not so fast, you're not going anywhere without me. You never know with these sorts, things could turn ugly and the last thing I would want is to miss out," Solley grinned.

"Ok, but let me do the talking. Oh, and you'd better get back to your room," added Paul, holding the door open for Frank.

—◊◊◊—

Philip returned to the table, nudging it and spilling the drinks as he sat down next to Reggie, "Ok, you have a deal," he said. "However, before we conclude things, I also want my job back and promotion."

"You're a bit of a clumsy bastard, aren't you?" said Roberts.

"Just a little nervous that's all," he replied. "I'm not used to this kind of thing."

"So where is she?" asked Roberts.

"Sorry?"

"That fucking bitch of a wife of yours nearly killed my poor Sylvia."

Reggie put his hand up, "That's no longer of any concern to us, is it Philip; now where are the documents?"

"I don't have them with me. We will make the exchange tomorrow morning at 11am, next to the boating pond."

"I'm afraid that's not acceptable, I want them tonight. You will meet me under the aqueduct at midnight. We'll do the exchange there and if you know what's good for you and that pretty wife of yours, don't get clever. Oh, and not a word to anyone," he snarled, looking up as Ian returned to the table with four cups of coffee precariously balanced on a tray.

"Excuse me gentlemen."

Reggie turned abruptly, his face contorted with rage.

"Mr Turnbull, could I have a word with you?" asked Paul. "I

was thinking it would probably be best to go through the insurance after all."

"Err, yes, I guess so," replied Ian, "but cash would save a lot of trouble."

Paul turned and started to make his way out of the bar.

"Sorry about this, it won't take long," smiled Ian, as he hurried out after Paul. "What the hell are you playing at?" he said.

"We know all about this little charade of yours," said Paul, "I've been talking to Frank and I know all about Philip Townsend."

"Oh shit!"

"And that it was Frank who got those documents for you. So, let's have it."

Ian glanced back at the bar but it seemed that Reggie and Carlyle were more interested in Philip at that precise moment.

"Look, I don't know what that lying bastard upstairs has told you but *I* am the victim in all of this. Philip has the documents, not me, and he's blackmailing Roberts and Carlyle for 300 big ones."

Paul raised his eyebrows, "They're willing to pay that much for them?"

"You'd better believe it."

"Ok, you'd better get back there. We'll speak first thing in the morning."

Paul and Solley made their way back upstairs and paused outside Frank's room.

"What are you doing?" asked Paul.

"I won't be a minute," he replied.

Turnbull returned to the bar, "Sorry about all that."

"Sit down," said Reggie. "You are to stay with Townsend tonight and keep him with you at all times. Do you understand?"

"I can't do that," protested Philip, "I have to get home."

"You'll do as I say and if for any reason you fail in your duties, then your wife will suffer, understood? Oh, and I have a little bit of insurance of my own."

Reggie showed him some of the footage taken of his wife, "Now

I'm sure you don't want this all over the Internet? Do as I say and in a few hours from now you will be £300,000 better off and if you forget all that has happened between us, then everything will be just fine for you and your wife. However, rest assured, if any of this gets out, I will kill both of you – do you understand?"

Philip nodded.

"Good."

Reggie addressed Turnbull. "He's your responsibility now. If he does a runner, then I'll always know where to find that lovely daughter of yours."

With this last statement he got to his feet and instructed Roberts to give Ian his phone back. Ian and Philip watched in silence as Carlyle and Roberts left the bar.

"What now?" asked Philip.

"We'll book into a B&B tonight," answered Ian. "Where exactly are you going to make the exchange?"

"He's not."

Turnbull and Townsend turned to see Frank standing before them.

"You lost your bloody mind?" said Turnbull. "Carlyle's only just left"

"No, I have all my faculties and you are trying to double-cross me."

"What the hell are you talking about?"

"£300,000 – and where's my share?" he said.

"Your share? I'm getting nothing out of this."

"And I'm supposed to believe you?"

"Wait a minute," said Ian, "how do you know how much money's involved?"

"Let's just say a little birdie told me, a Cockney sparrow if you like," answered Frank. "This is what will happen," he continued, "I'll do the business with Carlyle, and we'll split the money three ways or I'll tell Pinky and Perky upstairs that I am your so-called Russian and that you're trying to rip them off."

He then turned his attention to Philip. "And as far as you go, I still have that information on your wife. Additionally, Ian here has told me a few interesting things about you my lad," he added, looking directly at him.

Philip got to his feet, "I'll handle this my way."

"Be quiet and sit the fuck down," said Frank.

Townsend reluctantly returned to his seat as Frank sat down next to him.

"I'll tell you this, when you hand over those documents, you'll get nothing – fuck all – not one penny. If either of you want to get out of this with anything, and in one piece, you'll have to let me handle things."

"What makes you think you can handle Carlyle any better than me?" asked Philip.

Frank eased a little closer to Townsend and pulled his jacket back slightly, "This for a start," he said.

"Is that real?" he exclaimed.

"Of course it's fucking real and I'm not afraid to use it. After all, unlike you two, I have nothing to lose. I will need those documents now."

"No I can't do that," he protested. "I don't trust you."

"Ok then, let me spell it out to you so you understand how exactly this is all going to work. I know a forger that can make an exact copy of the files and it will be this copy that I hand over to Carlyle. We'll keep the originals."

"But if he thinks he's got the right documents, how's that going to help? And if what you're telling us is true and Carlyle won't honour his side of things, we'll have no choice but to keep the documents," replied Philip.

"He's right," said Ian. "If he thinks he's got the right papers, he will feel confident enough to do whatever he feels necessary, and I for one don't want to end up as pig feed."

Frank disagreed, "No, all we have to do is keep out of his way for 48 hours."

"What fucking difference will that make?" asked Ian.

"Quite simply this – these forged documents will start to decay after two days – the ink's not colour-fast and it will start fading to the point where all you'll be left with is several sheets of blank paper. We will have the protection of the original documents, plus 300 grand."

Frank's proposal was met with a certain amount of incredulity from them both. "You've been watching too many films," laughed Ian.

"I'm telling you the truth and what's more, do you have a better idea?"

He looked across at Philip. "I guess he's right, what do we have to lose?"

Reluctantly he agreed.

"Right – so where are these documents?" asked Frank.

"He doesn't have them with him," answered Turnbull.

"I didn't think he would – so where are they?"

Reluctantly Philip slipped his hand inside his coat and removed a pale pink folder tied with a red ribbon.

"You cheeky bastard!" exclaimed Ian. "I admire your balls. You've been sitting here all this time talking to Carlyle with them shoved up your jumper? Who'd have thought it?"

"Now come on, we'd better get these over to…" Frank paused. "Probably best if you don't know."

"There's no way I'm going to let these originals out of my sight," said Philip, shoving them back inside his coat.

"Fair enough, I don't blame you. Come on let's go."

Philip held the front passenger door open as Frank eased his leg into the foot well. Philip couldn't help notice small beads of sweat gathering on his forehead from the effort and pain, his face now sallow, almost green in complexion. Finally, after some time, he was seated.

"So what time and where are you to meet Carlyle?" he asked.

"Do you know the Kenning Junction Aqueduct?"

"Yes," replied Frank hoping against all odds this was not going to be the meeting place.

"I'm to meet him there at midnight. Will that give us enough time to get these documents printed?"

"Yeah, of course – if we get a move on," he said. "The guy I know is one of the best forgers around. Mind you he's not cheap, but then again that doesn't worry us does it Philip me old mate?"

—⁓—

Ian made his way to the bar just as Margaret was about to relieve Alan.

"I take it you're the owner?" he enquired.

"For my sins," she replied, carrying several bottles of locally brewed beer.

"My name's Ian Turnbull. I wonder if you could ask Mr Solomon and Mr Goodman to join me."

"Very well," she said, placing the last bottle on the shelf. "I'll just try their room."

"Paul? It's Margaret here."

"Yes Margaret, what can I do for you?"

"There's a gentleman here by the name of Ian Turnbull. He would like you both to join him in the bar."

"Oh would he?" he answered. "Tell him we'll be down in a couple of minutes. Oh Margaret…"

"Yes."

"Is there anyone with him?"

"No, there's only him and a couple of stragglers from the Murder Mystery Society."

"That's fine. As I said, tell him we'll be down shortly."

"What was all that about?" asked Solley, buttoning up his shirt.

"It seems our Mr Turnbull wants to have a word."

"Well then, we'd better not keep him waiting."

22

Joe answered his phone, "Ok, boss…"

He ended the call and placed the phone back into his inside breast pocket then turned to Frances. "Now, you listen to me carefully. You are to speak to no-one about what happened tonight; if you do you'll regret it. Does 14a Station Road ring a bell?"

"That's my daughter's address."

"That's right. Remember, nothing happened."

He grabbed her by the chin with his large hand, pulling her out of her chair. She could feel the power and strength of this big man and it felt as though his fingers could crush her jaw at any moment.

"Your daughter's a pretty girl," he said, "It would be a shame if anything happened to her."

He eased his hand from her face, leaving several red marks. "Goodnight Mrs Turnbull. Sleep tight."

Frances watched in stunned silence as Carlyle's henchmen left.

—⁓—

Ian began to grow impatient, desperate to get home to his wife.

"We understand that you wish to speak to us," said Paul.

Ian turned sharply, a look of relief on his face. "Look, I really don't know what to say but none of this fiasco was my doing."

"I have to say we both find that hard to believe, am I not right?" he added, turning to Solley who, with one arm resting against the bar, nodded his agreement.

"Ok, I'll be totally up front with you," continued Turnbull. "This Russian business was dreamt up by Frank. He told me he had made enquiries – suggested it could be a way of getting more money out of you, and if it didn't then we could just make up some excuse and say he had to pull out for some reason. Goodness knows why I went along with it. Well to be honest I do," he continued, "you see Frank's very useful if you know what I mean? But unfortunately, he has a bit of a hold over me so I don't want to upset him."

"Ok, let's suppose you're telling us the truth," said Paul, "what about these documents?"

"That's the thing – again I had no involvement until Frank asked me to set up this meeting with Roberts and Carlyle. The gammy leg he got escaping from Reggie. I didn't even know he was here until I arrived this evening," Ian lied. "I mean – what the hell's all that about? Arranging a meeting place for the person that just tried to kill you and you're just up the bloody stairs. I mean – come on."

Both Paul and Solley were familiar with Frank's type and it was just the sort of crazy thing they would do. But of course, the last place Carlyle would expect Frank to be would be in the room over his own head.

"So where's Frank now?" asked Solley.

"He's gone off with Townsend. Don't ask me where though, as far as I'm concerned, I'm finished with the whole bloody affair."

"Right this is how things are going to be from now on," said Solley. "You are to get full planning permission for the Sanatorium into apartments. Once that is in our hands in writing – then you have a deal. Oh, and the 20k I gave you – I want that back tomorrow."

"But I will need that for sweeteners," he protested.

"After what we have heard tonight, I think that your Councillor Roberts would be wise not to poke the hornets' nest," said Paul.

"Savvy? Now my colleague and I are going up to the old hospital tomorrow. We'll be there – say – 11ish. Meet us there with the money."

"It will have to be later, say 1pm? I'll need a bit of time to put that much cash together."

"Ok, but don't mess us around," said Solley, "we have plenty on you."

—⁂—

"Pull over here," said Frank.

Philip did as instructed and pulled the car tight into the kerb.

"This is it." He looked through the front windscreen at the rows of old terraced workshops long since abandoned.

"This whole street is derelict," observed Philip.

"Not quite, now help me out of this piece of shit."

Opening the passenger door, he leant in. Frank put his arm around his neck and with his assistance, lifted himself out of the small car.

"Are you sure this is the right place?" he asked, taking in the area in the half-light. "Are any of these places occupied?"

"One or two," Frank answered, pushing open one of the back gates with his shoulder. "Come on, what are you waiting for?"

Philip locked the car and reluctantly followed him into the small courtyard at what appeared to be the rear of a semi-detached Victorian miner's cottage. The door to the house was secured with a padlock which seemed odd. *If this so-called forger's here, how the hell did he get in?* Plus, there were no other vehicles about. *Perhaps he's on his way over?* he thought.

He then began to feel extremely uneasy, after all – he had good reason to. Not only did he have valuable documents on him, he knew virtually nothing of this Frank character. He was also armed, and from what he had indicated, he was not above using it.

Frank stood to one side, padlock in hand. "After you," he said.

He hesitated for a second. Should he make a run for it and just do the deal with Carlyle? His instincts were screaming at him to get out of there.

"Come on, what are you fucking about for? He will be here soon and we don't have much time."

"You mean he uses this place to forge documents?"

"Only sometimes," replied Frank. "Most of the time he uses his shop on the High Street. You probably know the one; it has a big flashing fluorescent sign '*Get your forged passports and documents here*'. What the fuck do you think?" he added sarcastically.

Philip could not argue with this reasoning and stepped into the black void. "Is there a light in here?"

"Hold on," replied Frank as he struggled to shut the door behind him.

A few seconds later a pale red light came on. The windows were completely blacked out. At the centre of the room was a table with several small printing machines, and scattered about were what looked like various types of blank IDs and passports. Philip felt an overwhelming sense of relief. For a time there, he had thought Frank was leading him on.

Philip crashed to the floor, a pool of blood starting to form around his motionless head like a dark halo.

Frank pulled him onto his back and retrieved the documents and the car keys. He then removed one of his gloves and took a glass phial out of his pocket snapping the top off and inhaling the contents. Now bolstered by the amphetamines, he made his way to Philip's car. High on this powerful drug, he started the vehicle, the pain of his now infected injury a thing of the past – if only temporarily – as he drove at high speed along the deserted streets.

—⁂—

"What do you make of all that?" asked Paul as the two men stood before their hoped-for acquisition.

"Bullshit," answered Solley. "But if he can deliver us full planning permission then that's all we have to be concerned about; his problems are his."

"You're not worried about any of this rubbing off on us by association?"

"Don't see why it should; are you worried?"

Paul did not answer at first. Had this been a couple of days ago he would have abandoned the idea, but after today and with the late afternoon sun shimmering on the old Sanatorium, he felt a strange affinity with the place; almost as if it was meant to be – and his gut feeling had served him well in the past. Not only that, the potential was really quite exceptional for the price.

"No," he answered. "As you say, we have had very little to do with Turnbull and nothing to do with anyone else mixed up in this nonsense."

—꘠—

Frank pulled off the road. "Yes, it's Frank here. I have what you want. I'll meet you at the same place you were going to meet Townsend in one hour."

He hung up, his heart rate and breathing now elevated. He would probably need another capsule to get him through this but he was reluctant to commit himself unless it was absolutely necessary. He knew that drugs were unpredictable.

—꘠—

Philip started to come to, doing his best to focus on the wall in front of him. What the hell had happened? He tried to get to his feet but his legs did not want to respond so he lay there trying to piece together events and where on earth he was. Finally he got to his knees and with one hand on the table, he managed to stand up. He felt sick. Reaching into his pocket, he retrieved a hanky then tried to wipe away the semi-congealed blood from his eyes.

He then pulled frantically at his sweater. The documents were missing. "That lying bastard!" he shouted as he made his way unsteadily towards the door, trying it several times but it was padlocked from the outside. Philip looked about him for something to break out with. He reached into his pocket and retrieved his phone but, as he suspected, there was no signal.

—⁓—

Paul and Solley made their way to the lounge with their drinks as Margaret's rowdy guests piled into the bar, resembling some kind of multi-limbed organism intent on devouring everything in their path.

With Alan now in the kitchen with Pauline, Margaret manned the bar with great skill, taking orders left, right and centre. Paul could not help but be impressed.

"Are you going to try Julie again?"

"Sorry?"

"You said you were going to phone Julie again to see how Kim's doing."

"Oh of course," he replied, "I'll do it right now. I would have done it earlier only there have been so many distractions this evening."

"That's true," said Solley, *and one of those is behind the bar,* he thought.

—⁓—

"Hello, Julie?"

"Hi, I've only just got back."

"How was she?" he asked.

"Oh you know Kim, it's hard to tell. She always puts a brave face on everything. She asked me to ask you how things were going with you and Solley."

"Err, ok," he replied.

"You don't sound very confident."

"Well you know how it is with these things, all last minute. Oh, and Julie…"

"Yeah?"

"Thanks."

"Thanks for what? She's my sister."

"I know, but thanks all the same. Look I have to go, tell Kim I love her and I'll see her soon, and give my best to Derek and the kids."

"Any news?" enquired Solley.

"She seems fine but as Julie said, hard to know with Kim, she's never been one to complain."

—⁓—

Despite Philip's best attempts, the door proved too secure for him. However, the small metal bar he'd found might be sufficient to prise away one of the sheets of ply that covered the two narrow windows. Sure enough, after considerable effort, he managed to force one of them loose.

Now able to grip it with both hands, he used every fibre of his being to force it back far enough to get through but in his rush to escape, one of the 3" nails that had held the ply in place, punctured his backside. He froze, half in and half out of the window. He tried tentatively to ease himself back inside and try again, but as he did so, the nail bit deeper into his flesh. There was nothing for it but to drop out onto the ground head first. Although he was on the ground floor it was still at least five feet to the cobbled courtyard below him.

Philip let out a piercing scream as he tumbled out of the window and onto the wet courtyard below him. The nail had ripped deep into the soft flesh of his buttocks and he could feel the warm blood running down the back of his leg. But there was no way he could stem the flow. The question now was how to get home and should he tell Turnbull what had happened?

He hobbled into the narrow road and it was then he realised things had gone from bad to worse as Frank had obviously taken his car. He didn't know this area well, but there must be a phone somewhere so he could call a cab.

—m—

Paul removed his mobile from his pocket. "It's Julie," he said to Solley.

"I'll leave you with that. I'll get us another drink."

Solley made his way to the bar, passing the Leeds Murder Mystery Society who had brought together several tables and were now deep in conversation with the occasional dramatic effect thrown in for good measure.

"They seem to be enjoying themselves" he remarked.

"Hopefully," replied Margaret, looking up from wiping the bar. "They like the hotel – well, most of it anyway. They said the location is perfect as they are planning on doing a short video film for their 20th anniversary."

"When's that?"

"Next May, so hopefully if they decide to stage it here, I'll have the place refurbished by then. Can I get you anything?"

"Two more Cognacs please Margaret."

She leaned forwards slightly, "Look, I know it's none of my business, but what was all that about with Councillor Roberts? And who was that horrible man with him? I didn't like the look of that character one bit."

"Well seeing as you're part of the team," answered Solley, "the guy with the dark suit, as you know, is Ian Turnbull – you will probably have dealings with him at some time in the future. As to the others with Councillor Roberts – I have no idea as to who they might be."

—m—

Frank eased the car off the road, turned the lights off and waited. It was not long before a black 4x4 drew up in front of him. The pain in his leg was now returning with a vengeance – he would have no choice but to use another capsule. Breaking the top off, he again inhaled the contents – his brain immediately flooded with endorphins, washing away the agonising pain.

He opened his door to find Reggie and his two heavies standing in front of their vehicle, the headlights still on, making it difficult for him to see their faces.

"You have the documents?" said Reggie. "And where's Townsend?"

"He chickened out," replied Frank, "left the dirty work to me."

Reggie laughed, "Spineless twat – doesn't surprise me. Ok, let's see them."

"No, give me the money first."

Reggie nodded and Joe stepped forward and handed him a holdall. Frank fumbled for the zip and undid the bag – it was full of £50s. There was too much to count but it was obvious there was a small fortune in there. He put the bag in his car under the supervision of Joe then took the papers from under his seat and handed them over.

Reggie took the documents from Joe and handed them to Roberts. A few moments later, he confirmed they were the ones.

"Well Frank, it's been nice doing business with you," said Reggie. "Oh, and before I go, I'll be taking that with me."

Joe pushed Frank out of the way and reached into the car for the holdall.

"Get your fucking hands off," screamed Frank, the 9mm pistol levelled at his head.

"Ok Frankie lad, no need to get all girlie over a few quid," said Reggie, at the same time indicating for Joe to back away. "I have to say Frank; I'm very disappointed in you. I thought you would have had the common sense to get rid of that thing while you had the chance. Do you really think, after that little spectacle earlier, we would come unprepared?"

"You're trying to rip me off."

"Now Frankie, did you honestly believe I was going to hand over 300 grand just like that?"

Reggie watched from the corner of his eye as Keith, unbeknown to Frank – high on amphetamines and struggling to keep his attention and focus – moved around behind him.

"Look Frank, we don't want anyone to get hurt do we? You can keep the money, just hand over the gun," he said, moving forward slightly.

"Stay the fuck where you are. I mean it – I know how to use this thing."

As Reggie eased forward once again, Frankie screamed at him to stay still. Keith was now in position and was just about to make his move when he stepped on a discarded drinks can. Frank turned, firing instinctively in the direction of the noise. The gunshot was followed by a loud scream.

He then fired several more shots, sending Reggie and Joe diving for cover. He tossed the gun into the car, the engine still running, and accelerated down the narrow lane at high speed.

Reggie and Joe rushed over to Keith who was holding his arm. Joe ripped his shirt while Reggie removed his belt, and with the blood flow now stemmed, they bundled Keith into the back of the Range Rover.

"Dr Hussein," said Reggie, "I have some more work for you. Go to the flat, I will meet you there."

—∭—

A light drizzle had started to fall as Philip had all but negotiated the area of waste ground that separated him from the lights and life of Lower End – one of the less than prosperous areas well known for its drugs and prostitution problems. However, he was in need of a different type of relief.

It then dawned on him that in his present condition, would any one of the many taxis that plied this notorious area, be willing to take him as a customer? There was also another problem – he was now devoid of cash. He would have no choice but to contact Turnbull for help.

Some 100 metres away the flashing neon sign, clearly that of a takeaway of some sort, flashed out like a beacon across the debris that lay all around him. Maybe there would be a payphone, although he would have to reverse the charges. Or perhaps he could coax the owner of the establishment into using his phone? Either way he would try his luck.

He pulled open the door to the telephone kiosk to find the vestiges of what was once a working phone hanging loosely at an acute angle. He glanced through the Perspex and into the plate glass window of the kebab house opposite. The two tattooed men behind the counter looked less than friendly but there was no-one else.

"What can I get you?" said the shorter of the two as he entered the shop.

"I'm afraid I've had a bit of an accident," he said, "and I was wondering if I could use your phone."

"You'll have to buy something first," answered the taller of the men.

"Don't be such a fucking arsehole Asil," came a female voice from behind Philip, "can't you see he's in a bad way."

Philip turned to see who his potential saviour might be. There before him stood two women of the night, both late forties, short skirts and long boots – archetypal prostitutes – the type of people he despised most. It was ironic really, that he now found himself in a position where his very future might depend on them.

"Ok, for you I do it," said Asil, "but make sure the call's local," he added, removing a phone from under the counter.

—m—

"It's Philip here."

"What the bloody hell do you want?" replied Turnbull.

"I'm injured and need help."

Turnbull checked his rear-view mirror and indicated before pulling into a layby. "What the hell are you talking about?"

"Frank knocked me out and took the documents."

"Look sunshine, you're on your own now. I want nothing to do with this anymore."

"I'm at the end of Harbour Road. If you don't help me then…"

"Then fucking what?" shouted Ian. "Go to the fucking police? See if I care. And do you know what? I'm glad he's got them – at least it's all over. Trying to blackmail Reggie Carlyle was a fucking stupid idea in the first place."

"Hello? Hello?"

Philip slumped against the counter.

"You all right love?" asked one of the prostitutes, holding him by the arm.

"Yes, I'll be fine."

"How did you come to cut yourself, and there of all places?"

"Stag do," he answered.

"Oh really?"

"Yeah, one too many and lost my way – not sure how I came by this." It was then he had an idea. "Please may I use the phone just one more time?"

"Ok," replied Asil. "Just one more time then you piss off!"

"Hello, Mrs Grayson?"

"Yes, who's this?"

"It's Philip Townsend here."

"Philip, what are you phoning me for? I don't think this is a good idea – not with your suspension and all."

"Look, I desperately need your help. I wonder if you could come out and pick me up? My car has broken down and Catherine's had one of her turns – she can't leave the house."

"Have you phoned the breakdown people?"

"Yes, but they can't do anything until tomorrow."

"Why, I thought they were 24 hours these people?"

"Well you see – it's not exactly a breakdown; I've lost my keys. If it were a breakdown they could help but my keys aren't covered and there's something else I have to ask you. I don't think Catherine in her present state will even answer the door at this time of night. I was wondering if I could stay with you until the morning."

This request was met by a long silence.

"I don't see why not," she answered.

The thought of this man she had secretly loved for years under her roof overnight was too good an opportunity to miss, and she obviously still had what it takes, judging by the other day with Nigel. And as for that wife of his – ok she may be a stunner, but surely he must be fed up to the back teeth with all of her phobias. Maybe after he spends a night with a woman who has all her faculties he might just realise what he's been missing.

"Ok," she said, "whereabouts are you?"

"I'm over at Lower End – Harbour Road."

"What are you doing over there at this time of night?"

"Oh it's a long story but it involves our mutual friend Councillor Roberts."

"Ok, I'll be about twenty minutes."

Philip replaced the receiver, left the shop and made his way to the end of the road that terminated in a sea of destroyed memories. He would cross the debris back onto Harbour Road and wait for her there.

Ian turned his key and rushed into the hallway, calling his wife's name but she was nowhere to be seen. He raced upstairs where he could hear the sound of sobbing coming from the bathroom.

"Frances, open the door, it's me."

He could hear her on the other side, scrabbling with the lock on the bathroom door. This pathetic attempt at trying to protect herself really brought home the fear she must have felt.

As she threw her arms around her husband, he could feel her body trembling against him. He led her into the bedroom and sat her on the edge of the bed.

"It's ok, it's over, it's all over. There's nothing to worry about."

"What the hell's going on?" she sobbed.

"Look, I didn't want to worry you but a deal with some land fell through. This guy that was interested got upset and said I had deliberately led him on and that it had cost him. But there's no need to worry now, I have sorted everything."

"So why did they come here?"

"They wanted to make sure that I would give them the money that they said they lost."

Frances removed a small hanky from her sleeve and wiped her tear-stained face, leaving smudges of mascara under both eyes.

"How much?" she asked.

Ian hesitated, "Oh, not too much."

"How much?" she repeated.

"£20,000," he answered.

"I thought you said it wasn't much."

"We can afford it. Anyway, when this Sanatorium deal goes through, we will get it all back, plus. You wait and see."

"I need to get out of here."

"Ok," he said, "first thing tomorrow you go over to the apartment at Grange, I'll come over later in the day."

"No," said Frances sharply. "I want you to come with me now. I don't want to be left on my own – not for one second."

Ian got down onto his knees and took her hands in his. "Look, what happened earlier will not happen again, they have what they want. Frances – look at me – you are in no danger, honestly."

"But who were they?"

"It's best you don't know," he replied. "Tomorrow I'll take them the money and that will be an end to it."

"Suppose they want more?" she asked.

"It doesn't work that way – this is not extortion."

"Oh no? It sounds like it to me."

"Ok, I'll be honest with you. I may have given the impression that they had the land deal in the bag. I was convinced myself and yes, I may have encouraged them to make certain arrangements that would have put them out of pocket."

"Oh, so coming over here, forcing their way into our home, holding me hostage and threatening our daughter is somehow acceptable?"

"No, I'm not saying that for one moment, but I am ever so slightly to blame. However, once I have put things right, we will hear no more of them – that's a promise."

Ian could tell she was less than convinced, although he had tried his best and he knew that Reggie would always be lurking somewhere in the background. Once he had his claws into you, it was nigh on impossible to escape.

—⁂—

"So where do we go from here?" asked Roberts.

"That's a good question," replied Reggie, lighting a cigar that took several attempts to ignite. "Once we have got Keith sorted we'll find out a bit more about the two London gentlemen, and if I'm not mistaken, if they get planning permission (and we will make sure they do) to convert the old Sanatorium into apartments, they will need a contractor – and who better than a trustworthy firm like

Carlyle Construction," he added, tilting his head back and blowing several smoke rings. "Oh, and I think Turnbull should continue to liaise with them."

"Suppose they have someone else in mind, or even their own contractors?"

"That's possible," he replied, taking another puff on his Cuban cigar, "but of course, none of this will happen without consent so if they choose the right contractor there will be no problem if you see what I mean Councillor."

"You know there's only so much I can do?"

Reggie eased his cigar slowly from his mouth and flicked a wad of ash into the ashtray. "You know as well as I do that you have people in your pocket. I know this because I put them there, so all you have to do is to use your abundant charm and gently guide them in the right direction. And if – and I repeat *if* – you should have any trouble, just let me know."

He pulled up outside Roberts' house. "Well here we are Councillor. I would come in for a nightcap but I want to see how Keith is doing so if you would be so kind... Oh and before you go, I'll take those," he added, relieving him of the documents.

He leant across and opened the door. Roberts left the vehicle and without a word Reggie slammed the door with a resounding thud, Roberts watching as the large 4x4 slipped into the night.

—⁊⁊—

"Hello Ian, it's Reginald here."

"Two minutes," he replied.

"Who's that?" whispered Frances, a worried look on her face.

"It's nothing darling, just business. Why don't you pop downstairs and put the kettle on, I won't be a minute. Oh, and just close the door on the way out."

"Look, I have nothing of interest for you. Philip's got the documents, I can't help you."

"Oh, but that's where you're mistaken. I want to know more about your clients from London."

"Sorry, I don't know what you're talking about."

"Ok, let me spell it out to you – the two men that were at the hotel."

"What two men?" said Ian, trying to sound confused.

"So now you're telling me that you have never met the two men from London that were in the hotel last night?"

"Oh, those two – I told you I caught their car on the way in."

"Well a little birdie tells me otherwise. Your wife's quite talkative, especially with a little persuasion. Ian…? You still there?"

"Yes," he answered quietly.

"So tell me all you know."

"They're making an offer for the old Sanatorium," he explained. "They're planning to turn it into apartments."

"I know that much but there must be more to it than that."

"No, that's all there is and the rest you know."

"Ok, for once – and don't ask me why – I believe you. How much are they offering?"

"£500,000," he replied.

"£500,000 you say? And it's going to cost to convert. What are you expecting them to go for?"

"The top range apartments I would reckon £210,000."

Reggie did some quick mental maths, "There must be something we are missing here. I reckon with costs and purchase price you're looking at £1.6million. That's a big investment for a little return. Now listen carefully Turnbull, I want you to find out what's really going on – if you want a peaceful life that is."

"And how exactly am I supposed to do that? If there is another angle to all this, they're not going to tell me."

"That's your problem my friend. You got yourself into this situation – this is your only way out. Oh, and if by any chance you hear from Frank, find out where he is and be sure to let me know."

Frank ripped at the lining of his jacket – there had to be some more – but to his dismay, his pocket was empty, he had used the last of the capsules. He knew he would have to abandon the vehicle soon so he turned off the narrow road and drove along a track for some 200 metres.

Stopping the car, he removed the holdall containing the money, and made his way unsteadily towards to the old towpath that ran parallel to the canal. He would need somewhere to hide the cash. He settled on one of the old arched bridges that crossed the canal every mile or so and pushed the bag into a recess under some old planks.

This exertion and the pain from his leg caused him to vomit several times until there was nothing left then, now retching every few seconds, he collapsed onto the ground. He lay there for several minutes trying to gain some strength from somewhere but it was useless, so once again he would have to turn to his old friend.

He waited for what seemed to be ages until he heard Ian's voice. "It's Frank."

"I know who it is," came the reply.

"I'm really in a bad way."

"Oh? And what do you expect me to do about it?"

"I have £300,000 here."

"What the hell are you talking about?" said Ian.

"I took the documents from Townsend, smashed him over the head," he explained. "There's fifty grand in it if you can help me."

So that's why Reggie was so keen to find him, thought Ian. "Ok," he said, "where are you?"

"Err, err, not sure."

"If you don't know where you are, how the hell can I help you?"

"Hold on, I'll check my GPS. Ok, these are the co-ordinates, have you got a pen?"

Ian wrote down the numbers. "Right, I'll put this in my Satnav, hold on."

He knew leaving Frances would be difficult so without saying a word he slipped out the back door. He had two choices – find Frank and tell Reggie or better still, find Frank and keep the money and then tell Reggie. No – that was too risky – Reggie was pissed off as it was. Ian knew he had much more to lose than £300,000.

—⁓—

"This is cosy, reminds me of our sleepovers. Do you remember that time Mickey Ward stole his mum's bingo money and we climbed out of your bedroom window by tying the sheets together?"

"Yep," answered Paul, "and you told me I was wasting my time in the Scouts."

"What's that got to do with anything?" said Solley, now raised up on his right elbow, looking across at him.

"Well if it had not been for my half-shank knots, one or both of us would have broken our necks."

"Oh come on – you make it sound like escaping from Alcatraz."

"It was high enough, take my word for it."

"That's as may be, but whatever possessed us to buy that bottle of gin?"

"No ID checks in those days. I remember it clearly, 'my mum wants some gin,' said Mickey, holding up a fiver."

"Anyway, that's enough reminiscing for the moment. Are you sure it's wise to involve Margaret?"

"What do you mean?" asked Paul. "I told you, there's only one woman for me and that's Kim."

"Yeah, I know all that but what I mean is, what if things get a bit…"

"A bit what?"

"You know – ugly," replied Solley.

"Don't see why they should. Margaret will be just working for us, that's all. We both agree she'll be the best person for the job and not only that, she needs the money. You heard what she said earlier about making a go of this place, and we could help her make it happen. Not only that, I'm sure the bar and restaurant will do very nicely once the apartments are sold."

"I guess you're right," said Solley, easing himself onto his back. "Goodnight mate."

"Goodnight."

Paul lay there thinking – was Solley right? Whoever that was with the Councillor, he was certainly not your average Joe, that was sure, and it was obvious that Turnbull could not be trusted. But then again, they kind of knew that from the start.

He let out a deep sigh as the sound of Solley's snoring filled the room. Paul always envied him for this – no matter where he was, as soon as his head was down, he was asleep. He always claimed it was a clear conscience that enabled him to do this – maybe he was right.

—⁓—

Turnbull pulled up next to Philip's car. "Frank, Frank," he shouted. "Where the fuck are you?"

He started to search the bushes and the surrounding area, calling out his name every so often. Finally, he found him lying against the bank. Ian knelt down next to him and touched his neck – he was still alive but barely conscious and in a really bad way.

"Frank, Frank, can you hear me?"

"Is that you Ian?"

"Of course the fuck it is. Where's the money?"

"Piss off."

"Look, don't be a stupid bastard, if Carlyle doesn't get that back, he'll cut your legs off – if you're lucky. You're in no state for this game anymore. Tell me where the money is and I'll see he gets it. It might just save your life. Frank…? Can you hear me…? Fuck you. Ok, please yourself but I'm out of here, I'm doing you a favour allowing you to die now rather than letting that bastard get hold of you."

"No, wait," he croaked. "It's under the old canal bridge."

"Can you be more specific Frank; whereabouts under the bridge?"

"It's behind some sheets of wood."

"Ok, leave it to me."

Ian started to make his way back to his car.

"Where are you going?" he pleaded.

"I shan't be a minute," he replied as he disappeared into the dark.

"Reggie? Turnbull here, I have him."

"Well Ian you have gone a long way to redeeming yourself. I might even go as far as to say there could be a position for you in Carlyle Enterprises, I am always on the lookout for resourceful people."

"Yeah, whatever. What do you want me to do with him?"

"Do you have a pen?"

"Hold on a sec … yeah."

"Now listen carefully, I want you to take him to this address…"

"He needs a hospital," interrupted Ian. "I'm not sure how long he will last."

"Don't concern yourself – there will be a doctor waiting to receive him, he will be well cared for. You have the money I take it? Ian…? Ian…? You still there?"

"Yeah, yeah, I'm still here – just lost you for a moment. It doesn't look as though the money's here."

"Oh well," he said, "I'm sure when Frankie is feeling a little more like his old self he will be more than willing to tell us where it is. But I'll send one of my people over to where you are, just to make sure it's not lying around anywhere."

Ian returned the phone to his pocket. *You fucking idiot, why the hell did you say that?*

He bundled the injured Frank into the back of his car for the second time then locked Philip's vehicle and hid the key.

—∞—

Philip stepped off the kerb just as Mrs Grayson turned the corner in her bright yellow hatchback. As the car drew slowly to a halt, he did not hesitate in jumping into the front passenger seat.

"What on earth happened to you?" she exclaimed.

Philip looked blank.

"Your head and face – it's covered in blood!"

"Oh that; I tripped on my way over that rubble."

"What on earth were you doing out there at this time of night?"

He was fighting for a plausible excuse but just before he could find an answer, his phone rang. "Please excuse me, I must get this. I won't be a second," he said as he stepped out of the car.

"Ian here – now listen carefully. Your car is a couple of hundred metres beyond Miller's Boat Yard, the one that does all the narrowboats. Do you know where I mean?"

"Yes," he replied. "Catherine and I used to…"

"Never mind all that. Turn left, it's parked on some waste ground. The keys are under a stone next to the rear nearside wheel. Go and get it immediately before it raises any suspicion."

Philip returned his phone to his pocket and got back into Mrs Grayson's car. "I need you to do me a really big favour," he said.

"What kind?" she asked, sounding a little hesitant.

He placed his hand gently on her knee. "You know I told you that my car had broken down."

"Yes," she replied, her heart beating a little faster.

"Well that's not strictly true, you see things have been a little strained recently – what with my suspension and everything, not to mention this," he added, pointing to his face. "I suggested we go for a drive. Catherine wasn't sure at first but I just felt we had to get out of the house. Finally, she agreed but insisted on driving, against my better judgement. However, for some reason it seemed to make things worse, her driving became faster and more erratic.

"I begged her to slow down and finally, after some persuasion, she agreed to stop the car. I suggested we get out and go for a walk. It was then she drove off and left me. As I said, this cut on my head was from falling over all that rubble. That phone call was from a friend of ours – he's seen my car parked by the canal."

"Oh my goodness, you don't think she might be planning to…?"

"I don't know, but I need to get over there right now."

"Maybe we should phone the police?"

"No, that's the last thing we should do; if they turn up there's no telling what she might do. Not only that they'll take one look at me and wonder what's happened, but if I can find her, I know she'll listen to me. This is not the first time this sort of thing has happened."

"Oh you poor soul," said Mrs Grayson as she turned on the ignition and accelerated away at high speed in the direction of the viaduct.

23

Turnbull drew up outside the flat that Reggie had given him directions to. It was an end of terrace in a less than welcoming neighbourhood. Most, if not all, of the large Edwardian houses had been converted to flats in the 1970s to house immigrants.

This once prosperous area started its inexorable decline after the Second World War as nearby industry that once supplied the British Empire with everything from toothbrushes to locomotives began to close down as the Empire fragmented and one country after another gained their independence from a bankrupt and war-weary Britain.

He climbed the stone steps and depressed the doorbell. Instantly Joe answered the door, "Drive round the back," he said, "I'll meet you there," and slammed the door in Ian's face.

Turnbull returned to his car and made his way into the rear courtyard. Between himself and Joe, they carried Frank into the kitchen to find Dr Hussein standing by the table, the floor covered in heavy duty plastic sheeting.

"Ah Ian, how nice it is to see you again," said Reggie, stepping into the kitchen. "So you tell me that the holdall containing the money was not with our friend here?"

"No," replied Ian.

"Mmm, how strange. I have just had a call from one of my

assistants and they have looked everywhere for it. I'm guessing he must have hidden it somewhere."

"I guess you're right."

"But the thing is what shall I do?" continued Reggie. "If by some chance Frankie should happen to say it was with him when he passed out…"

"Well it wasn't," protested Ian. "Do you really think I'm that stupid – to risk everything for a measly 300 grand?"

Reggie placed his large hand on his shoulder and gripped him tightly with his fat fingers. "That is something we'll find out, mark my words," he said. "And there's another thing I want to find out – what these two from London are really up to."

"Ok Reggie, leave it with me, I'll find out all I can on them."

"Damn right you will, now piss off."

—◊◊◊—

"Stop, Stop!" shouted Philip. "Pull over here."

Mrs Grayson did as instructed. "What's wrong?" she asked. "Have you seen Catherine?"

"Turn your lights off and wait here," he demanded.

He made his way onto the grass verge that partially hid them from the viaduct and on hands and knees, crawled his way up the steep bank. From his vantage point, he could just make out the 4x4 that had caught his eye as they turned the bend. However, there seemed to be no-one there.

Suddenly he dropped to the ground as two men emerged from the trees. They were just about to leave when one of them went back. He lay watching until the man returned and after a brief discussion they got into their vehicle and drove off.

Philip looked back to where Mrs Grayson was parked and indicated to her, in no uncertain terms, to stay where she was. He ran down the bank, stumbling as he went and eventually spilling out onto level ground, then made his way up the track that ran beside the canal until finally, after 100 metres or so, he came across his abandoned car. He immediately started to throw everything that had been ripped out of his vehicle into the boot, occasionally looking over his shoulder in the hope that Mrs Grayson's curiosity had not got the better of her.

Moving to the rear of the car he turned over a very large stone and there, as Ian had promised, were his keys. He ran back to Mrs Grayson.

"What's happened?" she asked anxiously.

"It's my car," replied Philip slightly out of breath.

"Is Catherine there?"

"No, but there is good news; I have just had a phone call from a friend over at Hollerton. It appears she turned up there about twenty minutes ago. I've only just got the message; I must have had my phone off."

"That can only be a mile, two at the most, from here. I'll take you over."

"No, that won't be necessary," replied Philip. "Fortunately, she left the keys in the car."

"Lucky it's still there."

"I'm sorry for being such a burden to you."

"Nonsense," replied Mrs Grayson. "I'm only too happy to help, as long as she's safe."

"Look, I must go just in case she has a change of mind and runs off again."

"I understand – I hope all goes well," she called as he ran back to his car.

—m—

Ian had checked his rear-view mirror several times to make sure he wasn't being followed, then pulled off the road into a parking place and waited for a few minutes before making his way along the narrow lane that was almost pitch black despite the fact there was nearly a full moon. He attributed the darkness to the high hedges that towered over him either side.

Finally he came to a small stone arched bridge that crossed this section of the canal. He scrambled down, slipping several times, until he finally reached the path below, then made his way under the bridge.

Many years of neglect had caused this off-shoot of the Manchester to Leeds canal to become overgrown. It had also, over the years, served the local community as an impromptu dump site – everything from old mattresses to the occasional car. He had even seen an old upright piano, once someone's pride and joy, half-submerged in the shallow stagnant water.

He removed several pieces of wood and reached in, a sense of panic hitting him as he fumbled around in the dark. Finally, to his relief, his hand felt the canvas bag then with his ill-gotten gains, he climbed back up to the road and threw the bag onto the back seat.

But what to do with it? he thought. Reggie was bound to want to search his house and the office. Of course, the old Sanatorium, it would be safe there – long enough to find a way of laundering it anyway. But before that, he would help himself to twenty grand to give back to Solley tomorrow morning, thus ensuring the deal went ahead.

However, as he made his way back to his car he was starting to have second thoughts – maybe he should take the money to Reggie, get into his good books, but then again, he needed that twenty grand and there was no way he could get his hands on that much cash by the morning as the original money was now part of a deposit on a new sports car. And as far as Carlyle was concerned it was all or nothing.

Ian turned off his lights and with the aid of the full moon – and a lot of luck – he managed to negotiate the pot-holed track up towards the Sanatorium in the dark. Not wanting to push his luck any further, he pulled over to the side. Removing the holdall from the back seat, he grabbed a torch from the glove box along with a set of keys and continued up the rest of the track on foot, the heavy bag of cash held tight to his chest.

—m—

"Who's there?"

"It's me."

"Oh Philip, why were you so long and what's that all over your face, it looks like dried blood? Have you been attacked again?"

Philip staggered into the hallway and made his way into the sitting room where he slumped onto the sofa, putting his head into his hands.

"I can't do this anymore," he sobbed.

"Do what?" said Catherine as she knelt down in front of him.

"All this – it's my fault."

"What do you mean your fault?"

"I was blackmailed into taking documents from work that an Ian Turnbull was going to use to force one of the councillors…"

"You mean Roberts?" she interrupted.

"Yes. Turnbull wanted to make sure things went the way he wanted them to."

"What was in these documents?"

"Evidence of false invoicing and that Roberts – or should I say his wife and brother-in-law – had arranged things so that they got the bulk of the construction work for the Commonwealth Games Village," he explained.

"But how?"

"Oh by giving bribes mostly. One councillor had a bit of a fetish thing – local prostitutes."

"You mean blackmail."

"Yes, for want of a better word. But there's more to it than that; I went to see this private detective and hired him to find these missing documents."

"How did they go missing?"

"Turnbull had his car stolen, the papers were inside. I think it might have been something to do with Frank."

"Who's Frank?"

"He's the private detective I hired, it seems as though he and Turnbull were in cahoots. I went to see him but when I got there his office was being cleared out by the owner who thought I'd gone there to collect the papers which had arrived that morning in the post. It was then I had this foolish idea – you see I wanted to get my job back."

"Your job?" asked Catherine. "What are you talking about?"

"Roberts and Nigel Hunter made up a bunch of lies to get me sacked. I also thought it was a good opportunity to get some money out of Carlyle and Roberts. It was all because of this that they did what they did to you. If only I'd had the guts to say no in the first place."

"So why didn't you?" she asked, taking hold of his hands.

"Because this Frank somehow found about what had happened to you all those years ago and threatened to make it public if I didn't get these documents. So you see – I did it to try and protect you but it all went wrong and now look at the mess we're in."

"So where are the documents now?"

"That's the reason for all this blood. I went with this private detective to a forger…"

"A forger, why?"

"He said he could get exact copies made – good enough to fool Carlyle or anyone for that matter. It was there he struck me over the head and took the original documents along with the car."

"So how did you get home then?"

"Oh that's another story."

"You're shaking," observed Catherine. "Go upstairs and have a hot shower, I'll light the fire and make some tea."

Philip reached and grabbed her arm, "No there's more I need to tell you. This cut on my face – I was attacked at the bus stop on my way home. The following day I saw two of the attackers while I was at the boating lake trying to kill time before I came home. I don't know what made me do it."

"Do what?" she asked anxiously.

"Well you see I tried to hide from them by looking in my briefcase hoping they wouldn't recognise me and pass by."

"And?"

"They carried on past; I should have left it at that but for some reason, don't ask me why, I took the paperweight from my case."

"Paperweight?"

"Yes, I took it with me after clearing my desk. You see I followed them into the woods and hit them with it."

—∞—

Paul threw back the covers and sat on the edge of the bed. The sound of Solley's deep breathing, interspersed with bouts of snoring, had kept him awake. Or had it? Was he mad? What the hell were they getting themselves into?

He decided that in the morning he would tell Solley that this was too risky and there was no telling where it might end. He felt sure that Kim would feel the same if she knew exactly what was going on with this Turnbull and his associates.

It was then he realised that without this contract he would probably never see Margaret again. Maybe Solley was right – being here had nothing to do with the Sanatorium after all. He knew there was no way he would abandon Kim but what he was really after was the best of both worlds. This contract would probably last for a year or more and then he would probably keep Margaret on to help manage the property. This whole bloody thing was about keeping contact with her. It would have to come to an end.

The problem was that Margaret was now depending on this work in order to save her hotel – she deserved that at least after what she had gone through recently and who knew, he may be facing the same fate. Was there a way they could make this thing work? He would leave his decision until after they had met Turnbull.

—~~—

"He's heavily sedated" explained Dr Hussein, "I have done my best to clean the wound."

"Are you going to leave it like that?" asked Joe. "Surely it will need bandaging."

"No, with a wound like this it's best to let the air get to it."

"It fucking stinks," said Keith, sitting in the corner of the small kitchen, his left arm bandaged to his chest.

"Well go and sit somewhere else," snapped Reggie.

"No," he replied. "I'm not going to let that piece of shit out of my sight. I want the first thing he sees when he wakes up to be my face!"

"How long will he be out for?" Reggie asked Dr Hussein.

"At least eight hours."

"The thing is – our friend here has some very important information. I need to talk to him."

"I'm afraid that's not possible, it's important that he rests."

Reggie placed his hand on Dr Hussein's chest, "No, you don't seem to understand. It's important that I talk to him."

"Mr Carlyle, you will not be able to talk to him if he is dead, plus you then have a body to dispose of. I'll be back later; here are some painkillers and antibiotics – you'll find the instructions on the labels."

—~~—

Ian turned the key in the lock and putting his shoulder to the door, forced his way into the old Sanatorium. Although the place was massive and contained many rooms, hiding a bag of money would not be that easy, it had to be somewhere out of sight. The basement – that would be the best place.

He turned back on himself and made for a set of double doors that would lead him down into the bowels of this edifice.

"Bollocks," he said as he pulled on the brass handles. He looked at the large bunch of keys he had – there must be twenty or more. It was obvious from looking at the lock that some were not suitable so he tried those that were most likely to fit.

As he came to the last key, he placed it into the lock and paused – this had to be the one, it just had to be. Tentatively he turned it but like all the others before, it would not unlock.

"Fuck, fuck," he shouted as he kicked at the base of the double doors.

It was then that he remembered the laundry chute. *That must go down there somewhere,* he thought. He would come back later with some tools and break the lock after Goodman and Solomon had been here.

Ian listened as the heavy bag slid down to the basement below before making his way back along the corridor towards the exit, his torch now starting to fade. To his relief he reached the main doors and pulled but it would not open. He pulled again, this time using all his weight, but still it wouldn't budge. He tried several more times – each time a sense of panic increasing inside him as his torch finally gave up, the only light now coming from the moon in sporadic bursts as it broke free from the scudding clouds.

He tried again, "Come on, come on," he cried, then turned around suddenly, "Hey, who's there? Show yourself; I know you're there," he said, his back pressed firmly against the exit door. It was then he felt something. He ran his hand over the lock and in the half-light he could just make out the stem of a key protruding from the large brass lock. He turned the key and burst out into the cool night air.

"You stupid bastard," he said to himself. "Why the hell did you lock yourself in?"

Ian pulled the door to and, fumbling with the key, locked it securely and started to head back down the track as fast as the faint light would let him, stumbling every so often into one of the many potholes that littered this upper section.

Eventually he reached his car and once inside locked the doors, a sense of relief washing over him. But then came the realisation that whoever was in there – if anyone – they would have seen him put the money down the laundry chute.

Hold on a second, he thought, *get a grip on yourself, who the hell would be in there? It's just your imagination getting the better of you –* which seemed reasonable enough after all that had happened recently. Anyway, the money would have to stay there until tomorrow.

Reaching the main road, he turned on his headlights and headed for home to an extremely anxious wife. But the uppermost thing in his mind was how to find out what Goodman and Solomon were really up to. Carlyle was right, there would be very little, if any, profit in the conversion and that was assuming everything went according to plan – which in a project of this nature invariably did not.

So, he thought, *what could possibly make this conversion so desirable to two businessmen from London?* Or maybe he was going about the wrong way – what is it that makes it less than desirable? Well that was blindingly obvious for a start – its location – stuck out here in the middle of bloody nowhere on a windswept hill. Had it been the other side of Hadley by the railway line or the A629, it would be a gold mine at that price.

That was it! "Shit," he screamed as he swerved the car hard to the right.

—⁓—

Frances sat on the edge of their bed, a carving knife held firmly in her right hand. *If anyone comes in here,* she thought, *I'll kill them, so help me!*

She got to her feet and made another of many trips to the window in the hope of seeing her husband's car pull into the driveway. *Where the hell was he?* She looked at her dresser where the keys to their holiday house lay in the top drawer. Should she put some things together and leave a note?

Ian sat there dazed, blood pouring from his nose, the result of the airbag exploding into his face. It then dawned on him that maybe he should get out just in case there was a fire, something which had always been a phobia of his ever since he had been a child. It had been while they were on their way to the coast – he had been sitting in the middle of the back seat between his elder sister and his Auntie Mavis – when the car travelling in front of them hit a motorbike and careered off the road, turning over several times. He could see those inside tumbling about as though they were in some kind of giant washing machine.

His father and two other motorists ran to their assistance but as they approached, the vehicle burst into flames. His father and one of the other motorists managed to open one of the rear doors and Ian watched transfixed as they dragged a young woman out of the back. She could not have been much older than his sister, her clothes and hair on fire. He could still to this day see his father and the other man trying to put out the flames with their coats and finally their own bodies. His dad had to stay in hospital for nearly two weeks with these plastic bags on his hands. The girl died some days afterwards.

Ian looked up as his door suddenly opened and someone leant in and undid his seatbelt. Still dazed, he tried to focus on his potential rescuer but for some reason he could not define any features. It was as if they had their face covered. *Whoever this was they were strong,* he thought, as he felt himself being lifted out of the vehicle.

He then felt a crushing blow to his already damaged nose and stars floated before his eyes. *What the fuck's happening?* he thought. And then he wondered if this was a necessary part of his rescue. Maybe he was caught in something? Then came another blow – this time to the base of his spine – sending him down onto his knees. But this he recognised, as a boot came into focus heading straight for his face. Instinctively he reached out and grabbed his assailant's leg, holding on as tightly as he could.

Then a sickening pain, caused by something heavy, hit the top of his head. Ian released his assailant's leg and rolled to one side as his attacker kicked and stamped on him, pausing occasionally to hit him with something heavy.

Now coiled up in the foetal position in an effort to protect himself, he suddenly became aware that the punishing blows had stopped. He lay there frozen – too frightened to move until eventually he opened his eyes but was blinded by a bright light.

"Are you ok, can you hear me?" called a voice.

Was this the same person that had beaten him so savagely? he thought. *Surely not – or was it some kind of sick joke?*

"I'll phone for an ambulance. Look I can't get a signal – can you get to your feet?"

"Yes," replied Ian, "I think so."

He forced himself onto his knees, then the young man who had been speaking to him put his arms around his waist and hauled him to his feet. Ian cried out in pain.

"Are you ok?" asked the young man.

"It's my back – I think the bastard might have broken it."

"It's not broken, if it were you wouldn't be able to stand."

He was led tentatively to his rescuer's car and helped onto the back seat where he lay, trying to make sense of what had just happened to him, as the vehicle he was travelling in swept down the narrow country lanes at high speed.

A few moments later the car stopped and he felt a rush of cold air sweep over him – it felt so refreshing. He then realised how thirsty he was and despite his injuries, the most over-riding thing on his mind was a drink of water.

"Yes, you can have a drink in a minute," said a voice as he was hauled off the back seat.

—⁓—

Who the hell's that? thought Margaret, putting on her dressing-gown, as she made her way to the front door.

"Alan, it's you, what the hell's happened?"

"His car came off the road," he explained, "I tried to phone for an ambulance but couldn't get a signal."

"Ok, I'll… Oh Paul, what are you doing down here?"

"I couldn't sleep; I heard all the commotion and wondered if you might need some help."

"He's been in some kind of road accident, I'm just going to phone for an ambulance."

Paul looked at the injured man. At first he didn't recognise him as his face was all swollen and bruised. "No don't do that," he said.

"Why?" she replied, "He needs help."

"Trust me – just do as I say. Ian… Ian… it's Paul Goodman. You are at the High Gate Hotel; Alan found you – do you want an ambulance?"

Ian shook his head slowly.

"Are you sure?"

"No ambulance," he mumbled.

"I thought as much," said Paul.

Margaret took him by the arm as Alan helped Ian to a chair. "Do you mind telling me what the bloody hell's going on here?" she said in a low voice.

"Look, you know that man who was with Councillor Roberts earlier this evening?"

"Yes – I'm not going to forget him in a hurry, he looked like a truly bad type."

"Well you're right there, and what's more, I think – in fact I'm sure – this was his doing and if you phone for an ambulance you too could end up on the wrong side of him – and so could Alan for that matter."

"So long as he's not going to die he can stay here tonight."

"Do you have any old clothes?"

"Err – yes; why?"

"Don't ask questions, just get them. And some rubber gloves too."

Margaret returned a few moments later with a black plastic bag. "These are some of my husband's old working clothes," she said. "I was going to throw them out."

"And the gloves?"

"Oh, two secs."

She went into the kitchen and soon returned with a large pair of red rubber gloves. "These any good?"

"Perfect," said Paul, taking them from her. He called Alan over. "How far is his car?" he asked.

"About two miles."

"Ok, take me to within half a mile of his vehicle."

The short journey was made in silence.

"It's just at the top of the hill," said Alan.

"Right, stop here. Now I want you to go back to the hotel and help Margaret."

Paul stripped off and put his clothes into one of the black bags before putting on some of Margaret's husband's old things. He put the gloves on and made his way up the lane to the car.

The drizzle that had been falling all evening was now getting heavier and the once tiny particles of water now coalesced themselves into big fat rain drops.

The keys to the vehicle were, as Paul had thought, still in the ignition. The front end of the car had buried itself into a hedge, coming to rest against the stump of a once heavily coppiced tree while the rear wheels remained on the road.

He put the transmission into reverse but traction between the road and the rear tyres had been reduced by the now heavy rain so he tried driving forwards slightly and then back again, repeating this several times until finally the car – with the revs high – lurched back out onto the narrow lane and almost into the ditch on the other side.

After a quick inspection, he drove it back to the hotel and parked it inside the old garage that at one time had served the occasional motorist brave enough to venture this way, with its single five-star petrol pump. Squeezing past several old oil drums he made his way outside, closing the large wooden doors, one of which was barely on its hinges, behind him, then satisfied with his work he went back into the hotel.

—⚏—

As she tossed a bag of clothes onto the back seat of her car, Frances realised she had not left a note for Ian, but for some reason she could not face going back into the house now she had summed up the courage to leave.

He will know where to find me, she thought as she turned the key in the ignition.

—⚏—

Paul put the clothes he had been wearing, along with the gloves, into an old oil drum and set fire to them before crossing the yard, tucking his shirt into his trousers as he went. Just then a movement in one of the top left-hand windows of the hotel caught his eye.

Was that someone? he thought. It was too late now.

He went to the back of the hotel and into the kitchen to find Alan replacing the First Aid box.

"Where's Margaret?" he asked.

"She's in the storeroom with Turnbull."

Margaret looked up to see him standing in the doorway.

"How is he?" he asked.

"I'm ok, a little sore that's all," said Ian, wincing as Margaret pushed another pillow under his back.

"Who did this?" asked Paul.

"Did what?" he replied.

"You know what I'm talking about."

"No I don't. I came off the road that's all."

Paul turned to Margaret and asked her if she would be kind enough to leave them alone for a minute.

Margaret was less than pleased with this whole situation, let alone being ordered about in her own hotel by someone she had only met a few days earlier. "Ok, but he's gone first thing tomorrow morning," she said.

He waited for her to close the door behind her. "Ok you can cut the bullshit now," he said. "Let's have the truth."

"I told you – I had an accident."

"I know," replied Paul. "Your car's out the back of the hotel."

"A badger ran out in front of me," continued Ian. "I swerved to miss it, that's all. Silly I know – just one of those things I guess."

Paul moved a little closer and looked down on him. "You're in the shit right up to your neck and I don't want to end up in it with you so unless you tell me everything you know; the deal is off."

"I have told you all that I know. And you're not exactly up front either," he continued.

"What the hell are you talking about?"

"I don't know why I didn't see it myself at first. But then again I guess it was none of my business."

"See what?"

"It doesn't add up."

"What doesn't add up?"

"This project of yours, even at the price you're paying, there's no bloody money in it. Not as things stand anyway."

"Look I have no idea what you're talking about," said Paul, now sounding a little defensive.

"You know something don't you, you and that partner of yours? Something that will increase the value of this whole venture, and I want to know what it is."

"Even if there was something, as you said earlier, it's none of your business, you're just the go-between."

"Oh no," he retorted, "it's gone way beyond that. My wife was held hostage in our home and our daughter's life has been threatened."

"Threatened," repeated Paul, "by whom?"

"That fucking animal Carlyle – that's who."

"Look I am truly sorry for any trouble you may be in but my partner and I are just two property speculators trying to make a few quid – that's all – end of story."

"Ok, so why all the way out here?" asked Ian.

"The property market in London is being taken over by money-laundering Russian gangsters. Solley and I thought we could try somewhere different so to speak. We reckoned this project would only see us break-even but once we got ourselves established as it were, and made a name for ourselves, we would have a good platform to work from. However, it seems that you have your very own gangsters."

"If you don't help me I'll go to the police and tell them you tried to bribe me with twenty grand to get you planning permission from Councillor Roberts."

"You have no proof of that."

"Just because you're from London you think you're so bloody clever don't you? Come up here and throw your weight around. Well I have some news for you – we are not all as thick as you think. I was wearing a wire when we last spoke, I recorded the whole thing."

"Bollocks," said Paul. "You just made that up."

"Ok, if you don't believe me, go and look in the glovebox of my car."

"I'll go." They looked over to see Solley standing in the doorway.

A few moments later he returned and tossed the recording device to Paul.

"And if that doesn't convince you then I have a copy of the recording," explained Ian.

"So what is it you want from us?" asked Solley.

"There is something behind this hospital conversion that makes it worth your while, and I want to know what it is."

Paul was just about to speak when Solley raised his hand. "Check him."

"What?" he replied.

"Check him for recording equipment."

"I would hardly think he was wired," said Paul. "Look at him."

"I'll do it – I don't trust this bastard any more than I could throw him."

"I'm clean," protested Ian.

"What the hell's going on in here?" said Margaret entering the small room. "You'll wake everyone up in the hotel with all the noise he's making"

"We need to make sure he doesn't have any recording equipment on him," replied Solley.

"Have you all gone stark raving mad?"

Paul showed Margaret the wire. "He was wearing this at our last meeting," he explained. "He may have recorded things that might be awkward for Solley and me."

"Right; that's it – all of you out now!"

"It's too late for that," said Ian. "You're in this like the rest of us – like it or not."

"What the hell are you talking about?" she asked. "I have nothing to do with any of this."

"Try telling that to Carlyle."

"Who the hell's this Carlyle?"

"Carlyle's the man who was here earlier with Roberts," explained Paul. "The only way out of this is to work together."

"He's clean," said Solley, getting to his feet.

Ian tried to raise his head, "It's my back," he said.

"I'll get you another pillow," offered Margaret.

"No, that's ok," he replied, easing himself back down. "Now, tell me, what's so special about the Sanatorium?"

"Ok," said Solley, looking at Paul. "I guess it's time we owned up."

"If you must know it's because of what's underneath," blurted Margaret.

They looked at her, trying to hide their bemusement at this unexpected intervention.

"What the hell are you talking about?" asked Ian.

"The hospital and surrounding grounds are honeycombed with tunnels hewn out of the granite. The nuclear power plant at Hay Meadows is looking for somewhere to store their vitrified waste and this is the perfect site – not too far so little danger in transporting, nice and isolated."

"Is this true?" asked Ian, "and if it is, how do you know about it?"

"Ok," said Solley. "I'm going to tell you this – but listen, this must stay between us and I mean it – if it gets out it will be the end of us. My uncle's a politician."

"Is that true?"

"Yes," replied Paul, "you can check it out for yourself. He's on the Committee for Rural Affairs and Development."

"I knew there was something. How much could this be worth?" he asked, now somewhat oblivious to his injuries.

"It's hard to be exact," replied Solley, "but we could expect a fee of somewhere in excess of £10million a year – perhaps more. Of course, the amount would reduce over time but this stuff would be stored for decades, so it's safe to assume there's a good twenty years in it. However, you must understand that if a word of this gets out, the whole thing could be in jeopardy.

"This is top secret and if you think Carlyle is something to be worried about then you haven't met MICA9."

"MICA9," interrupted Ian, "who the fuck are they?"

"Ministry of Intelligence and Clandestine Affairs," explained Solley before continuing. "I don't need to tell you that if this gets into the public domain, there would be a national outcry."

Ian knew there was no way he could tell Carlyle about this, he would have to keep it to himself, but he would worry about that later. First, he needed to make sure he was involved with this project – although keeping Carlyle at bay would not be easy.

"I want to be part of this," he demanded.

Solley looked across at Paul and then back at Margaret. "Ok," he said, "you can have the job of local co-ordinator. Margaret will be your boss, but first we must secure the hospital and its grounds."

"That's no problem, leave it to me."

"And planning permission," added Paul.

"That won't be so easy," said Ian, "and why do you want that anyway, if you only want what's underneath?"

"To alleviate suspicion," he continued. "The building will be converted but it will be occupied by those managing the site."

"Ok, leave it with me – I know a way of putting pressure onto Councillor Roberts."

"You mean those documents?" asked Solley.

"Yes," he replied, knowing full well that Carlyle had them, but if this was what it seemed to be, he would find a way.

"Anyway, you need to rest; we'll discuss things more fully tomorrow."

Solley was the last to leave the storeroom, closing the door behind him. "I need a drink," he said, turning the key in the lock.

"Come on," said Margaret, taking him by the hand. "This one's on the house."

"So where did this nuclear waste thing come from?" Paul asked as she poured brandy into three glasses.

"I saw you were in trouble and it was the first thing that came into my head."

Solley raised his glass, "See – I told you she would be an asset"

"Well," she continued, "it's not all strictly off the top of my head. I was reading an article the other day and there's been quite a big discussion where to store nuclear waste after it's been vitrified and put into steel drums. There are rumours of old mine workings in the area so I just put two and two together and hoped for the best. I must admit MICA9 was rather good."

"Well I couldn't let you down," replied Solley, "but this doesn't really solve our problem – what about the long-term? We can't string Turnbull along for ever before he smells a rat. We have to get him off our backs somehow."

"Well if he does have a recording of us talking about dubious dealings," said Paul, "then we need something on him."

"But surely he would be in as much trouble for accepting a bribe?" said Margaret.

"Oh, he would have made sure he didn't say anything that might incriminate himself," answered Solley, moving a tray of salted peanuts to one side.

"I'll take those," said Margaret, tipping them into a black bin liner. "Is Turnbull married?" she asked.

"Err, yes," replied Paul, "why?"

She took a deep breath, "Do you have your phone?"

"Yes."

"Ok, come with me."

They followed her to the storeroom. "When I call out," she said, "I want you to come in and turn the light on. And don't forget to have your camera ready."

With that she unlocked the door and disappeared inside.

"Who's there?" asked Ian nervously.

"Shh, it's ok, it's only me."

He tried to make out what she was doing in the small amount of light that found its way under the door.

"I have another pillow for you," she said, pulling back the cover and exposing Ian's half-naked body. "Now!" she shouted.

Paul opened the door quickly and switched on the light to find Margaret sitting astride Ian in her bra and panties.

"Take the bloody photo!" she shouted.

"Oh yeah," replied Paul, raising his phone, taking several pictures as Ian struggled beneath her. However, all this served to do was make the pictures even more convincing.

Margaret got to her feet and gathered her clothes. "That's going to cost you," she said to Ian, as she passed an open-mouthed Paul and grinning Solley.

"I'll be down shortly, I'm going to have a shower," she added as she left the storeroom.

"You said you thought she was resourceful but that takes the biscuit!" remarked Solley, as he followed her out.

Paul now turned his attention to Ian. "Now Mr Turnbull, it seems as though we have a level playing field," he said, looking at the four images on his phone. "I would like to see you talk your way out of this one."

"My wife will never believe those photos," he protested.

"No? Well there's one way to find out."

"Ok, ok, I'll destroy the tape if you delete them."

Paul smiled. "The trouble with that is we both know that either of us could keep a copy. We'll just have to trust one another."

Ian knew that if his wife saw those photos after what had happened six years ago with that Ann Richardson, she would leave him, and what's more, the house was in her name, along with their holiday home.

"Ok," he said, "I guess, as you say, we'll just have to trust each other."

"I guess we will," replied Paul, placing his phone into his jacket. "Oh, and there's another thing – that twenty grand you had to give to Councillor Roberts…"

"Yes?"

"You can keep that as an advance payment as you now have those documents to twist his arm with."

"Thanks, you won't regret it."

"That's no problem; you can't do business without giving bribes. Tell me Ian, do you make a habit of this sort of thing?"

"That would be telling," he grinned.

"Come on, we're partners now – you can tell me."

"Well of course I've taken the odd sweetener, who doesn't?"

Paul removed his phone from his jacket, "Oh how silly of me – it's on record. Sleep tight," he added, closing the door as he left the storeroom, locking it behind him.

He joined Solley in the bar just as Margaret came into the hallway, her long raven hair wrapped tight in a pink towel in the way that only women seemed to know how to manage.

"I see why you had that large brandy earlier," laughed Solley as she joined them.

Paul handed her his phone.

"What's this for?"

"Those photos, I want you to delete them," he explained.

"Wait," said Solley, "won't we need those? After all, you can't see Margaret's face and I don't trust that Turnbull one bit. We might need them as a reminder."

"No, it's best if they're deleted. Anyway, have a listen to this," he added taking his phone back from Margaret and pressing the Play button.

"Hah, you are more than just a pretty face Paul Goodman!" retorted Solley as they listened to Ian incriminating himself.

"So tomorrow, we'll get rid of Turnbull and head home and put all this behind us."

"What about my twenty grand?"

"Never mind your money," said Margaret, "what about me? Suppose that…" she paused.

"Carlyle," interjected Paul.

"Whatever his name is… What if he comes back here? He knows there's something going on and he may well think I know what it is – and of course, now I do. So where does that leave me?"

"She's right," he agreed, "Carlyle's not one to give up easily and if Turnbull doesn't give him what he wants, then there's no telling what he might do."

"Look," she said, "I'm relying on you to think of something. After all, I am in this mess because of you. Now if you'd excuse me, I still have things to do and I have an early start."

24

Catherine knelt down in front of the wood burner, screwed up several sheets of newspaper into tight balls and placed them into the grate before carefully arranging the kindling. Using her thumb, she prised open the box of matches that sat on the mantelpiece, then struck one and rested the yellow flame against the paper and watched it take hold.

Soon the flames had engulfed the kindling, causing it to spit and crackle, sending tiny sparks out onto the hearth – one landing on the back of her hand. She looked down at the tiny ember as it faded, leaving a pink mark on her skin. It was strange – the pain was almost gratifying, it made her feel alive, something she hadn't felt for a long time – until now that was.

She looked up to see Philip standing over her, "I know what you did," she said.

He did not reply immediately but sat down on the sofa, his eyes fixed on the fire.

"That night I was dragged from my car; I've known all along it was you who walked out in front of me."

He still did not reply.

"Oh come on, the time for pretence is over especially after what you have just told me."

"But how?" he asked, almost pleadingly. "I had my face covered."

Catherine got to her feet and went over to him, "It's the way you move, nobody I know moves like it. It's almost… automaton."

"So why did you call the police?"

"Because that's what you would have expected and I didn't want you to think I knew it was you."

"Look, I never intended for anything to happen, they were only supposed to frighten you not…"

"They didn't."

"I don't understand, the doctor's report said they found three different types of semen."

"That's because I'd had sex with three different men that night. Not those you hired to scare me. And I know why you did it, you thought I was having sex with Tobin, and of course you were right. But not only him, there were others."

"But why?" he asked.

"I don't know really, it all started off innocently enough but I guess I was bored, I was longing for some excitement in my life; it had always been one of suppressed emotions. The first time it happened I could hear you next door cutting the grass, it felt so exhilarating and things just went from there."

"But if you needed this sort of thing why didn't you tell me, I had no idea you felt like that; and why are you here now?"

"Because of all this," she replied looking about her, "I didn't want to lose it and despite what I said I do have feelings for you, I always have. And not having intercourse with you for the last eighteen months was my way of punishing you for what you did. But things are very different now; you see you're not that boring little office boy, are you? You're a man, and a dangerous one."

Philip looked up as she stood astride him, her skirt hitched up over her thighs, her large firm breasts just inches from his face. "And that turns me on," she added, unfastening his belt.

—w—

374

"It's ok for us to bugger off back to London," said Paul, standing in the doorway of the en-suite, toothbrush in hand, "I very much doubt Carlyle's going to bother us down there, but what happens to Margaret?"

"I don't know," replied Solley, laying his trousers over a chair before heading for his bed.

"Well we'd better think of something. We can't just abandon her; after all, we owe her big time. That performance with Turnbull earlier could not have been easy for her, now it's our turn."

"To do what?" he asked as he pulled the duvet over himself.

Solley was right, if Carlyle wanted to make life difficult for Margaret, there was nothing they could do. Paul sat on the edge of his bed – his feelings for her had clouded his judgement. All he wanted to do was help her but all he had succeeded in doing was put her in a situation of danger, and one they had little or no control over. Plus, all the way out here, she would be vulnerable.

He jumped to his feet and made his way back into the bathroom, "We'll go ahead with the conversion," he said.

"What?" asked Solley, raising himself up on his elbow.

"We'll take it on. Fuck it, I'm not going to let some flat-capped northern thug change my plans. If he wants to make trouble, well fucking well let him – and see what he gets when he messes with the London boys."

"That's fighting talk and you know me – when was the last time I ran away from anything?"

This statement of support brought back memories for Paul of the time they and a few of their mates left the Palais Ballroom only to be followed out by a mob of about twenty blokes hell-bent on trouble. Their first reaction was to run for it but Solley stood his ground. Paul could still see him standing there in the middle of the street, feet apart, jacket tossed to one side, a length of wood in his hand.

Although they had been outnumbered, with Solley's encouragement, they had put up a hell of a fight. The whole thing ended with everyone making a run for it as the police arrived, but as

Solley said afterwards, if they had bottled it, they would have picked us off one by one. He was not only brave but wise.

However, Paul knew there was an ulterior motive to go ahead with the project and he knew that Solley knew that too.

—ᵚ—

The next morning Paul and Solley made their way downstairs to find the jovial Murder Mystery Party in full swing over breakfast, with Alan and Margaret busying themselves with orders.

"Better check on Turnbull," said Paul.

"I did, a couple of hours ago, I took him to the loo and got him a drink."

This admission of Solley's made Paul feel slightly guilty. He had all but forgotten poor Turnbull. After all, he had only done what a lot of people would have done. He hadn't really designed this; or had he? And who was Turnbull anyway? What he had told them seemed to add up and he was a victim of this Carlyle as much as they were. He's bent but surely not stupid – well not enough to get involved with the likes of Carlyle deliberately. The person he needed to speak to was this Townsend character.

"Sleep well?" Paul addressed Ian, holding a mug of sweet tea.

"Like a log – what do you think?" he replied, wincing as he reached up for his drink.

Paul sat down on one of the many plastic chairs that lined the storeroom as Ian sipped at his tea.

"Ah, that's just what the doctor ordered," he sighed.

Paul took the mug from him.

"Hey, I haven't finished yet!"

"You can have it back in a sec after you have told me the truth. There's no point in hiding anything now, not with this tape recording. We have just as much on you as you have on us, plus there are those photos."

"What is it you want to know?"

"I want to know how you and this Townsend bloke got mixed up with this Carlyle?"

"I told you," replied Ian, "now can I have my tea back before it gets cold."

"So you're sticking to your story?"

"It's not a story, it's the truth."

"Ok," said Paul, handing Ian his drink back, "tell me where I can find this Townsend."

"What?"

"You heard me."

"You'd better stay away from him for all our sakes!"

"Oh, why's that?" asked Paul, making himself a little more comfortable.

"Because he's not like us, he's just a regular bloke; he doesn't have the stomach for this sort of thing. As I say, he's best left alone, he could break at the slightest pressure and go running to the police and if you show up out of nowhere asking questions, it could tip him over the top."

"In that case, you had better tell me exactly what's going on."

"How many times?" Ian complained. "I told you all that I know."

"Fair enough, if that's the way you want it. You could be right about this Townsend character but I think it's worth the risk," said Paul as he made his way to the door.

"Ok, wait. I blackmailed Townsend into getting hold of some old documents that gave an account of Carlyle's dealings regarding his part in the development of the Commonwealth Games Village."

"So what Frank was saying was true, but that must be over twenty years ago."

"Nineteen to be exact," he replied. "The thing is, Councillor Roberts' wife is Carlyle's sister and she was the Chief Executive of an Aggregates Company which in turn was closely linked to her brother's construction business."

"How did you come to know all this?"

"Purely by chance," answered Ian. "I was up in the loft clearing out some old rubbish when I came across a local rag. Anyway, there was an article regarding the construction of the Commonwealth Games Village and how there had been public disquiet in the region due to the fact that most of the jobs seemed to be going to companies outside of the area.

"I knew Councillor Roberts' sister was heavily involved and it was then I noticed a name I recognised, it was someone I sold a house to years before, so on the off-chance I paid him a visit to see if he knew anything. It turned out he knew quite a lot. Apparently, he'd been given these files regarding the construction of the Village when he was town clerk along with instructions to destroy them. It was made quite clear to him in no uncertain terms, what would happen to him and his daughter, if he told anybody about them.

"The thing is, he didn't destroy them, but hid them away in a filing cabinet with a load of ancient documents relating to some old mine workings on the Albright Estate. I'm guessing it's because this is where they illegally dumped most of the waste."

"But why on earth would he do that? Why not just get rid of them as he'd been told to do?"

"He felt very uncomfortable about complying with what he knew was not only immoral but illegal so he decided on a compromise; also, it made him feel safe knowing where they were; a kind of insurance."

"So why did he tell you where these documents were and that they still existed?"

"Money I guess, he was in a right state. Not that it did him much good; the poor bastard topped himself shortly after I had spoken to him. It seems they found him in his bath tub full of sleeping pills and with his wrists cut. That's why it was important to keep this contact of Frank's out of Carlyle's way."

"So you're telling me it was Carlyle that killed him?" said Paul.

"Hard to tell – I mean he was full of pills – seemed like a

straightforward case of suicide but I guess he could have been made to take them. He's a clever bastard that Carlyle."

"What about his daughter?"

"Well that's a bit of a sad story too. You see the reason he had to sell his house was because he had taken out a second mortgage to help his daughter buy a place of her own. He lost out big time during the financial crisis."

"Yes, but that doesn't explain about her."

"I'm coming to that. A year or so after she moved into her new house, it appears she was trying to replace a lightbulb on the landing using a kitchen stool. He went round there to visit and found her at the foot of the stairs in a crumpled heap, her neck broken. So you see – he really had nothing much to live for, that's why I'm guessing there was no investigation."

"Ok, so how does this Frank fit into all of this?"

"Well, obviously once I found out about the documents, I knew if I could get hold of them I could put pressure on Councillor Roberts for your planning permission. Frank was just the man for the job; it was he who blackmailed Townsend for me."

"Townsend didn't strike me as the type who had much to hide."

"No, you're right there," answered Ian. "It was something that had happened to his wife, something he was desperate to keep secret."

"Let me get this straight – you found something on Townsend's wife and used that to make him get you these documents so you could blackmail someone like Carlyle? Are you fucking mad or just plain fucking stupid?"

"No – I had no intentions of blackmailing Carlyle – I got them to blackmail Roberts into getting planning permission for the Sanatorium."

"But that's what the twenty grand was for. Oh I see," he continued, "you got greedy, keep the twenty grand for yourself and then get consent by blackmailing Roberts."

"The thing is," said Ian, "when the documents went missing

from my car a few days ago while I was up at the old hospital, somehow – and don't ask me how – Townsend got them back. But then – and you might find this hard to believe – he tried to use them to blackmail Carlyle and Roberts. It was him who got me to set up this meeting. I chose this place because it's out of the way – the last thing I expected was to find you two here."

"And Frank?"

"That was my doing – it was me that got Frank to come here. I thought if things went wrong I could hand him over to Carlyle as a peace offering."

"You are one hell of a fucking maggot Turnbull," said Paul.

"That's as maybe," replied Ian, "but this maggot could worm his way into places that could be very useful to you."

"What happened to his leg?"

"He did that escaping from Carlyle."

"So why did an intelligent man like you get mixed up in all this? You could have told Townsend to arrange things himself? Or did he offer you a slice?"

"No – the opposite; he wanted half of whatever I got out of you, plus fifty grand. Can you fucking believe it?"

"And why would you do that?"

"What I told you earlier about Townsend is not strictly true. Well – the part about him being unreliable is – but one of the reasons I went along with him this far is that the man's a fucking psychopath, that's why. You know I said we blackmailed him with something that happened years ago to his wife?"

"Yes," he replied, listening intently.

"Frank found out that she had been dragged from her car one night on a lonely country lane and attacked by three men. Her identity had been kept secret – as it is with these sorts of things and they never found out who was responsible. But get this – Townsend set the whole thing up to punish her."

"Bollocks! Surely you don't believe that?"

"I have to admit, I had my reservations," agreed Ian. "The other night he came round to my house. At first he seemed perfectly normal then, just like that, almost as if a switch had gone off in his head, he had me by the throat. I really thought the bastard was going to kill me. Underneath that mild exterior there's a fucking homicidal maniac, mark my words."

Paul could see the fear in Ian's eyes, "Ok, for once I believe you," he said. "But there's another thing – why was Frank running from Carlyle?"

"Frank has this key witness who used to work for the Inland Revenue – I believe he goes by the name of Billy Quinn. It was him who noticed there were some anomalies and that something was not quite adding up. He did some sniffing around and took what he had found to his superiors but was told in no uncertain terms to bury it. You see it was so sensitive at the time – you could hardly have the Queen rocking up to open the Commonwealth Games with all that shit floating about. So the combination of these documents and what Frank's contact knew is nothing short of dynamite."

"How did Frank know all this?" asked Paul.

"He was in the police force at the time," explained Ian. "He had just made detective when Billy came to him about it. It was shortly after that they both lost their jobs."

"And Frank told you all this?"

"So to speak – bits came out over the years. He hit the bottle pretty hard, I guess I felt sorry for him. I used him for this and that but it was when I found this old newspaper it all made sense."

"So you thought you would try and take advantage?"

"I guess so."

"So where is this Frank now?"

Ian shrugged his shoulders, "I have no idea."

"And this contact of Frank's, do you know where I can find him?"

"Oh fuck," exclaimed Ian, sitting bolt upright as if hit by lightning.

"What the hell is it?" asked Paul, leaping off his chair, not sure whether Turnbull was having some kind of seizure.

"I must get out of here," he said as he hauled himself out of the makeshift bed, beads of perspiration breaking out over his forehead.

"Where the hell do you think you're going?"

"Don't just fucking stand there – help me get dressed, I have to get out of here. Is my car driveable?"

"Yes, the front end's a bit scratched, that's all, but you're not going anywhere until you tell me what's so important."

"Look – this contact I told you about – it was imperative I kept him away from Carlyle at all costs so I made arrangements to have him taken somewhere safe but he can't stay there any longer, I have to move him."

"Ok," said Paul, handing him his shirt. "You're on your own with this one."

"I don't care about that; just help me get to my car."

"Where exactly is this contact?"

"He's holed up in a client's house – they're in Spain at the moment. I'm trying to sell it for them."

"When did you take him over?"

"I didn't," replied Ian, "Townsend took him there last night, that's why he was late for our meeting."

"Well why don't you get Townsend to get him?" suggested Paul.

"Oh yeah, and then what?"

"I don't know – what were you going to do with him?"

"I had a text from my wife, she's gone over to our place in the Lake District, I was going to put this Billy up at my place for a couple of days in the hope that this might have sorted itself out by then."

"Come on, even you can't be that naïve surely, that's the first place Carlyle would look?"

"What the hell else am I supposed to do?" said Ian, "Put him back out on the streets so Carlyle can turn him into dog food?"

"I admire your concern for your fellow man," said Solley, closing the door behind him, mug of coffee in his hand.

"Fuck that," replied Ian. "As long as we have this key witness we have a chance. Ok, he might be an alcoholic and a bum, but sober him up and he's as sharp as a razor. If we have Billy, we have a major advantage over Carlyle."

"I know where we could take him," said Paul.

"Where?" replied Ian, sounding a little dubious.

"The old Sanatorium – it's out of the way, and no-one's going to look for him there."

Turnbull almost jumped out of his skin, "No, not the Sanatorium. I have a place in the Lakes, I'll take him there."

"I thought you said your wife was going there? She was too frightened to stay in the house after what had happened."

"No, I remember now, she changed her mind at the last minute; she's gone to her mother's."

"You're telling me you're going to drive all the way to the bloody Lake District with a half-deranged wino in your condition?"

"He's right," said Solley, "what about a hotel?"

"Makes sense," said Paul.

"How much is that going to bloody cost me?" Ian complained.

"I would look at it this way," said Solley. "Think of it as an investment, there's a lot at stake here. Are you really willing to risk everything for a few quid?"

"No, of course not; you're right, give me my phone."

─ ⁘ ─

Catherine made her way downstairs and into the kitchen. She half-filled the kettle and placed the teapot onto the Aga to warm, her eyes blood-shot and stinging from a sleepless night. Opening the silver tea caddy, she put three teaspoons of tea into the pot, poured the boiling water in sending a sweet woody aroma spiralling up into the air carried on thin wisps of steam, then went over to Philip's jacket to answer his phone.

"Hello?"

Ian looked at Paul and held the phone away from him, "It's Townsend's wife," he whispered.

"So? Just ask for Philip."

"Hi, I wonder if I could speak to Philip please."

"Who shall I say is calling?" she replied.

"I'm a friend, that's all."

"I'm afraid he had rather a late night last night, can I take a message?"

Ian paused.

"What is it?" mouthed Paul.

Ian covered the mouthpiece, "She wants me to leave a message," he whispered.

"So?" said Paul in a low voice.

"Could you tell him…?"

"Hold on," she interrupted, "he's just here."

Philip took the phone from her, unsure who would be calling him. "Hello?"

"It's Turnbull here."

"What do you want?" he snapped, making his way out of the kitchen in order to be out of earshot of Catherine. "I don't have the money or the documents."

"I know," he said, "Frank sold them to Carlyle. We need to move Billy."

"No – *you* need to move Billy – I have done with all this."

"Look, you don't understand how important he is."

"Of course I do, that's why I went to all the trouble to find him, but he's your problem now, you deal with it."

"It's not that simple," replied Ian, "I was beaten up pretty badly last night. I don't think I can drive or even if I can handle Billy, plus you have the keys."

"Where are you?" asked Philip.

"That doesn't matter but you must get Billy out of there."

"But what am I supposed to do with him? There's no way I'm bringing him back here."

"Ok, give me a minute to think. Take him to the motel, the one at Pine Way roundabout – do you know the one?"

"Yes."

"Get a double room – I want you to stay with him, and keep your head down."

"Why there?"

"It's as good a place as any to hide him. What you must realise is now that Carlyle has those documents, he's our only insurance. As long as Billy's safe, we have a chance."

At first Philip did not reply, but maybe Turnbull was right? And what difference did it make anyway? He was up to his neck in all this. "Ok, leave it to me," he said.

"Well?" said Paul, looking anxious.

"He's going to take him the motel at Pine Way," replied Ian.

—m—

Philip returned to the sitting room and found Catherine sitting in her favourite armchair. "I have to go out," he said.

"What about your tea?"

"It'll have to wait," he replied as he picked up his car keys.

As he turned the key in the ignition he was immediately assaulted by a loud blast of electronic music and quickly adjusted the radio to Radio 4. *It must have got altered last night,* he thought. He had always favoured the melodic sound of this particular station, somehow it helped him think, with its informed views and interesting and diverse plays. And now was a time to think – and carefully. Maybe there was a way out of all this?

He pulled into the long drive. *Well at least he hasn't burnt the place down,* he thought, opening his door, for some reason feeling self-conscious. Although the house was really quite secluded, he still felt as though the eyes of distant neighbours and passers-by were focused on him as if they were aware of his guilt. He placed the key into the lock and eased the front door open cautiously.

"Billy – it's Philip," he called, but there came no reply.

He paused in the hallway, the door still open and once again he shouted for Billy. He went to the foot of the stairs, "Billy, you up there?" but still no answer. Probably asleep or unconscious from all that brandy he thought as made his way up the stairs.

But Billy was nowhere to be found. Philip went back down and thoroughly searched the rest of the house. "Where the hell are you?" he shouted at the top of his voice, regardless of who might hear through the open door.

All the windows were locked and the doors had deadlocks so there was no way he could have got out unless somebody had let him out.

"Oh shit!" he exclaimed, "where the bloody hell did you materialise from?"

"The loft," answered Billy, brushing pieces of fibreglass from his clothes. "You can't be too careful."

"You're sober?"

"You sound surprised."

"I was led to believe you were an alcoholic and leaving you with all that brandy I naturally assumed you wouldn't be in a fit state."

"Me?" replied Billy, a tone of indignation in his voice. "I may live with alcoholics and drug takers but that doesn't mean to say I am one. Ok, I might have one too many on occasion, but then again, who doesn't? And to be fair, I did go through a period where my only friend seemed to be the bottle but I realised the errors of my ways."

"So why are you still on the streets?"

"Quite simply, after all these years, I fit in and I make use of myself. I help people with their social and tax problems."

"Tax?" exclaimed Philip, sounding surprised. "I didn't think that was a profession much sort after in those circles."

Billy smiled, "You'd be surprised. At this very moment I am acting on behalf of Lord Stokes – he had been given bad advice from those who were supposedly acting on his behalf. This was compounded by incompetent staff at the Inland Revenue. His case comes up in three weeks."

"You're telling me this Lord Stokes lives on the streets with you?"

"Not with me," replied Billy, "but he is homeless. You see it's here that I can make a real difference to people's lives. Not everyone you see on the street is there because they have been feckless – most are there due to others' selfishness and inconsideration."

"Look, you know why you're here don't you?" said Philip.

"Turnbull wants to keep me out of Carlyle's way on account of what I know regarding the Commonwealth Games Village construction."

"That's right," he confirmed.

"So what now?" asked Billy, scratching the back of his neck that was now slightly inflamed due to the small glass fibres embedded in his skin.

"Turnbull wants you…" Philip paused, "to come with me," he continued.

25

"Frank!" shouted Reggie as he grabbed his hair and shook his head violently. "Chuck some more water over him," he demanded.

Joe did so but it was no use, Frank was out cold.

"We need to find Turnbull," said Reggie. "The question is – where would he be if he was not at home?"

"Maybe he pissed off for a few days with his wife," suggested Joe. "Let the dust settle."

"This dust ain't never going to settle Joey boy, you mark my words. Not until I'm satisfied – and it takes a lot to satisfy me."

"So where to boss?"

"I think a chat with our London friends might be in order."

"What about him?" asked Joe, looking across at Frank's unconscious body stretched out across the table.

"Keith can take care of him, even with one arm, eh Keith?"

"It will be my pleasure boss."

"Oh, and I want him in one piece when I get back, I need to talk to him and once I have what I need, you're free to do with him as you please."

—m—

Paul moved a little closer to Solley and lowered his voice, "You know those bruises on his right shoulder?"

"You could hardly miss them."

"Do you think his collar bone might be broken?"

"Quite possibly."

"So do I," agreed Paul, "but do you know what I reckon?"

"No," answered Solley.

"Those blows were meant for his head."

"I don't think Carlyle's that stupid. I know that road is pretty deserted at night but to take a chance like that is not his style I'm sure."

"No, exactly my point."

"Ok so what are you getting at?"

"Whoever did this to him somehow got him to swerve off the road," explained Paul, "and Alan said nobody passed him before he found Turnbull."

"Ok, so they went the other way?"

"Maybe – but to where?"

"Wherever they came from."

"That's the thing – I had a look at the map earlier, it runs for at least 14 miles before it joins the motorway."

"So they came up the motorway."

"No – it just doesn't seem to make any sense. That's in totally the opposite direction to where Carlyle's based. And there's another thing," he continued, "if it was Carlyle, how did he know Turnbull was going to be there? And what the hell was Turnbull doing there in the first place, *and* at that time of night? There's nothing out there except the old Sanatorium. Come on."

"Where are we going?"

"To the old hospital."

"What about him?" asked Solley, looking in Ian's direction.

"He can come with us," answered Paul, "I think he might have some explaining to do."

"What?" he exclaimed. "We can't take him with us, surely."

"Why not, he's the vendor's agent after all."

"He needs a doctor, that's what he needs."

"All in good time," replied Paul. "After the breakfast Margaret gave him earlier, he's not going to die any time soon and he seems to have perked up a bit."

"Did he eat all of it?" asked Solley, a tone of disbelief in his voice.

"Every last frigging morsel – and toast to boot," answered Paul.

"Huh, and there's me thinking he was at death's door."

"The question is; how the fuck do we get him to the car? He's had one hell of a beating."

"I know that," replied Paul curtly, wondering how they would get Ian out without anyone seeing him.

Finally, after some effort, they managed to get Turnbull dressed.

Solley tossed Paul the keys, "Right, you get the car."

He made his way out of the storeroom and into the short corridor that led to the lobby. "Shit!" he said to himself as he was confronted by a raucous and somewhat excited group of middle-aged failed actors all vying for attention.

Getting Turnbull out of here without anyone noticing the state he was in would be far too risky, he thought. Their only other option would be to take him through the kitchen but Alan was in there which could be awkward, as Margaret had told him they were going to take Turnbull to the hospital. Not only that, there was Pauline of course, she was in to help with breakfast on account of this bloody Murder Mystery group. They could hardly drag Turnbull through there in his state.

"Margaret," he called, pushing his way through the melee that had for some reason, organised itself around the reception desk.

"Do you mind young man?" said a lady in her late sixties as he pushed past.

This reference to his age was rather flattering but he had no time for courtesies, he was on a mission. "Margaret, please, I need to speak to you now."

She looked across at him and smiled, "Ladies and Gentlemen, I am afraid you will have to excuse me for a moment."

Paul took her to one side.

"Can't it wait?" she asked, "As you can see, I'm extremely busy."

"No it can't. You need to get Alan and Pauline out of the kitchen so we can get Turnbull to the car without anyone seeing us."

Margaret felt a sense of relief at this news, "Ok, but remember, once he's out of here don't, under any circumstances, bring him back."

"You needn't worry about that," he reassured her, "we won't."

She reached out and grabbed his arm as he was about to leave, "What about his car?"

"Shit! Err, leave it with me."

"Ok, but first give me five minutes to sort this lot out. I'll knock on the storeroom door when the coast is clear."

—⁂—

Paul entered the storeroom to find Solley kneeling down next to Turnbull.

"What took you so long?" he asked.

"Never mind that, is he ok?"

"Not really, I guess all the excitement earlier has taken it out of him."

"Well we can't take him through the front of the hotel, that's for certain," said Paul, "those Society people are all over the bloody place.

"What about the kitchen?"

"That's exactly what I thought. Margaret's going to get rid of Alan and Pauline first then she's going to give us the all clear. When we get Turnbull into your car, you can take him to the old Sanatorium, I'll follow you in his motor."

"Then what?"

"We'll take him home."

"Oh yeah?" replied Solley. "'*Here's your husband Mrs Turnbull, sorry he's a bit broken only he fell off a cliff*'. We're not bloody ten

391

years old anymore, turning up at Peter Jeffries' house with him after he fell through that warehouse roof when we were trying to pinch cigarettes to sell to Nicky Baker."

"Ok, we'll leave him outside in his car."

"And then what? Run up the drive and ring the bloody doorbell?"

"What the fuck else do you suggest?" retorted Paul. "We can't hang onto him forever. Not only that, he's going to need some medical attention at some point, especially if that collar bone is broken."

Their heated conversation was interrupted by a sharp knock. "That'll be Margaret."

The two men lifted a somewhat disgruntled and apathetic Turnbull to his feet and with Solley holding him steady, Paul unlocked the door and was just about to open it when Margaret burst in, telling them to be quiet in a low voice, locking the door behind her.

"What the hell's going on?" asked Solley.

"It's that man who was here last night."

"Which one?" Paul urged.

"The redhead and he's not alone."

"That's all we fucking need – Carlyle turning up."

"Did he say what he wanted?" asked Paul.

"He wants to speak to you two."

"What did you tell him?"

"I told him you had gone out for a stroll over the moors."

"Why did you tell him that?" asked Solley.

"What else was I supposed to say – that you're in my store cupboard with a half-dead estate agent?"

"You could have said we had checked out," he remarked, raising his voice slightly.

"Oh that's right, I forget," she answered sarcastically. "You couldn't pay your bill so you left your 100 grand Merc here as security."

"Err, yeah, I see what you mean," he answered apologetically.

"Did you say how long we would be?" asked Paul.

"I told him I had made you sandwiches and a flask of coffee so you could be some time."

"What did he say to that?" enquired Solley.

"He wanted to know how long you had been gone, and in what direction you went. I said you had left about an hour ago and I didn't know which way you had gone."

"Did he believe you?" he asked anxiously.

"I'm not sure. He seemed a little surprised, said you didn't strike him as the outdoor type."

"Ok," said Paul, "we'll just have to sit tight, there's nothing else we can do."

Margaret took a deep breath and grabbed one of the chairs then made her way back out into the hallway to find Reggie waiting by the desk, his two companions sitting in the bar. She made her way over to him.

"Can I be of any more assistance to you?"

Reggie sniffed the air, "No, you have been most helpful." He looked across at the two men and gave a slight nod of his head. They got to their feet and to her relief, made their way to the exit. He turned to follow them but paused, "Margaret isn't it?"

"Yes," she replied, her heart racing.

"I like that name, mine's Reginald. I do prefer first names, don't you? Before I go, there is something you could perhaps help me with."

A sense of panic welled up inside her, "Certainly, if I can."

"Could you tell me why Ian Turnbull's car is parked in your old garage and why it is all scratched?"

As if rehearsed, the two heavies came back into the hotel and stood either side of Reggie, their massive bulk casting a shadow over her.

"He had too much to drink," she said, "I offered to get him a taxi but he refused, he only got 100 yards down the road and came off. You can see where he hit the wall if you like. I phoned for a taxi to take him home."

"Home you say?" enquired Reggie. "Are you sure?"

"Oh yes, I got his address from his car."

"And how did the car get back here?"

"I took the liberty of driving it back; it was only a short way."

"Do you have the keys?"

"That is none of your business Mr Carlyle," she replied. "I believe that is your surname."

"And how would you know that?" he asked.

"Mr Turnbull mentioned it last night."

"And what else did he have to say?"

"Nothing," she replied. "He was sick shortly afterwards. Well Mr Carlyle, it has been very nice talking to you but I have a hotel to run so if you would please be kind enough to leave…"

"You must forgive me Margaret – if I may call you that? I forgot my manners. You see Mr Turnbull is a dear and trusted friend of mine and after he did not go home last night, his wife phoned me to see if I knew where he was. I said I would see if I could find him but I think I know what might have happened after he left you. He probably got the taxi driver to take him to another hotel to sober up before going home and I can't blame him; Mrs Turnbull is a force to be reckoned with – somewhat like you I imagine. Good day."

Margaret watched as Reggie and his colleagues made their way out of the hotel.

"Bollocks, bollocks," she said to herself as she ran to the storeroom.

Paul opened the door.

"He knows Turnbull's here," she blurted.

"How?" he asked.

"His bloody car, that's how."

"But it's out of sight."

"Well he, or one his gorillas, obviously had a good look round and found it."

"So where is he now?"

"He left and took his henchmen with him."

"But if he knows Turnbull's here, why leave?" said Solley.

"Well if you're quick enough you might be able to catch him and ask him yourself," she retorted. "I tried to fob him off with some cock and bull story about how Turnbull got drunk and pranged his car and that it was me who brought it back and that I sent him off home in a taxi but he's not stupid, he knows that's all bullshit. I think we should go to the police."

"With what; what's he done?"

"Well *that* for a start," she said, looking at Ian, now stretched back out on the makeshift bed.

"We don't know that do we? Not for sure anyway."

"Oh come on, be serious, who else would have done it?"

"You tell me," he said, "because it was not Carlyle."

"You don't know that for certain," added Solley, "everything points to him."

"Ok, so why were they looking for him?"

"They were looking for *us*," he corrected. "They just happened to have found Ian's car."

"Ok," said Paul, now pacing up and down the small storeroom, "but I just know it was not Carlyle that did that to him."

"So we'll forget taking Turnbull to the Sanatorium, we'll do as you suggest and take him home, leave him outside his house. Now Margaret," he continued, "I would like you to do us one last favour. Go outside and make sure they have gone. Are Alan and Pauline still in the kitchen?"

"No, I sent them into town to get some supplies. They looked at me a bit strange but anyway you can get out that way without being seen."

"Give me my car keys."

They turned to see Ian standing, his left hand holding up his trousers.

"You can't drive," said Paul.

"Yes I can," he replied; "just give me the fucking keys. Look, it's not your responsibility to look after me, just let me go."

Paul looked at Solley, "If he thinks he's ok to drive, give him his bloody keys," he said.

He handed the keys over and the two men watched as Ian slipped on his shoes, even this simple task causing him much pain.

"It's all clear," said Margaret from the doorway.

They guided Turnbull through the kitchen to his car, where after some effort; they got him into the driver's seat.

"It's a good job it's automatic," remarked Solley. "There's no way he could drive the thing otherwise."

They then watched as Turnbull tentatively reversed the car out of the garage and into the car park, pausing for several seconds before driving out onto the narrow road and disappearing slowly down the hill.

Paul answered his phone, "Ah Julie, how's Kim? I was just about to call," he said, walking out of earshot of Solley. "I know I should have phoned earlier but things have been a bit hectic here and the phone reception's not that good either."

"Well you know exactly how I feel with Kim in hospital. You could at least phone now and again to see how your wife is, especially after being attacked."

"I spoke to Kim last night, not only that, this is not where I want to be at a time like this. I was quite happy to… Hello… hello… Julie, can you hear me?"

"Yes, I can now," she replied, only to have the line go dead again. "Bollocks," she said as she tried Paul's number only to find it unavailable. *Maybe he's right, it must be the signal,* she thought, as she placed her phone onto the granite worktop.

—m—

"Bloody hell, where did you come from?" exclaimed Solley.

"Sorry, I didn't mean to frighten you," replied Margaret, sounding a little indignant. "Where's Paul?"

"He's…" he looked about but couldn't see him anywhere. "He was here a minute ago – just over there."

Solley called out but there was no reply. "Paul," he shouted, "come on, stop playing silly buggers. That's strange," he said, turning to Margaret, "he can't be far away." Solley called his name several more times as Margaret went to look for him.

"Over here!" she shouted.

Solley ran over to where she was standing. "What's that?" he asked.

"I think it's his phone," she said, handing it to him.

"It is," he confirmed as he started to shout Paul's name again at the top of his voice. "You know what this is?" he said.

"No," she replied.

"It's some kind of ambush; Carlyle's lured us into a false sense of security and has taken Paul. Well one thing's for certain, that ginger prick's messing with the wrong person this time; no-one hurts my friends and gets away with it."

Just then Alan pulled into the car park with Pauline in the passenger seat. Solley ran over to the car and asked him if he'd seen anyone.

"Yes," replied Alan, "it was that bloke that came off the road last night. Anyway, what was he doing out here? Should he be driving in his condition?"

"He was in a bit of a panic," said Margaret, "lost his wallet."

"Don't look at me," he said defensively, "I didn't take it."

"Nobody's accusing you of taking it," she replied.

"Never mind all that," said Solley, "was that the only vehicle you saw?"

"Yeah, unless you count David in his tractor."

So where the hell is he? he thought. *They can't have taken him that way – you can see the road for miles. He must still be here somewhere.*

"What the hell's going on?" asked Pauline, getting out of the car.

Solley placed his hand on Alan's shoulder, "I want you to do me a favour," he said, "it's very important. I want you to go to the top of that hill and see if you can see anyone. I'll take a look over here."

"Whoa, hold on," he said. "Is somebody going to tell me what's going on here?"

"It's Mr Goodman," explained Margaret, "he's gone missing."

"Gone missing? What the hell are you talking about?"

"Pauline, would you please take that box of groceries into the kitchen," she added.

As Pauline disappeared inside, she turned to Alan, "Look you mustn't say anything to anyone, you understand?"

"Yeah, of course," he answered, looking a little concerned.

"Mr Goodman is on medication for depression. Apparently, according to Mr Solomon, he hasn't been taking it recently, so you see it's important we find him."

"Well I'll be…" he breathed. "You can never tell can you; didn't seem the type…"

"Well that's as maybe," she continued. "But if you'll just do as Mr Solomon asks, I will be most grateful."

"Leave it to me," he said as he took off towards the hill.

—⁓—

"Ah Frank – nice to have you back with us, I hope Keith's been looking after you?"

"I need help," he pleaded.

"Oh, you mean this," said Reggie, pressing his thumb into Frank's infected wound.

"Oh please, just get me to a hospital."

"You don't need a hospital Frankie – does he boys?"

"No boss," they replied in unison.

"What you need," he continued, forcing his thumb deeper into Frank's flesh, "is to learn how to tell the truth."

Frank screamed and grabbed his arm. "You fucking bastard Carlyle!"

"Now, now Frankie, you know how much I hate profanities." Reggie looked over to Joe, "Get our guest a glass of water."

Joe handed him a plastic tumbler.

"Steady," he said as Frank gulped at the cold liquid. "You don't want to choke yourself, do you? It seems Frankie, as though we have a bit of a mystery on our hands and I think you might be able to help us solve it. And if you do, then maybe I can get Keith to forgive you for shooting him."

"What the fuck are you talking about? I didn't shoot anyone."

"Oh but you did – last night. Surely you remember?"

"Oh shit, did I?"

"Yes Frankie. Fortunately for Keith – and not so fortunately for you – he still has full use of his other arm."

"Look you have to believe me," he pleaded, "I didn't mean to shoot anyone, honestly. I just panicked, that's all."

"Ok, we'll forget about all that for the moment. First things first – where's my 300 grand?"

It then dawned on Frank that that bastard Turnbull must have taken it and kept it for himself. The question now was, could he talk himself out of this situation and get to Turnbull first?

"It's in the car," he said.

"No – try again."

"No, I remember now," he said, pulling the tumbler towards him.

"You can have some more when you tell me where my money is."

"It's all coming back to me now. I hid it in some bushes, it must still be there."

"I see," replied Reggie, making his way round the table menacingly. "We'll come back to that. What happened to Turnbull?"

"I don't know, it's all a blur. I was taking these poppers you see – to keep me going and kill the pain."

"Ok," said Reggie, "let's see if this helps."

Joe stepped forward and grabbed the flesh on either side of

Frank's wound while Reggie pulled him onto his back. Joe then started to rip open the wound, almost to the bone.

"Ok, ok, I'll tell you!" he screamed. "Turnbull's got your money. He promised me he would give it to you; he said that if you got your money back you would be lenient on me."

"Oh please, please Frankie boy, surely even you can do better than that. And even if you are telling the truth, there's nothing I hate more than a snitch," said Reggie, looking at Joe and giving him the nod.

Frank screamed again as Joe ripped his would open even wider.

"That's enough," said Reggie. "We don't want our friend here to pass out, do we? There's one more thing I want you to help me with," he added, pouring the cold water over Frank's face. "Now this is something I really want to know – what do you know about those two so-called business men up from London?"

"What two from London?"

Reggie sighed, "You know Frank – this makes me very, very cross having to repeat myself time and time again. I will find out what I want to know somehow – it either comes from you or someone else."

He leant forwards and placed his lips next to his ear, "What you can't seem to get through that thick skull of yours Frankie boy, is that I'm giving you a chance to redeem yourself."

Frank grabbed his arm, "Look, you have to believe me, I really don't know what you're talking about, but if you let me go I can find out and I'll get your money back."

"He wants us to let him go boys," teased Reggie. "Of course you can go – go on, what are you waiting for? Oh, I forgot – you can't can you?"

He looked at Joe again and nodded, who then grabbed Frank's arms and secured them with cable ties while Reggie opened one of the kitchen drawers and brought out a saw then ran his finger tentatively along the sharp jagged teeth and flexed the blade.

"What the fuck's that for?" asked Frank, eyes bulging.

Reggie waved his hand and Joe grabbed his feet as he stepped forward, "Seeing as you can't walk, you won't be needing these."

"You can't be fucking serious?" he screamed as Reggie placed the cold steel against his thigh.

"You know Frank, you're right – I'm not serious, it's all a big joke and the joke's on you."

Frank screamed, his sinews tightening, as the off-set teeth of the saw ripped through his thigh. "Stop, stop!" he screamed. "I'll tell you everything."

But Reggie was oblivious to his pleas for mercy as each stroke sent the saw blade deep into his leg until it hit bone.

"Please, please!" he screamed, but it was no use, Reggie was now in the zone. "Turnbull and the two from London are in cahoots."

Reggie stopped and lifted the saw out of Frank's leg, pieces of skin and flesh stuck between the teeth.

"It's Dr Hussein," said Keith as he came into the room, "he's back to see Frankie."

"Let him in," replied Reggie. "It seems as though you might be lucky Frankie boy. I would say – and I'm just a layman you understand – but it does appear your femoral artery is still intact. One more stroke and you'd be on your way to the ferryman. Now listen if, and I mean if, I ever ask you a question in the future and you lie to me, I won't be so nice to you. Understand? And another thing, don't be thinking this is all over."

Frank nodded, his face contorted with agonising pain.

"What the hell's going on here?" exclaimed Dr Hussein, pushing Reggie to one side.

"You know our arrangement," he said, "ask no questions, tell no lies. And another thing – don't you ever touch me like that again. Now, see what you can do for him, and if by any chance he does not make it, leave him for me to deal with."

"This man needs a hospital, what have you done to him?"

"Me?" he replied innocently, "nothing. This was self-inflected wasn't it Frankie boy?"

"I can't go on like this," pleaded Dr Hussein, his face buried in his hands.

"In that case my friend," said Reggie, "your brother and his family had better start packing for Iraq."

Dr Hussein took a deep breath, "Ok, ok, I'll do my best."

"Joe."

"Yes boss."

"I think it's time we found our local friendly estate agent and got to the bottom of this after all."

26

"Over here!" cried Margaret.

Solley ran over to the old garage.

"In here," she shouted.

It took a few seconds for his eyes to adjust to the gloom and there, in the corner, lying between two oil drums was Paul with Margaret kneeling next to him. He felt Paul's neck for a pulse. "He's still alive," he announced.

"I found this," she said, holding up a piece of gauze.

Solley sniffed it and drew his head back immediately, "It's chloroform, or something very much like it."

"But why would anyone do that?"

"Well whoever it was, it wasn't Carlyle, what would be the point?"

"Perhaps it was a warning?" she suggested, lifting Paul's head into her lap.

"Maybe, but to do something like this doesn't make any sense. If it was Carlyle wanting to scare us off, he would have used his heavies to give us a good hiding, that's more his style."

"He's coming to."

"Help me get him over there out of this shit."

"Whoa, what the hell's happening?" asked Paul, waking to find himself being dragged slowly across the garage floor.

"You were knocked out," explained Solley.

"Do you remember what happened?" asked Margaret as they sat him against the wooden doors beneath the enamelled sign for Dextor Motor Oils.

"I was talking to Julie," he began. "I wandered over here to see if I could get a better signal and the next thing I knew there was a hand over my face and that's all I can remember until now. What are you doing?" he asked as Solley checked through his coat, removing his wallet.

"Well their motive was obviously not theft," he said, placing the wallet back into Paul's jacket.

"I didn't think it was," said Margaret.

"Why's that?" asked Paul.

"Well for a start they didn't take your phone and there's another thing, where did they come from and where did they go?"

"Well that's a question we need to answer," said Solley. "My guess is that whoever did this is still here."

"But who?" she asked. "Look for yourself, there's nobody here for miles, unless you think it might have been one of my guests trying out a theory for one of their murder mystery plots on an innocent bystander? There's fresh coffee in the kitchen," she added, getting to her feet. "Now you must excuse me – I do have a hotel to run."

"She's right," said Paul as she went inside, "we've become a real burden."

"Not of our making," replied Solley.

"That's as maybe, but it's up to us to sort this mess out one way or another. I feel as though I ought to go and apologise."

"We've done that once already. As you've already said, it's not apologies Margaret needs; it's an end to all this nonsense."

—⁓—

Ian pulled into a layby, his neck now almost impossible to move. As he eased his seat back, the sound of the electric motor was almost soothing. He lowered the window and took a deep breath of warm morning air scented with the smell of newly-mown hay.

—∞—

"Where are you going?" asked Solley.

"To the Sanatorium," replied Paul.

"Whatever for?"

"We need to draw a line under this while we still can and get the hell out of here. This whole project is more trouble than it's worth."

"If it's more trouble than it's worth, why go back there?"

"I know it sounds crazy, but I have a gut feeling the answer to all this lies in that building somewhere; that's where Turnbull was last night; I mean, where else could he have been? I was in two minds as to whether to carry on with it as things stood, but after your show of determination not to be beaten by Carlyle, I felt this whole thing was do-able. But now this – it's too weird for me – I like my enemies where I can see them and know their measure."

Solley sat down next to him as the early morning sun started to heat the door, sending the smell of warm oil into the air about them, "You've lost me old man," he said, "we know who our enemy is – Carlyle."

"There's something else – and I know we've been through this – but that morning I went to the Sanatorium, I know what I saw."

Solley gave him a look as he continued, "Not only that, you should have seen the way Turnbull reacted when I suggested taking this Billy Quinn and hiding him at the old Sanatorium. I know for a fact he told me his wife had gone to their place in the Lake District. The thing is, he told me he was going to take this Billy there and when I mentioned his wife, he changed his story and said she'd gone to her mother's in Derbyshire. I'm certain there's something there that we need to know about."

"Ok, if it makes you feel any better, we'll go back and have a good look around the place, but I still think this figure at the window is just a figment of your imagination. There's just one thing…"

"What's that?" he replied, getting to his feet.

"We don't have the keys."

"That's where you're wrong. I took them out of Turnbull's car last night."

"Where are they?"

"They're in our room."

"Ok, have it your way, get the bloody keys and let's put our minds to rest. I'll wait here for you."

Pausing half-way to the hotel, Paul looked back at Solley who sat there – eyes closed, face raised to the sun – a sight which brought back memories of when he was a kid, standing with his back next to the fence of their rented home in the early Spring sunshine, soaking up its trapped warmth.

—m—

Turnbull closed his eyes, the early August sun feeling good against his face. Suddenly he sat bolt upright, the pain in his lower back shooting up his spine like an electric shock.

"Sorry to disturb you," came a voice.

Ian could not believe his eyes, there – as clear as day – stood Carlyle.

"What a pleasant surprise," said Reggie, "I never expected to see you out here?" He moved a little closer to the open window. "My, my, Ian, what have you been up to? I hope you haven't been upsetting other people, but if you have I must congratulate them on their thoroughness."

"You mean to say this was not your doing?"

"Please Mr Turnbull; what do you take me for? I am just a simple businessman trying to make a living, nothing more, nothing less."

Ian thought about trying to drive off but what was the point?

This meeting between the two of them was inevitable at some time, might as well get it over with now.

Reggie opened the driver's door, "I would like you to come with me," he said. "Joe, Alex, help this poor gentleman into our vehicle."

Ian was manhandled into the back of the Range Rover. "I'll drive," said Reggie, "you take care of our poor friend here. It's such a lovely day for a drive wouldn't you say Mr Turnbull?" he added, getting into the driver's seat. But Ian did not reply.

"So where to?" he continued. "Oh come on, don't be so churlish, any suggestions from anyone? My, you are a dull lot I must say. Ok then, it's up to me, now let's see." Reggie paused, "I know, we'll take a drive up onto the moor, how does that sound? No objections? Good."

—⁓—

"We'll have to walk from here," said Solley.

"Don't like the look of those dark clouds," remarked Paul, "looks as though we could be in for some rain. Can't you get the car up any further?"

"Not without damaging it I can't. We'll park here, it's not far." He made his way to the rear of the car and opened the boot, taking out two pairs of night vision equipment.

"This next section of track's not too bad," observed Paul.

"I'm not fucking my car up just to go on some wild goose chase to satisfy your curiosity," he retorted.

"Ok, ok, no need to get all bitchy on me and it's not just about us, we are doing this for Margaret remember."

Solley slammed the boot of his car with great force and stared angrily at Paul. This show of displeasure was not unexpected as he knew Solley hated that turn of phrase, but at least now he was fired up and for some reason Paul felt that might not be a bad thing.

"Hold on a minute," he gasped as they started up the track.

"What now?"

"I'm a little out of breath."

"That's because you're a fat bastard and need more exercise."

Fair enough, he thought, "I guess I deserved that. But fat, where did that come from?" he added, looking down at his belly. "It's ok for you," he said, "*You* weren't knocked out with chloroform this morning, were you?"

This retort brought Solley out of his sulk. He realised this was no game and who knew what they might be getting themselves into. However, he still felt convinced there was nothing here worth all this effort.

—⚹—

"Do you know what Ian?" said Reggie, leaning his head slightly to one side, revealing his bald spot.

"No," he replied, wedged upright in the back seat between Joe and Alex, their combined heavy bulk compressing his ribs, causing him to whimper every now and again, especially over uneven ground.

"I think while we're out this way we should play a visit to the old hospital, don't you think?"

"If you want to," he answered in a low voice.

"Oh I do want to. By the way, in your absence, I took the liberty of having your house searched."

"Why?"

"Why?" repeated Reggie. "The same reason why I searched your car earlier, you have something of mine and I want it back."

"No I don't," he said, trying to make himself comfortable.

"Well I think you do and I have it from a little birdie that you do know what I'm talking about and where exactly it is."

"Oh, you mean the money. Frank's got that hidden somewhere."

"Now that is strange because our mutual friend tells me otherwise and having spent a little time with him, helping him with his memory so to speak, I don't think he was lying. And if he was not, then you must be.

"The question is – where did you put it?" he continued. "It occurred to me that having searched your domicile and found nothing; I began to wonder where you might have stashed it. It was then I had an epiphany – of course – where better than the old Sanatorium? And there is something else about that place isn't there old friend, something that makes it valuable – valuable enough for two London businessmen to travel all the way up here. So now is the perfect opportunity for you to tell me what exactly it is that had brought them this far out of their comfort zone.

"As we know Ian, there's two ways of going about this – first there's the easy way and second, for you this is, the not so easy way. To be honest the latter is my preference but we'll start with the former."

"Ok, I'll tell. The jokers up from London, one of them has an uncle – he told me he's a politician. I did a little research and it's true – he's none other than the Minister for Rural Development. It seems as though the place is a honeycomb of tunnels dug out centuries ago, mining for lead."

"Very interesting, but I don't see how that can be a positive unless one's looking for a giant wine cellar."

"The reason these two are so desperate to get their hands on the place is quite simple – the government's looking for somewhere to store its nuclear waste and it looks as though everything about this place fits the bill – the location, the type of rock – everything. Whoever owns that land will get millions every year for decades."

"I knew it," said Reggie, slamming his hand down on the steering wheel, "I damn well knew it, the old dog hasn't lost it yet eh boys?"

"No boss," came the reply from the back in unison.

"Do you know what Mr Turnbull? You may have just saved your badly bruised neck; I think we can make use of you. All we have to do is get rid of our two London friends and the rest is up to you wouldn't you say?"

Ian did not reply.

"Never mind," he continued, "you concentrate on conserving your strength."

Paul stepped out, his left arm outstretched slightly, impeding Solley, "Look."

"What?"

"There."

"I can't see anything."

"Mud."

"Mud?" repeated Solley. "There's bloody tons of the stuff or haven't you noticed. We're in the middle of the bloody countryside."

"No, you don't understand," he continued. "It's wet."

"So fucking what, can't we just get on with this?"

"Look, it goes through this door – someone's been through here recently."

"Hold on a minute, I need a leak."

"Ok, but don't take all day about it."

"Hold this," said Solley, handing Paul his night vision goggles.

"Are you sure these things work?"

"Find out in a minute, first I need that piss."

Paul stood back slightly in the doorway to shield himself from the constant wind that never seemed to cease. If it was fresh air they were after – which seemed to be the case as it was once a TB clinic – there was certainly plenty of it.

Come on, where the hell is he? he thought. *How long does it take to have a leak?*

Having relieved himself, Solley bent down and picked up a piece of paper, "I don't fucking believe it," he said, "it can't be." He read some more, "Huh, well I never."

"About time," said Paul as he returned. "What's that?"

"You'll never guess in a million years," he answered, handing over the sheet of paper.

"This refers to the construction of the Commonwealth Games Village and Carlyle's Construction Company, plus there are a few other names here that ring a bell. Where did you find it?"

"Over there in the bushes."

"Oh, I guess that's why it's wet then."

"Oh – yeah – that's why," he answered as they made their way to the building.

Paul placed the key carefully into the lock and slowly eased the door open, stepping to one side to allow Solley to enter. Once inside, he closed the door and locked it.

"What the hell did you do that for?" asked Solley. "If there is someone or something in here, I want to know I can get out quick like."

"That's why I locked it; to stop whoever might be in here from getting out – or anyone getting in."

"You forgot one thing Sherlock."

"What's that?"

"If there's someone in here, they must have got in here using a key otherwise it wouldn't be locked."

"Huh; no of course. Have you got those glasses?"

Solley handed him a set of the night vision goggles.

"Blimey, they're heavy," he remarked, slipping them over his head. "Bloody hell, they actually work and what's more, someone's definitely been in here, there are footprints all over the place. See – I told you," he added excitedly. "I wonder who it could be."

"Us, the other day, you prick."

"You think you're so clever Solley Solomon – then what do you make of that?"

Solley looked closer to where he was pointing, "It looks like a laundry chute."

"Yeah, I know what it is, but look at the dust."

"Oh yeah – someone's put something down there by the look of it; try the lock."

"It's no use," said Paul, "none of these keys fit."

"Ok, wait there."

"Where are you going?"

"Never mind, I'll be back in a minute."

Paul stood with his back to the wall, periodically checking both ends of the corridor until finally Solley returned with a large piece of iron piping.

"Saw this the other day," he announced. "Stand back." With the pipe in both hands, he brought it down onto the lock. "Fucking Norah!" he exclaimed as the vibration shot up each arm.

Several more blows followed, each a little more frantic than the last. "It's no bloody use," he said, "This place is built like bloody Fort Knox."

"Maybe there's another way down," suggested Paul, looking along the corridor. "We'll try along here, and take that with you."

Solley picked up the pipe and followed him to a flight of stairs.

—w—

"Looks like we have company boys, isn't that your client's car?" asked Reggie.

"Yes," replied Ian quietly. Although he was basically a selfish man, he had grown quite fond of Solley and Paul and felt sorry for what might happen to them.

He grabbed Joe's arm for all he was worth as Reggie put the 4x4 into off-road mode and forced his foot down on the gas, sending the three-ton monster hurtling up the remainder of the rutted track, chunks of mud and stone flying in every direction, stopping the vehicle just feet from the door.

"Right, give me the keys," he said, turning to Ian.

"I don't have them."

"What do you mean you don't have them?"

"They were in the car – I thought you must have taken them."

Reggie looked at Joe and Alex, "The only keys in the car boss

412

were these," said Joe, holding out his hand with Ian's car keys looking a little lost in his large palm.

"Goodman and Solomon must have them," said Ian.

"And what on earth would they be doing with them?"

Ian thought about lying, saying he had given them the keys so they could have a look round on their own, but time for lying was over. "Last night I came up here and hid your 300 grand."

"Now that's more like it," replied Reggie.

"After I hid the money I drove down the lane but something shot out in front of me. I swerved off the road into a ditch. Someone opened my door – at first I thought they were going to help me but they dragged me out of my seat – fuck were they strong. To start with I couldn't quite make out what was happening, I was still dazed from the airbag, but then realised I was getting seven bells of crap kicked out of me."

Reggie told Alex to check the doors of the Sanatorium. A few moments later he returned.

"It's no use boss, they're locked."

"Ok, you know what to do."

Alex unhitched the hawser from the winch that sat fastened to the front bumper of the massive 4x4 and hauled it out, fastening the hook to the door handles. Reggie turned the winch on and watched as the cable tightened, then put the vehicle into reverse and eased it slowly backwards. Bit by bit the strain increased until the lock could take the pressure no more and the doors burst open.

"You stay here," he said to Ian.

Ian picked up his car keys that Joe had tossed onto the seat and wondered whether he would ever get to use them again.

—∞—

"That's it," announced Solley, pulling open the door.

Paul placed his hand on his arm, "Did you hear that?"

"No, what? All I could hear was me trying to smash our way into here."

413

"I am sure I heard something else."

"Probably an echo," he said as he made his way into a large room. "This must be it, look at all those sinks."

Paul noticed that the floor sloped slightly to the centre of the room which was dissected by a shallow channel that led to a large drain cover at the far end. "Well this must be the laundry room all right," he said as he watched Solley make his way to the corner of the wash room where he bent down and picked something up.

"What's that?" he asked.

"Not sure," he replied, bringing the holdall over to Paul, "but whatever it is, it's what was shoved down that chute that's for certain," he added, placing the bag on the ground in front of him. He took hold of the zip.

"Wait," cried Paul.

"What now?"

"Suppose it's a body?"

"It would have to be a small one."

"Ok; or even part of one – a head maybe?"

"It doesn't feel like a head," he said, lifting the bag.

"And how the fuck would you know what a head feels like?" replied Paul, the pitch of his voice slightly raised.

"Head or no head, here goes," answered Solley as he opened the holdall.

"Shit! How much do you think's there?"

Solley looked up, "Do you know, that's funny, I haven't had chance to count it yet" he quipped.

"You know what I mean."

"Well it seems mostly to be £50s so a couple of hundred at least, maybe more."

"What the fuck is 200 grand doing down here?" said Paul, kneeling down to take a closer look.

The two men looked up.

"I heard that!" said Solley.

"They're upstairs."

"Might be kids messing about," suggested Paul hopefully.

"What, all the fucking way out here in the middle of nowhere? Not only that but I locked the door remember."

"Well it's not Turnbull with a spare key that's for certain."

"So we have two choices, go up there and confront whoever's there or hide down here."

"The laundry chute."

"What?"

"The chute – we could climb up, get out that way," suggested Solley. "It's near the exit. Better than being trapped down here like rats."

"It's worth a try," replied Paul, hoping to avoid any sort of confrontation.

Solley was the first to try, "It's a bit of a squeeze," he said, "but I think we can make it. Give me the bag."

Paul handed the holdall to him and he placed the bag into the chute before forcing his way up, pushing the bag along in front of him with his head as he inched upward, his hands and feet pressed hard against the sides of the metal duct. "Come on, what the fuck are you doing down there?" he hissed as quietly as possible.

"It's a bit tight."

"It's not tight – it's that you're fat."

Maybe he was right after all, thought Paul.

Solley's arms and legs were trembling as he braced himself against the sides, waiting for Paul to join him. After all, what was the point of him getting out and leaving his friend behind?

"About fucking time," he whispered as Paul's sweaty face appeared from below.

—m—

"Did you hear that boss?"

"No, what?" asked Reggie.

"It came from back there," said Alex, "by that chute."

"Ok, check it out."

"Hey, boss, over here!" shouted Joe shining his torch at the door that led down to the basement. "Someone's tried to smash their way in – it looks recent too."

"Someone's after my money," said Reggie, "and I bet it's those two bastards from London."

Alex stood by the chute and slid back the metal cover plate, "Hey, who's down there?" he shouted.

"Fuck!" said Solley, losing his purchase at the same time, sending him and the money crashing down straight into Paul. Regardless of his snug fit, Solley's 18 stone was enough to dislodge him in spite of his best efforts to resist, sending the pair hurtling back from whence they came, spilling out onto the laundry room floor with the bag of cash close behind.

Blood was now pouring from a deep gash in Paul's head just above his right eye.

"Are you ok?" asked Solley.

"Yeah, just a cut, must have been those goggles, probably looks worse than it is."

"So what the fuck now?"

"Down there."

"What?" he replied, trying to see where he was pointing.

Paul knelt down and examined the heavy metal drain cover.

"Are you out of your fucking mind? I'm not going down there; the place could be swarming with rats."

"It's either that or face whoever's up there," he replied, "and if I'm not mistaken, it'll be Carlyle and his heavies, and knowing that bastard he'll probably be tooled up as well. Another thing, that accent was Russian and you know how handy those bastards are with a blade so you can either go down there as you are or in little pieces. Now are you just going to stand there or are you going to help me?"

Reluctantly, Solley joined him on the stone floor and between them they managed to lift the heavy metal grating. Paul dropped down into the deep drain before Solley tossed the bag of money down and climbed down after him, dragging the cover back into place behind them.

"Fucking hell," he said, "it's like the bleeding underground down here. Why do you think the tunnel's so big?"

"I don't know," replied Paul impatiently, "could be some kind of storm drain. Now come on."

The tunnel was just high enough for them to negotiate without having to resort to using their hands and knees. Bent almost double, the two men made their way along the perfectly engineered Victorian brick-lined passageway.

"Where do you think it goes?" asked Paul.

"Your guess is as good as mine."

Alex burst into the laundry room followed by Reggie and Joe, guns at the ready. "There's no-one here."

"But there must be," said Reggie, shoving him to one side and shining his torch round the room as if he could not quite believe the evidence of his own eyes.

"They must be here boss, I heard them falling down," said Alex, focusing the beam of his torch up the laundry chute.

"What's that on the ground?" demanded Reggie.

Alex shone his torch onto the stone floor next to his feet. He knelt down and placed his fingers onto a dark stain near the drain cover, then brought them to his nose and sniffed. "It's blood boss and it's fresh."

Paul stopped.

"What is it?" hissed Solley.

"Up there," he indicated, pointing to a metal hatch just in front of him.

The two men tried to shift the metal grating but it was no use, decades of corrosion had welded it shut.

"We'll have to go on, see if we can find somewhere else to get out."

"Mind out," he replied, pushing Paul out of the way.

"What the hell are you doing?" he asked as Solley lay down on the floor of the tunnel, the water cascading over his face, causing him to cough and splutter. Drawing his legs back and lifting his head, he took a deep breath.

"Here goes," he said, kicking out with both feet.

"It moved," said Paul excitedly, "go on, try again."

Solley drew his legs back and with every ounce of his strength he made one last desperate effort. The heavy cast iron cover dislodged itself and between them they managed to force it to one side and climb out before pushing the hatch back into place.

—⚬—

Ian watched the raindrops grow fatter as the bright morning sky gave way to billowing black clouds rising high into the atmosphere where they flattened out into that characteristic anvil shape of a thunderstorm.

—⚬—

Alex followed the trail of blood with his torch, "It goes down here boss."

"Lift it," demanded Reggie.

Joe and Alex lifted the grating.

"Come on," said Reggie as he stood down into the drain, water around his ankles. "Those bastards are down here somewhere."

The three men began to make their way along the tunnel.

—⚬—

Solley tossed his soaking wet coat to one side, "What?" he said, looking at Paul. "It's ruined anyway, and what's more, it weighs a ton, I'm better off without it. So where do you think we are?"

"Your guess is as good as mine; it's a cave of some sort."

"Well the only way out is up there by the look of it," he said, pointing to a row of metal rungs fastened into the rock face.

Paul made his way over to take a closer look at the iron ladder.

"It's a fucking long way up," noted Solley craning his neck as he joined him,

Paul placed his foot on the first rung and started to climb. He paused some three metres off the ground and looked down, "Come on, what are you waiting for?"

"I don't like heights," he replied, looking up.

"In that case, don't look down."

It was then Solley remembered Carlyle and his henchmen so he took a deep breath and followed his partner.

About halfway up Paul noticed some of the iron staples that had been fastened into the rock face were quite badly corroded. He remembered Solley's 18 stone and for the first time since the news of Kim's cancer, he felt truly afraid.

He reached the top and waited for Solley, watching his slow and almost painful ascent, occasionally giving words of encouragement. He could do nothing now but pray that the 200-year-old mine workers' ladder would hold out long enough for one more ascent to be completed.

Finally, Solley joined Paul who instinctively grabbed him and pulled him towards him in a firm embrace.

"Nice to see you too, but I don't think this is the time or place," he quipped, still being held firmly.

Paul realised how much he loved this man and if anything should have happened to him, he didn't know what he would have done. "Look, there's something down there," he indicated.

The two made their way along the old mine workings towards what he had spotted.

"What the fuck's that?" asked Solley, stopping in his tracks.

Paul moved forward and took a closer look, "It's cheese!" he exclaimed.

"Piss off!"

"It is – I'm telling you, take a closer look, it's a type of blue cheese and there's tons of the stuff."

Sure enough, as Paul had said, there before them, stacked row upon row of identical metal shelving, were large round blocks of cheese.

"That explains it," said Solley, sniffing at one of the gauze covered cheeses.

"Explains what?"

"Your so-called mystery man and those fork-lift tracks; whoever is responsible for this wants to keep it a secret."

"But why?"

"Fucked if I know, you'll have to ask them but I'll tell you one thing."

"What's that?" he replied, examining the shelves.

"You had a piece of this on your plate last night – the Moorland Blue, remember?"

"Oh yeah – Margaret said it was local. Apparently, it had won several gold awards.

"But do you remember what she also said about its recipe being a closely guarded secret, and nobody knew how they managed to get it to taste so good?"

"Well maybe not anymore," smiled Paul as he grabbed one of the cheeses.

"You can't take that, it's stealing."

"It's not," he replied indignantly, "it's payback for knocking me out this morning."

"Oh come on, you don't think they would go that far."

"Why not? And look at this gauze – I'm sure it's the same one that had the chloroform on. Not only that, I reckon one of these blocks has got to be worth a couple of hundred quid, maybe more, and if I'm not mistaken there must be hundreds of them. This place is a bloody gold mine; you can't blame them for wanting to keep it to themselves."

"The thing that I don't understand is that these places are highly regulated – EU rules and all that crap – so how could they get away with it?"

"Farm shop," replied Paul simply, "and online."

"I'm not quite with you."

"Look – it's quite simple – when the inspectors come round you show them the shop full of cheeses and storerooms. When you sell some you just come up here and replace them. Who's to know? Everyone would think it was made and cured down there. This place is its secret, that's why it's won so many awards."

"That's as maybe," replied Solley. "Anyway, it's about time we got the hell out of here and not only that, I'm bloody freezing."

—⁓—

Ian looked across to the hillside, now almost obscured by the heavy rain, as a bolt of lightning ripped across the moor, shortly followed by a thunderous boom that seemed to shake the car.

He noticed thin rivulets of water cascading off the moor and down the track, turning into torrents of mud-stained water channelled along the ruts and furrows, adding to the erosion that had, over the years, eaten the once metalled road into almost non-existence, only the occasional thicker patch of tarmac remaining as evidence as to it ever having been there.

—⁓—

Reggie, followed by his two faithful companions, ploughed on, the water now knee-deep and still rising.

Joe's torch was the first to fade, "I think we should head back now boss."

"I give the orders around here," barked Reggie, "and don't you forget it."

The water had now reached their thighs.

"Boss, I think Joe's right," said Alex, trying to resist the pressure of the water against his legs.

By now even Reggie was having second thoughts, "Ok turn round," he said.

But as Alex turned to face the ever-increasing current he lost his footing. Desperately he reached out but his fingers could not gain any purchase on the slimy brickwork and his legs were swept from under him, plunging him into the murky water, forcing him down the tunnel into Joe and Reggie, their torches extinguished as they were knocked down like two skittles in a bowling alley.

The three men floundered in the total blackness, grabbing one another in a desperate attempt to try and regain their footing but no sooner than one of them managed to get to their feet, they would be pulled down again by their panicking counterpart.

Finally, their inexorable descent into oblivion was arrested by the iron bars of the filter gate and their bodies, now impeding the water's exit, caused it to rise steadily, filling the tunnel.

—◊—

They came to another ladder, but to Solley's relief, it was only a short climb this time and they now found themselves in a large chamber stacked with packing cases and pallets, some already loaded ready to be shipped out, a fork-lift truck parked to one side.

"See, I told you it was a fork-lift truck," said Paul. "They probably use it to load up that sheep trailer then tow it down using the quad bike. No-one would be any the wiser."

But Solley was totally disinterested in Paul's self-vindication, "Over here!" he shouted.

Paul made his way over to where he was standing by a door.

"It's locked."

"Well of course it's fucking locked," replied Paul. "Get out of the way – it's time for you to see a fat bastard in action. Go on, get out the way," he repeated, placing his precious cheese on the floor.

Solley stood back as he charged the door bull-like, smashing it off its hinges, sending him cartwheeling out the other side. He looked up to see Solley standing over him, the roundel of Moorland Blue tucked under his left arm, his right extending to help him up.

The two men continued to make their way along the mine-workings towards a distant light where Solley stopped and removed his night vision goggles, Paul doing the same.

"It's getting lighter," he remarked, "We must be near the exit."

However, their hopes of escaping their troglodyte existence were shattered as they came face to face with an iron gate forged into the very bedrock of the hillside.

"There's no way we're ever going to get out of here," said an exhausted Solley as he slumped to the ground.

Paul made his way to the gate and started to search though his pockets.

"What the hell are you doing?" asked Solley as he retrieved a bunch of keys.

"It's worth a try; after all, we've got nothing to lose."

"You have more chances of winning the bloody lottery than one of those fitting." However, the second key Paul tried opened the door to their freedom. "I don't believe it, I don't fucking believe it!" he exclaimed, getting to his feet

They made their way out into the rain and looked down the moor to the old Sanatorium. Paul grabbed Solley's arm just as he was about to bound off down the hillside.

"What's the matter?" he asked.

"It's Carlyle's Range Rover, and I think there's someone in it."

"This way."

Paul followed him as he crawled through the wet heather, finally stopping some 20 metres from the 4x4.

"It's Turnbull," hissed Paul. "That fucking little bastard sold us out."

"Maybe; come on."

"Where are you going?"

"To get that little shit and then we're out of here."

"No, leave him, let Carlyle sort him out. That's what a piece of shit like him deserves."

"No," replied Solley, getting to his feet, "he's coming with us. The last thing we want is Turnbull's body turning up in the old Sanatorium just after we have been there and that bastard Carlyle blaming his demise on us."

"Come back!" shouted Paul.

But oblivious to his pleas, he tumbled down the hillside to Reggie's Range Rover.

Ian jumped as Solley opened the door, reached in and grabbed him by his left arm, pulling him out onto the wet ground where he cried out in pain.

Paul joined Solley and between them they managed to drag the injured Turnbull down to their car, Ian doing his best to explain what had happened; that he had pulled off the road on his way home to try and make sense of things. It was then that Carlyle had turned up like a bad penny.

It was only when they came across Ian's car parked in the lane did they start to believe him but even then they had their doubts.

Could this habitual liar ever be trusted to tell the truth? thought Paul as they pulled in in front of his car.

Solley got out and opened Ian's door, "Go on, piss off! I never want to see you again."

With great trouble Ian eased himself out onto the roadside as Solley got back in and slammed the door before accelerating hard down the half-flooded lane. He stood there in the rain holding his ribs, watching the two men disappear into the distance.

—᠁—

"What the hell was Carlyle doing there?"

"I don't know for certain," replied Paul, "but my guess is that it had something to do with that money – and Turnbull of course. Anyway, we'll call in to see Margaret and try and work something out before we go."

"Fine by me," he agreed. "I could do with a shower and one of those excellent meals of hers. Paul, Paul, are you all right mate?"

He stopped the car and hauled Paul onto the grass verge where he turned his head to one side and threw up. "You might have concussion," he said, a note of concern in his voice.

"I'll be ok, not the first bash to the head I've had. Come on, let's get back."

Solley drew into the car park and stopped close to the entrance, "I'll give you a hand in."

"No, I'm fine now."

The two men made their way into the hotel to be greeted by Margaret.

"What the hell's happened to you?" she exclaimed.

"Minor accident that's all," said Solley. "As soon as we're cleaned up, everything will be back to normal."

She put down the freshly cut flowers she was holding and grabbed Paul by the arm, "I think you'd better get him upstairs."

"He said he was all right a minute ago."

Between the two of them, they managed to get him up to their room, fortunately without being seen.

"I'll get him showered off," offered Solley. "You wouldn't have something for that cut, would you?"

"Of course, there's a First Aid kit downstairs, I'll fetch it, just give me a minute."

Solley removed Paul's clothes and tossed them into the bath before helping him into the shower where it wasn't long before the warm water revived him somewhat.

He answered the knock on the door to find Margaret holding a First Aid box.

"That's great – I'll have him fixed up in a sec. Oh, by the way Margaret."

"Yes?" she replied, looking a little concerned.

"That venison wouldn't be on the menu by any chance?"

"With juniper sauce you mean?"

"Yes, that's the one."

"Well you're in luck."

"That's good – oh, and thanks again."

He shut the bedroom door and turned to see Paul coming out of the bathroom, towel wrapped round his waist. "That's better," he said. "I'm starving, I could eat a horse."

"There's venison on the menu tonight."

"With that juniper sauce?"

"Yep," he confirmed.

"Good, I can't wait."

Solley opened the First Aid kit and removed a plaster, "That's quite a gash you've got there. At least it's stopped bleeding."

"Funny, can't feel a thing."

"There you go; that's better," he said as he covered the wound. "At least now it won't put the other guests off their food tonight."

"You know I'm still worried about Margaret; this whole episode must be a worry to her and it may not be over yet."

"Well not for her anyway. I understand your concerns but I really don't know what to do if Carlyle wants to make a nuisance of himself."

"There are a couple of things," suggested Paul.

"And what's that?"

"Well we have that sheet from those documents and there's some pretty damning evidence in there."

"Yeah, but we need this Billy bloke as well," answered Solley. "That on its own won't be enough."

"Damn," replied Paul.

"What is it?"

"We should never have left Turnbull like that."

"Why not?"

"I'm not sure whether he was in a fit enough state to deal with this Billy."

"Oh he'll manage all right. He knows how important he is."

"Of course, we could give Carlyle a clear message to stay well clear of Margaret?"

"I'm not sure that's a good idea with someone like him, it might just make things worse. Not only that, I've a feeling that it wouldn't be worth his while to bother her. After all, once we're out of the picture, Margaret's of no interest or value to him and she's no threat."

"I guess you're right."

"Are you ok for travelling back tonight after dinner?"

"Err, yeah, I think so," said Paul, sitting tentatively on the edge of the bed.

"I'll take that as a no then. I'll phone Julie and tell her you had a minor accident – nothing to be concerned about just that you're not up for travelling tonight."

"I don't know if that's a good idea. She'll only think I'm making up some excuse to stay here."

Solley took a photograph of him on his phone. "What's that for?" asked Paul.

"There's all the evidence she needs," he explained.

"Anyone could stick a plaster on their forehead and take a photograph."

"How stupid of me," he replied, ripping the plaster off.

"Ouch, what the hell was that for?"

"Show Julie you're not messing about," he said, taking another photo.

"She gave me a difficult time this morning," moaned Paul.

"I heard the beginning of your conversation with her. Wasn't hard to get the gist of what was being said."

"Solley?"

"I know I'm not going to like the sound of this."

"I've been doing some thinking."

"I'm definitely not going to like the sound of this."

"How do you fancy going into the hotel business?" he continued.

"That blow to your head must have been more serious than I thought."

"No, seriously – when that railway line goes through here, this place could be a little gold mine. The thing is, that could be three years away and there's no way Margaret could keep this place going until then – she just hasn't got the money to invest, but we do."

"What is it exactly that you're suggesting?"

"We'll buy half this place, finish doing it up and then make a killing – so to speak – when the line comes through. Not only that, we could remove the old garage and outbuildings and either extend the hotel or put in a couple of self-catering units. What do you think? After all, it's not going to cost us anything is it?" he added triumphantly, lifting the valance to reveal the damp holdall stuffed with cash.

"You might be on to something, maybe this wasn't a wasted trip after all. We'll run it by Margaret, see what she thinks."

They made their way downstairs and into the bar to find Alan serving two elderly gentlemen.

"Good evening," he said as they approached the bar. "What can I get you?"

"Two brandies," replied Solley, "large ones."

"I take it you're staying the night then," he remarked as he poured the drinks.

"Yep, one more night, we'll be off first thing tomorrow. Do you think you could do me a favour, would you see if Margaret has got five minutes?"

They took their drinks and sat next to the fire. "Can't beat an open fire," said Paul.

"I thought you were going to have one fitted?"

"I wanted to," he replied, "wood burner, but Kim would hear none of it. She said they were messy and I would only get bored bringing wood in to light it."

"Ah, Margaret," said Solley, getting to his feet as she approached.

"I can only spare a couple of minutes," she answered. "I'm in the middle of preparing dinner."

"This will only take a couple of minutes," said Paul. "Please sit down I'll come straight to the point; we have a proposition for you."

"Oh?" she replied, looking a little uneasy.

"We would like to buy a fifty percent share of the hotel and invest in refurbishing the remaining rooms – of course to the standard you have already set."

Margaret did not reply at first, but sat there, her mouth open. "But what about the fire escape to the staff quarters?" she blurted. "Don't forget Councillor Roberts refused planning consent."

Paul eased slowly back into his chair, "Don't you worry about him, his interfering days are over."

"Look," said Solley, "I know this is all a bit sudden and on top of everything else that's happened it's a major decision. If you need time to think, that's fine by us."

She knew that making a go of this place on her own was wishful thinking as there was no way she could raise the capital to refurbish the rest of the hotel so as to make it a viable proposition. This was indeed a lifeline shot to her out of the blue.

"I don't need time to think," she said, "the answer's yes, very much yes!"

"Alan!" called Solley, "a bottle of your finest Champagne!"